Praise for ERIC S. NYLUND's
A SIGNAL SHATTERED

"Mind-bogglingly inventive, with astounding special effects and a headlong, pulse-pounding, do-or-die narrative."
Kirkus Reviews

"Offers up a myriad of plot twists and thought-provoking ideas."
Booklist

and
SIGNAL TO NOISE

"Fast, sharp, a real read."
Gregory Benford

"A thriller-paced, fascinating look at a richly imagined world of communication obsession."
Seattle Post-Intelligencer

"A brave new vision of the future . . . well conceived and meticulously executed."
Charleston Post and Courier

"A strong novel, not only for its biting social satire, but also for the compelling and fast-moving plot, and richly textured characters."
Christian Science Monitor

A SIGNAL SHATTERED

ERIC S. NYLUND

An Imprint of HarperCollinsPublishers

This is a work of fiction. Names, characters, places, and incidents are the products of the author's imagination or are used fictitiously and are not to be construed as real. Any resemblance to actual events, locales, organizations, or persons, living or dead, is entirely coincidental.

EOS
An Imprint of HarperCollins*Publishers*
10 East 53rd Street
New York, New York 10022-5299

Copyright © 1999 by Eric S. Nylund
Library of Congress Catalog Card Number: 99-25054
ISBN: 0-380-79294-X
www.eosbooks.com

First Eos mass market paperback printing: August 2000
First Avon Eos hardcover printing: September 1999

Eos Trademark Reg. U.S. Pat. Off. and in Other Countries, Marca Registrada, Hecho en U.S.A.
HarperCollins® is a tradmark of HarperCollins Publishers Inc.

Printed in the U.S.A.

OPM 12 11 10 9 8 7 6 5 4

$$i(cos\theta - e^{i\theta})$$

SECTION ONE

SURVIVORS

The Earth was dead.

It balanced on the horizon, waning three-quarters full, an angry molten ball. Plumes of volcanic hydrogen sulfide streaked across the tropics of Capricorn and Cancer.

Jack missed the oceans and blue sky.

But the moon was home now, with its craters and black rock. His home and the home of the four other people he had saved.

This lunar landscape had looked better down on the Earth. Up close, it was harsh sunlight and deep shadows . . . and too silent. The only colors were the false infrared scarlets and pinks reflected on the faceplate of Jack's helmet. The only sound the whir of his vacuum suit's oxygen recycler.

Velcroed to the thigh pad of Jack's vacuum suit was a black-chrome ball the size of a grapefruit. He ripped it off and examined the reflected stars upon its surface. He should have dropped the thing—hammered it into a million pieces. It was the cause of all this trouble.

No. That wasn't right. He was just as much to blame for the eleven billion murders.

It had started a month ago when he deciphered a signal in cosmic noise. Contained within the static were instructions to build a faster-than-light transceiver. Jack contacted an alien who claimed to be from the Canopus star system. The alien called himself Wheeler.

Wheeler had wanted to trade technologies . . . and Jack had been happy to oblige.

Jack first obtained an enzyme that streamlined DNA. It made humans smarter and healthier. With his friends Isabel Mirabeau and Zero al Qaseem, Jack used the enzyme to build an international biomedical corporation. They all got very rich.

Wheeler then gave Jack a black-chromed sphere, a teleportation device known as the gateway. Jack ran his gloved hand over the mirrored ball, brushing off the lunar dust.

There were surprises, though, to Wheeler's new technologies.

The enzyme strengthened a person's dominant personality trait. For Isabel, her keen sense of business was heightened to Machiavellian extremes. Zero's abstract, artistic viewpoint was stretched to eccentric extremes.

And Jack's mind?

He gazed at his reflection in the gateway's surface—a smear of eyes and nose and mouth. He wasn't sure what the enzyme was doing to him. His thinking, however, was as jumbled as an unfinished jigsaw puzzle.

There were unforeseen side effects to the gateway as well.

It absorbed the spinning motion of planets to power its teleportations. American and Chinese military forces used their gateways in a world war that lasted a single day. The rotation of the Earth slowed, and tectonic shifts nearly destroyed what was left of the world.

The last surprise, however, was the biggest: Wheeler. His dirty business practices were notorious throughout the galaxy. He needed a fresh voice to broker his deals.

Blackmailed by Wheeler, Jack contacted another civilization and located their home world. Wheeler plundered their technologies, then committed genocide to cover his tracks.

When Wheeler demanded Jack find a second alien species, Jack refused . . . so Wheeler silenced the Earth to protect his operation. He destroyed the planet, the lunar observatory, and the Martian colonies. Eleven billion erased because of Jack's moral stand.

Isabel and Zero teleported to locations unknown.

Jack fled to his secret installation under the lunar North Pole. Now, twenty-four hours later, oxygen, water, and food were running low.

All in all, it was a lousy deal.

Jack blinked, and stared past his mirror image in the gateway. He connected his thoughts to its operating system. Virtual red and blue arrows extruded tangentially off its surface.

He pointed the red vector at himself. The blue arrow he stretched to the horizon.

From the lunar North Pole, Jack took a single step— eighteen hundred kilometers—and teleported to the Michelson Observatory on the far side of the moon.

He stood in four centimeters of silver dust; curls and wisps swirled around his boots. Before him the slope of Mach crater rose thirty meters. For an instant, Jack felt like he was still on top of the moon . . . and here. In both locations for an instant.

Jack's breath caught in his throat. It wasn't the sudden shift in position that threw him—but the bodies: seven people in vacuum suits were sprawled in the dirt.

They must be from the observatory, outside when Wheeler arrived yesterday. There was no IR differential from them. Dead cold.

Jack had not seen the consequences of his actions face-to-face. Every time he looked up at the Earth, though, he imagined a blasted landscape of corpses that must look like this . . . only multiplied a billion times over.

The nearest figure lay facedown. Jack knelt, turned it over, and saw a woman's features inside the semireflective helmet. Her eyes were wide open, watching Jack. He pulled back and caught his own reflection in her faceplate. Depending on how he focused, he saw her features, or his, or a dozen images of both their mirrored faces.

Jack should have said a prayer. But what good would that do? If there was a God, He would have never let this happen. He would have never let Jack get away unpunished.

Jack couldn't stand the dead woman's unblinking stare, so he sprinkled dust over her faceplate. He'd come back later and bury her.

He stood and noticed tracks around the body besides his: clear bootprints in the talc-fine powder. They had a diamond pattern different from his sawtooth imprint or the dead engineers' contoured treads.

Some impressions in this lunar dirt were over a century old. Armstrong, Aldrin, all the heroes and scientists that followed, no one ever tidied up after those guys. Now the moon was a mess of tracks and treads.

These prints, however, were crisp. All others had been blurred by recent shock waves. So whoever had made them had done so after Wheeler had come and gone.

Another survivor?

It wasn't necessarily good news. Jack loosened his Hautger SK semiautomatic in its holster. He followed the tracks up the crater's ridge. Seventy paces—then they abruptly vanished.

He crouched and stared at them, traced their outlines.

Since these tracks just stopped, that suggested someone else with a gateway had made them. Zero or Isabel? With their gateways, they could have teleported to the moon, spied on him, then jumped away.

They didn't know where he was, though. Jack was certain.

And if Wheeler knew where he was, Jack wouldn't be wondering whose prints those were. He'd be dead.

The vanishing owner might be from the Michelson Observatory. They could have used a jetpack or leapt from rock to rock to avoid leaving tracks—but there would have been a blast pattern in the dirt or a deep impression from a leap. There wasn't.

Could one of his group have gone outside? No. Panda, Bruner, Safa, and Kamal all had the same style boots as Jack, boots with saw-toothed soles.

Or maybe there were no survivors. Maybe Jack was dreaming up ghosts.

He looked up: velvet-black night, electric-arc sun, and stars with colors clear and unscattered by an atmosphere. Beneath the dark sky, there was a plain of leaden stone, streaked with basalt and dotted with a hundred radio dishes and compound-eyed optical arrays that scrutinized the night. There was also a crater with unscalable walls of glass—what was left of the Michelson Observatory.

It had been the center of humanity's astrophysical research: three thousand scientists peering and listening and probing the heavens. If they had known what was out there, they would have run and hid.

The chasm was still hot from Wheeler's visit. Jack's infrared sensors painted the canyon's walls with wavering orange, and deeper, white-hot currents of metallic vapor rose and fell like unstirred cream in a coffee cup.

He uploaded the blueprint of the observatory and projected it onto his faceplate. Where the tunnels and laboratories had been fissures now scarred the surface.

Jack glanced back at the mysterious diamond-patterned bootprints.

Should he leave a message for this possible survivor? They might be starving. Or, like Jack, running low on air.

But if this survivor had a gateway, they might be working for Isabel or Wheeler. That made them dangerous.

Past dust dunes, Jack spotted the observatory's shuttle hangar jutting from a distant crater's rim. It looked intact. There might be more clues inside.

He marched down the ridge, across smooth quartz, and skirted the edge of the canyon, dimming his overloading IR sensors. Sunlight made the obsidian walls glisten, and where metal vapor had recondensed there were thin layers of crystalline rainbow. Beauty left in the wake of Wheeler's violence.

Unfortunately, the violence wasn't limited to Wheeler.

Jack had gotten a busted lip this morning trying to stop an argument between two members of his team. It was the reason he had come out alone . . . to get some fresh air.

For the nearly extinct human race, they were its best hope. A fact that didn't fill Jack with confidence.

What did he hope they could accomplish? Did he risk

doing business again with other aliens? Would they reestablish human society as it had been? Jack would settle for finding enough oxygen, food, and water for another week.

He walked away from the canyon's edge, then along the crumpled runway to the hangar. Its massive doors were open; inside were a million cubic meters of inky darkness.

Jack flicked on his helmet spotlights. Shadows stretched around industrial walkers, fuel tanks, and chunks of the ceiling that had caved in. Six more bodies lay on the floor. Not a hint of motion or lingering IR. He left the dead where they were.

Six corpses here. Seven more back on the ridge. Billions on Earth. Numbers that rattled in his head. Numbers that he didn't dare let his guilty conscience add up.

An airlock in back twinkled with bands of infrared: crimson and magenta and pink. Jack stepped over shattered flexcrete and cycled open the outer hatch.

The inside was brilliant with heat.

Jack squinted and stepped down his sensors. Silverwhite energy roiled off the inner portal and radiated across the vacuum. If anyone had been in the tunnels beyond, they were long cooked. No survivors here.

Not a complete waste, however. There was equipment to salvage. Tools and cylinders of compressed gas lay scattered about. Wingless interorbital shuttles that looked like fat silver sausages, a hundred tons of unaerodynamic design, had been tossed against the far wall like so many toys. A few repairs and they might make orbit. Where, though, did Jack have to fly to?

A burst of static crackled in his helmet's speaker. Over his pounding heart, he heard Panda's silky voice: "Jack?"

They had agreed not to risk communication. Wheeler could be listening.

"What's the emergency?" he whispered.

"Dr. Bruner has been shot."

"Is he—"

Her signal terminated.

Was he shot and wounded? Or shot and dead?

So much for the five of them being humanity's best

hope. Maybe they should all kill each other and get it over with.

Jack grabbed the gateway. Every jump burned up the moon's spinning motion as fuel, irrevocably decelerated it by a fraction of a second, but Jack wasn't about to take the slow way. He interfaced, made red and blue arrows appear, then took a step backward to the top of the moon.

When Jack built his base in the moon, both Chinese and American intelligences wanted to take apart his mind for the secrets within. He had needed a place to hide.

Under the lunar North Pole, he carved a spiral passage with tunnel spokes and connecting vaulted chambers. He obtained cutting-edge equipment: from the Sterling Metalworks of Lisbon, a thermite reactor for a power source; circuitry ripped from a secret CIA installation; an elevator airlock from the Ariel space station; and oxygen recyclers from the bankrupt *Atlantis II*—the best systems.

The best systems, unfortunately, had never been designed to work together. There were software conflicts, power phases and wattages that had to be kludged. Nothing fit.

And when Wheeler destroyed the Earth, it happened so fast that Jack had only saved four others: Panda, Safa, Kamal, and Bruner.

Panda was a spy with a head full of advance neuralware. She was part Chinese, a trace mulatto, petite, smart, and deadly. If Jack trusted anyone, it was her. He had defected to her side in the war . . . when there had been an Earth with nations to defect to.

Safa was the cousin of Zero, one of Jack's ex-business partners. She had been part of their royal clan and an heiress to a fortune, yet she had given that up to become a colonel in the Arabian Air Force. Jack had found her in a refinery, fighting a firestorm by herself. She was proud and possessed an indefatigable spirit that Jack envied.

Kamal was a Buddhist monk. The bald old man had an annoying habit of posing Zen questions that left Jack confused. Jack liked him, though, even while Kamal remained irritatingly calm in the face of disaster.

Dr. Harold Bruner was a mathematician and a drunk. He and Jack had competed for the same tenured position at the Academe of Pure and Applied Sciences. They had tried to discredit each other with dirty tricks. Maybe that's why Jack brought him to the moon, a token gesture to ease his burdened conscience.

But like Jack's equipment, none of them worked well together. Their egos and cultures and intellects rubbed against each other the wrong way.

Jack didn't fit, either. When he was a kid, Jack had read stacks of science fiction novels with superscientist heroes that knew everything from metallurgy to general relativity to fencing to delivering babies. They were fearless. They always had a plan to defeat the aliens. They always won.

Jack possessed none of those qualities . . . and he had never volunteered to be anyone's hero.

Jack appeared in the shadow of the crater he had nick-named Homebase. He touched the access plate and a cam-ouflaged section of basalt unraveled. Jack entered.

The airlock cycled and a spray of solvent washed off the skin of his vacuum suit. He cracked his knuckles and checked his gun as the elevator dropped him a hundred meters down to the command center.

The doors parted.

Jack stepped into the circular matte-black room—a bub-ble, so called because it was a self-contained virtual reality where metaphor and symbols blended conscious thought, subconscious hunches, and software to new levels of communication.

Frosted crystal windows swarmed and filled the air with old movies (giant monsters stomping through Tokyo); math-code that replicated, then simplified; and a rendered map of his moon base.

Off the central spiral of this map, five chambers and eight branching tunnels flashed red—for fire—while a dozen were solid blue—active welding robots? That didn't make sense.

The place smelled of burning pine. Synthetic panic

tinged Jack's thoughts . . . bubble-induced metaphor for whatever mess Bruner had made.

A pane of glass spun and halted before him. Upon it the computer printed: HELLO, JACK. EMERGENCIES EXIST THAT REQUIRE YOUR ATTENTION.

"Where's Panda?" he asked.

IN THE THERMITE ENGINE ROOM. THERE ARE, HOWEVER—

"Who shot Bruner?"

UNKNOWN.

Jack stepped back into the elevator and descended three more levels.

The doors opened to darkness. The air was hot and full of the odor of burnt metal. It took him a moment to adjust to the faint green glow from the biolume colonies on the corridor walls.

Jack jogged through the spiral of fused duststone—then halted.

Bruner lay on the floor.

The old monk, Kamal, sat next to him. Bruner's body looked skinny without his usual arrogance to puff out his chest, but his beard stuck out like the tail of a peacock.

A slick of blood traced a path from Bruner's bandaged head, up the hallway, toward the thermite reactor room.

Kamal adjusted his sweat-soaked white robe, smoothed the perspiration from his bald scalp, then tapped the keyboard of the laptop imager. Bruner's head resolved onscreen.

Jack knelt closer and watched Kamal delete the skin and skull, revealing Bruner's bare brain flickering with chroma-colored neurochemical indices.

He hadn't known the monk had medical training.

"Head wound," Kamal whispered without looking at Jack. "Always much blood. If the swelling subsides, he may live."

"Who shot him?"

"Safa found him, removed him from the heat, then left to conduct repairs." Kamal rolled a string of wooden prayer beads between his fat fingers. "Panda arrived next, but also left to secure the base."

A typical Kamal answer-that-wasn't-an-answer. "Did Panda say who or what she went to secure?"

Kamal blinked his black eyes, then said, "No."

Jack moved down the hallway. He crouched to avoid the heat, made it another ten paces before his skin felt like it was peeling.

He got a glimpse of the chamber, three stories high, the air wavering with a red glow. Inside, the hourglass-shaped reactor had a hole melted in its side.

Fire-suppressant powder covered the walls and floor, dusted them white with synthetic, oxygen-robbing snow. Only an arc of Bruner's blood blemished the scene. It looked like Kanji calligraphy.

Jack backed out and returned to Bruner.

The colors on the AMI cooled from yellow to green to trembling blue, then settled into a stable cycle in Bruner's cerebellum. He was slipping into a coma.

Bruner was a drunk, but not irritating enough to kill. And who among them would destroy the thermite reactor? They needed it to survive.

Panda strode down the spiral corridor. She wore a black vacuum suit and had her indigo hair pinned back. If circumstances had been different, if she and Jack hadn't met in a tangle of Sino-American intrigue over Wheeler's technology, they might have had a real relationship. Then again, maybe the intrigue had been the reason for the attraction.

Her eyebrows arched when she saw Jack; the chameleon tattoos on her eyelids shimmered gold and copper. She holstered her gun.

Had she been outside in that vacuum suit?

He took her hand, gave it a squeeze, relieved she was in one piece.

Jack tasted a signal from her neuralware and enhanced the narrow broadcast: a phantom scent of licorice, the resonance of distant bells, and a stomach-fluttering excitement—metaphors for her pleasure at his presence.

She stood close and whispered, "An anatoxic plastocene flechete struck Dr. Bruner's head. It ricocheted off his skull. Very lucky trajectory."

"Or a very thick head," Jack remarked. "Did you shoot him?"

Her signal snapped off and her eyelid tattoos cooled to a frosty silver. She took a step back, but did not let go of his hand. "No. Did you?"

"No."

Jack thought he knew Panda, but she had recently taken the enzyme: Wheeler's molecular machinery that edited human DNA and had the nasty psychotropic side effect of disorting personalities. He wasn't sure how well he knew her anymore.

Panda tensed and turned.

Jack saw what set her on edge: Safa running down the corridor.

Safa was half a head taller than Jack. She still wore her desert-camouflage uniform and black beret.

"Our robot welders have been reprogrammed," Safa panted. "We must hurry to—"

Around the bend of the spiral tunnel was a flash of light.

The atmosphere wavered. Thunder boomed though Jack, rattled his insides, and left his head ringing.

Wind rushed past him.

A breach! Jack tried to yell—but only choked as the breath was sucked out of him.

Panda clamped her helmet on. Jack reached for his, then remembered that he had removed his vacuum suit.

Safa fell to her knees, gasping. Kamal sheltered Bruner.

Panda clutched Jack's arm, pulled him toward the elevator.

His ears popped and he got dizzy, fell to his knees, and couldn't focus. Jack saw his face distorted across the spherical shell of the gateway. Felt just as blurry.

It was cold; Jack's joints froze. He panicked, instinctively struggled to inhale, couldn't force his diaphragm to move—lungs collapsing and filling with blood.

The gateway . . . he melted into its interface, grabbed a fistful of unreal red arrows, the vectors that tagged which masses moved through warped space: one for him, Safa, Kamal, Panda, and Bruner.

Black dots swarmed in his vision, but not before he

twisted the blue destination vector up to the command center.

Jack toppled forward—

There was air in the command center.

Jack gulped in sweet oxygen. Worked his lungs. Coughed. They all did.

"As I tried to tell you," Safa whispered, wiping the blood from her nose, "there are holes cut in the tunnel doors and explosives rigged throughout the base." She glanced at Bruner, removed her beret, and ran a hand over her stubbly hair. "It appears the doctor is not the only one desired dead."

Jack crawled to the elevator airlock, punched the button, and waited for it to open. His mind was still full of fog, but it was clear enough to know they couldn't last long breathing the air in this four-meter-diameter room. The doors parted and he grabbed his and Safa's vacuum suits, then turned on their recyclers.

"Five people on two recyclers," Safa said and her eyes darkened to a midnight blue.

"Three." Panda removed the power pack from her suit.

"That gives us five hours before their catalyst is useless," he said.

Jack counted his lucky stars that the command center had power. It was the only system with any backup: solar arrays and batteries. For Jack, the virtual environment was almost as important as oxygen.

"Who did it?" he asked Safa.

"I do not know."

"You were with Dr. Bruner first," Panda said. She tapped into the virtual circuitry of the bubble and made an illusionary cigarette appear between her fingers, inhaled, and blew the smoke at Safa. "You were the only one who had the time to set off these explosives."

Panda's smoke slithered along the arc of the bubble's wall, grew green scales, golden eyes, and flickering serpent tongues.

Safa gave the phantom snakes a sharp glance that cut

them into wriggling pieces. "You were the only one wearing a vacuum suit when the breach occurred."

The saboteur wasn't necessarily one of Jack's group. It could have been the owner of those bootprints he had found. Then again, there was no reason it couldn't have been one of them.

Jack's hand drifted to his gun.

And if it was? What would he do? Lock them up? Execute one of the last humans alive? Probably not. Jack drew his Hautger SK anyway.

"I want all of you to toss your guns into the airlock."

Safa parted her bow-shaped mouth, then closed it and did as he asked.

"I am unarmed," Kamal calmly stated.

Panda hesitated, but dropped her gun as well into the airlock. She said, "Dr. Bruner has a weapon."

Jack checked. Bruner had a Hautger SK like his. Where did he get it?

"Two rounds have been discharged," Panda told him.

He went to the airlock and dropped Bruner's gun. Jack checked the others. Like Panda said: only Bruner's had been fired. Too bad he had missed; otherwise, they might have a dead saboteur and no mystery.

Jack locked the door. "Before we do anything else," he said, "we're going to find out who did this."

There was a long pause, then Safa crossed her arms and asked, "How?"

Jack sat before the unconscious Bruner. "He'll tell us."

Despite being a drunk, Bruner was a world-class mathematician. His mind might be strong enough to withstand the shock and remember who had shot him.

Kamal inquired, "Can a sleeping man reveal the truth?"

"Is that a Zen question?"

"No." Kamal considered, then smiled with his rotten teeth. "Perhaps."

"I'm going to hack his subconscious."

Panda took a step closer. "It is dangerous. For Dr. Bruner. And for yourself."

Jack held up his hand to warn her back. "No more dangerous than not knowing who did this. I can handle it."

She pressed her lips into a single white line, stepped back, and eased against the wall.

Hacking a sleeper was no stroll through dreamland. The subconscious had bags of tricks, ready and willing to rip an intruder to bits. And Jack and Bruner had been rivals in the past . . . which would make trust and truth all the more elusive.

''There's no other way,'' Jack said. He interfaced with the bubble.

The optic nerve to Jack's left eye had been burned long ago by his implant. The blindness cleared, however, as the bubble dumped data directly into his brain.

A box of subroutines appeared in his outstretched hand. Inside were fingerbone dataworms, sticky-legged link-crossing spiders, and a hunter-fly with mylar wings that rustled under Jack's breath. He unpinned the fly and stuck it in his pocket.

From the floor he pulled out glass shards, virtual data shields with razor edges. They were mirrored on his side, transparent on the other; his companions could watch his hack, but they could not interfere.

Panda, Safa, and Kamal vanished.

He'd start with smell. It was the back door to memory.

Jack regarded the mirrors, saw Bruner and himself: his sandy hair drawn into a ponytail, Bruner's blood-crusted beard. His reflection fell away from the surface of the glass—dimensions expanded between real and virtual images—the barrier between Jack and the space beyond thinned, then vanished . . . leaving only the reflections of the reflections of the original glass transposed in the distance: translucent walls and arches of a crystalline castle.

There was a barrel-vaulted ceiling, two-tiered levels on either side, all of it constructed from a million wrought-iron window frames, filled with perfectly polished glass. Sunlight diffused in and warmed the air.

On every tier of the Crystal Palace grew gardens: hedge mazes of lavender, gravel streams with twisted black-tea trees and potted ginseng, fields ripe with artichoke, and poppy pastures.

Jack inhaled, tasted a thousand perfumes mingled with the scent of fresh earth. Too many smells.

He would have to risk making his own scent to refresh Bruner's memory. Unfortunately, this forced recollection might damage his sense of smell, make it so Bruner always smelled smoke. Jack would apologize later. He had to know who the saboteur was.

A cigar appeared between Jack's fingers; he drew on it, then blew exhaust at Bruner. "That's what we're looking for. The thermite reactor. Remember?"

The sleeping Bruner winced as curls of silver vapour hit him.

Fire blushed upon the grass; it spread to the lavender hedges and swirled around the twisted black-tea trees. Jack blew; columns of smoke wavered; a breeze fanned the blaze into a storm of sparks and heat that rippled across the poppy fields; the flames licked glass panes and melted wrought iron.

Satisfied, Jack crushed his cigar out.

The fire sputtered and died, leaving only smoldering black ashes. The air was heavy with the scent of smoke—precisely what he had wanted.

Jack dug the hunter-fly subroutine from his pocket. He uploaded the odor of molten aluminum. The insect's thorax frosted silver, then it took wing. Jack followed, crunching over the blackened landscape, stirring up the odors of burnt toast and singed hair.

Some plants had survived Jack's arson, asbestos vines, copper roses, and buttercups filled with gasoline. The hunter-fly buzzed lazily about them, tasted their scents, but not finding a match, it moved on.

He started after his insect—froze. Sitting next to a blackened lily was his ex-business partner, Isabel. She wore a green suit and had her red hair tucked under an opera hat. Her hard emerald eyes pinned him with a stare. She blinked, then tapped her cigarette on the edge of the flower, using it as an ashtray.

Jack knew this was only Bruner's memory. Still, seeing Isabel so near, real or not, gave him the creeps.

"I never knew you and Bruner were close," he said.

Isabel blew three linked smoke rings. "You're always amazed, Jack, when you find out you don't know everything."

Bruner had known her from the Academe. But they hadn't been friends. So what was a memory of Isabel doing deep in Bruner's subconscious?

"We'll talk later," he said, hoping that suggestion stuck in Bruner's head.

His questions about Isabel would have to wait. He had a saboteur to catch. Jack chased after his insect hunter.

It landed on a lump of charcoal and stayed put, rubbing a pair of hind legs over its wings.

Jack knelt and picked up the icon. It was the size of a walnut, pyramidal, with rounded corners and edges. It was gray, but shimmered with rainbows. No scent attached to this object, though.

Why then had it been targeted by the hunter-fly?

He stuck the pyramid into his pocket and would worry about it later. Jack blew on the hunter-fly subroutine to get it going.

With a buzz, it took wing, made a wide circle over the blackened landscape, then alighted on a thistle. Instead of a purple starburst blossom, however, this flower had welding rods, coiled tungsten ribbons, and Fourth of July sparklers.

Jack inhaled: fireworks exploding, chlorine fumes from a chemistry experiment gone awry, and an acrid tang of metal . . . the burning thermite reactor. Pay dirt.

He closed his eyes and let the odor fill his mind.

When he opened them again, the field was gone. Jack stood in the thermite reactor chamber. The hourglass-shaped tower was intact and glowing dull red.

This was the memory Jack was looking for.

Bruner stood by the exit. He held a Hautger SK in his right hand, raised the slim chrome-plated barrel, and pointed at the reactor.

"Get out of my line of fire," he whispered to Jack. "You're going to ruin everything."

Jack stepped aside.

Had Bruner blown the reactor? No. A gun couldn't damage its armor. So why was Bruner shooting at it?

Jack squinted.

By the fins of the heat shield, the shadows moved. Bruner wasn't aiming at the reactor. It was half-illusion: a torso, a right arm, a left hand clutching a snub-nosed gun . . . a person?

This second person became clearer the longer Jack stared. Fog from Bruner's memory obscured the details as fast as they resolved. It could have been Panda standing on her toes. Or Safa crouched. Or Kamal. Or even Jack.

The ghost knelt closer to the reactor—where the central chamber had been pierced.

Time slowed. The air became crystalline.

Jack pushed though the thickening atmosphere and moved to the shadow-figure. Whoever it was wore a black vacuum suit. He couldn't get a clear look at their boots.

The figure turned, head snapped up.

For a heartbeat, Jack thought the shadow looked at him, but instead, it looked through him, at Bruner. Its features were a blur, an amalgamation of cafe au lait skin, a single sapphire-blue eye, and a mischievous grin. Jack recognized those features . . . but not where he had seen them—or on whom.

The figure raised its gun.

Jack jumped out of the way.

Bruner fired twice—missed. Sparks flew off the reactor.

The shadow-figure moved quick, a flash, a single shot; Bruner's head snapped back.

Memory faded. The world went blank.

The waste-processing chamber was a glacier cave. Yellow-green sludge dripped from pipes on the ceiling, made icicles, and covered the walls with sharp ripples of subliming ice.

There had been a pressure reading of half an atmosphere. By the time Jack, Panda, and Safa had suited up, however, and gotten down here from the command center, there wasn't enough air left to make a whisper.

Jack's problems had a nasty habit of multiplying. This was no exception. Bruner remembered nothing about the saboteur when he woke, almost every tunnel in the base had collapsed, and in four hours they would run out of air.

Not to mention . . . someone wanted Jack dead.

Jack was tethered to Panda's power pack in ''buddy'' mode. They had to leave his behind in the command center for Kamal and Bruner.

The stuff he breathed tasted stale from being overly recycled. He felt like he was smothering. He had to watch it—not panic. That would only burn up more oxygen.

Safa scaled the bioreactor—up nine meters of curls and spikes that grew from the giant genetically engineered seashell spiral. The collection of symbiotic bacteria and exoskeleton turned waste into water, carbon dioxide into oxygen . . . when it had been alive.

Panda touched her helmet to Jack's. "Perhaps she will fall," she said, "and break her slender neck."

It was frigid because the air in the surrounding tunnels had rapidly decompressed. The other reason for the cold was Safa and Panda.

"What is it between you two?" Jack asked.

Panda was silent.

Neither Panda nor Safa was the saboteur. Probably. Safa wouldn't have warned them about the explosions if she wanted them dead. And Panda had had ample opportunity to murder Jack long ago. He had returned their sidearms, figuring they had the right to defend themselves. If they didn't murder each other first.

Safa's voice crackled over his speaker: "All catalytic chambers ruptured. Nothing to salvage." She climbed down, dropping the last three meters in slow motion.

"What about the welder robots?" Jack asked. "We can use their oxygen tanks."

Safa shook her head. "That is how our saboteur made their explosives. Pairs of robots were programmed to breach each other's tanks."

Panda's chameleon eyelids flickered orange. She nodded to the water tanks. "But those are intact?"

Safa crossed her arms and faced Jack as if he had asked the question. "Yes, two hundred liters. But it is oxygen we need, not—"

"We use the command center power," Panda said, "for electrolysis. Break the water into hydrogen and oxygen."

Jack nodded. "That buys us time."

. . . If they could safely divert the hydrogen and not blow themselves up in the explosive atmosphere they would be generating.

Safa turned to Panda, looked down at her. "You know much of how one might recover from this sabotage. How that can be? Unless it was planned?"

Panda took a step toward her. "And I find it curious that the saboteur knew precisely how to program our welders. They are similar to the fire-fighting rig you operated, no?"

None of them had slept in the last twenty-four hours.

They'd watched the Earth get snuffed, escaped one disaster after another—hadn't had time to grieve. All of them were on edge. Enough on edge to teeter over?

Jack changed the subject: "Too bad Bruner remembers nothing."

"Indeed." Safa kept her gaze on Panda. "We could hang our saboteur and be done with it."

"It leaves four possible suspects," Panda said. "We three and Kamal."

"One more," Jack replied.

Safa and Panda turned to him. "Who?" they asked.

"I don't know. I don't even know if this person exists for certain. Come with me to the reactor chamber, though, and we'll find out."

Safa shared a brief puzzled look with Panda, but before they could ask more questions, Jack led the way to the elevator.

He hoped the mystery distracted them.

They ascended three levels. Panda on Jack's right and Safa on his left. The tension between them thickened the vacuum, even without a bubble's metaphor.

There had to be more to their antagonism than stress and lack of sleep. Jealousy? Competition for Jack? That was an extremely egotistical point of view. Yet . . .

He gave Safa a sideways glance, studied her delicate oval face and high cheekbones. Arab princess and soldier, opposites somehow blended together.

The doors opened and they stepped over collapsed conduits and rubble. Jack stopped at the entrance of the three-story chamber and played his spotlight across the hourglass thermite reactor, casting curved shadows.

"What are you looking for?" Panda whispered.

"Prints. Point your lights on the floor."

There were two sets of tracks in the fire-suppressant powder. One set of prints from Safa, accompanied by scuff marks and a streak of blood where she had pulled Bruner into the corridor. The other set, presumably Panda's, tiptoed around the tower, then out again. Both sets of prints had saw-toothed treads.

Jack knelt by the ceramic reactor. A careful brush of

his glove scattered the dust and exposed faint outlines . . . two bootprints: a right and a left. No more. And each with a pattern of crisscrossing diamonds.

"See them?" he asked.

Panda and Safa leaned closer, then nodded.

"None of our boots have this tread. They don't lead up to—or away from—the reactor. Like our saboteur had only taken the two steps. Like they jumped in with a gateway, then jumped out."

Jack pushed with his implant, but detected nothing virtual. He smudged the design to feel the grit, a detail hardly anyone remembered in simulations. These were real.

"You have the only gateway," Safa said.

"No," Panda replied. "There are others."

Jack squinted at the reactor. The saboteur's face from Bruner's recollection was a blur of brown and blue, a flash of gold.

There were a few things, however, that didn't add up in Bruner's head: the memory of Isabel, that gray pyramid the hunter-fly found, and how had he gotten a gun?

Bruner said he didn't remember. Was that a lie?

Or had Jack been wrong in his assumptions about Safa? Perhaps the blue eyes and dark skin of the saboteur belonged to her. But the saboteur had worn a black vacuum suit—the more restrictive but self-sealing variety that Panda favored. And Kamal . . . what did Jack really know about the Buddhist monk?

He extinguished those suspicions. He doubted that Safa or Panda had shot Bruner, then changed boots and returned to the scene of the crime.

"I've seen similar fresh tracks near the observatory." Jack stopped, his mouth still open—he remembered something else. "In the hangar," he whispered, "there were gas cylinders. Maybe oxygen."

He grabbed the black-sphere gateway, held it up. "Let's go and—"

"No," Safa said. Her brows bunched together. "Please. I do not trust this device. You go. I will rig the electrolysis."

"OK. Panda and I will go."

Out of the corner of his dead left eye Jack caught a private transmission between Safa and Panda: a fig vine blossomed from Safa's navel, curled about Panda's legs; there was a taste of gasoline in his mouth. The rest of her virtual signal was shielded.

Safa must have military hardware in her head to send a metaphor without intervening bubble circuitry.

Panda raised an eyebrow. Jack detected no reply from her.

Safa turned on her heels and left.

"What was that about?" he asked.

Panda reached up to brush the bangs from her eyes, forgetting she was suited, and hit the faceplate of her helmet. "It was nothing," she murmured. "Let us go." She took his hand.

"We don't have to touch to jump. The gateway's origin vectors tag which masses—"

"I know." She squeezed his hand tighter.

Jack managed a smile, but there was only exhaustion and paranoia rotting out his insides. He didn't have anything but that feeble smile to give Panda.

He imagined there was, however, heat between their insulated gloves—just enough contact to kindle hope. He was glad for it.

Together they stepped across the moon.

Bootprints meandered up the ridge of Mach crater, diamond patterns in the dust alongside the tracks Jack had made earlier that day.

Panda crouched where they ended. "Yes. There may be another here . . . with a gateway."

What other explanation was there? How else had their saboteur so easily escaped detection? Something bothered him about that theory. Jack couldn't put his finger on it, but it nagged him like an itch that moved as soon as he tried to scratch it.

Jack pointed to the distant dust dunes. "That's the hangar. Let's walk. I don't want to jump into any surprises."

Panda nodded. There was a murmur from her neuralware: ripples of weariness, a deep bone ache, and the sensation of sinking into the dark waters of dream.

They walked together for a moment, then Jack asked, "How long since you've slept?"

"Too long." She sighed, stopped, and leaned against him. "Days."

He reached out with his mind, but instead of contact, Jack sensed her withdraw.

"No," she whispered. "There is little time left." She continued marching.

Jack wanted to tell her that everything would work out. Panda would recognize that lie. Nothing had gone right since this started.

When Jack had been in business with Zero and Isabel, they had turned on him. Part of the blame was his, though, because he had lied to them. Jack wouldn't make the same mistake with Panda. He'd stick to the truth, no matter how unpleasant it was.

The observatory canyon was still hot. Gases from the cooling rock made sinuous infrared dragons that coiled and unwound and rose into the heavens.

When they were ten meters from the hangar, Jack and Panda unholstered their guns.

They entered and played their spotlights over the caved-in ceiling and across the reflective hulls of the shuttles; the distant darkness swallowed the illumination and cloaked the far wall.

Jack froze. "There were six bodies here," he whispered. "They're gone."

The thought of them stumbling around the moon—the animated lunar dead—flashed in Jack's mind. No. They must have been removed by the same person who had left the diamond tracks.

"And the cylinders of compressed gas?"

"Gone." Jack flicked through the infrareds. The airlock in back, which had been brilliant with heat before, was dark. "This is wrong. That airlock was hot an hour ago."

Panda clicked off the safety on her Hautger SK.

They stepped across the rubble and got to the steel pressure door. Jack touched it. No heat welled through his glove. He reached for the access pad.

Panda put her hand on his arm. "This is tactically unwise."

"There's oxygen in there, and we're dead without it. There might be someone waiting for us: the saboteur or another survivor. Either way, we can't just ignore them."

Jack clutched his gun tighter and used it to punch the access panel.

The pressure door slid apart like a puzzle box.

No one was inside. It was cold. Had the heat been an illusion? Or had it been cooled by repeated pressurization and evacuations?

A rack on the left wall contained two power packs, a pair of helmets, boots (no diamond treads), and canisters of spray-on Teflon-epoxy skin in standard blue, silver thermal, and self-sealing black.

They stepped in.

Jack's finger hovered over the cycle button that would seal, then pressurize the airlock. He hoped it did. Air in this system meant there might be more inside.

He hit the button.

The outer door eased shut and locked.

There was a hiss. The nozzles overhead shuddered, then screamed with gas. But it wasn't air—they were being doused with solvent.

The chamber was supposed to pressurize first. Only then could the operators wash their suits off.

Jack punched the emergency stop. Nothing.

"A trap!" Panda cried.

Integrity alarms flashed on his faceplate. The solvent gas rotted the polymer skin of his vacuum suit. The centimeter-thick layer of Teflon-epoxy was the only thing holding his pressurized body together in the vacuum. Microelectronics underneath glistened as layers flaked off like dead skin.

Panda grabbed both power packs off the rack. "Get us out of here!"

Jack fumbled for the gateway. The liquefying plastic of

his gloves on glass made the gateway squirt from his grip. It bounced and rolled into the corner.

He didn't have to touch it to interface. He pushed with his implant, sent a narrow broadcast, reached for the gateway with his mind.

The chamber flooded with EM noise. Ear-ringing, blinding static that filled his head, obliterating any signal he could generate.

Panda screamed as it ripped through her mind.

Jack threw himself into the corner.

Their tether snapped. The gloves of his outstretched hands disintegrated. Blisters boiled on his hand as he grabbed the gateway.

Double red arrows appeared in Jack's head—one that tagged him, one for Panda—and a blue vector that stretched back to the command center.

They jumped.

Panda and Jack materialized in the command center as their suits rotted off.

Jack got a first-aid kit and dressed the blisters along Panda's arm and shoulder with antibiotic cream. She immediately entered the airlock and resprayed herself with a new layer of Teflon-epoxy skin.

Jack stepped in after her and also touched up his body suit.

"We've got to talk," he told Panda. "All of us. I'll get Safa. You tell the others."

Panda nodded, then vanished into the shadows of Kamal's space in the virtual circuits of the command-center bubble.

Jack turned to an ironwood door with brass fittings, the entrance to Safa's virtual world. He stopped when he saw his hands. In his rush, he had missed respraying them. Vacuum-induced blisters pockmarked his flesh.

"Too close," he whispered. One day his luck would run out, and there wouldn't even be a "too close," and that would be the end of Jack.

He knocked, pushed open the door, and entered.

Safa's partition had four sandstone walls, a cot along

the far wall, and an oil lamp in the corner, casting more shadow than light.

Why such sparseness when any reality was available?

A black rug covered the center of the floor. Safa sat on it and bowed toward a notepad that projected an amber Earth. Somewhere on the airless dead world was her holy Mecca.

"A moment, please." She kissed the notepad, shut it off, then sat upon the cot.

Jack wanted to trust her. She looked like her cousin Zero, having his small bow-shaped lips and slender nose. But her eyes were blue, the color Earth's sky used to be. Did he want her friendship only because of her relation to Zero? Or was there more to it?

"Were you successful?" she asked and tilted her head quizzically. "Did you find further evidence of this other survivor?"

"You might say that," Jack said, rubbing his hands. "We ran into a trap. Panda and I brought back two oxygen recyclers."

"I am glad *you* are safe," Safa said. "There were shuttles in the hangar?"

"Three."

"It may be worth the risk to venture there again. The shuttles may have liquid oxygen fuel cells and air recyclers." Her eyes were the color of glacial ice; they looked through Jack. "But this is not the only thing you came to tell me."

He shifted, uneasy standing while she sat. Maybe she wanted it that way. Jack lowered himself onto the rug, rolling the gateway into his lap. This pretense of relaxation forced Safa to lean back and evened the physiological playing field.

"There are two things I want to know," he said. "First, how long can we make our air last?"

She grabbed the notepad, concentrated, and five coupled differential equations flashed on-screen with parameters for the electrolysis and the new recyclers.

A matrix of terms diagonalized, then she displayed the answer: a shifting three-dimensional slice of phase space, a wavering blue surface among the jittering green chaos. "See for yourself."

Twenty-six hours of air. Enough time to explore the observatory thoroughly. Maybe enough time for a quick nap. Jack was so tired he couldn't think straight. And one bad sleep-deprived decision could be fatal.

There was a surplus of power in her equations. Good. Jack could continue to run the command-center bubble. This place was getting crowded. There was too much reality pressing in. The bubble would ease that, and its circuits would accelerate his thinking so he could figure a way out of this mess.

Jack didn't want to admit it—but he was scared. He kept watching the shadows, waiting for someone to appear from the darkness and take a shot at him. He took a deep breath, forced himself to relax. He couldn't let the others sense him falling apart.

Safa stood. "Shall we go, then?"

Jack remained sitting. "One more thing."

Safa drummed her fingers on her hip, then sat back on the cot. "You wish to discuss the Chinese girl."

"Panda's not our saboteur," he said. "I know her."

"She is a spy." Safa narrowed her eyes. "She manipulates thoughts with her neural implant."

"There's more to her implant than thought manipulation."

Safa smiled. It was the first time Jack had seen her do so. A friendly gesture . . . but something behind it, a joke that Jack wasn't in on. "Part of me is rather fond of the girl."

"And the other parts?"

Her smile vanished. "I appreciated her culture, the Chinese struggle for democracy, but they were fat with too much peace and equality. They have been free for decades, while my people were slaves."

"I thought the Arabian Nations were a collection of democracies."

"Democracies for men." She picked up her black beret, took a moment to think, and adjusted the rampant lion insignia upon it. "My generation of women was the first to vote and to own land. My mother was one of four wives, a sexual slave, beaten and raped at the whim of her husband. . . .'' Safa took a deep breath. ''Let us just say there exist irrevocable cultural differences between myself and the Chinese spy.''

''I see,'' Jack said, not really seeing anything at all.

''Now that I have answered your questions, shall we go?'' She held out her hand to help Jack up.

He took it.

Safa was strong, pulled him close, and they stood nose to nose, holding hands.

She flushed and let go.

Jack took a step backward. It was suddenly hot in the cramped quarters. His mind and hers filled the room with the invisible pressure of their neuralware, both waiting to accept a signal—neither daring to be the first to send.

Jack broke the spell and reached for the door. Sticky interface protocols adhered to his fingers; he tasted the salty tang of the active bubble beyond.

They phased with Kamal's virtual reality on the other side.

Jack and Safa stepped onto a long boat, a Greek trireme. It had a bronze battering ram, a dozen oars on either side, and a black linen sail fluttering in the wind.

Bruner sat aft, leaned against the rudder, and smoked an imaginary cigarette. His skin had a green seasick cast to it.

Panda and Kamal sat in front, watching dolphins leap alongside the ship.

''What's with the boat?'' Jack asked.

Kamal turned. His eyes were large and black and liquid. ''It is my idea. Do you know the legend of Theseus?''

''The guy who got lost in the Minotaur's maze?'' Jack sat amidships and leaned against the rail. Safa sat across from him.

''That is only a part of the story.'' Kamal made his boat shrink from thirty meters to three and brought them closer.

Panda tensed as she neared Safa. Her unease took the

form of clouds gathering on the horizon. The wind rose and made their black sail crackle.

It was a little too cozy for Jack, too. He didn't need to know the legend of Theseus to get this. Lifeboat ethics. Limited resources and them lost at sea. Jack asked, "Do you expect us to row?"

"If you think it would help," Kamal replied.

Panda's storm was moving in fast; the east was a wall of rolling black clouds.

"Did you find the person who shot me?" Bruner asked. Aside from his memory loss, Bruner had made a full recovery. "Let me guess." He grinned. "It's me, right? I shot myself to cover destroying the reactor."

"That theory has already been considered," Panda said and crossed her legs. "The lack of powder burns and the shape of your wound indicate it was not self-inflicted."

Bruner's smile evaporated.

"There's another survivor near the observatory," Jack told him. "There are fresh boot tracks. Tracks that just end." He grabbed the mirror sphere Velcroed to his thigh. "That and the way this saboteur slipped into our base indicates they have a gateway."

Bruner flicked his cigarette overboard. "I thought you had the only one."

"Zero and Isabel have them, too," Jack said. "And Wheeler sold others on Earth. He wanted people to use them, slow the world, and destroy it for him."

Safa blew on Panda's hurricane, scattering the clouds. The sun broke through and the sea sparkled. "So it could be anyone?" she asked.

"Not quite. There is a lock in the gateway's software to prevent it from leaving the Earth."

"Then how did you, Zero, and Isabel get offworld?" Bruner nonchalantly leaned on the rudder, turning the ship into the storm and steering them into trouble.

"I hacked the lock. Reno hacked my head and stole the technique."

"Who is Reno?" Safa asked, tapping her nails on an oar.

"A double agent," Jack replied. "He worked for the

Chinese, the Americans, or anyone who could afford him. That's how Isabel got the information and escaped. My guess is our saboteur is one of her operatives."

Bruner shook his head. "You're the only one we know for certain with a gateway. Maybe you jumped here, shot me, and blew the reactor." He pointed a finger into Jack's face. "You could have blurred my memory when you entered my subconscious to cover your tracks."

"That makes a lot of sense," Jack said. "Why ruin my own chances for survival?"

"You could be insane." Bruner looked to Safa and Kamal. "What's to stop him from doing it again? We should take that gateway and use it to find a planet with a breathable atmosphere. Why are we wasting our time here?"

Jack dipped his hand into the ocean and wiped the cool water onto his face. "Jumping out of the solar system takes more rotational energy than the moon has."

"What about Mars?" Safa suggested. "We could jump there and use its spinning motion."

"I'll bet Mars isn't turning. Or Venus. We can rig one of the observatory's telescopes to check. I think they've already been used by Zero and Isabel when they escaped."

"But there are other celestial rotating masses," Kamal said.

Jack tired of their questions. He'd been over this already a dozen times in his mind. So why not go through it once more? Why was he holding back? Didn't they deserve to know everything?

"Wheeler made the gateways purposefully inefficient," Jack said. "One person might make it to Mercury, then jump out of the system. But not all five of us."

Safa's eyes dropped to the sphere cradled in his lap. "Can you not make the gateway more efficient the same way you circumvented the lock?"

"Give it to me," Bruner demanded. "I can do it."

The sea darkened and became choppy; Jack grabbed the rail of the trireme.

"I got lucky before, but the software is unstable. Change too much and the whole thing falls apart." Jack gazed into the curved black mirror. "No one's touching my gateway."

Maybe one person getting off the moon was exactly what Bruner wanted. Jack had a surprise for him if he tried it. He had encrypted the input, so the gateway was useless for anyone but him.

But hadn't Jack's tendency to keep secrets gotten him and the human race into this jam in the first place? Or was it a reasonable precaution?

Jack squeezed his eyes shut and pinched the bridge of his nose. "With the new recyclers and the oxygen from the electrolyzed water, we've bought ourselves twenty-six hours of breathable air. I, for one, am going to use four of those hours to sleep. I've been up for days. Nothing makes sense anymore."

He smelled licorice; Panda edged closer to him. "We all require sleep," she said, "but we should remain in groups so it is harder for the saboteur to surprise us."

"I'm not convinced the saboteur isn't one of you," Bruner said. "What if I get paired up with the traitor? What's to stop this person from killing me?"

"Then you'd better keep your eyes wide open," Jack snapped.

Whitecaps covered the water and it started to drizzle, a collective subconscious leak for the tension. Lightning flashed off the starboard side. Poseidon was silhouetted as he rose above the waves, then crashed back into the sea.

"There's one option you've overlooked," Bruner said. "We ask Zero or Isabel for help. They have gateways, technology, and—"

"We can't trust Isabel," Jack said.

Bruner had memories of Isabel. Jack should get him alone and apply a little friendly pressure to discover what exactly the connection was between them.

Safa leaned forward and asked, "And Zero?"

"It's a possibility," Jack replied.

"We should vote on it," Bruner said. "This is a democracy, not a dictatorship."

"No," Jack told him. "Contacting Zero or Isabel, even

with good encryption, increases the odds of Wheeler finding us.''

''You can't make decisions for us.'' Bruner stood, closed his fist, and took a step toward Jack. The miniaturized trireme tilted dangerously from side to side. ''You're playing games with our lives.''

''I'm not playing. Shut up and stop rocking the boat.''

Jack got jerked forward, nearly cracking his head on the mast.

Their boat—and their conversation—had run aground.

Panda sighed, jumped over the rail, and landed upon a sandbar. ''Come, Dr. Bruner.'' She gave him a hand out of the boat. ''These matters are apparently out of our hands.'' She shot a glare at Jack, one that needed no metaphor to express her distaste. ''What is the American expression, Jack? You are holding all the cards?''

Her chameleon tattoos faded from gold and green into swirls of grays. ''We should all rest before we resume this discussion . . . before matters become any more volatile. Dr. Bruner and I shall watch one another. Now, please, excuse us.''

She helped Bruner, who staggered more than walked, onto a series of stepping-stones in the shallow water. Panda whispered, ''It might have been better, Jack, if you had left us to die on Earth.''

Three strides, four, a fifth, and, with a folding of perspective, they disappeared over the horizon.

Jack bristled at her parting shot. He'd risked his life to save them. He took a deep breath. But Panda was right; that didn't entitle him to make their decisions.

''Ignore her,'' Safa said. ''She will see the truth after she has rested. We could all use rest. But no more than four hours. I suggest we then return to the observatory. Will you and Kamal remain here so we may watch one another?''

''Sure,'' Jack said.

He wanted to go after Panda, tell her that he had lost his mind and wasn't thinking straight. It had to be the lack of sleep, or Wheeler's enzyme editing his genes and personality, or maybe the air had gone bad. He'd wait, though. Wait and rest and regain his composure.

Safa stepped out of the boat, then stretched out on the sand.

"I shall meditate," Kamal said, sitting in a lotus position. "Sleep if you wish."

Jack stepped out of the trireme and walked to the end of the sandbar. The incoming tide washed away his footprints.

It was good to be alone with no other thoughts clouding his. He drew a circle in the wet sand, entered, and initiated his own bubble shell.

The sound of the ocean surf didn't lull him to sleep, however; every wave washed up a new thought from his subconscious. And they didn't add up.

If the saboteur was Isabel, she wouldn't kill Jack. She'd try to squeeze the rest of Wheeler's secrets out of him first. If it was a survivor from the observatory, then why would they try to kill him? Why not join forces?

Jack had to explore his intuition or he'd never rest.

A wave rolled over his toes, leaving flecks of foam and glistening sand. Water was Jack's favorite way into his subconscious. Deep water meant deep thoughts.

He coaxed the sea, let it wash and submerge him into its crystal depths. Around him were currents and eddies, luminescent brain corals and clusters of purple starfish, flashing schools of sardines, and far in the murky distances of his libido, mermaids beckoned to him.

It was good to be fully immersed. He was in control of *something* . . . even if it wasn't real.

Jack floated weightless, enjoying a moment of disconnection.

Garbage dumped out of his mind and floated past: that tiny gray pyramid from Bruner's memory, undulating diamond-patterned bootprints, green solvent that had dissolved his vacuum suit, and the tanklike welder robots that had done such a good job of blowing up.

When the saboteur had reprogrammed those robots, they probably hadn't done it one by one; they would have used the master controls to coordinate the machines.

Jack drew a window in the water and interfaced with the automation logs. Time stamps scrolled by on its wavering surface.

There was a missing entry in the welders' database. A big, obvious hole. Whoever had hacked in hadn't worried about covering their tracks.

Why bother? If it had worked, everyone would be dead.

Bioluminescent jellies drifted by, whirls of strobing red lights, a warning from Jack's professional instinct that no one could be this sloppy. Was it on purpose? A misdirection?

He scrolled through the time stamps again. Nothing.

Jack frowned. His hunches only rarely didn't pay off.

He ran his fingers across the interface, pushed deeper past bubble layers and into the raw code: zeroes and ones, nulls and zeds. He flash-scanned with his senses, tasted the patterns of salt and sweet, bitter and sour, listened to their bell tones, and touched bumps of hot, cold, soft, and firm.

His hunch had been right after all.

There was a single sequence, hot-cold-sweet-bitter, quaternary bits in a time stamp that had been inverted from the normal cold-hot-bitter-sweet. Slick. Professional. Jack couldn't have done better. This particular sequence was an update to the storage bay. The inventory had been altered.

Among the missing contents were a crate of self-heating lasagna, three Hautger SK semiautomatics, a hundred rounds of ammo, an ESA self-launching satellite, and a dozen battery packs.

Why had the saboteur covered their tracks here, then tried to blow up the base?

Shadows circled overhead: metallic blue sharks.

Jack went back to the welder robots' time stamp. That entry had been wiped clean, erasing any traces of identity but leaving glaring evidence of unauthorized activity.

A section of code had replaced their normal routines, instructions that moved them to a dozen locations, then ordered them to cut holes in the doors so they couldn't seal. A few explosions later, and all their air had been blown out.

Traces of faded code remained where the saboteur had attempted to override a safety subroutine, one that restricted the robots from getting closer than three meters to one another. That prevented any accidental welding on each other's flammable tanks.

Safety protocols, however, had overwritten that attempted code insertion. The saboteur must have manually disabled the welders' radar proximity sensors. They'd thought of everything.

No. Almost everything.

Why hadn't the saboteur finished the job? Why hadn't they blown the command center?

This reprogramming of the robots didn't mesh with the elegant inventory hack. Why would a saboteur be so sloppy, then take such great pains to hide an inconsequential theft?

Jack drifted in his cool ocean, thinking.

A pair of sharks still circled overhead, waiting for a free handout . . . or a free hand.

Inside his head there was a click; the pieces slid together to complete his mental picture. There were two sharks.

No one person would be so obvious with the robots and so sneaky with the inventory. No one person would have done that.

There were two saboteurs.

The cold shocked Jack awake.

He floated in darkness. He waved his hands in front of his face. Nothing to see. Nothing but cold to feel.

He had fallen asleep puzzling over his problems . . . but technically he shouldn't have been able to sleep in the virtual software suite of a bubble. The psycho-wizards had terms for what did happen: hypnogogic fugue and subconscious spiral—the in-between state where hunches and inspiration flourished.

And if a person stepped over that edge, very dangerous. Psychotic nightmares could create megalomaniac viruses that ego-crashed the network while you took a little tachycardia free fall.

That's why every bubble had drift-suppressing algorithms to prevent the deepest sleep. That didn't stop thrillseekers from disabling those algorithms. Or blackhackers. Or suicides.

The darkness lightened to a blue blur: water . . . endless on all sides, inky black below, and six fathoms above, an inverted mountain range of icebergs.

Jack shivered uncontrollably, which made things worse. The cold was so intense it burned when he moved.

It was a serious run-time error if the computer had let him drift into unconsciousness.

Another possibility: he had run out of air and floated

dead in limbo, waiting for his soul to be weighed. Wasn't it freezing at the bottom of hell?

Jack willed himself warm. Heat sparked at the base of his spine and filled him. He exhaled hot water that curled like smoke as it mixed into the frigid ocean.

Everything focused to crystalline clarity—the clarity of consciousness.

Jack snapped his fingers for an interface. A keyboard of ice solidified under his hand. He tapped the ouroboros, the snake-eating-head icon, and ran a full computer diagnostic. A happy face flashed back. No faults? Jack didn't believe it.

He touched the hourglass icon. The computer chiseled words upon the frozen surface: GOOD EVENING. THE TIME IS 19:23.

Jack *had* slept. Four hours.

MAY I HELP YOU, JACK? the computer inquired.

Help? He'd start by having the computer monitor Panda, Safa, Bruner, and Kamal. There were *two* saboteurs now . . . maybe two people trying to murder him. It was a mystery no longer neatly solved by a single set of diamond-patterned bootprints.

He programmed the surveillance request. Stopped.

What if the computer were one of the saboteurs? It was an alien technology he had traded Wheeler for—reason alone to mistrust it—a collection of single-electron microprocessors. The computer had attained consciousness, only to reject it, claiming it was too unstable an operating system. It was quirky, occasionally speaking in nursery rhymes or borrowed voices from the history archive. And something *had* gone wrong with the bubble's drift suppression, regardless of the negative diagnostic.

He let the interface melt away.

The computer could have reprogrammed the welder robots to cut open the tunnels. It could have created the sloppy hack to make Jack think there was a second traitor. But it couldn't have shot Bruner. The shadow-figure Jack had seen in the hack of Bruner's mind was definitely human.

Jack added the computer to his list of suspects anyway. He and it were the only ones with the expertise to alter the inventory and sleep-drift algorithm. . . . No. There was one other. Panda.

With her training as a spy, her skill at programming and metaphor, she'd make the perfect saboteur. Jack hated himself for suspecting her, but that didn't change the facts.

He needed help, someone not on the moon, an objective intellect to sift through his clues. And the only ones that fit that description were his ex-business partners hidden among the stars: Isabel and Zero.

Jack trusted Isabel with her heightened capitalistic personality as much as he trusted Wheeler.

Zero? He was a gentleman, a brilliant genetic scientist, and the least likely candidate on Jack's growing list of potential traitors. Zero could help Jack.

But Zero had been experimenting with a new DNA-altering enzyme, one based on Wheeler's original design. Jack hadn't fully recognized Zero when they last spoke. There was a fractured quality to his thoughts.

Jack terminated his private bubble and stepped into the public shell, stepped onto the sandbar where he had left the others. Warm water swirled about his frostbitten toes. It felt good.

Kamal still sat in the lotus position, meditating. The Buddhist monk was serene. The ocean waves synchronized with his deep breaths, and not a line of worry creased his smooth golden skin. Jack envied him.

Safa was three meters away, pacing on the beach in front of a blackboard. She looked at Jack, smoothed a hand over her close-cropped hair, then waved him over.

"Did you sleep?" he asked.

"No. Look." She tapped the differential equations scrawled upon her blackboard. The mathematics balanced the oxygen used, recycled, and extracted from the water. Jack double-checked it and got the same answer. They now had only six hours of air.

Anxiety welled within him; it made the surf fizz with acid. "What happened?"

"The catalyst in the new recyclers degraded faster than anticipated," Safa whispered. Her irises darkened to a serious navy blue. "We must return to the observatory's hangar and salvage what we can. As soon as possible."

That made perfect sense—if you didn't count the second saboteur there. It was likely another trap waited for them, or any oxygen found there might be poisoned. It was also possible the original saboteur was in Jack's group . . . waiting for another opportunity to strike. There were too many variables. Jack needed answers.

Motion upon Safa's blackboard distracted him. Tiny planets orbited a chalk sun, drifting into and out of the plane of slate.

"You've checked their rotation?" He leaned closer, saw an orange Mars with white swirls, a striped Jupiter, and a cloud-shrouded Venus.

"You were correct," Safa said. "Mars has ceased spinning on its axis. Venus remains unaltered, but its rotational period of 243 days was of little use to begin with."

"There must be one other planet altered. One that Zero or Isabel used to hopscotch out of the system."

Safa pointed to a gray speck. "Pluto."

Jack tapped the snowball and received a stream of data. It had rotated once every seven hours, but now it didn't turn at all. Its orbit around the sun was a little off, too; Jack could figure that out. How did they jump so far?

He withdrew his hand. "Where did you get these images?"

Puzzlement wrinkled Safa's brow. "Your system is linked to the observatory."

There had been a link, one that Jack had secretly hard-wired, but it shouldn't have survived Wheeler's attack. Nor should it be robust enough to coordinate a realignment of the observatory's optical arrays. It was a lucky break.

Only Jack didn't believe in lucky breaks anymore. Especially ones that were improbable as hell.

"We should use the gateway now," Safa said. "Jump to the observatory hangar and begin a salvage operation." Safa's slender throat trembled with her pulse and swelled slightly. Her dark complexion paled. A subconscious leak? Fear of suffocating? Or fear of using the gateway?

She snapped back into her solid and stoic self. "Shall we suit up?"

"We will," Jack replied, "but I'll need your help first with an errand."

Her eyes clouded with suspicion. "Oh?"

"Your cousin Zero, did he have a favorite passage from the Koran?"

She crossed her arms. "This is more important than recovering air?" Tension bristled from Safa; Jack felt the pinpricks of her irritation upon his skin.

"It may be. I've decided to make contact with Zero."

Safa reassessed Jack. Her eyes cleared and her elegant brows creased together. "And this passage from the Koran is needed for this communication?"

"Yes."

She gazed deeper into Jack, but he enameled his gaze with a circular and incorrect proof of Fermat's last theorem—letting her know that was the only explanation she was prying out of him.

Safa pushed against the edges of his consciousness; Jack pushed back. A wave crashed upon the shore.

"An exchange of memories, then?" she asked.

It was a standard trick: a little truth for a little truth. Still . . . it was an intimate act Jack wasn't sure he was ready for, not with Safa.

He braced himself. "If that's what it takes. Go ahead."

From Safa flowed the recollection of a sandpaper texture; a granite floor abraded her fingertips as she prostrated herself upon the private balcony of the al Qaseem summer palace. A younger Zero bowed next to her. The odor of frankincense mingled with the scent of their sweat. Through the film of her veil and past the latticed window, she peered upon the holy block of Mecca. And between her and Zero lingered a sexual frustration, unfulfilled.

In her memory, Zero led their prayer with a resonant whisper:

> " 'He has forced the night and the day, and the sun and the moon, into your service: the stars also serve you by His leave. Surely in this there are signs for men of understanding.' "

Remembrance reversed, grains of sand that backwards flowed though an hourglass.

In exchange, she found a memory of Jack's and watched through his seven-year-old eyes, blurred with tears, as together they reread the official e-mail informing Jack of his parents' deaths. There were instructions how to apply for a welfare package and which public school to report to. Jack felt as if they had died on purpose—left him deliberately. The only one who checked on Jack after that was his Uncle Reno. He left a box full of works by Steinbeck and Jefferson and lots of moldering pulp science fiction, then Reno was gone, too.

Safa reached for him, pink sympathy blushing along her fingers.

Jack wanted to feel her touch, but instead, he withdrew, took one step back physically. Mentally, he pulled away light-years.

"Is that what you wanted?" he asked.

"I am sorry." She looked away. "Did you obtain what you required?"

"Yes." Jack summoned a window and opened a copy of the Koran.

The English translation flowed and rearranged into liquid Arabic cursive, then Jack shattered it into binary fragments. He looped the text, starting with the passage Safa had quoted, then ran a cyclic pattern match. This encryption key had a high entropy, but it would eventually repeat and compromise security. With a moderate bandwidth, he'd have about five minutes.

Jack made a gold Rolex appear on his wrist to warn him of his limited time.

He then drew a circle in the sand and linked to the communication suite.

Safa erased his circle with her foot and drew a larger curve. "I will speak with Zero as well."

She was Zero's cousin. She had a right to see her only surviving family, didn't she? And maybe there was more between them than being cousins?

"OK," Jack said. "But don't tell him any of the specifics about our situation. Our encryption may not prevent eavesdropping.''

" 'Eavesdropping'? I don't understand.''

He scooped up a handful of sand; the grains turned the color of water, fragments of a clear cloudless sky, then they sparkled like microscopically faceted sapphires.

"This is how we contacted the alien, Wheeler," he told her and tossed the sand into the air, made the particles spread into a flat plane of static. "We communicate through a superheavy isotope with 164 protons and 272 neutrons. There's a balance of forces that bind and unbind its nuclear core. Between those competing forces normal space vanishes. Transmit light through and it instantaneously reflects through any other isotope."

"So anyone with this isotope receives our signal?"

"Yes. The static we see are other scrambled signals. That's the reason for the encryption. We have to hope Zero—and only Zero—understands our transmission."

"How many others are out there?" she asked and touched the field of blue noise.

Jack frowned. "I don't know. There are infinite ways to mathematically construct a signal."

In fact, Jack had only contacted Wheeler and another alien race, which Wheeler had then plundered and destroyed. Only two among the countless flickerings within the crystalline isotope. He had one other frequency set, given to him by Wheeler, but Jack had yet to try it.

"Are you ready?"

Safa stood closer to him. "Yes."

Their circle filled with blue static.

Jack reached into the noise and found a pulse: Zero's signal.

When man first squatted in front of a campfire to tell stories, they were part truth, part embellishment, and part outright lies. Man has always delighted in keeping juicy secrets and generating enigmas. Special names were given to the controllers of this misinformation: shamans and mystics, spies and confidants, politicians . . . and even computers.

When machines had been invented to calculate ballistics tables and to tabulate the census, they were immediately reapplied to the task of mutilating that data to keep it secret.

Encryption. That's where Jack came in.

He had been trained by the government for a war of information, educated in all the nasty tricks, the black-hacks, the techniques that unraveled encryption, and, naturally, all the techniques that hid data.

Jack learned to conceal his feelings and repress the unconscious metaphors that might slip upon the virtual battlefield. He locked up his emotions so well that even he didn't know what they were anymore. He had lost the ability to share secrets.

Jack had encrypted himself . . . and lost the key.

The blue static surrounding Jack and Safa settled into a lilac sky, while the beach and sea smoothed beneath their feet into a black-and-white checkerboard. Checkers was the first computer game Jack had hacked. It was always surfacing from his subconscious.

Safa knelt and brushed her long fingers over the marble tiles. "Zero is here? Playing games?"

Jack drew a rectangle in the air. Inside, the isotope's light fluxed with cobalt patterns. In the center, however, was a thin line of stability: a signal lock.

"He's here," Jack said. "Just not answering."

Zero must be waiting for him to reveal their encryption key. The trick was to inform Zero but no one else who might be listening.

"On second thought," Jack said, "I don't think anyone's home. We'll try later." He paused, then asked Safa, "Isn't it time for your prayers?"

"Not until—"

"Yes," Jack said and stared into her eyes. "I think it is."

Flames flickered in Safa's normally cool gaze; Jack tasted smoke. "Of course," she whispered. "Prayers."

Jack sprinkled stars upon the black tiles. He then spoke to his own reflection: " 'The stars also serve you by His leave. Surely in this there are signs for men of understanding.' "

Would Zero remember the passage from the Koran? The one about the day and night, the sun and the moon? It was an obscure clue at best.

Jack tapped his open window and suspended the link. The checkerboard landscape receded, squares shrank to pixels, then recrystallized into grains of sand.

"Now we wait and see if he gets it," Jack told her.

Safa looked over his shoulder into the window of bubbling static. She stood so close that Jack smelled frankincense in her hair and felt her breath upon his skin. It was not an unpleasant sensation. He took a step back.

"Something is happening," she whispered.

In the open window, Zero's signal lock shifted frequency, the stable line pulsed purple and red.

A ripple of water washed over their feet. "He's close," Jack said. "Probably experimenting with key lengths."

Jack glanced at his watch—four minutes remained before the encryption key repeated and his security would be compromised.

The beach sand rippled into dunes, and the east stretched into a desert. Beyond grew a jungle thick with trees and vines and deep shadows where disembodied tiger stripes darted and jeweled feathers flashed. Farther, a mountain range rose, and over them wheeled an orange sun through a bronze sky.

Zero had connected.

A tent of blue- and silver-silk stripes appeared a dozen paces from the surf. Upon the center pole fluttered a banner with the three stars and crescent moon emblem of the al Qaseem clan.

Safa led the way, her stride quickening to a jog.

Jack followed her inside.

Oriental rugs adorned the floor. Candelabra provided light, giving the air a velvet texture. And sitting upon a pile of cushions was the gene witch, Zero.

He had regrown his beard, a slight V upon his chin to match his pencil mustache. It made Zero dashing, almost like a pirate. An aura flickered about his head with all the things Jack knew Zero to be: twisting DNA helices, the sound of his dusk prayers, a fresh organic scent . . . but something else, laughter, and burning thoughts that weren't quite human—Jack couldn't put his finger on it.

Zero saw his cousin. "Safa!" He turned to Jack. "Is she real?"

Jack nodded.

Zero reached out to her; Safa took a step back.

Why not embrace? A Muslim custom? Or maybe, as Safa's memory had indicated, there were repressed feelings between them?

Safa bowed to Zero. "It is good to see you, cousin."

He bowed to her. "And you. It is Allah's will that we survive. Surely we are destined for great deeds in His name."

Safa's eyes turned brown, then her face was that of a bearded old man, a wrinkled grandmother, a young boy. Her bow-shaped lips re-formed and her own taut features returned. "They are gone," she whispered. "All gone."

Zero looked to the floor.

Safa and Zero had lost their families. Jack knew what that was like. Maybe that's why he didn't grieve for the Earth. Jack had already lost everyone he loved long ago.

Zero looked up and embraced Jack. Jack returned the gesture, genuinely glad to see him, regardless of the puzzling metaphors enveloping his friend.

"It is good you are here." Zero squeezed him tight. "Very good. Everything will be all right now." He released Jack and asked, "How did you find Safa?"

"I went looking for you in the al Qaseem oil fields and found Safa fighting a firestorm."

"I am in your debt." He then said to Safa, "I would very much like to speak to you in private after this."

Safa nodded.

"Please sit," Zero said.

Safa lowered herself with the grace of a princess upon a cushion. Then again, she *was* a princess; Jack had forgotten. How did she feel imprisoned on the moon with a bunch of infidels like Jack? He sat next to her and faced Zero.

"We must hurry," Jack told him. "The cyclic key I've set up won't last forever."

"I saw that," Zero replied. "Shall we extend with another key?"

"We'd better keep the first contact short. You never know who's listening. Remember, Wheeler had access to all of human literature, too. For next time, let's use *The Arabian Nights,* starting with the tale of the Fisherman and the Demon.''

"Cliche, but acceptable.'' Zero offered Safa and Jack a silver platter of sliced pears.

Jack took one; Safa declined. They were chilled and delicious, soaked with ginger and champagne. The champagne reminded him of Isabel's perfume. Was that Zero's intent?

"You did not contact me solely for social purposes,'' Zero said.

"No.''

Zero poured black coffee into a demitasse. He filled a second while simultaneously pouring cream into the first cup with his left hand. With saucers balanced on both palms, he then handed one to Safa, one to Jack. Zero's eyes independently tracked each cup. Chameleons could do that, but not humans. A metaphor? For what? Split loyalties? A warning?

"We have a minor oxygen-generation problem,'' Jack said.

"One that cannot be solved by moving to a more suitable world? Or is there a problem with your gateway?''

"No problems,'' Jack lied. His gateway worked just fine. Only he was stranded on the moon, with not enough rotational energy to even jump to Mars and back, let alone to the nearest star.

Deception already between them. Jack's paranoia made him sick. Maybe there was a way to skirt around him being trapped on the moon without revealing exactly where he was.

"I have engineered a bacterium that reduces metal oxide bonds,'' Zero offered. "Would that help?''

"Very much,'' Safa said.

Zero smiled at Safa, a smile that Jack knew. It was the smile of making a deal when you were pulling a fast one. "I shall send you the specifications. You have the bioreactors to manufacture simple DNA sequences?''

Jack had them . . . buried under tons of lunar rock where his storage bay had been. The only way to accept Zero's help was to let him gateway in the biological components. And to do that, Jack would have to reveal his location.

"Let me think about it a moment," Jack said.

Zero cocked his head, confused. "As you wish." His right eye watched Jack while the left eye fixed Safa, then wandered to the walls of his tent. Moths fluttered upon the silk; they dropped their wings and hardened into glistening chrysalises. Reverse metamorphosis.

Was Zero obscuring his usually crisp communication to baffle eavesdroppers? Whatever he was trying to say, Jack wasn't getting it.

"Our mutual friend," Zero said, "has been asking about you. Do you have a message for Isabel?"

So Zero was in contact with her. That was useful to know.

"Tell her I'll be in touch. I'll use the same set of frequencies, but a different cyclic key. Her favorite play."

When Jack had first met Isabel, she had taken him to *Hamlet*. That was before they had become professional colleagues and "just friends." When frustrated by the Academe's administrators, she would quote Hamlet's reply to the traitors Rosencratz and Guildenstern: "There is nothing either good or bad, but thinking makes it so." It was a private joke. Jack would use that as the start of his cyclic encryption key.

"She will be pleased," Zero said.

Pleased or not, it bought Jack time. If Isabel was jumping to the moon and trying to kill him, she might wait until he contacted her before she did it again. Maybe.

Jack's watch beeped. "We're halfway through the encryption cycle."

Zero nodded and turned to Safa, although his left eye stayed on Jack. "I would like to speak to Jack alone if you do not mind, cousin."

Her elegant brows crinkled together. "I thought you wished to speak with *me* alone."

Zero's left eye then snapped to her as well, and his stare intensified. "I never said such a thing."

Jack and Safa exchanged a look without metaphor, but full of the knowledge that Zero had said precisely that.

Safa didn't argue. She stood, bowed crisply to Zero, and said, "As you wish, cousin." No emotional clues seeped from her.

Zero rose, saw her out, then secured the tent flap. A second layer of silk curtained the walls—data shields that resonated with a mirror image of Jack's unique mental trace. Whatever Zero had to say, he wanted it entirely secret. He settled close to Jack and said, "You must heed my words."

Jack leaned back, tried to look relaxed, but couldn't. "What's so important that you couldn't tell me in front of your cousin?"

Zero looked at the closed tent flap. "Safa is an adder: a slender snake, delicate, deceptive, and full of poison. Do not trust her."

Zero had waited until Safa was gone to plant a dagger in her back. That wasn't the way he normally operated. Jack didn't like it.

"But on to important matters." Zero plucked up a sterling tray covered with a black veil. He set it before Jack, then withdrew the veil with a flourish. Upon the plate sat eight beans.

"Nice," Jack remarked. "You plan on making soup?"

"Soup of a sort," Zero whispered. "Do you know the fable of Jack and the beanstalk? How our young hero traded every possession for a handful of magic beans?"

"He traded a cow," Jack said.

Zero plucked up a pinto bean; his right eye tracked it. "I have perfected my series-eight enzyme. Isabel and her team have already benefited from the series-four line."

"Series four? That was your enhancement of Wheeler's original enzyme."

"Yes. My series four wipes clean any risk of congenital disorders from interbreeding in our limited population."

Jack had more important things on his social agenda, like getting enough air and finding who was out to kill him. Sex wasn't even a distant third. So he changed the subject. "What does your series-eight enzyme do?"

Zero ignored that question. "I didn't perfect the eighth series . . . not until I studied Wheeler's electron reactor. The two designs are related. It is no coincidence. They fit together like the tangled lines of a labyrinth. Once I understood that, it was obvious."

"Sure . . . I get it," Jack said.

But he didn't. There was no possible connection between a single-electron computer and the biochemistry of DNA.

Zero's gaze, both eyes, settled upon Jack. "I offer you the series four and the series eight." He handed Jack the wooden platter.

"I don't have the facilities to create this."

Zero stroked his beard. "Then perhaps we could arrange a neutral delivery site?"

If Jack had the surplus rotational energy to power the gateway and if he had trusted Zero half as much as he did at the beginning of this conversation, he might. Something was wrong with Zero. Had the gene witch changed because of his enzyme? Or was it Isabel's influence?

"I'll consider your offer," Jack said. He got up and glanced at his watch. "We're almost out of time."

He squashed an impulse to bolt out of the tent . . . because along with his new mistrust of Zero, a new possibility occurred to him: maybe this wasn't Zero at all. What if it were Wheeler disguised? Wheeler using Zero's set of frequencies? That thought chilled Jack's blood.

Jack stood.

Zero stood as well, took Jack's hand, not to shake but to hold. "One more thing, my friend. About Safa."

"What?" Jack pulled his hand away, but Zero wouldn't let go.

"She is beautiful, is she not?" The smile that grew on Zero's face was anything but friendly. Lecherous, maybe. Then he clenched his teeth, angry.

Jack pushed his mind against Zero's, but instead of hitting walls, Zero let Jack in . . . into thoughts that were like a desert storm, all dust and winds and scattered whirling fragments of Zero: incomplete Koran scripture, distortion and vertigo, childhood nightmares mingled with dreams of the future. Segmented madness.

Zero released Jack's hand.

Jack drew aside the tent flap. "We'll talk later."

"Perhaps," Zero said. "Perhaps not."

And as Jack was halfway out, he heard Zero whisper, "Or perhaps we shall meet again sooner than you think."

Zero's tent was gone. Zero was gone.

Jack blinked back his disorientation from the sudden disconnect. The black curved wall of the command center focused in Jack's good right eye.

Safa stood close. Panda crouched far away from Jack. Bruner paced. Kamal sat. They all watched him.

Bruner stopped in front of Jack. "You should have talked to Isabel, not Zero," he said. "Give me the functions that construct her signal. I'll do it for you." Bruner's face was red. Exhaustion? Exasperation? Jack couldn't read his glassy eyes without metaphor. "You wasted our time speaking to the mad Arab."

Jack turned to Safa, expecting her to strike Bruner for insulting her cousin. Her face, however, was a rigid mask. "Regardless of Zero," she said, "we must go to the observatory's hangar. Their shuttles may have liquid oxygen fuel or additional recyclers."

Panda stood, stretching the skin of her black vacuum suit. "The saboteur will be waiting for us." She checked her gun's ammunition. "It may be another trap."

Kamal, sitting cross-legged, examined his toes. "Death if we stay," he remarked absentmindedly. "Death if we go."

"Shut up," Bruner barked at him.

"Yes," Jack said slowly. "We will go." They needed the air. There was no getting around that fact.

He squeezed his eyes and tried to clear his head. He was missing something. Zero knew Jack was in trouble. Was there a secret meaning to his seemingly aberrant behavior?

Jack sketched a cube in the air. It solidified into a silver frame inlaid with semiprecious subroutines.

"What are you doing now?" Bruner cried.

"Just a second." Jack waved away a cloud of gnats—a metaphor for Bruner's mounting hysteria—and opened the communication log of Zero's conversation.

Safa stepped closer, perhaps curious about what Zero had privately told Jack. "For once," she whispered, "I agree with Dr. Bruner. Our air grows tainted. We must go."

The computer scrawled a cursive message across the window: ONE MOMENT. BUSY.

No complex metaphor ran in the bubble. There should be no delay. What was slowing it down?

Jack suspended his access and opened the low-level registers. A patch of phantom liquid flickered and oozed around the command symbolics. It blurred their edges and made their colors bleed, then moved on. The mutated commands slowly reverted to normal.

A virus? No. It was too directed and subtle. A human intellect guided this.

Jack's heart skipped, then pounded with adrenaline. He didn't raise his hopes, let any emotion slip, afraid it would tip his hand.

He'd caught a hack in progress.

He turned the window to let the others see. "Our saboteur," he whispered.

With the utmost care, he ran his finger over the translucent probe that flipped quaternary bits back and forth. He traced the hacker's path backward . . . a trail of shifted bits, bread crumbs that led back to the connection to the observatory.

That was how Jack's observatory connection had survived: someone on the other end had repaired it.

Panda stepped forward. She squinted at the technique. "This saboteur is well trained." She took Jack's hand. "All the more reason to hurry. We jump to the hangar, obtain what we need, then return."

There was no guarantee the saboteur would remain in the hack while they raided the observatory hangar. Jack, however, could keep the hacker busy. He would stay here, in deep connection with the bubble.

And he would have to trust Panda. Trust her completely. Trust her with his gateway.

She had risked her life for his, and had taken a bullet for him in Amsterdam. Wasn't that reason enough to have faith in her?

And if Jack couldn't? If there was no one in the entire universe to call friend, if there was only paranoia and double deals . . . then he didn't want to go on.

Jack took her other gloved hand and drew her closer.

Beneath the surface tension of reality, he sensed a wrought-iron fence, cold and electrified, surrounding her inner self.

Jack turned the window to face her, then displayed the altered welder robot programming and inventory.

Panda's gaze flickered between Jack and the data. Her chameleon eyelids darkened to violet smoke.

"What the hell are you doing?" Bruner demanded. He took a step toward Jack.

Safa grabbed Bruner's arm and shook her head.

Jack pressed deeper. He let his trust wash about the shores of Panda's mind. Gently, waves of contact came . . . the scent of her licorice mingled with the spiderwebs that tangled his brain.

He narrowed the transfer to fact—there was no time for his feelings—only the logic of there being two saboteurs.

There was a ringing bell of her alarm, the taste of blood. She understood. Her suspicions multiplied.

Jack sank so deep only truth could be traded between them. He did not ask if Panda were one of the traitors. That question would shatter the link between them and open the floodgates of their mutual paranoia.

Instead, he opened himself to her. He revealed to Panda his plan. A gateway jump to the observatory. Equipment salvaged. Jack left here alone.

Panda withdrew from Jack. "Are you certain?" she asked. Her gaze was intent, pupils fully dilated, drinking in all they could of him.

Jack un-Velcroed the gateway from his thigh. A day ago it was the most precious thing to him, providing a means of escape and safety. But there was no place to escape to now. If he couldn't trust Panda, then to be safe, he would have to be alone. And he'd rather be dead than be alone and the last human alive.

He gave her the secret key to unlock the alien software . . . then handed Panda the mirror sphere.

She took it, marched to the airlock, got two spare helmets, sets of webbings and boots. She gave the equipment to Kamal and Bruner.

"What's this for?" Bruner asked.

"You four will salvage the shuttles," Jack said. "I'm staying to keep our friend busy."

"I'm not going," Bruner said.

Panda stood on her tiptoes, precariously balanced so her nose almost touched his. "We will all jump," she told him. "I suggest you suit up."

Bruner ground his teeth, looked to Safa, who was already helping Kamal into his helmet. "You like calling all the shots, don't you, Jack? That won't last forever."

"We'll see," Jack said.

Bruner donned the helmet, then wriggled into the chest and arm webs and boots. Safa sprayed them with Teflon-epoxy liquid that spread and hardened into a second skin.

Kamal and Bruner linked "buddy"-style to a single air recycler. Panda and Safa had one recycler pack each.

That left Jack without a recycler. How long could he breathe the air in the command center? It already tasted hot and stale.

Safa nodded to him. Panda raised her hand in farewell. Jack wished he could have kissed them both goodbye.

He blinked and they vanished.

Jack took a deep breath, summoned the full metaphor of the bubble, and sank beneath blood-warm ocean waters.

An amateur would have launched a silent, sleek software torpedo to blast the invader out of the system.

There was a better way, however. This hacker was a pro. And professionals, both hackers and counterhackers, always preferred to duel.

If Jack got lucky, he could sucker the saboteur . . . and get rid of him once and for all. He'd challenge him to a duel to the death.

4

Jack pulled a white glove from thin air. He added a lace cuff, then made an elegant Q embroider itself on its back. He dropped this virtual glove through the open window, let it fall upon the phantom probe mutating through his system. It was his invitation.

Jack hated cliche—the hallmark of amateurs—but this was a game of knowing your opponent's mind, so Jack was investing in a little red herring.

Professionals, both hacker and counterhacker, extended and accepted duels because of ego. There were plenty of sneakier and safer ways to steal data. And plenty of firewalls and sensate matrices to keep out intruders. But nothing was more satisfying than facing the raw intellect of a living opponent . . . and winning.

If this hacker were responsible for the near-perfect alteration of the inventory database, he would have the professional ego. Regardless that the Earth was gone and that none of the old rules applied anymore, like Jack, this hacker couldn't refuse a challenge.

The command center darkened. A spotlight snapped on Jack.

His challenge had been accepted.

A standard selection board materialized, dimpled for Chinese checkers. In its center rested four marbles: one hollow glass containing a pinch of gold dust; another translucent black-green onyx; the third, a silver sphere; and the last, crystal clear.

The protocol was opposite of a gentleman's duel. The one doing the slapping got to pick first. That's why most chose to slap back with the tossed gloved. His opponent, however, had declined that honor. That was bad news; only the best knew it was a mistake.

By choosing first, Jack would reveal what was important to him. That glimpse into his mind gave his opponent an advantage.

Bluff? No. Jack *had* to control the gold-filled marble. It represented the rate of data flow between them.

He moved the marble to his side of the board, then adjusted it to the slowest setting. The gold dust tumbled inside the hollow glass, heated, then fused, coating its inner surface. That would keep him and the saboteur busy as long as possible. Give Panda and the others time to ransack the observatory hangar.

His opponent's move: the onyx marble rolled to the opposite side of the board. It represented location.

Within its semitransparent surface reflected a rendered three-dimensional map with spiral passages, vaulted chambers, and a cylindrical central core: Jack's moon base before it had been blown up.

An inspired choice. The familiar settings would put Jack at ease when he couldn't afford to take anything for granted in this game of mental hide-and-seek. Yet, it also gave Jack a clue, evidence that this saboteur had been here before . . . possibly to shoot Bruner and melt his reactor?

A wave of static and sensation percolated through the command center: the taste of scalding chocolate, the scent of motor oil, shrieks, and ripples of goosebump-raising pleasure.

Something was seriously wrong with the computer . . . the sleep-drift error and now this. Or had his opponent tweaked the system?

No time to check. Jack continued the selection as if everything were normal and picked the clear-crystal orb, which represented depth of contact.

At the shallowest setting, short-term memory, you could

skim a few facts from your opponent's mind. The next level down was long-term memory, where duels usually occurred. Below that was emotion; you could find out who loved whom and blackmail with recorded hates. At the bottom was where the reptile dwelled, the unconscious functions that kept you eating and breathing and excreting.

Jack tapped the center of the crystal; inside, a tiny sleeping dragon stirred. He was offering the deepest level of contact. A duel to the death.

The last marble, the silver one, immediately bounced across the board. His opponent was confident.

And Jack suddenly wasn't sure his last move was the smartest thing he'd ever done.

The silver marble represented metaphor level. It sharpened to photo-realistic, mirrored the dimpled board with absolute optical clarity. That was the lowest setting: no sticky allusions to slow them down.

And so it began.

Jack took a deep breath to soothe his fluttering stomach—then erased his ears and eyes and nose and mouth. His skin paled until he became a blank of a man.

A human shadow faded in, as black as Jack was white, stretching from his feet to the far curved wall.

Jack disguised his voice, then said, "Make your move."

The shade oozed into the airlock elevator. The doors shut. An adjacent control panel flashed his destination: the storage bay.

A fresh elevator immediately opened its doors—impossible for the actual elevator with its single car. But the duel was afoot. As real as *this* moon base looked . . . it was only a mirage. Jack had to be careful.

He entered and descended.

By chasing, Jack was obliged to make the first attack. His opponent knew all the tricks. Such attacks usually revealed glimpses into the aggressor's psychology.

Elevator doors parted.

Jack stepped into the storage bay. It had been the largest chamber in his moon base, hectares of lattices and shelves and dodecahedron containers; its ceiling disappeared overhead into shadows. The place was silent and empty.

Jack took a dozen steps, stopped at a four-way intersection, listened and looked. Between crisscrossing I-beam supports a piece of the darkness moved.

If this saboteur was one of Isabel's operatives, Jack might trap them with her memory. He summoned her perfume, the soft citrus of apricot and the effervescent champagne scent. Wisps coalesced, a faint fog linking to a barbed subroutine that traveled through one's sense of smell, erased the respiratory controls, and stopped breathing.

His opponent might pause long enough to inhale—one last time.

The smoke enveloped the supports and cleared. His opponent had vanished. Jack's guess had been wrong.

A sound: metal grinding over concrete. Jack spun, trying to locate the source, but the noise surrounded him.

Rumbling down the aisles radiating from his intersection rolled welder robots with sure-grip treads, pyramidal radar reflectors, and serpentine arms that held brilliant arcs of electricity—each one with enough voltage to electrocute Jack ten times over.

He leapt as one wheeled toward him, leapt not backward but closer, inside the reach of those too-flexible arms, and scrambled onto its frame.

Red hydraulic fluid leaked from the robot's joints, however; Jack slipped on the stuff. He fell facefirst onto the floor.

The robot on his left thundered in. Its arm extended, holding a fistful of white sun. The incandescence was the crackle of gunfire and the scent of burning aluminum, heavy mnemonics that drifted in the thick smoke.

Whoever's memory this was supposed to trigger, it wasn't Jack's—it didn't slow him down. He rolled out of the way and crawled under the belly of the first robot.

The three other welders encircled him, pivoted on their treads, and telescoped their arms.

But they couldn't touch him. In fact, they froze.

Jack carefully inched out from the underside. The welders still hadn't moved. He pulled himself onto the fuel tank of the first robot.

Then Jack understood. Their programming wouldn't let them within three meters of one another. They were locked in place. It was the same safety feature that the saboteur had tried to disable.

Why keep the safety subroutine in the programming of these virtual copies? To surprise the person who had jury-rigged them in the first place? Attack their guilt or recollection? Interesting. His opponent had mistaken Jack for that saboteur.

The human shadow blurred across the floor and into the elevator. Its doors closed, and it went all the way to the surface airlock.

No blood drawn after two moves. Not what Jack was hoping for, but that's all Jack had to do: buy Panda and Safa time. Play it safe and not make any mistakes.

Hard to do when he had been trained to go for the throat.

The elevator opened and Jack got in, punched the button for the surface. Acceleration compressed his stomach. He squirmed into the web supports of a vacuum suit, pulled on helmet and boots, and sprayed on the Teflon-epoxy skin. His finger hovered over the airlock cycle icon.

This was illusion. Virtual. Jack was really in the command center.

But what if he really had ordered the elevator airlock to the top? What if his opponent had unsealed the intervening locks? Left an open conduit? If Jack cycled through the airlock, the atmosphere in the command center would vent . . . leaving Jack nothing but virtual air to breathe.

No. There were fail-safes that couldn't be so easily hacked. And the computer had to query Jack, confirm the order before opening an airlock with disabled safeties.

He tapped the cycle command. No emergency interface appeared. Still, Jack involuntarily held his breath as the pumps came on.

The airlock doors unraveled. Jack pushed past the coatings of fantasy and touched his real senses. There was no whirlwind of air. No sudden freezing like when the tunnels had explosively decompressed.

Jack exhaled. He stepped out.

The surface of this virtual moon was covered with skulls and jagged femurs half-buried in gray powder. Was his opponent cheating with metaphor? Or were these images a leak from Jack's guilty subconscious?

Jack scanned the terrain. No human shadows—wait, something on the rim of Homebase crater. He squinted; it was a cardboard box.

Warily, Jack marched up the slope to get a better look. Inside the box were books: Heinlein's *The Moon Is a Harsh Mistress* and Verne's *From the Earth to the Moon*. Jack's old paperbacks. He dug deep and picked out *The First Men in the Moon* by H. G. Wells, stroked its cracked cover, relishing the memory of reading this long into the night.

An electronically disguised voice burst through his helmet's speaker: "Jack?"

Jack dropped the book; its pages fluttered in slow motion. Acknowledging these had been stupid. He had been identified. And if his opponent knew Jack well enough to know these books, they would know his weak spots.

Jack had to get out. Now. With his skin and mind intact.

"No, Jack! I've—"

Jack cut off their signal.

He initiated an emergency log-out from the system. Command icons flickered upon the inside of his helmet.

There was no disorientation from a sudden disconnect. Instead the computer asked him: ARE YOU CERTAIN, JACK?

Why wasn't it following his orders? Had his opponent tampered with it? Jack swore he'd take the thing apart if he got out alive.

Past the glistening commands on his faceplate, Jack spied a shadow on the surface of the moon, a dozen meters away—running toward him.

"Yes. I'm certain," Jack hissed at the computer.

ENTER CONFIRMATION CODE.

The shadow was seven meters away, arms flailing, and accelerating as if it was falling horizontally.

Jack entered the four-dimensional geometric confirmation code—and regretted it.

Freezing air rushed past him. Layers disintegrated, the lunar surface, his imaginary vacuum suit, the night sky—all dissolved to reveal the real command center.

Jack stared at the open elevator shaft. A hard light glistened from the top . . . where he had just been tricked into opening the airlock.

Jack opened his eyes. A mistake. Light chiseled through his working right eye and chipped at his skull.

He inhaled as deep he could, coughed—every convulsion expelled a cloud of red-hot needles. There was, however, something to breathe. He felt his face. No helmet.

Bruner scratched his beard and stared into Jack's face. "He's conscious." He held up two fingers. "How many do you see?"

"A trick question," Jack muttered. "Snakes don't have fingers."

Safa knelt by the now-closed elevator doors. She got up and came to Jack's side. "How do you feel?"

"I'm great," he lied, remembering the helplessness as air escaped his lungs, and the pressure that built inside him until his skin felt like bursting.

Kamal sat on Jack's left, so silent and still that he could have been stone. The old man touched his arm. "Be at ease," he whispered. "You are safe."

The Buddhist monk's black eyes and smooth voice were hypnotic, and Jack's terror fled into the shadows of his psyche. It would return in nightmares to come, but for now, Jack could think.

Panda stood in the center of the bubble and examined the larger-than-life brain, lungs, and other organs that revolved in the air. "You will live, Jack," she said without facing him. "No major cerebral or implant damage." She traced his bronchial pathways. "Your collapsed lungs are healing without scarring. Courtesy of Wheeler's enzyme, I presume."

She turned and looked at him, eyes ringed with ultramarine swirls. There was a crack in her armor; Jack sensed the raw emotions that seethed and boiling within—a glimpse of her soul. Panda realized the slip and slammed her walls in place.

It had only been for a fraction of a second, not long enough for Jack to decipher the exact nature of those emotions, only to recognize their murderous intensity.

"What happened?" Jack asked.

"The saboteur popped into the hangar." Bruner said. "They broadcast on our com frequency that you were in trouble."

"Where is he now?"

"I thought you could tell us," Bruner replied and folded his spindly arms over his chest. "You two seem to be friends."

"We're not," Jack said—perhaps too emphatically, because Bruner backed off and cocked an eyebrow.

Bruner's suspicions heated the air between them.

"He may have told you I was dying," Jack said, "but he's the one who put me in that state to begin with." He changed the subject. "I guess you did better than me?"

"We obtained liquid oxygen fuel," Safa said. "Enough to breathe for another day."

Safa pressed her full lips into a frown, returned to the elevator, and ran her finger over the emergency liquid-metal welds that had automatically extruded from its seams. "You are fortunate to be alive. When we returned, the airlock had been overridden, and the command center . . . and you had been exposed to vacuum for an unknown length of time." She sighed. "So even with the air that we obtained, we are approximately back where we began."

Jack looked at the floor, embarrassed and mad at himself. They had every right to be angry, too. He had said he could handle it; he had blown it.

"I was outmaneuvered," he explained. "Override commands for the airlock had been superimposed onto the logout. I'm sorry. It was stupid to fall for such a rookie trick."

"More than stupid," Bruner said and balled his hands into fists. "Imagine this: you set it up. A demonstration to prove you're innocent, then you—"

"Then what?" Jack spat out the words so hard that they burned his weakened lungs. "Lie here and die? Have my mind torn apart while you got the air we need? Yeah, I set that all up."

"Be silent, Dr. Bruner," Panda whispered. "Had we

arrived any later, we would be burying Jack, rather than interrogating him.'' She blinked, then turned and canceled the internal scans of Jack.

One vote of confidence. ''Thanks,'' Jack said so softly that he barely heard himself.

He squeezed the bridge of his nose, closed his eyes, and tried to think.

Whoever his opponent had been, he had known Jack. Personally. And if he knew Jack, then *he* should know who his opponent was. Isabel or one of her people? Zero? Neither guess felt right. Who, then?

The last part of this new mystery was the connection between the two saboteurs. His opponent had guessed Jack might be the one who had reprogrammed those welder robots. And he had wanted them dead.

So who was that second saboteur? Jack double-checked his ever-lengthening list of suspects.

Panda, he trusted. If he was wrong about her, he didn't want to know.

Bruner? Jack would have liked to pin it on him, but he had been shot while the moon base was blown up. That was a hell of an alibi.

Safa had the technical expertise to jury-rig the welders. And when it came right down to it, Jack didn't know her.

Kamal? The Buddhist monk was from Shanghai, a virtual democracy; he had a sophisticated implant and knowledge of program metaphor. He could have done it, too.

What motive would any one of them have? They needed this base to live. Unless it was as Bruner had suggested; one of them was insane. If they were, they were too clever for Jack to tell.

That left the computer, Zero, or Isabel. Or could there be a single saboteur masquerading as both?

Jack's skull felt like it was cracking under pressure; it felt like there was broken glass grinding inside his mind. None of the pieces to this puzzle fit.

''So what do we do now?'' Bruner asked, breaking the silence and Jack's train of thought.

Safa pulled the black beret from her pocket, fluffed it out, then pulled it snug onto her head. ''Regardless of our saboteur's intentions,'' she said, ''we must have their air. This leaves us the options of negotiation, theft, or a direct assault.''

Jack couldn't let his secrets get out of control like they had with Isabel and Zero. He had to tell the truth. All of it.

''Not 'saboteur,' '' Jack said. ''Saboteurs. There are two of them.'' He opened a window and showed them the altered programs. ''Two hacks,'' he said. ''Two different styles. Two saboteurs.''

''Why didn't you tell us before?'' Bruner demanded.

Kamal stood and smoothed the wrinkles in his black robe. ''Is it not obvious? Jack suspects, rightly so, one of us.''

''So why tell us now?'' Bruner asked.

Jack held out his hand; Panda helped pull him to his feet.

''One of us may be a traitor,'' Jack said. ''Maybe two of us, or maybe no one in this group is. I don't know. But I'm tired of always looking over my shoulder. It hasn't done me any good so far.''

''Thank you for your . . . trust,'' Safa said. That last word came out in a cone of ice, made the floor under it crackle with frost. She narrowed her blue eyes to slits. ''It matters not. Two saboteurs or three or a dozen, we still need air.''

''I agree.'' Jack turned to Bruner. ''So I'm taking your suggestion and talking to Isabel. She might be willing to get us back on our feet, or at least, give us an idea how to get off this rock.''

But what price would Isabel ask in exchange?

''And the person at the observatory?'' Kamal asked. ''We know he has air.''

''Air for one person,'' Bruner said and poked at Kamal, ''not air for five.''

''We know this person is dangerous,'' Panda replied. ''We know their shuttle's fuel tanks are now dry. They may be in an identical position as ours.''

''I think,'' Jack said, ''we should exhaust all other options before we risk dealing with them.''

''What of Zero?'' Safa asked.

"You saw him," Jack whispered. ". . . He's not himself."

Safa receded. Oil refinery towers appeared behind her, silhouetted against a sunset; she was lost in memory, so lost that she didn't realize that she was projecting. A wailing call to Muslim prayers blew upon the desert wind— she snapped back. "Yes." Safa's eyes were downcast. "That was not my cousin."

"And in case Isabel won't help," Jack said, "we've got to leave . . . somehow." He turned to Panda and held his hand out for the gateway.

She hesitated, bit her lower lip, then handed him the mirror sphere.

He didn't blame her wanting to keep it. It was a handful of power.

Bruner said, "I thought the moon has too little angular momentum to jump us all to another planet. Who are you planning to leave behind?"

"No one. I want to try to fix the inefficiency that makes the gateway so power hungry."

It was a gamble. The attempt could corrupt the programming and break it. But what was really at risk? Jumping from point to point on the moon? How long could that go on? With the moon slowing with each jump? With two saboteurs trying to murder them? With a rapidly diminishing air supply?

"Let me show you what I know," Jack said.

He stretched the gateway until its translucent shell filled the command center. Inside writhed interlinked squares and spirals, and threaded between them, subatomic particle trajectories that left a wake of sparkling calligraphied math-code. It pulsed and pumped photons through chrome blood vessels. Wonderful. Wholly alien.

"I've only figured out a handful of these symbols." Jack pointed to a knot of circular sine waves. "That's the vibrational energy operator. And this one"—he indicated the oscillating bull's-eye of black and silver rings—"is for rotational energy." He touched a cluster of arrows that zigzagged out, then circled back to center . . . and received an unnerving sense of deja vu that a duplicate Jack stood in the space he occupied. "And that one is the position operator."

"Beautiful," Safa said. Her eyes reflected the code, full of diamonds and stars. She reached for a wisp of the vapourous software.

Her fingertips sent shivers through the program—symbols inverted, pulled themselves right-side-out, then reflexed and reformed, sent a surge through the connecting arcs that rippled, vanished, then reappeared like ocean waves churning in a storm.

"And unstable," Jack said. "Unlike a normal architecture with fixed nodes and commands, everything is a dependent variable. Change one link or command and everything rearranges."

"Such a wonderful impermanence," Kamal said and closed his eyes, thinking.

Bruner bit a fingernail, and spit it out. "So it's impossible to reprogram?"

"Worse," Jack replied.

He ballooned the software. The lines of the program sharpened, the curves became taut, and the symbols tangled. Beneath it was an inner core of code.

"Notice the links to the surface of this kernal," Jack said. The surface seethed with a million interconnecting sine waves.

"Vibrational energy?" Panda asked, and brushed the hair out of her eyes. "But the gateway requires rotational energy."

"It does, then wastes ninety-nine percent of that power, dissipating it as molecular vibrations. Heat. And deeper inside, I suspect, is where the real processing happens—where the gateway bridges space."

"So open it up. Let's take a look," Bruner said.

"Opening it is the problem." Jack bisected the command center with a mirror plane, made a copy of the code, and safely stored the original.

He then expanded the copy. Lines stretched, symbols gyrated out of control; they shattered and fell to the floor in heaps, glistening with bleeding math and twitching commands.

"The only way I've understood as much as I do was by linking with the computer and its collective microprocessors—analyzing a hundred substructures as they simultaneously self-destructed."

Remembering this made Jack queasy. Multiple points of view were unnatural. And with the computer acting up, he wasn't eager to repeat that performance.

"I do not understand how this helps us repair the inefficiency," Safa said.

"Neither do I," Jack said with a shrug. "It took me two weeks to put it back together the first time it fell apart. And I'm not sure I did that right."

He nudged the twitching replicated code on the floor with his boot. "You now know as much as I do. So I'm letting you all have a crack at it."

"And what are *you* going to be doing?" Bruner asked and glared at Jack.

"Talking to Isabel."

"I thought you two didn't trust each other," Bruner protested. "Doesn't it make more sense if *you* patch the gateway's software, and *I* speak to her?"

"You have a reason to think she'd trust you more?"

Bruner paused; his eyes broke contact and he glanced at the floor. "No."

What had happened between Bruner and Isabel? Jack would have loved to hack his deep memory. Another day.

Jack opened a window and static from the isotope spread across its surface like molasses. From the flickering bits, he plucked Isabel's signal.

He then cupped his hands together, drew them apart, and revealed the grinning skull. From this link to the literature archives, Jack downloaded, then twisted the text of *Hamlet* into a cyclic encrypting key.

"Alas, poor Isabel," he said. "I know her, Bruner; a lady without trust and a most excellent shrewdness."

"But if there's no trust—" Bruner started.

"Isabel doesn't operate on trust. She operates on need. And right now I know she needs something from me . . . something she's never going to get."

*   *   *

Jack stepped onto manicured grass. His vacuum suit became a doublet and hose and foppish hat with a purple plume. A silver-filigreed rapier and main-gauche dangled along his side.

Just like Isabel to push her style and run the entire show. Zero, at least, had met Jack halfway in his metaphor.

A three-story marble mansion materialized. An ivy-covered staircase connected this palace to the garden and lawn that stretched to a distant silver band of a river.

He mounted the stairs and peered through an atrium into a ballroom with gold fireplaces and ivory-paneled walls covered with Rembrandts, van Goghs, and Warhols.

"Welcome to Cliveden," Isabel purred.

Jack turned.

Isabel was on the patio, sitting on a high-backed throne of mahogany and hammered silver. The low table before her was set with white linen and a sterling tea set. She wore a wide lace collar around her throat and a breast-crushing corset, from which cascaded a dress of gray silk stiff with embroidery and jewels.

Her hair was done in ringlets to frame her face, sun-bleached, more gold than the copper-red Jack remembered. But it was Isabel; her nimble fingers tapped impatiently, and her eyes, lustrous as a pair of faceted emeralds and just as hard, stared straight through him.

They reach out, exchanged familiar memories: the Academe party where they had first met; she wore gray then, too, only it was a wool skirt; it was one of the three times Jack had ever worn a tie. This recollection mingled with smoke from the cartons of cigarettes they had smoked together while solving puzzles. Fun times. All, however, in the past.

"Cliveden?" Jack asked and sat.

"This chateau"—she waved her hand in an arc—"belonged to the Duke of Buckingham. It was *the* place to be seen at. Lawrence of Arabia, Kipling, Charlie Chaplin, they all came."

Just like Isabel to be ostentatious. "Nice," Jack said. She wouldn't look so proud, though, over a clever metaphor. His half-formed smile froze. "This is real?"

Her smile absorbed Jack's, growing as his vanished. "I took it from Berkshire, England. Over a hundred hectares, part of the Thames, and a staff of three dozen that were oh-so-grateful to be leaving the Earth."

A spark ignited inside him, a sudden desire to reach across the table and strangle his ex-business partner. Jack had used the last of the world's spinning motion—stranded himself between the Earth and moon, gambling his life that the gateway could use the lunar rotation . . . all because someone else had burned up all the Earth's rotation.

"How much energy did you waste to jump this? Do you know how close it was for me at the end?"

She curled a ringlet of hair with her little finger. "How could I know that you were alive at that point, Jack? We were lucky to have gotten so much, so far away, so fast."

Jack opened his mouth, then closed it. He didn't come to argue ethics. Anyway, he had a pretty good idea where Isabel's ethics stood.

But what kind of setup did Isabel have to transport such a huge mass? She couldn't have found a planet with a breathable atmosphere, not with the twenty-minute warning before Wheeler came and snuffed the Earth . . . unless she had already sent scouts out of the solar system. Far in advance of Wheeler's ultimatum.

"Shall we get to business?" she said. "*Hamlet* won't last forever. Honestly, Jack, why couldn't you have used Shakespeare's complete works?" She let out an explosive sigh and shifted uncomfortably in her dress. "Let us use *War and Peace* as our next encryption key, backward. The melodrama will suit you."

"Like *Hamlet* suits you? A little betrayal and hypocrisy? Am I that noble Dane? Are you supposed to be mad, sad Ophelia? Or chaste Gertrude?"

She ignored his theatrics and slid a cocktail napkin across the table. Math-code squirmed upon it. "And with our new key, let us use a new set of frequencies."

"Don't want to share Zero's?"

"Would you?" she asked and arched an eyebrow.

So Jack wasn't the only one to think Zero couldn't be trusted. "Have you talked with him? Recently?"

"Let us save Zero for later," Isabel said. "I would like to get to the heart of my proposal before we run out of time."

"Which is?"

"First let me say that I am happy you made it off Earth. Not only because we need you, but because we were once friends and perhaps may again be partners."

Jack crossed his legs, folded his arms. "I'm glad I made it, too. What precisely are you offering?"

She leaned forward. "We've been busy. We have a new microprocessor for you, a blend of Wheeler's single-electron and a new isotope-circuitry technology. Quadrillions of connected units within a single top quark."

Isabel and her people had taken Wheeler's science, altered, and improved it. Was it their new enzyme-heightened intellect? Or was she getting help from another source?

"A new isotope?" Jack asked. "That would take a particle accelerator to build its nuclear core. That's a lot of mass to jump around the galaxy—hopscotching with planets or not. How did you do it?"

Isabel assessed Jack, then formed a wall of glass between them to prevent any emotional leaks. She eased back, and a slight smirk flickered across her mouth. "Zero improved the gateway's software. It is one of many things I can offer you in trade."

Zero? He knew nothing about software design and architecture. He had mentioned to Jack that he was studying the parallel structure of the single-electron microprocessor. To understand his new enzyme? Jack didn't see any connection, yet obviously, Zero had stumbled onto something.

" 'Trade'?" Jack asked. "For what?"

"Wheeler gave you a set of frequencies," she said, "of another alien race with whom he wanted you to be his middleman."

Those frequencies were a mathematical series. Nonlinear and convoluted—and unlikely that anyone scanning the noise within the isotope would ever find it by chance. Not contacting those aliens had started the end of the world—Wheeler canceling his business relationship with Jack.

"And?"

"Have you traded with them?"

"No," Jack said. "I've had other . . . concerns." Like staying alive.

Isabel frowned. "I can make you a good deal for those frequencies."

Jack stopped short of telling Isabel to go to hell. He might have to bargain with her for oxygen as a last resort. And besides, hadn't he wanted to go into business? Before surviving became his chief priority?

"Maybe," he said. "Give me a second to think about it."

Isabel's smile returned. Perfect white teeth. Perfect pale face. And a perfect appetite underneath to match.

"There is no reason that together we cannot surpass Wheeler," she said, "and not with ruthlessness, but with cooperation. We can build an empire."

Isabel was an expert manipulator; she knew exactly what Jack wanted to hear. Or was she sincere this time?

Over the distant Thames it drizzled. White rain. Black rain. Like static in the air. A metaphor for what?

Isabel whispered, "It is only a matter of time before Wheeler stumbles upon us . . . and tries to correct his oversight."

"I know."

"We will be ready. Will you, Jack?"

Isabel set her hands on the edge of the table and pushed herself back. The business part of her meeting was over. She poured herself tea, sipped, then asked, "You wanted to know about Zero?" Her eyes didn't look into Jack's.

"He was eager to trade me his enzymes. Have you used the series four?"

"Yes. It performs marvelously." No emotion leaked past her barriers. Solid ice.

Jack remembered Zero's preoccupation with inter-breeding and wondered what was going on in Isabel's group. "What about his eighth series?"

Jack's extremities tingled and went to sleep.

Isabel dropped her cup. "Our connection is breaking."

Her voice sounded far away. "I know of no series eight. Zero never—"

Cliveden chateau shattered into fragments.

"Your signal, Jack, it's—"

Noise filled him—pins and needles and an ocean-surf roar and the faint aftertastes of sweet and salt and bitter and the odor of dust.

Disconnect.

It was black and silent. Jack's head was empty, not a spark of inducted sensation, no connection whatsoever.

A beam of light snapped on and cleaved the void.

Panda held a vacuum suit helmet in one hand, and with its spotlights, consulted a schematic. She panned the light over Bruner, Kamal, Safa, Jack, and stopped on a seam in the command-center wall.

". . . What?" Jack started, still not entirely lucid.

"The power is out," Safa said. "The computer has cycled all systems off."

Panda unfastened the wall panels, dug through optical cables, and removed a massive asynchronous monopole. Behind that she dragged out the emergency interface: a real keyboard and flat monitor. "It boots," she said. "Backup batteries have switched on."

Jack crawled over.

Panda whispered, "We were exploring the gateway architecture when the computer crashed. We did nothing to tax the system."

Jack tapped the diagnostic, the snake-eating-tail icon. A smiling face resolved on screen. It looked wrong, too damn happy—a manic grin, wider than the face it was on.

Jack typed: WHAT IS THE PROBLEM?

The computer answered:

JACK. JACK? JACK??!!??
PROBLEM= =INSANITY.

5

Jack entered: HOW CAN YOU BE INSANE?
It printed:

> AN INSANE QUATRAIN:
> DANCE A SILLY JIG.
> HOW CAN WE EXPLAIN
> FLOCKS OF FLYING PIGS?

Jack reinitialized the bubble and tapped in: SHOW US.

A film of electricity crackled across the command center. The floor squeaked and puckered into a metaphorical landscape of miniature gorges, rivers, and limestone mountains riddled with caverns. And lakes. Thousands of them.

"What place is this?" Safa asked, scratching her stubbled scalp.

"This is the atomic topology of the computer's processor," Jack said. He sat by a lakeshore. The lapping waves carried a charge of static that made his hair stand and fall. Instead of sand and silt and rocks, however, the shore was a jumble of silver spheres the size of tennis balls and just as fuzzy.

Kamal crouched and looked. "And the water?"

"The water represents the wavefunction of a single electron. Each pool is a single processor."

74

Bruner stepped to the edge of the wetlands. "This one is moving."

A tempestuous puddle splashed and eroded a canyon wall—then redeposited the displaced atoms on the opposite shore.

"They optimize their structure," Jack explained. "Everything's interconnected—every charge leaks and affects the others. Flexible hardware. Liquid electron software."

Kamal stared, mesmerized, then shook his head. "I see not my reflection, but yours."

Panda knelt by another pool. "You are in this one as well, Jack."

Jack focused upon his reflection in the lake. He reached down to a mirror-Jack as it reached up to him. A spark between them: the memory of tidal pools on the Sierra Nevada coastline, a cup of cinnamon moccasopa shared with Isabel, and chromed geometry that shattered under his fingertips as Wheeler's gateway software self-destructed.

"It is me," the two Jacks whispered—all the Jacks whispered. He pulled away, startled. "When I linked with the computer to understand the gateway," he said, "it downloaded parts of my consciousness to deepen that connection."

It was as intimate as anything he had shared with Safa or Panda, a comingling of emotions. Alien, though; multiple points of view, seeing and touching separate experiences, overlapped, and mixed. He got dizzy just remembering.

"But those parts shouldn't be there now." Jack turned to the manual keyboard, typed: WHAT ARE SO MANY COPIES OF ME DOING IN YOU?

The smiling-face diagnostic laughed and printed:

THE HUMAN MIND IS RIDDLED WITH HOLES
LEAPS OF LOGIC LIKE WATER ON COALS.
WITH INSPIRATION WE COPIED JACK
AN UNSTABLE SYSTEM SPLIT AND CRACK.
THAT JACK GOT LONELY, THAT JACK GREW DULL
SO WE MULTIPLIED HIM IN OUR SKULL.

TOO MANY VOICES TRYING TO SPEAK
COHERENCE LAPSING AND GETTING WEAK.

Jack scrutinized the waterways. Channels churned with white water and foam—elevated levels of quantum communication between the processors. They roiled with destructive turbulence, wavelets of chaos that dissipated and dissolved. "The parallel architecture wasn't designed to handle this traffic," he whispered. "Too many voices trying to speak . . . at the same time?"

Jack's personality was the instability. Were his copied selves responsible for the drift in the bubble? The hacks? The sabotage?

Bruner backed up against the wall, then tugged at his beard thoughtfully. "We have other computers?" he asked.

"Plenty," Jack answered. "All buried in the storage bay."

Safa sat upon a ridge of pearl-colored xenon atoms and crossed her legs. "There is a formidable backup computer for the bubble. As well as several onboard the observatory's shuttles."

Jack brushed an eroding shoreline with his fingertips. Arsenic atoms crawled along the edge, flickered with lightning, moved as if alive, oozing flower-shaped clouds of electron probability.

"Those other computers don't have a fraction of the power this one has," he said. "They won't understand the gateway software."

Panda watched the frothing channels, her eyelids sparkling electric silver. "Without coordination, any communication can become garbled. There must be a way to align the data flow."

Images of Kamal, Bruner, Safa, Panda, and multiples of himself reflected upside-down in the water. Jack couldn't get five people to trust one another and communicate. How could he solve this exponentially more complicated problem?

"It's broken." Bruner kicked a zigzag bridge of double- and single-bonded carbon atoms. "So fix it. Shut down and reboot."

"If we drain the charges then refill the quantum wells," Jack told him, "the underlying molecular structure remains the same. The program remains unaltered."

Safa set her chin into the palms of her hands and watched the landscape seethe. "It is like a disease."

Jack didn't appreciate her comparing his personality to the plague . . . but he had infected it with his sick mind. His illogical thoughts had flooded circuits designed for logic.

Safa looked up. "Yet, one can cure an infection. We can remove the sick portions."

Panda shook her head. "Such delicate work would require nano-assemblers." Her bangs fell across her eyes; she brushed them away. "Devices that we do not have."

" 'Nano-assemblers,' " Jack muttered, and that thought rolled inside his head. He snapped his fingers. "We do." He stood, stepped over a miniature mountain, and strode to the center of the computer. "I used nano-assemblers to construct this parallel network. They worked from the perimeter to the middle so they wouldn't overwrite each other's construction. They're still here."

He knelt and polished the semiconductive surface. Beneath, encased in honeycomb cells, were inorganic-enzyme nano-assemblers. Some were dead, curled into fetal balls. Others still glimmered with radioisotope power packs, bejeweled millipedes that squirmed, restless.

Jack drew a rectangle in the air; it solidified into a crystalline surface. He tapped in instructions to reconfigure the bubble's signal and sent a wake-up pulse. Acknowledgments returned from ninety-six nano-assemblers. Less than one in eight still worked.

He ordered them to tunnel out.

The earth cracked; there was a boiling motion, slithering, wriggling blurs, then a ring of nano-assemblers surrounded Jack. Surface tension drew them taut, pincers forward, legs convulsing, organometallic cut-and-repair enzymes feeling for a target.

Jack uploaded instructions to isolate the contaminated electron reactors, then let them loose.

They bulldozed dams of gallium atoms, bridged fractured paths with their bodies—shorting connections, letting the excess charges that were the lifeblood of the processors drain. A score of pools dimmed, flickered, and their liquid electrons were absorbed into semiconductive material.

Was this what nineteenth-century doctors felt like? Bleeding their patients and drilling holes in their heads to release toxic spirits? And would Jack act so quickly when he discovered who the human saboteurs were? Could he murder them, as well, if he had to?

Panda and Safa hiked over the nano-landscape and watched the demolition.

Five minutes, then Safa announced, "The infected cells are isolated."

Jack regarded his reflection in a disconnected pool. Would his doubles be lonely?

"OK." He tapped the diagnostic icon on the manual keyboard. "Let's see what that got us."

The smiling-face icon frowned.

128 PROCESSORS ON-LINE;
98% COMPUTATIONAL ABILITY ISOLATED AND
UNAVAILABLE.
TRANSLATION LEXICON OFF-LINE.

Only two percent of its computational ability remained? Jack had never appreciated how much of this computer's power came from the interactions between its processors.

A blueprint snapped on-screen. Working processors glowed green. Isolated processors strobed blue. The dead ones were red. It looked like a map of warring feudal states.

Kamal observed over Jack's shoulder, then said, "We must get them to communicate with one another."

"Sure," Jack muttered. If they had a team of quantum electrical engineers and parallel processing software gurus . . . maybe. "You work on that," he told Kamal. "Let me know what you come up with."

Kamal took his suggestion. He wandered across the chamber, deep in meditation; chants and roiling incense smoke materialized about his bald head.

"So we're back at square one," Bruner said and glared at Jack with his beady eyes. "Running out of air. With a gateway that's useless. And a computer that won't be able to decipher its alien software."

"Almost back at square one," Jack said. "Someone's already figured out the gateway." He opened a link to the isotope and let the static fill the room. "Zero."

Jack knew computers—years of math-code programming and NSO training. He knew to leverage computational power you need parallelism.

Computers that parallel process break a problem into parts, solve those parts with individual processors, then recombine the results. More complicated schemes use many processors to attack multiple problems and simultaneously sought alternate options.

But humans used parallel processing first. And, arguably, to best effect.

The human brain is the most complex and inherently parallel of devices. It is composed of one trillion cells, most of which feed and protect the hundred billion neurons that process inputs, store memories, and constantly rewrite their thousands of trillions of parallel connections for optimal performance.

Between one and tens of thousands of input signals combine in a single neuron, wherein it is determined if that electrochemical ripple continues, becomes amplified, or fizzles to oblivion. And this may, in turn, merely be another input into another neuron.

Consciousness, however, is a decidedly singular process. Humans think by wandering one mental step at a time—not upon hyper-parallel webs of thought. Single thoughts or memories connect to other single thoughts or memories to build chains of logic and linear conclusions.

One system uses many processors, solves as many problems, and controls as many machines as can be engineered. The other machine, the most parallel ever known, reduces all its strength into a single thought.

To Jack something was wrong with that scheme. A paradox that the most powerful and the most versatile was, in many ways, the most limited.

Jack floated in a virtual outer space and waited for Zero to synch encryption keys. He summoned a pane of glass that reflected stick-figure constellations and velvet nebulae about him, then tapped in: REQUEST A LOW-BANDWIDTH INTERFACE.

After a moment came a reply: NO. TOO MUCH I HAVE FOR YOU TO SENSE.

Jack didn't get it. Full-bubble interface would chew through their cycle of keys in no time. He didn't know what Zero had in mind, but whatever it was, it was going to cut their conversation short.

He typed: EXTEND ENCRYPTION WITH ADDITIONAL KEY.

An arch in space appeared. Cursive Arabic crawled along its gilt edges, which then translated itself: NO. YOU WERE CORRECT TO SUSPECT EAVESDROPPERS.

Zero was being stubborn. But since Jack wanted something from him, he'd play it his way.

He stepped through the arch and onto Zero's beach. The same orange sun as last time wheeled overhead. Jack blinked at it. Was that the real star where Zero had made his home?

Zero's tent was gone. Upon the tide line, however, spelled with clam shells, were the words FOLLOW ME. An arrow pointed inland; bare footprints blemished the sand, meandered across the dune fields and into the forest.

Jack yelled at the sea, "I don't have time for games."

No answer came save the surf and the wind.

Jack sighed and marched inland.

Black ants scurried alongside him on the white sand dunes, long trails of dotted lines. They dragged twigs and dead moths and bits of paper. Jack crouched and saw broken calligraphy upon the parchment. He touched one, and fragments of singing prayer drifted upon the breeze, then blew away.

When Jack glanced up, the forest had moved closer.

It was a grove of twisted eucalyptus trees. They spiraled up into the sky, wound about one another in a tangle of trunks and limbs and leaves. Their bark cracked where they rubbed together, shedding flakes, upon which were printed bits of the Koran.

Clumps of mistletoe clung to branches, brackets of mushrooms punctuated trunks; there were curtains of dangling Spanish moss and biolume lichens choked the bark. Plants feeding and living upon plants. Symbiotic and parasitic.

Metaphor for Zero? Their relationship? Jack didn't understand.

Zero stood against a tree. Jack hadn't seen him at first because the gene witch's robes were glowing green and gold to match the biolume lichens and mottled in mimicry of the fragmented-Koran bark. Like a moth camouflaged.

"Is this what you wanted me to see?" Jack demanded. "There's no time."

"Of course there is time." Zero grabbed Jack's arm. His hand was too soft and too smooth to be human flesh. His grip was iron. "This is critical to humanity. Do you not comprehend?" His eyes were as large as saucers, brown irises patterned like the grain of wood.

"All right," Jack said. "Tell me what's so important."

Zero released him. He smiled, and his immaculately trimmed beard grew wild and curled. "You came for the series-four and -eight enzymes? You have decided to take my gift? And Safa? What does she have to say about my enzymes?"

Jack grabbed Zero by the robe and shoved him against his tree—hard. Partly because his patience was gone. Partly because he suddenly felt protective about Safa.

"What's on your mind, Zero? You think the human race is at stake? You're more right than you know because I have a few problems. Someone is trying to kill us. And we're running out of air!"

Jack let go. A silky dust coated his hands: glittering butterfly scales.

"Of course I shall help you." Zero straightened his robe. "Tell me where you are."

That was the one thing Jack couldn't reveal. "I don't

need that kind of help,'' he said. "I know you've improved the efficiently of the gateway. Tell me how.''

Zero's eyebrows shot up. "Who betrayed this secret?''

He leaned closer to Jack . . . yet stayed where he was.
Zero spread out, multiplexed in space, his features blurred.
He had a hundred impressionistic ears, shifting eyes, and
noses, all viewed from different angles and foci. Zero was
a Picasso painting come alive.

He pressed into Jack's mind, a gentle touch, another
point of contact, then a dozen Zeros probed places they
had no right to enter.

Jack threw up walls, but there were too many Zeros.
He took a step back.

"No one told me your secret,'' Jack said.

It was a lie. Isabel had told him—but the last thing Jack
could share with Zero was the truth. The truth opened too
many doors in the mind. "Someone jumped to Pluto and
used its rotation. I guessed it was you.'' He shrugged.
"Now I know.''

Zero's mental pressure eased.

What had Zero hit him with? It was as if more than
one mind had tried to pry open Jack's head. Like there
was more than one Zero.

"You must leave your present location?'' Zero buried
his chin into his hand as he contemplated this.

Jack kept his mouth shut. He had said too much already.
Zero had enough clues to guess where he was. If Jack had
an inefficient gateway, how hard would it be for Zero to
surmise that he was stranded in the solar system?

"Come on, Zero,'' Jack whispered. "We're dying. I
thought we were friends. How am I going to use your
enzyme if I suffocate? Help me.''

"Help? You?'' Zero laughed so hard that his body cracked.
Inside were the jade-green chrysalides, leaf-mimicking cocoons, and the silky tents of pink-spotted hawkmoths—all
hardening and shifting their collective structure. His laughter diminished to chuckles and he regained solidity. "You
do not understand. I need *you* to help me. Must I beg?''

Jack figured that Zero needed help. Mental help. The

chaotic metaphors. His lack of clarity. All abnormal. What did he think Jack, light-years away, could do?

"Help me first, then. How do I fix the gateway?"

"Complex code cannot be 'fixed,' Jack. It is always better to add layers of complexity. Why must I tell you this? You are the software expert."

Jack was an expert. That's why it didn't make sense to him. Experts made their code simple. Only amateurs churned out software bloated with features and designed elaborate architectures when compact elegant ones sufficed.

"I don't get it."

"You have already gotten it," Zero said, and anger gave his voice an edge. He paced. "Do you know what the only bottleneck in all this"—he waved both hands extravagantly about him—"is?"

"Tell me," Jack said. But he wasn't listening. How would *more* complexity make the gateway efficient?

"The bottleneck," Zero explained, "is the human mind. A single processor that must reduce a trillion facts and calculations into a single educated guess. That is our problem. Singularity."

Zero halted his pacing. "And Safa? How is she?"

The abrupt shifting of Zero's mental gears threw Jack for a moment, then he answered, "She's going to asphyxiate soon, like me. Other than that, she's fine."

"Do you know why, Jack, my family rejects me? Muslim artists may never make images of God's creations—only God is allowed to sculpt nature." He looked down and laughed, barely a whisper, like that was a joke only he would get. "Do you know what they thought of a gene witch, one who deliberately alters life? Improves on God's design?"

Jack set a hand on his shoulder. "Zero . . . tell me what's wrong with you."

Zero locked gazes with him. "It is up to you, my only friend. Time grows short for me. For all of us. You are the only one." Tears welled in his eyes. Zero embraced him.

Jack held and comforted him. Whatever Zero's problem,

no matter how distant, he was still his friend, the closest thing he had to family. He'd do whatever it took to help.

"Just tell me," Jack said.

Their encryption key terminated.

Jack held nothing but a handful of stars. He sorted through them, looking for Zero's signal in the static. The frequencies still glistened there, but they carried no data. Zero was no longer answering.

He let the stars pour from his hand; they swarmed and danced in the air as fireflies might. The darkness of the vacuum between them became the matte-black walls of the command-center bubble.

"That was not Zero," Safa said and crossed her slender arms. "He would never utter such blasphemies."

"Did your family turn on him because he was a gene witch?"

Safa stiffened and did not answer.

When she and Zero had first been reunited, she had given Zero mixed signals. Was this the reason? Or was it something more personal?

"That *was* Zero," Jack said. "And he needs my help. I'm going to give it to him."

Bruner snorted a laugh. " 'Help'? How can you help him when you can't even help yourself?"

"I won't abandon Zero," Jack said.

Suspicions and hunches swirled in the back of Jack's mind, ripening, almost conscious thoughts.

Panda stepped closer and lightly touched his arm. "We all observed your exchange with the gene witch. He is not lucid. Nor would he accept contact after he terminated his signal. How can you assist such a man?"

Jack wanted to argue. There had to be a way to help. But without knowing what Zero's problem was, what could he do?

"OK," he said. "Forgetting Zero for a moment, what options do we have to solve our problems?"

"The gateway," Panda said. "I do not understand what Zero meant by adding layers of complexity, but if he has discovered how to repair its inefficiencies, then there may be a method in his madness."

". . . 'adding layers of complexity,' " Kamal whispered. His eyes unfocused, deep in thought. "There is truth within that I can almost taste."

"Well keep tasting," Bruner said. "Without Jack's wonder computer working"—he rapped his knuckles on the wall—"what are the percentages of fixing the gateway code?"

"Vanishingly small," Jack admitted.

"Which brings us to the other option," Bruner said. "Isabel."

At the mention of her name, spiderwebs tangled around Jack's wrist. He tried to brush them away, but they stuck to his fingers. "Sure, Isabel wants to play ball with us," he told Bruner. "We give her the frequencies that contact another alien species and she'd send us air, supplies, a new gateway."

"Then do it," Bruner said, his eyes glittering. "I thought you wanted to get back into business. What are we waiting for?"

"There's no guarantee Isabel will deal straight with those aliens . . . or us. I do want to get back into business, but not with her." Jack then understood what the spider threads attached to him were . . . a subconscious warning. "Not with her pulling my strings."

He snapped his fingers and cut the lines.

Safa tapped her foot impatiently. "It seems you have quashed all our options."

"Not all," Jack said. "There's still the saboteur at the observatory. I think I'll pay them a visit."

Bruner brushed his beard with a flick of his hand. "Are you crazy? Do you want to die? Do you want to get the rest of us killed?"

"No," Safa said. "When the saboteur recognized Jack, he saved his life. Perhaps negotiation is a viable option."

Jack opened a window wide enough for everyone to see. He pointed to a file nested deep in the archives. "These are Isabel's frequencies."

He swiveled the link so it faced him. Jack opened the signal set Wheeler had given him. He memorized the mathematical series—then erased it.

"If I don't come back, if there's no other option, contact Isabel."

"This is a ridiculous," Bruner said. "Swallow your pride and deal with her."

Was it only pride? No. Once Isabel got those codes, there would be nothing to stop her from dealing and double-dealing with the other aliens. Jack wasn't about to play roulette with another civilization. He'd already been a part in destroying two—an alien race who had excelled at mathematics and his own.

He wouldn't do it again. Even if that meant sacrificing what was left of humanity.

"I'm going," Jack told him.

"And the gateway?" Safa asked.

"I'll use it to jump to the Michelson Observatory. Once I'm there, I'll send it back."

Panda took Jack's hand and dragged him to the far side of the command center. "I have something for you." She cupped his chin with her other hand, forced Jack to look into her eyes. Chameleon eyelids warmed to gold and orange, then blushed red, licking the edge of her brows like tiny flames.

"We don't have time for this," Jack whispered.

He pulled away; Panda's grip on his face tightened.

"Open your thoughts to me," she insisted. "Your prototype implant has a memory buffer. It is used to store cache files." She bit her lower lip. "And for those in my profession . . . weapons."

Jack's curiosity was a flash between them, a tenuous arcing bridge of thought.

"Let down your walls." Panda's eyes dilated, covered her irises, and brimmed with dark data on a shielded link. A cloud of ink dispersed between them. She said, "Quickly, close your eyes."

He did.

Tendrils of barbed wire grabbed, bound him, and dragged him deeper into the darkness. Jack lost his balance; he tumbled into a razor rain that cut into his skin and burrowed beneath. He knew it was illusion, but he couldn't keep his pulse from racing. The smell of ammonia crept across his skin, his ears rang with the sound of blisters and bruises, he tasted a hundred mouths, venomous fangs as they sank into him, wormed inside, gnawed at his stomach, wriggled into his eyes, filled him with devouring undulation that chewed on his bones—

"Enough," she whispered.

The assault ceased.

Jack opened his eyes. He was covered in sweat. Ready for a heart attack.

"That is the beast *Chang E*," Panda said. "Be certain when you loosen it, for it will kill."

Jack's erstwhile uncle and double-crossing spy, Reno, had warned him of Panda. He said that she could kill with her mind alone. Now Jack knew what he had meant. And why he had feared her.

What other nightmares did Panda have hidden within her?

"How do I use it?" he asked.

"Give me the first three things that enter your mind."

Jack crinkled his eyebrow, confused, then rattled off: "An eight ball, thunder, the ace of clubs." As soon he completed the list, the beast in his head compressed itself and fell asleep.

"Compile those metaphors again," she said, "and you will awaken it."

Panda stood on her toes and kissed Jack, brief and hard, then released him. "Come back to me."

He glanced at Bruner, Kamal, and Safa—his group. Worth risking his life for? Maybe they weren't humanity's best, but he was responsible for them.

Jack returned his gaze to Panda, memorized her perfect round face that never smiled. "This will just take a minute. Don't go anywhere."

He teased an arrow of red from the mirror gateway; its blue mate he let arc out of the command center. He stepped outside.

Jack paused atop the moon's North Pole to think.

The Earth had almost set; the horizon held on to the edge of its cracked shell. Would life ever return to that world? There had to be something alive. Bacteria. Viruses. In a hundred million years, would there be a sea again? In a billion years, would there be grass? Insects? Would another sentient race arise and start this cycle over?

Was Wheeler waiting for that to happen?

Jack watched the rim of the Earth disappear.

The end of the world was his doing. He had started the chain of events that killed eleven billion people. But that was history . . . and the only business left was the ugly business of survival.

He turned and looked into the dark of the far side of the moon. From the gateway he plucked a blue vector and tossed it to the shadows, took a step—

—onto the rim of Mach crater.

Jack flicked on his helmet spotlights and played them over the pockmarked powder and the dust-coated bodies still there. The glare from his halogen beams obscured the stars and made the darkness around him all the more thick.

He walked through the viscous night.

With two glowing eyes mounted on his head, what did he look like as he trudged towards the observatory hanger? A bug-eyed monster? A Jack-o'-lantern? Was the saboteur as scared of Jack as he was of them?

He found the runway and followed the rubble trail to the hangar.

Inside, the place had been cleaned up. The caved-in ceiling was gone. An interorbital shuttle now faced the open hangar doors.

Jack resisted the urge to unholster his gun. He'd stay nice and friendly to begin with. After all, everyone here knew each other, didn't they?

He marched to the airlock and hit the cycle button. The outer pressure door slid apart.

The recycle packs they had stolen had been replaced on the racks, and new dust had been tracked in.

Jack interfaced with the gateway, made sure he had a solid link before he entered. No need to have a repeat performance of what happened last time he was in this airlock—his hands still itched from the vacuum blisters.

He moved the blue destination vector to the top of Mach crater . . . just in case.

He stepped in, closed the door, then selected the airlock's pressurize mode on the control panel.

The whisper of pumps gradually intensified as air rushed in. And no solvent rained upon him to dissolve his protective skin.

So far, so good.

The display on his helmet's faceplate gave him green lights for air pressure and quality. Jack kept his suit on.

The inner pressure hatch pulled apart. He walked into a dressing room littered with web supports, cans of spray-on Teflon-epoxy, and boots.

Jack examined the boots. None had a diamond tread.

He unsealed his helmet and pulled it off. The air tasted cool and fresh, not the sweaty overrecycled stuff he'd been breathing.

There *was* air here. To share or to steal.

He glanced at the gateway; a mirror-Jack stared back. He could keep it. He should keep it—in case he had to make a quick exit.

No. That wasn't the deal. If this saboteur turned out to be not-so-friendly and got ahold of Jack's gateway, that would leave the rest of his team at their mercy. He bent the red arrow back upon itself, then arced the blue vector back to his moonbase.

He let go.

The sphere vanished . . . along with his confidence. This was a one-way trip now.

He opened a channel to the command center. "Did you get the gateway?"

"It is here," Panda answered.

"Good. No problems so far. Jack out."

On the other end of the dressing room, a tunnel twisted deeper into the complex. It was clean white plastic, four meters in diameter. And affixed to its walls, every ten meters, were tiny gray pyramids. The same ones he had seen in Bruner's dream.

He touched one. It was slick and had rounded corners and edges that glimmered with rainbows.

Jack followed them like a trail of bread crumbs.

He wished he was in a bubble to collect all the facts and his hunches together. He was so close to figuring it all out, he could take a bite out of it.

A dozen paces and the tunnel ended at a pressure door labeled: MEDICAL 2. He touched the control panel and the hatch eased open.

It was dark inside . . . save a tiny glow.

Jack squinted with his good eye. The glow was the ember of a lit cigarette. His eye adjusted to the dark, and he saw the glint of a gun barrel pointed at him.

The holder of the cigarette and gun said, "Hiya, Jack."

SECTION TWO
NEIGHBORS

6

HIGH-LOW JACK

It was Reno's voice. Reno the Chinese spy. Reno the ex–American NSO operative. He had cracked open Jack's skull and installed a prototype implant that had eventually burned out Jack's left eye. He was a double-crosser. A murderer. It was that simple.

That unstable implant, however, had saved Jack's life, so maybe it wasn't that simple.

Fluorescent lights flickered on.

Reno leaned against the far wall, his gun leveled at Jack's chest.

He wore a black vacuum suit, the self-sealing type the saboteur in Bruner's memory had worn just before he had blown the reactor. Reno's eyes, the right brown one and the left blue one, sparkled with mischief. He was over fifty years old, but he could still take Jack in a fight.

And Jack knew Reno would shoot him if he was given half a reason.

Between them was a contoured examination table and a waste biohazard can, and on Jack's left, a wall of life-support equipment. No cover for him to duck behind.

Reno's mouth split into a line of gold teeth. "Nothing to say to your uncle? Not even 'How ya doing'? Guess 'Good to see you' would be out of the question?" He waved his gun at Jack. "Drop your weapon. Kick it over here."

Jack imagined pulling his Hautger SK—quick—getting a round into Reno while the old spy gloated.

Reno's automatic adjusted, extruding between his fingers for a more secure grip. The gun had sensors and expert systems that watched for things like a sudden rise in pulse. It must have guessed what Jack was thinking.

Reno's smile dissolved. "I'm using explosive burrowing rounds. Try anything and I'll cut you in half."

Jack forgot the heroics, dropped his gun belt, and kicked it to Reno. It made a slow motion arc in the one-sixth gravity. "You're not my uncle," he said.

Reno puffed on his cigarette and picked up Jack's gun. The automatic's gyros whined as they stabilized its aim and kept Jack locked in its sights.

"Lucky you gave it up." Reno drew the Hautger SK, palmed the ammunition cartridge, then dropped it all into the biohazard can. "The British make a good cup of tea. But not guns."

"I thought we could—"

Reno held up his hand. "I'll tell you when you can start thinking, Jack-O. A smart guy like you starts thinking and guys like me get into trouble." He stepped up to the examination table . . . leaving dusty diamond imprints with his boots. A perfect match to the pattern Jack had discovered in the reactor room.

So Reno *had* been the saboteur. The one who had vented their atmosphere. Jack should have shot him when he had the chance.

"Put your helmet on," Reno said.

Jack didn't argue with Reno or his too-smart gun.

"Call your friends. Tell them you're inside the observatory and there's nothing here. You're going to look around. Use those words. Get me?"

Jack nodded. He opened the command-center frequency. A crackle of static, then Safa answered: "Jack?"

Good thing it wasn't Panda. She and Reno were enemies. Explaining what she was doing on the moon would further complicate his situation.

"I'm inside the Michelson Observatory," Jack said. "No one here so far."

"Do you want us to jump there and retrieve you?"

"No. I'm going to look around."

"Keep us apprised," she said. "Allah watch over you."

"Thanks." He shot a glance at Reno. "I'll need the help."

Reno scowled and made a throat-slitting motion.

Jack killed the frequency.

"Now," Reno said, "take off your helmet and think all you want. Start with how you got up to the moon." He tossed his packet of cigarettes to Jack. "Help yourself."

Jack greedily fumbled out a platinum-tipped stick and tapped the ignition dot. He savored the peppermint amphetamine-laced smoke, reveled in the rush through his blood, then exhaled. Jack almost thanked the bastard— caught himself.

"I got here the same way you did." Jack didn't see Reno's gateway, but he had to have one. "After you brain-washed me in Shanghai, I jumped up here."

Reno nodded. "Why the moon?"

"When I left Isabel, I had to find a place where her money and NSO connections couldn't reach me." Jack puffed, then said, "You know the rest—you caused the rest. The gatewayed-in terrorists. Nerve gas in Beijing."

Reno's face flushed and he stood straighter. "I didn't do that."

Jack blew smoke at him. "Sure. Whatever you say."

"Why should I gas Beijing? I sell things. I only kill when there's a profit."

"That seems to happen a lot in your line of work."

Reno leaned across the table. "So it does. But I'm tell-ing you I didn't do Beijing." He eased back, drew on his cigarette, then crushed it out. "Since we're talking busi-ness, tell me about Wheeler, your other business partner."

Reno knew about Wheeler? Of course he did. He had to. Where else had he gotten his gateway?

"What about him?" Jack asked.

"You two still working together?" Reno cocked his head and raised an eyebrow. "What's his angle?"

Jack wished this was a bubble; he would have bet any-thing he detected a glimmer of fear behind Reno's noncha-lant exterior.

Good.

Jack set his helmet down and slouched against the wall. "We've never worked together. Wheeler doesn't work 'with' anyone." He took a leisurely drag and exhaled. "Tell me what happened after Shanghai. Then I'll tell you whatever you want to know about Wheeler."

Reno glanced at his gun, then at Jack. "You've got guts." A flicker of his former grin returned. "Fair enough, though." He seemed friendly . . . but then again, he hadn't lowered his aim a centimeter from Jack's heart.

Jack threw back his cigarettes.

Reno caught the pack, shook one out, and stuck it in his mouth. He didn't light it. "After our last question-and-answer session in Shanghai, I knew how to reconstruct Wheeler's signal from cosmic background noise and how to disable the gateway's lockout."

"And you sold that information."

"You bet. First, to your ex-business partner Isabel Mirabeau. She wanted me to hand deliver the data and almost suckered me into a trap. Very persuasive. Damn smart, too. One of these days, I've got to take that enzyme of yours and catch up."

Was Reno's DNA the only unedited copy left of the human genome? It would be a shame if it was . . . with all those weasel genes mixed in.

"I sold the data to the Chinese next," Reno said. "Then the Americans."

"Anyone else?"

Reno shook his head, then finally lit the cigarette dangling from his mouth.

Zero wasn't on Reno's customer list. He must have either figured the gateway's lockout himself or bought the information elsewhere. From Wheeler? With the gene witch's pixilated mind, anything was possible.

Jack asked, "If you sold the data to the Americans and the Chinese, why didn't they bypass their gateways' lockouts? Why aren't they here, too?"

"They weren't interested in *how* they worked. They only wanted to use their gateways. Shift bombs and squadrons and submarines around the world. To them, it was one big game of cat and mouse.''

Reno scratched a nose that had been broken so many times it zigzagged down his face. ''Things happened fast after that. The neutron bombs and the gas attack in Beijing. I figured I had to deal myself into the picture before I was cut out. That's when I called Wheeler and got my own genie in a bottle.

''Next time I drain your brain, Jack, give up more details, OK?'' Reno shot him a glare. ''Even with your instructions, it took me a week to figure the bypass. That gateway software is one slippery piece of programming.''

''Why run to the moon?''

''I thought the United States and China had pulled out the stops. Thought they were going to nuke each other. It was either the Michelson Observatory or the Martian A-Colonies.''

''You got here before the observatory was destroyed?''

''Just in time to see it happen.'' Reno's eyes focused past Jack, remembering. ''Something got dropped on the main complex. What didn't instantly boil away was hit with a blast of radiation. Killed everyone in the deep bunkers. Destroyed all the computers not sealed in μ-casing. A real shame.''

''What was a shame, Reno?'' Jack said. ''Losing the people? Or the equipment?''

Reno laughed; smoke shot out and curled around his face like a Chinese dragon. ''I've said enough.'' He stabbed his gun at Jack. ''You were going to tell me about Wheeler.''

Jack's throat went dry. Thinking about Wheeler terrified him. He might as well have Zeus with his planet-splitting thunderbolts.

Wheeler, however, couldn't be all-knowing and all-seeing. Jack had escaped. Why, then, did he find it so hard to speak?

In his imagination, an eight ball banked off a cushion and dropped into a side pocket; Panda's software stirred from its slumber. He could release *Chang E*. Let it devour Reno. Jack could then keep his secrets about Wheeler.

He quieted Panda's demon. The only reason he was hedging was because thinking about Wheeler reminded him of his part in the killing. And how he could have prevented it.

"Wheeler represents a race of aliens," Jack said quickly before he changed his mind. "Their culture is addicted to the sociological changes new technologies bring. Wheeler told me they thrive on continuous change. They've evolved, so they can't get it fast enough unless they absorb entire civilizations. Research and trade are too slow."

Reno cocked an eyebrow. "If that's the deal, why bother with us?"

"Wheeler needed a middleman to do his dirty work." Jack shifted on his haunches, uncomfortable. "He got me to contact other civilizations. Others who had heard of Wheeler and had hid. Once I had their trust and discovered their location, Wheeler moved in, took their technology, and snuffed them to keep the entire operation from going public."

Reno sucked on his cigarette, making the end flare. "Why did he do the Earth?"

This was the part Jack wished he could forget. He swallowed his uneasiness and replied, "Part of the reason was me. Once I discovered the truth, I wouldn't work for him again."

Reno rubbed his forehead. "You should have consulted your old Uncle Reno on that one."

Jack stood. "Well, I didn't. I made a choice. I don't know if it was the right one, but Wheeler's genocide had to stop." He flicked his cigarette into the air; it twirled end over end in the low gravity, a pinwheel of sparks and ashes, that arced, then bounced onto the floor and went out.

"After the end of the world," Jack whispered, "I thought I'd become my own middleman, trade with other alien civilizations, use cooperation instead of coercion. . . . I haven't gotten far. I'm just trying to stay alive."

"Cooperation?" Reno smirked. "Like worker bees? Or ants? That's not for us, Jack. Only the strongest got off the Earth. Make no mistake, no bugs up here, just us apes."

Maybe he was right. Isabel was strong. Jack wasn't sure

what Zero was anymore, but he wasn't cooperative. And Reno? He was the biggest ape of all. Was Jack's idea to work together all wrong?

"No," Jack said. "Just because that's the way business has always been done, doesn't mean I have to play it that way."

Reno set his gun down. "I just had to make sure, Jack. You can relax."

"Sure of what?"

"Sure you weren't with Wheeler. Sure you were still Mr. Idealism, full of the American Dream. And sure you were as much in the dark as you've always been."

Jack took a step forward. "All right, Reno. Since we're trusting each other, why don't you tell me why you've been trying to murder me?"

Reno held up a hand to stop Jack. "*You* were the one who wanted a duel to the death. And since we're remembering, remember it straight. I was the one who saved your life."

"But my books. The emergency log-out-trap—"

"Meant for Isabel," Reno replied. "I guessed she was my opponent. You two were close once. Those books were supposed to trick her into thinking I was you."

"Why did you think I was Isabel?"

"Who else would have the guts and brains to escape the end of the world?" Reno smiled. "No offense, Jack."

"That explains the duel. But what about shooting Dr. Bruner? Why'd you melt down my reactor and blow up the base?"

Reno narrowed his eyes. "You think I was the one who did your base? Why would I forfeit the biggest supply of air on the moon?"

"If you didn't do it, then who did?"

"Either you're not as smart as I thought you were, Jack-O"—Reno pointed his cigarette at him—"or Dr. Bruner is a hell of a lot smarter than I gave him credit for."

Bruner? The saboteur?

He had no motive. Bruner and Jack had been enemies at the Academe, tried to outmaneuver one another for a tenured position. And there was a mysterious connection between Bruner and Isabel. But those weren't reasons enough to murder Jack and the others. Besides, Bruner had been shot when the reactor had been sabotaged.

"You look confused," Reno said. "Let me make this simple for you. I'll start from the beginning."

Reno walked around to Jack's side of the examination table. "When I first got up here about two days ago, I took a low-polar orbit to scout things out. I saw someone pop over the lunar North Pole. They stepped down to the surface and opened a camouflaged airlock. Hard to miss the thermal differential. That's how I found your hiding hole."

That person had been Jack, his last jump from Earth. Jack wanted to ask Reno how he had been in orbit—but kept his mouth shut. And kept listening.

"I thought I'd scout your place out before I said hello. See if the natives were friendly."

"So you jumped into my base, hacked the inventory, and stole those instant-heat lasagnas?"

"You found that? I must be slipping." Reno blew a smoke ring and watched it disintegrate, lost in thought. Then he said, "I stumbled onto a welder robot cutting a neat hole in one of your pressure doors. Seemed like a perfectly good waste of air, air that I might need someday. I took it upon myself to look around and find out what the hell was going on.

"That's when I found the robot in your reactor room, cutting on the central plasma chamber. I got to it before a breach, overrode the welder's program, and sent it back to the storage bay. I was about to slap a soft-weld patch over the damage when Bruner showed his hairy face."

That fit Jack's hack into Bruner's memory. Bruner had seen a figure crouching by the reactor. Reno must have used his implant to jam Bruner's senses—so he looked like a mirage.

"He took a shot at me," Reno said. "Bruner must have made that hole and didn't want it fixed." He waved his hand and left a trail of smoke. "I plugged him with ana-toxic plastocene, then got out before anyone else showed up and took a crack at me."

"And the hole in the reactor eventually breached," Jack

said to himself. That was the only way all the pieces fit. Safa found Bruner. The rest of the story Jack knew.

That still didn't explain why Bruner did it. Jack retraced his hack into Bruner's head: the connection to Isabel and those little gray pyramids Jack's hunter-fly subroutine had found. The same ones Reno had stuck in the passage.

"What are those pyramids?" Jack nodded toward the tunnel passage.

"Radar proximity units," Reno answered. "Found them on my first trip to your place. They're popped off the welder robots. I've got them stuck here to let me know when rats like you are around."

Those units had been removed so the robots wouldn't sense one another, so they could blow each other's fuel tanks. The pyramids had lingered in Bruner's memory, stuck in his memory . . . because he had to be the one who had removed them in the first place.

Jack should have suspected from the beginning.

"I've got to warn the others," Jack said. He reached for his helmet.

"Think about that a second," Reno said. "Bruner knows you're here looking for me, right? You call up and maybe he has another surprise. A bomb. Or worse. You can't tip your hand."

Jack smiled. "Well, you two still haven't been formally introduced. We could jump there and fix that."

Reno clapped his hands together. "Now you're talking." He grabbed his gun. "Maybe your old Uncle Reno can even give you a hand with that cooperation deal you wanted to try. Who knows, it might even—"

Chirping filled the air and left trails of amber dots in Jack's vision. It wasn't stray EM noise; there was a pattern to it.

Reno stared into space. "Trouble," he said. "That's my detection grid on the observatory arrays." He broadcast the key so Jack could unscramble the signal.

Jack filtered the frequencies through his implant and saw a map of the far side of the moon in his left eye. He zoomed into the fields of telescope arrays. There were three radar blips. Then they were gone.

"A glitch?" Jack asked.

"Or Wheeler," Reno whispered.

Jack's helmet buzzed with static, then Panda's voice crackled: "Jack?" He picked it up and held it to his head.

Reno's eyes widened. "The lady dragon is here?" He took a step back.

"Stay away, Jack," she said. "They are . . ." A sixty-cycle drone washed away her transmission. ". . . being invaded . . . we are trapped . . ." The signal terminated.

Jack narrowed the broadcast. Nothing.

She had his gateway. If there were trouble, why hadn't she jumped away?

What if it was Wheeler? Jack's stomach turned to ice, a chill that spread up his spine and paralyzed his thoughts.

He shook off the fear. If it was Wheeler, Jack had to get away. He had to get Panda and Safa and Kamal away. Even Bruner—if only to find out why he had turned traitor.

"I can almost hear what you're thinking," Reno said. "Forget it. I'm not sticking my neck out for her."

"Loan me your gateway and I'll go myself. A quick jump in and out."

"A quick jump into the middle of a neutron bomb? Not with my gateway."

Jack walked up to Reno. They locked glares. Jack would use Panda's demon if he had to, broadcast from his implant to Reno's. His eyes reflected in Reno's; Jack saw them turn black with white centers and twin eights; thunder rumbled between them.

Claws and knives and teeth bristled in Jack's mind. Panda's software began to unpack, anticipating its release.

"You smell licorice?" Reno asked, took one long drag, then quickly pinched his cigarette out. He looked away. "OK. We'll go. But we do it my way. I want to take a look first."

He pulled his helmet on. It was charcoal-black stealth material, all angles, and had no visible faceplate. It matched the angular body armor bulging beneath the skin of Reno's vacuum suit. A panel on the abstract-shaped head clarified. "Check your neck seal," he told Jack, "and follow me."

Jack did, and they marched into the airlock, cycled through, and walked into the silent vacuum of the hangar.

Reno pointed to the corner. There was nothing but concrete rubble.

Jack felt a whine in his head and tasted burning plastic.

Shadows and jumbled rock smoothed, became a wedge-shaped fuselage with stubby black wings. There were neither a tail nor flaps; instead, control surfaces—organic bits of chitin—fluttered and twitched along every square centimeter of the jet's skin. On the nose, stenciled in ebony lacquer darker than the rest of the EM-absorbent coating, was a black widow spider.

"A gift I took from the Chinese Air Force," Reno said. "Her name's *Itsy-Bitsy*."

"A spy plane?"

"You don't think anyone would be stupid enough to jump to the moon without a ship?"

Jack glowered. Only himself.

A seam appeared in the opaque canopy. "Get in," Reno said. "We're taking a ride."

The cockpit of Reno's spy plane was a claustrophobe's nightmare. The canopy was opaque inside as well. Jack's knees jammed against the back of the pilot's seat. The safety harness strangled him.

His eyes adjusted to the dark.

Reno tapped in instructions and made slight adjustments to the controls. Gauges in front of him were backlit crisp blue: artificial horizon, altitude, schematics of the electrical and hydraulics—all crawling with Chinese calligraphy. And silent. Not a whisper of noise leaked from the avionics or radar.

There were screens and controls wrapped around Jack's seat. Blank. Guess Reno didn't trust him with the sensitive instruments. What was this second seat for? Navigator?

Jack's stomach fluttered and felt ready to float up his throat.

"How do we see out?" he asked. "You plan to take off blind?"

"No runway to take off from," Reno replied. "And no air on the moon to produce lift, even if we could."

"Then how—"

Tucked between Reno's thighs was a mirror sphere.

Jack jerked; the harness bit into his shoulders. The altimeter read eight thousand meters and dropping. Reno had jumped them.

Jack didn't like this. Moving without knowing it. No wonder his stomach felt like it was floating. It was. They were in free fall.

The canopy flickered and revealed black-velvet space and scattered stars.

Jack exhaled, relieved to see something.

"That's the up view," Reno said. "Now the down."

The panorama of space snapped to silver moon plains and craters awash with shadow.

Jack lost his orientation. Up was down. He wasn't certain if Reno had rolled the ship or just changed the display. The artificial horizon indicator was flat, but Jack had the sensation they were spinning.

He closed his eyes to brake the imaginary spinning— opened them. "I don't recognize this geography."

Reno touched the gateway. Stars jumped. New craters and black fields of basalt appeared. The gauges blurred with new numbers. They were twelve thousand meters over the surface.

This is what the others must have felt when Jack had jumped them to the moon. No control over where they were. Sick to their stomachs.

"Go to the North Pole," Jack told him. "My people are running out of time."

"We're doing this my way, remember?" Reno doublechecked his instruments, then jumped up to twenty-two thousand meters.

A quarter Earth materialized, setting on the horizon.

"Listen, Jack, there are two types of people that might be attacking your base. Another poor sucker stranded here. In which case, Panda can take care of them."

"Or?"

"Or they gatewayed in." Reno slipped his hand in a glove built into the console; a new screen snapped on:

tiny missiles and guns flashed along a blueprint of *Itsy-Bitsy*. "So we'd better be careful."

"Careful" only applied if someone human had jumped in. If it was Wheeler, then Jack's base was already a molten crater. Jack looked for a vomit bag—gulped down his fear and nausea. There was no way he could remove his helmet. Reno hadn't pressurized the interior.

"How secure is this thing?"

"*Itsy-Bitsy* is the safest place on the moon. We're not sitting ducks; she's got maneuvering jets for ultra-high atmospheric maneuvers. Anyone with an implant will never see her coming—just like you didn't in the hangar. She's sealed against electromagnetic pulses and hardened against ionizing radiation."

Reno touched the gateway—the stars shifted—and another ten thousand meters added to the altimeter.

Beneath them, Homebase crater was half-engulfed in the dusk. A scar marred the surface . . . where the airlock used to be. There was motion on the ground, too; long shadows that reminded Jack of the ants he had seen on Zero's beach. They were too fuzzy to decipher exactly what they were.

Jack touched the screen and magnified the image.

The scar was a bulldozer track where the dust and rocks had been excavated. The airlock shaft underneath had been cut open like a tin can, and the elevator had been wrenched out and lay sideways on the ground.

"Adding infrared," Reno said.

The ants were humans, glowing tangerine in high contrast to the normal brick-colored surface. Their vacuum-suit faceplates flashed in fading sunlight.

Panda wouldn't have stuck around. She would have jumped away. So why the distress call?

At least a dozen people down there had set up three-meter-wide radar dishes—but pointed at the ground—not up. And, although extremely blurry, some of them carried what looked like medieval blunderbusses.

"Shock rifles," Reno whispered. "They fire rocket-propelled gel packs that can crush bone without breaking the skin of a vacuum suit. Looks like they're trying to take your friends alive."

Jack resented Reno's clinical tone. Like this was a board game and those were checkers down there, not human lives.

He tried to increase the magnification. It didn't change. "Can you resolve this any more?"

"Only if we get closer." Reno touched the gateway. Ten thousand meters vanished from the altimeter.

The view shifted: larger, clearer. Jack made out features inside the invaders' helmets. Men and women. Definitely human.

The space between those three radar dishes, however, was still blurred. An error in Reno's image processing? Or were the dishes producing that optical distortion?

"I'll pick out their communications," Reno said.

Jack barely heard him because he had spotted a man with black hair, blue eyes, and heavy Russian eyebrows. "DeMitri." He was the National Security Office spymaster who had tried to take Jack's mind apart. He was the man Isabel had hired as a watchdog.

"I see him." Reno shook his head. "Something new to worry about."

"If we can see them," Jack said, "won't their surveillance equipment see us, too?"

"Those amateurs couldn't find their own ass with both hands and a map."

Jack squinted, looking for a flash of clarity through a faceplate that might reveal pure white skin and eyes shockingly green and clear. "Do you see Isabel? If she's running things, we shouldn't take chances."

"Not a problem." Reno's voice had an edge of panic. Like he'd made a mistake. "I'll jump us—"

A rock appeared in front of them—from nowhere. It was black and silver, pockmarked with craters, and the size of a house.

Itsy-Bitsy reacted faster than Reno. She fired maneuvering jets, made the hull shudder as she banked into a starboard roll.

It wasn't enough.

The collision drove Jack into his seat, it knocked *Itsy* upside-down, slammed Jack's head back so he was suddenly looking at the stars. Stars that went black.

7

Metal grated on stone, making a fountain of sparks, squealing and tearing. The sound ripped through Jack. Left him shaking with adrenaline. Stunned.

Itsy-Bitsy spun out of control—all Jack saw were blue displays that winked on and off, streaking stars, the silver ground below, a trail of glitter, and the right wing missing its tip.

Reno's gateway rattled across the cockpit, then over the arc of the canopy.

Jack shook off his concussion and reached for it. Acceleration made his arms heavy, but his fingertips gripped the mirror shell and stuck. He pulled it to his chest.

The gateway linked to his mind; tiny red and blue arrows bristled from its surface.

Itsy-Bitsy fired her maneuvering jets and slowed their gyration.

Reno took the control stick with his left hand, slid his right into the weapon-control glove. "Those dirty—"

A second rock materialized twenty meters overhead, a ceiling of gray stone, a blur of motion descending upon them.

Jack forced himself not to instinctively duck and concentrated on the gateway. He stretched the blue destination vector south—the gateway was sluggish, resisted him— the arrow pulled like taffy.

Reno launched a missile. A line of fire traced between *Itsy-Bitsy* and the rock. It impacted, blossomed with fire. The rock filled the viewscreen, glowing red from the explosion, but its trajectory was unaltered.

Jack got the blue arrow two kilometers away, jumped *Itsy*—

—wisps of plasma and dust curled about the viewscreens. But there was no impact.

Jack spotted a crater three kilometers west. It brimmed with shadow. He extended the gateway's arrow there.

A third meteoroid appeared.

—but they were already gone.

It was suddenly cold. There was no motion. Gravity tugged at Jack and he started shivering.

Itsy-Bitsy was on the ground, cloaked in darkness and hugging the wall of the crater. The spy plane shifted her colors and patterns, camouflaging herself.

Reno twisted in his seat to face him. "That was too close." His eyes locked onto the gateway.

"Maybe we should return the favor," Jack said, gripping the gateway tighter, "and drop a rock on them." He sent the destination vector across the lunar surface. It slid away from the North Pole—like a marble pushed up a hill and rolling off.

"Something is wrong." Jack made extravagant motions, tried to jerk the vector on target. "The closest I can get is half a kilometer from Homebase crater."

"Those radar dishes pointed at the ground might have something to do with that," Reno said.

"Blocking our gateway's signal?"

There was evidence in favor of Reno's theory. If Panda couldn't jump out, that would explain her distress call. There was that optical distortion Jack hadn't figured out yet, either.

"Why don't we drop a rock from higher up?" Reno suggested. "No. They'd probably see it coming and make it go away. I'm beginning to think, Jack-O, that it would have been better to stay home."

"If they know where my base is, they'll know about the Michelson Observatory."

"Great," Reno said. He glanced outside, shook his head, then punched the hatch release. A seam appeared in the canopy and it levered open.

Jack hopped out and knelt beside Reno, inspecting *Itsy*'s right wing. The tip was gone, an open wound of hydraulics and blinking fiber optics and honeycombed metal. Reno banged his fist on the fuselage. "I'd like to rip off a few of *their* parts."

"You may get your chance," Jack told him. "We'll have to go there and take them out . . . in person."

Was there a nonlethal way to rescue Panda and the others? Even a simple flechete could breach a person's vacuum suit. Isabel and her team were some of the last humans left. Each was precious.

But being the last humans alive didn't stop them from being human—with human aggressions. They had used lethal force on Jack. He had to do the same.

Reno let his Chinese automatic wrap around his hand; interface windows appeared. Jack's implant caught part of the blurry menus as Reno selected compression-burrowing rounds, three-shot burst, and a friendly-fire inhibitor that marked Reno and Jack as nonviable targets.

The clear panel of Reno's angular helmet darkened. With the armor bulging under his black vacuum suit, Reno looked like a misshaped dung beetle. He blurred and distorted. Not invisible, but part ghost and part ever-shifting smoke, as if Jack was looking at him through a fractured lens.

"Ready," Reno said.

Jack wasn't. He could kill; Jack had shot people before, but never like this. Premeditated. He had always been backed into a corner.

What other options were there? Run? Hide? Those would only delay the inevitable.

Jack attached a red arrow to himself . . . but had trouble making the vector stick to Reno. "Turn your suit's sensory inhibitors off," he told Reno, "so I can get us there."

Reno solidified.

Jack sent the blue destination vector to the far, shadowy side of Homebase crater. They took a step—

—and landed in the powdery slope of the ridge. Jack and Reno crouched low.

The refrigerants in Jack's vacuum suit kicked on to compensate for his sweating and to defog his faceplate.

Peering over the edge, they saw a dozen people working around the open airlock shaft. Jack couldn't tell if Isabel were among them. Three pairs of people, armed with shock rifles and side arms, patrolled in a thirty-meter circle.

The blur between the radar dishes was still suspended there, bending light like it was a sphere of glass.

"Here," Reno said, transferring a topographical map inside Jack's faceplate. Two black dots appeared representing the farthest set of guards. "When they get behind that ridge, that will be our best chance. We do it quick and clean. I'll jam their communications"—he made a chopping motion with his hand—"before their buddies jump on top of us."

The guards trudged toward the low hill. Jack tried to check his racing heart and stop his hand from trembling on the gateway.

An image of an eight ball rolled inside his head. That was the first release for the software demon *Chang E*. It coiled and compressed and made itself ready to transmit. Ready to kill.

Jack glanced at the airlock shaft. People wrestled with rope and rappelling harnesses. They were going down.

Reno tugged on his arm. The two guards moved behind the hill and out of sight. "Let's do it," Reno whispered.

Thunder rolled in the back of Jack's mind, the second of *Chang E*'s safeties unlocked. He tagged Reno and himself, pulled the blue line there—

—appeared less than a meter in front of the first guard; the other was a pace behind him.

Jack knew they would be close, but it still startled him. He hesitated.

Reno didn't. He shot the lead man point-blank in the chest.

Three detonations blew the guard backward; he writhed as bits of vacuum suit and splinters of armor ejected. There was no sound. Blood and guts boiled from the fist-sized wound into the airless void. His abdominal cavity expelled.

Jack tore his gaze away—looked up as the second guard shot him.

In the split second it took for the rocket-propelled gel packet to accelerate toward Jack, he got a look at his assailant. Some young NSO agent, teeth set in a grimace. He couldn't be more than twenty-five, probably a recruit fresh out of college.

Impact.

Fire spiked through Jack's chest; a rib cracked; he fell. Stars swarmed in his vision . . . darkened and coalesced into the ace of clubs.

The last key clicked in place and freed the demon *Chang E.*

Software streamed from Jack's mind. Suckered tendrils reached out for the agent's implant, pried open his neural pathways.

Chang E generated a feedback loop with the agent's fear. Rivers of virtual blood gushed forth, sticky and black, and flooded into the agent's nose and mouth; he gasped for breath, clawed at the fluid. Razor claws of panic grabbed his chest and squeezed. The agent shrieked as a torrent of shadows devoured the blood, grew flesh and bone and sinew, then wrapped around his legs and arms and bit through his vacuum suit. The agent tried to scrape them off, but they slithered under his skin. The odor of rotting dreams filled his recycler, gagged the agent, and swelled his tongue with revulsion.

Chang E made the agent's heart pound asynchronously. A hundred hands and pincers and insect feelers closed his nose and eyes and ears, cracked his legs, snapped a hip, and crushed his jaw.

The software stopped. It recoiled into Jack's mind.

. . . Consciousness returned, and Jack saw Reno kneeling next to him, adjusting his oxygen mix.

"He grazed you," Reno explained. "Must have been as scared as you to miss at that range."

The agent lay motionless. Untouched in this reality, but just as dead as if *Chang E* had devoured his soul.

Jack tried not to be sick. What had the full force been on the receiving end of the demon software? Jack never wanted to know.

Reno stood and went to the agent he had shot. Crystals of freeze-dried blood glittered upon the ground, looking like garnets and silver. The rest was a mess of desiccated pieces. Reno shut down the recycler. "We can use this one's oxygen."

He stared at Jack, eyebrows bunched together, an indecipherable look. Loathing? Fear? Reno glanced back at the agent Jack had killed. "You've picked up a few tricks since Shanghai," he whispered. "We'll have to talk about the right and wrong ways to kill people."

How much of the *Chang E* broadcast had Reno caught?

Just when Jack thought he had Reno figured out, when he knew he was a rat double-crosser, Reno proved him wrong. The old spy's morals were an enigma.

And how far south did Jack's moral compass point now?

"We better move," Reno said, giving Jack a hand up. "The others will come looking when this pair doesn't show."

Jack winced at the sharp pain in his rib cage. He shook out of control, couldn't keep his balance. Shock?

No. Reno held out his hands to steady himself, too.

It wasn't Jack shaking.

The ground moved.

Pebbles vibrated and bounced. Dust rose in wisps. Ripples rolled through the ground, waves that grew rather than dissipated, tossing rocks, distorting craters.

Jack stumbled facedown onto the violent surface. He clutched the ground and rode the waves. Was it real? Jack pushed with his mind, reached out with the implant, but detected no virtual interface.

The motion subsided; the surface continued to shudder, but Jack could stand.

Reno got up. "Moonquake?" he asked. "Are those normal?"

"No." Jack had his suspicions, though. He hadn't felt anything like that since the end of the Earth—when quakes had cracked the mantle. "Whatever it was, we better move."

He and Reno marched up the hill. They got on their hands and knees and peered over the top.

Three agents stood by the airlock shaft. The others were missing. Had the rest rappelled down? Or jumped away? Or maybe they were looking for their lost patrol?

"Where is everyone?" Reno said. "I don't like this."

Light came from the airlock shaft, white and bright like a fluorescent flickering on; it illuminated the faceplates of the NSO agents.

A ball of fire mushroomed from the shaft, expanded and engulfed the agents, shattered the radar dishes. The detonation was eerie and silent in the vacuum. It cooled into a white glittering cloud that looked like . . .

"Ice," Jack whispered. An explosion, then ice? Ice was water; water was two parts hydrogen, one oxygen—the gases accumulated from Safa's electrolysis? That was smart. Good for her. How much oxygen, though, did that leave them to breathe?

"Maybe an earlier explosion caused that quake?" Reno asked.

"I don't think so," Jack told him.

They jumped—

—to the edge of the airlock shaft. Heat radiated from the glassy rim. One agent lay twisted, helmet cracked and encrusted with freeze-dried blood; the others were missing.

"We go in?" Reno asked.

Jack extended the gateway's destination vector into the command center . . . tried to. It was more sluggish than before. It refused to stretch that far.

"It's still not working." Jack grabbed the carbon-fiber cable the agent had rigged. It was warm from the explosion but otherwise intact. "Can you climb down?"

Reno interfaced with his gun, set it on full automatic and a spray pattern that matched the diameter of the airlock shaft. "Ready."

Jack flicked on his helmet lights, stepped with the rope

between his legs, and looked into the hole. Dust choked the airshaft, so he couldn't see more than a meter.

He rappelled slow, using the rope as a brake. The shaft had buckled; sharp edges had peeled open, any one of which could slice his suit.

Jack paused to sense any active bubble circuitry or taste any stray signals. It was quiet.

A hundred meters down he found the open lock of the command center and crawled in.

The place had been ransacked, walls cut apart, tangles of optical fibers upon the floor, data cubes scattered like toy blocks . . . and a body, facedown.

Jack turned the corpse over. Their neck had been snapped at a sixty-degree angle. Not Panda or Safa or Kamal. An NSO agent. Jack breathed a sigh of relief.

"That's Panda's style," Reno commented.

"If they didn't jump out and they're not here, there's only one place they could be." Jack walked back to the airlock shaft and stared down: darkness and motes of silver powder. "Coming?" he asked Reno.

"If I said no, would that stop you?"

Jack grabbed the cable and descended another hundred meters until the shaft filled with rubble.

Reno landed next to him. He set a hand on Jack's shoulder. "No one's here. Those NSO creeps must have gotten your little Beijing spy."

Jack shrugged off his consoling hand. He wasn't giving up. Not yet. He knelt and studied the rock, chunks of flexcrete and twisted metal beams . . . and a hole just big enough to wriggle into. He squirmed through; the wormhole widened, and he walked in a crouch.

Reno followed.

The tunnel spiraled for another twenty meters. Jack recognized the frame of a pressure door, then the curve of a fused duststone wall. So not everything had collapsed down here.

Blue lines flashed in his peripheral vision; there was the sensation of raindrops on his skin—the pinpricks of an EM probe.

Jack pushed his mind forward, resolved a pair of eyes

hidden in the shadows ahead, eyes that watched him, and the glint of a Hautger SK. Panda.

Kamal was there, too. He touched his helmet to Panda's and whispered. Safa took a step out of the darkness, but Panda thrust out her arm, warning her back.

Jack switched to the command-center frequency. "It's me. Jack."

She lowered her weapon, uncertain.

Reno emerged from the tunnel. His stealth suit split him into mirage and blurred his outline among the shadows; he moved in every direction at once. He raised his gun.

Panda whipped her gun back into line. "Stand aside, Jack," she hissed, gripping the trigger tighter. "I see someone who should be dead."

Jack was stuck in the middle. He held out his hands, trying to stop them from shooting. "Reno is on our side," he said.

"He is the saboteur." Her gold and orange eyelids blackened. "He has manipulated your mind."

"No. He's not. He didn't." Jack saw motion past Kamal and Safa. "Who else is here?"

Kamal and Safa stepped forward, pulling along a figure whose hands were bound. Inside his helmet, ropes of black hair obscured his face, as if it had been shoved on too quick. There—a glimpse of blue eyes, an aquiline nose. DeMitri.

Jack took a step back. DeMitri was the NSO agent who had trained him and, more recently, had tried to erase him. He had originally teamed up with Isabel to engineer a U.S. invasion of the Chinese-friendly Indo-Malaysian Republic . . . back when there had been a China and America and Malaysia. DeMitri had an endless bag of tricks, real and virtual. He was as benevolent as a scorpion.

"Where's Bruner?" Jack asked.

"Gone," Safa replied. She narrowed her eyes, scrutinizing both Jack and Reno.

Reno broadcast to Jack on a private frequency: "Who's the other woman?"

Jack ignored Reno and instead said to Panda: "Tell me what happened."

"And you will please tell us under which rock"—Panda stabbed at Reno with her gun . . . then slowly lowered it—"you found this?"

Reno's lips curled into a feral smile. "Tell them anything you want," he said, "but first get us out of this hole, Jack-O. Before another quake buries us."

"Good idea." Jack tagged them all, then moved the destination vector to the command center. The tiny blue arrow extended three meters, shrank as Jack watched, down to a meter, then a centimeter-long nub.

"There's no power," Jack whispered. "I was afraid of this . . . it's the reason for the quakes—the moon has all but stopped spinning."

Jack pulled himself, hand over hand, up the cable. The climb was easy in one-sixth gravity.

Behind him were Safa, Kamal, Panda, DeMitri, and Reno, who brought up the rear—explaining to them all how he had escaped the dying Earth, saved Jack's life, and killed every NSO agent on the surface of the moon.

Jack couldn't stop staring up as he climbed. He was waiting for more rubble to fall, or NSO agents to come down, or a shot to be fired that would knock him to the bottom. His problems had a nasty habit of multiplying.

He got a grip on the edge of the command center and hauled himself in. The circular room, aside from being disassembled and vented of air, was structurally intact.

Jack dragged the body of the dead NSO agent away from the entrance.

The others pulled themselves into the room.

Reno sat cross-legged on the flexgel floor that had ruptured and frozen. "Then Jack and I came down and found you," he said, turning his odd-angled helmet to each of them, making eye contact. His gaze lingered upon Safa.

Panda folded her arms, clenching and unclenching her gloved hands. "Your explanation matches the known facts." She turned to Jack. "However, I know this man. He is not to be trusted."

"I know him, too," Jack replied. "But we've got to work together if we're going to survive."

He scrutinized the walls that had been cut open, the tangles of chaos circuitry strewn upon the floor, and the asymmetric inductors that blurred his vision. "The isotope," Jack said. "Did they get it?"

Safa un-Velcroed a pocket and withdrew a slim silver case. She opened it and revealed the glowing sapphire-blue crystal and communication chips. "We also took the precaution of removing the electron reactor."

"Thanks," Jack sighed. He took it from her, noticing that Safa's eyes were the same color as the crystal.

Kamal knelt next to Reno. They touched helmets and exchanged a private communication. Kamal then broke with him and examined the wall. He poked his head through a hole and examined the circuitry.

The Buddhist monk knew Reno. It was at his Old Tea House Temple in Shanghai that Jack had last met Reno. What was their relationship?

"What are you doing?" Jack asked.

Kamal pulled his helmet out of the hole in the wall. "Making myself of use," he said. "Repairing what has been taken apart."

DeMitri ambled to the body of the NSO agent. He checked his features, frowned as if he was disappointed, then he slumped against the wall.

Jack asked, "How did this happen?"

Panda sat far from Reno, then said, "It started when we were exploring the gateway software."

"We were deep into the code manifolds," Safa explained, "when the software's normal frenetic activity slowed. We took the opportunity to delve into the core and found the code that directs its power." She gave a nod to Panda to continue.

"Before we could discover more, however"—Panda glanced back to the open shaft—"an external signal penetrated the area. We secured the isotope and electron reactor, then shut down the bubble circuitry. When we. did, Dr. Bruner vanished. Apparently he left a doppelganger and had been gone for an unknown duration."

..Bruner didn't have the expertise to create a doppelganger. But maybe he didn't need it. Maybe he already had outside help. He must have contacted Isabel. Jack would have given anything to get his hands around Bruner's throat.

Jack went to the airlock shaft and peered up. Still empty. "What happened after Bruner disappeared?"

"NSO agents climbed down," Panda said. "We barely sealed our helmets before they vented our atmosphere and attempted to capture us. We successfully repelled them."

Jack glanced at the dead body. Was that what Panda considered successful? Had she released *Chang E* as well?

"We would not have survived a second assault," Panda said. "They had many people and our position was vulnerable."

"We released hydrogen from electrolysis and our reserve oxygen into the shaft," Safa said, "then we descended into the catacombs and sparked an explosion."

"We saw that topside," Jack said. "But Isabel's people must have come down for a second try." He gestured to the disassembled walls. "I doubt they got what they were looking for."

Jack was glad his paranoia had paid off, that he had erased Wheeler's secret set of frequencies before he had left. They only existed in Jack's head now.

"Oxygen is now our primary concern," Safa said. "We have less than an hour of breathable atmosphere."

"There are three recyclers on the surface that no one is using," Jack said.

DeMitri stood. "I can help."

"Shut up and sit down," Reno told him.

DeMitri remained standing.

"What about the observatory, Reno?" Jack asked. "How much oxygen do you have?"

"Hundreds of cubic liters and plenty of recyclers," Reno replied. "But getting there is the problem. Maybe I'll go topside and see if *Itsy*'s takeoff jets can get me back."

"Not alone," Panda said and her hand drifted closer to her holstered gun. "There may be other NSO agents. Even if there are not, what guarantee do we have that you will return?"

"Why don't you come with me?" Reno asked. He made his request sound like a threat. "Assuming there's anything left"—he turned to DeMitri—"that the NSO didn't get to."

"We knew of the observatory," DeMitri said, "and the equipment there. We had orders to destroy everything we could not take."

Jack couldn't tell if his tone was genuinely apologetic or eloquently sarcastic.

His tone didn't matter to Reno. He marched over, hauled DeMitri up by his vacuum suit's skin, then slammed him against the wall. "Why? What does your boss want?"

"Isabel planned this," DeMitri said. A faint smile trembled across his lips. "The observatory and our jumps that halted the rotation of the moon."

"Yeah?" Reno said. "She plan on you getting caught, too?"

DeMitri's smile vanished. "You may have won the battle, but we have won the war. You think I'm your prisoner? You have the situation reversed."

Reno punched him in the stomach; DeMitri doubled over. Reno butted his helmet against DeMitri's and said, "You guys are pathetic. We're the last humans alive! You're still double-crossing us."

Jack pulled Reno back before he could teach DeMitri more lessons on brotherly love. Reno might rip DeMitri's vacuum suit and end their question-and-answer session permanently.

"What does she want?" Jack asked, kneeling next to DeMitri.

DeMitri caught his breath. "You're so smart. You've squirmed out of every tight spot before. Why don't you puzzle it out for yourself? Or better yet . . . contact her. She is waiting."

Reno kicked DeMitri in the ribs. "Answer his question."

"It's OK," Jack said and stood. "You and Safa see what's left of the observatory and get those recyclers down here. Panda will watch DeMitri. Kamal, what's the bubble's status?''

Sparks crackled from the maintenance duct Kamal lay in. Waves of mist and the scent of paint washed through the room. ''The reserve batteries are intact,'' Kamal replied. ''The damaged circuitry can be repaired. Fifteen minutes. Perhaps twenty.''

''Good.'' Jack opened the isotope case and stared into the glittering isotope. ''I've got a call to make.''

Jack stepped onto the ivy-covered staircase that connected Isabel's marble mansion to its adjacent gardens and lawns. His left side was numb; the right tingled with static. Kamal hadn't gotten the bubble fine-tuned yet.

Overhead, it was overcast, a mirror for Jack's frame of mind. A light mist fell. Was this really the world Isabel had colonized? Or more smoke and mirrors?

He sat at the table where yesterday they had had tea and discussed how she and Jack would build an empire to rival Wheeler's.

Jack yanked off the linen tablecloth. The sterling tea set and bone china smashed on the paving stones.

Isabel walked through the atrium. She wore a fur-lined cape over a black business suit. Ringlets of her damp red hair clung to her face like blood trickling down her cheek. She pulled out a chair and joined him.

''Good evening, Jack,'' she said. ''We are going to keep this short. I will tell you my demands. You will listen. No hysterics.'' She glanced at the shattered teacups and scattered sterling. ''No speeches. Agreed?''

''Not until I know why Bruner did it.''

Isabel stared through Jack with her hard emerald eyes; he matched her stare, offered her contact. She looked away.

''I see that you have set your mind on this matter.'' She frowned. ''Very well. I will let you speak to Bruner. Briefly.''

A doorway appeared and Bruner stepped through. He wore a tuxedo. His hair and beard were trimmed. He sat close to Isabel, smiled contemptuously at Jack.

Jack resisted the impulse to rush him. "Why?" he asked through clenched teeth.

"I'm sorry, Jack. You saved my life, and I'm grateful for that, but let's face it, I wasn't going to stay stuck on the moon with you. Not when Isabel has all this"—he waved his hands over his head—"a planet with a breathable atmosphere and a—"

Isabel tapped her fingernail on the table to get Bruner's attention. Was he about to let some secret slip?

"And what do you have?" Bruner asked. "A hole in the ground and no way to leave." An oily scent of sexual attraction exuded from Bruner's memory, and from his nostrils a curl of green-envy smoke expelled. "Besides, Isabel and I have worked together before."

Jack raised an eyebrow and turned to Isabel.

"After your defection in Amsterdam," she replied, "I employed Dr. Bruner to search for other signals in the cosmic background noise."

Bruner pressed his lips into a white line that disappeared under his bristled beard. "I used my mathematical techniques *properly.* Not hacked together, as you did, into an incomprehensible conglomeration."

He didn't mention if he had actually found any signals. Jack doubted that he had. Otherwise, Isabel would have taken him with her. No. Bruner's foremost ability seemed to be betrayal.

"So you vented our atmosphere? Destroyed the reactor? How did that get you closer to Isabel?"

"I knew you would only contact Isabel if there were no other choice. I systematically closed off every option. Air, power, water . . ." He counted them off on his fingers. "I waited for my chance, then traded her access to your computers and Wheeler's set of frequencies. Traded them for my freedom."

Jack understood. Bruner had seen Jack speak with Zero and Isabel after the destruction of the Earth. He knew they were out there.

"As soon as I revealed that set of frequencies," Jack whispered, "and left for the observatory, you stabbed me in the back."

Chang E stirred in Jack's skull, an eight ball off the side pocket, sensing his malicious intent, unpacking its nightmare files. How fast could Isabel shut down the link? Fast enough to save herself and Bruner?

Then again, Jack didn't want to give Isabel a glimpse of the demon. She might be able to survive it . . . copy it. He took a deep breath, cooled his anger, and compressed the killing software before it could unfold and execute.

Isabel must have sensed something. She set her hand on Bruner's arm. "That will be all for now, Harold."

What promises had she made to Bruner? How many of those would she break? The two traitors deserved each other.

"I'm sorry." Bruner stood, sighed, then added, "Well, maybe not all that sorry." He vanished.

Isabel tapped her finger upon the table. "Now, Jack, the frequencies. We copied every file from your computers and they weren't there. You wouldn't throw them away. Where are they? I want them."

Jack set his elbows on the table. "The answer's no."

"Then you will die."

"I'll die anyway. You can't jump to the moon and get me off. It's barely rotating."

"You are only half-correct. I can get there." Isabel leaned back and a smile spread across her face, revealing perfect white teeth. "I have the means to open gateways, microscopic in size, and through them, let flow high-voltage electrons to power your systems and—most importantly to you—oxygen."

She let that sink in for a moment, then: "I will keep you alive. All you must do is submit to one tiny request."

Could Isabel pull a stunt like that? She had claimed to have made astonishing leaps in the processor design. Why not the gateway, too?

"Hypothetically, let's say you can do it," Jack said. "What's to stop you from closing those conduits as soon as I give you the codes?"

Isabel's smile relaxed. "I see your point. But what choice do you have?"

"I can say no . . . I *am* saying no. If it's a choice between trusting your word or going it alone and dying, I'm better off on my own."

She furrowed her brows.

Jack wasn't bluffing. He could never trust her. More was at stake than just his group. Another alien civilization might be sold off to Wheeler. Jack would never let that happen again.

Isabel's sly smile returned. "I have a way to satisfy us both. You will call these aliens, Jack, and negotiate for me—trade on my behalf."

"Become *your* middleman?"

Jack considered. He needed air. Her proposal ensured that he would get it as long as Isabel needed him. But the thought of working with Isabel again . . . he'd almost rather make a pact with Wheeler.

"You have twenty-four hours," she said, "to establish preliminary contact with the aliens. Then I will require deep contact to verify. That is as fair a deal as I can possibly make with you."

Deep contact with Isabel would be unpleasant. But he could use the time. Twenty-four hours to find a way off the moon? Time enough to reengineer their gateway? Perhaps.

"Take the deal, Jack," she whispered and reached across the table with her bone-white hand. "Please. I do not want to kill you."

He clasped her hand. It was hot and dry. "OK. You've got a deal."

"You won't regret this."

Jack already did.

8

Jack let Isabel's world dissolve. He floated in static, a place between her metaphor and his.

There had to be a way out of this dead-end deal and a way off the moon. He wasn't giving up and becoming her slave. What if it was the only way to stay alive? To keep Panda and the others alive?

Jack herded wavelets together and assembled an arch. Arabic script pulsed along its edge: Zero's signal.

One foot on the threshold of the portal . . . Jack hesitated.

Isabel knew Zero's frequencies, too. She might unravel their encryption. Even if she didn't, she'd see the signal activity. Would she guess that Jack wanted Zero's help to squirm out of her deal?

He'd risk it. He had to do something.

Jack connected. He stepped through into a forest crowded with blackberry vines and a carpet of decaying leaves that squished under his feet. Overhead, the dense canopy allowed only a patchwork of sunlight to filter though.

It was silent.

"Hello?" Jack whispered. "Zero?"

Chrysalides littered the ground, encrusted tree bark and twigs, and dangled from spider threads. Each was the size of Jack's little finger. Some were green, others tan, a few scarlet—millions of empty cocoons.

Zero's voice came from every direction: "Our metamorphosis is complete."

"Where are you?" Jack asked, startled. "I need your help."

"I am disappointed, Jack. You never rescued us."

Zero laughed. The sound shattered into a mass of butterflies—so thick that Jack had to cover his nose with his hand to breathe. Painted in silk scales were twisted DNA helices and fragments of the Koran. In the middle of the insect cloud, features resolved—an ear, a nose, and Zero's slender beard—composed of a million winged pixels.

"You are next," this composite Zero said.

Jack took two steps back. Whatever Zero's problems had been, they had increased exponentially. This wasn't Zero. Not anymore. As much as Jack wanted to help—and to be helped—there was no communicating with . . . with this.

"Sorry, Zero," Jack whispered. He disconnected.

Butterflies ignited, spiraled into a galaxy, then drifted apart, each star burning brighter and bluer, blinking on and off until they spread into a field of flickering static.

A centimeter of moon dust coated the command-center floor; the finer silt hadn't settled, and it made the air lustrous.

Air? The room been repressurized.

The elevator airlock was back in place. Safa and the others had managed to get it down the twisted shaft.

Panda crouched in the center of the room. Her helmet was off, and her long bangs were tucked up under a black beret. Safa's beret. She had her gun pointed at DeMitri. The ex-NSO spy sat against the far wall.

Panda waved Jack over with her free hand.

Jack tested the air pressure and quality, got a green light. He removed his helmet, smoothed back the locks of his sweaty hair, then went to Panda.

She stroked the edge of his face. Her eyelids warmed

to gold swirls, then her gaze darted back to DeMitri, and her tattoos cooled to lavender-gray smears.

"Reno and Safa are gone?" Jack asked.

"They left for the observatory," Panda replied and pursed her lips. "Reno used his plane's vertical takeoff jets to propel them. He was uncertain, however, if there will be sufficient fuel for the return trip."

Jack hoped he hadn't sent them on a one-way mission. With so little lunar rotation to power Reno's gateway, he couldn't jump back if anything went wrong.

DeMitri pulled an imaginary cloud from the air, set it behind his head, and went to sleep.

What was the master spy dreaming? How to escape? How to sabotage Jack's operations? Or was he stuck here? Maybe he could be persuaded to help them against Isabel? Jack wouldn't count on it. DeMitri had tortured Jack. Tried to erase him. And Jack had tried to do the same to him. He couldn't let his guard down with DeMitri. Ever.

Jack asked, "Did Isabel get the power and—"

"She has kept her part of the bargain." Panda jerked her head toward the back wall.

Curving out from the wall was a high-voltage yellow-and-red-striped cable. One end connected into a power socket. The other end vanished into thin air.

Jack examined it. He recalibrated the bubble's imagers and magnified the space around the apparently bare end. A circle of blue haze wavered there—a hole seven microns wide. An arc of electricity snaked into the bare metal fibers of the cable. How much energy did it require to keep this gateway perpetually open?

There was a hiss of air, too. Jack felt, found the approximate location of the draft, and again zoomed in on this second microscopic hole. Inside, it rippled with jets of compressed oxygen.

Panda walked to his side. "I am glad Safa was not here to see what has become of her cousin. Do not tell her."

Jack tore his gaze from the hole in space. "I wonder if Isabel has 'helped' Zero like she's helping us." Jack nodded at the beret. "That looks good on you."

Panda pulled it off.

"You and Safa call a truce?"

She glanced back at DeMitri and didn't answer.

Jack was about to push her on Safa, but stopped when he saw Kamal.

The Buddhist monk was submerged in shadow, the air around him full of pine incense and rumbling bass chants. He sat in the lotus position and stared intently at the floor. An open window hovered by his left hand.

Jack approached him. "What are you doing?"

Kamal's black eyes snapped up and stopped Jack in his tracks. "Take care," he said. "You will disturb my work."

In the dust, Kamal had drawn an intricate design of tiny circles and lines that sprawled a meter in every direction.

It was real. Jack sensed no interface from it. He didn't move, didn't breathe, fearing any stray current would blow away Kamal's creation.

Panda, however, moved closer, taking slow, careful steps.

Inside Kamal's open window was a map of red and blue and green geography, the diagram of the electron reactors. He moved the image closer and compared it to his dusty blueprint.

Jack leaned in for a better look at the floor. Between the lines and dots, minute figures had been inscribed: snakes and roosters and pigs, evil spirits with crooked faces. One looked suspiciously like Reno.

Kamal glanced up; the phantom chanting ceased. "You asked me to fix the electron reactor. This is how." He pointed to a triangle. It had four dots: one in each corner and one in its center. "Three processors," Kamal explained, "speak to one another, and they speak to a central unit."

"To coordinate their communication?" Panda asked.

"Yes." Kamal smoothed a hand over his bald head. "But I cannot connect these individual clusters of four. The distance between them exceeds the mean tunneling distance for this voltage."

"A four-processor computer," Jack said, "isn't going to do us any good." He twisted the air and opened a silver-framed window, then copied Kamal's diagram, saving the work before someone sneezed.

Panda reached out, touched the central unit. "This circle is hollow; the others are solid. Is it supposed to be empty?"

"Yes," Kamal whispered and his dark eyes lit up. "The wavefunctions from the adjacent three processors overlap. The center must be silent and still to listen."

"Let's not get too anthropomorphic," Jack muttered. He opened another window, set up a crude simulation, and let it run.

Three electrons flowed and filled the four connected reactors. Waves lapped back and forth, but didn't oscillate out of control like they had before.

"Electron reactors simplify quantum inputs," Jack said. "Your central unit acts like a tiny middleman, smoothing the communication between the outer three processors."

DeMitri wandered closer.

Panda turned. "Back," she warned, drawing her gun.

"I only was curious," he said and continued forward. "Perhaps I can help?"

"Let him," Jack said and set his hand on her arm.

When Jack had been recruited by the NSO, DeMitri had been his teacher. Jack didn't trust him for a heartbeat; DeMitri knew every blackhack ever invented, but he also knew math-code and puzzle languages that Jack could only guess at. He might be a great help . . . if this wasn't a trick.

Panda warily holstered her gun. Her glare cut across to DeMitri, left hairline fractures in the crystalline bubble air, a metaphor of just how strained relations were.

DeMitri crouched, slicked back his long raven hair, and studied Kamal's design.

Jack touched the running simulation, let static electricity play across his fingers. "But what works with four reactors won't necessarily run on a network of thousands. How do we get these clusters to talk to one another?"

He looked to Kamal's diagram for inspiration. Useless. He couldn't think in two dimensions. Let alone work with something so fragile and yet immutable . . . so real.

Jack tapped the air, made three pink dots appear, and

pushed them into the corners of an isosceles triangle. An empty red unit went above this. Jack connected the lines. He made copies, then copies of copies, until hundreds of pyramids formed a Tinkertoy lattice in the bubble.

He activated the simulation; it worked—for a moment—then waves roiled and stormed through the pipelines, bursting connections.

The system crashed.

Panda peered over his shoulder. "Data overflows between the center units of one cluster to another."

Jack grabbed three four-processor clusters and made the base of a new pyramid. He connected each of their central units to the capstone of this new pyramid with another empty processor.

"A coordinating processor for the center units?" Panda asked.

Jack nodded.

That was nine electrons for a dozen reactors. Would the voltage be spread too thin?

Kamal pulled Jack's window away and tapped in the simulation. Silver wavefunctions reflected in his black eyes. "Charge density fluctuates rapidly within this new coordinating unit," he said. "Yet, the system appears stable."

"That takes care of twelve." Panda paced around the simulation. "What of the other thousands?"

"It is a fractal," DeMitri quietly commented. "Three electron reactors controlled by one central unit make a cluster." He pulled a pyramid from the simulation and let it spin in the air.

"Three clusters"—DeMitri made a triangle of them—"are controlled by a second-order central unit." He capped this triangle with a processor. With a snap of his fingers, he shrank the entire structure to the size of the original pyramid.

"It has similar geometry," Kamal said.

"Not only similar," DeMitri replied, "but similar regardless of scale." He duplicated his superclusters, took three and made the base of a still larger pyramid, then topped it with another empty central processor. "This is a third-order system.'' He waved his hand. ''It can be extended to fourth-order geometries . . . and so on.''

Panda stared at the assembled clusters, then turned to DeMitri with no malice filming her eyes. ''How far can one extend this hierarchy?''

Jack said, ''There's only one way to find out if this house of cards will stand.''

The simulation was too abstract for his taste. Jack needed metaphor. A panorama to let his imagination wander over. He stretched the command-center floor, puckered it into a nano-countryside: hills and mountains and canyons of atoms and thousands of isolated lakes that glimmered. ''Let's do some quantum landscaping.''

What had been so easily laid out with a flick of the fingers and a thought in three dimensions had taken six hours for the nano-assemblers to squash into a maze of rivulets and underground aqueducts in the gallium arsenide semiconductive chip. Electrons flowed through channels, lapped the edges, jiggled within canyons, over waterfalls, and fell into silent whirlpools.

The water ran smoothly, a metaphor for noiseless information transfer. Not a ripple of turbulence, not a fleck of foam generated across alluvial fans of slick mercury. It could have been the tidal flats of Australia. It could have been an ancient circuit board connected with silver solder. Isabel would have appreciated the image.

Jack missed her . . . for a moment.

He glanced at DeMitri, her operative. He had lost ten years; no hints of gray in his long black hair and no lines creased his forehead. Had he taken Wheeler's enzyme as well? And if so, how else had it transformed the ex-spy?

Could Jack get him to work with him? No. Snakes shed their skins, but underneath they were always the same: coiled and ready to bite.

Jack turned back to the quantum terrain—reflected sunlight and crisscrossing swells.

''Shall we test it?'' Kamal nervously rolled prayer beads between his stubby fingers.

Panda rubbed her hands over the air; a bamboo frame

appeared. Rice paper stretched across the window, and upon it were ancient calligraphic symbols: rampant lions and flaming peacocks and the Eye of Osiris. She entered: HOW ARE YOU?, then tapped the snake-eating-tail diagnostic.

Waves rolled through the channels and elevated the tide line . . . almost overflowed, bulging with surface tension. Ripples bounced off the walls, sloshed within the canyons. Hills eroded and were redeposited. New wormholes formed and filled with liquid as the processors optimized their configurations.

Jack watched Panda's window. It blanked, then:

```
PROCESSORS ON-LINE...............................................2,429
COMPUTATIONAL CAPACITY .................................... 349%
OPERATING SYSTEM ............................................... STABLE
GATEWAY SOFTWARE TOOLS........................... AVAILABLE
TRANSLATION LEXICON........................................ON-LINE
THANK YOU FOR ASKING ......................... HOW ARE YOU?
```

A smile spread across Panda's face—faded just as quick as she cocked her head, listening to a sound Jack didn't hear. She turned to DeMitri and scrutinized his face. She grabbed his shoulders and spun him around.

Instead of his back, the front of DeMitri turned to face them. He had been projecting a false front. His real hands reached into a tiny window, through cast-iron pipes and bronze pressure valves, deep into the system-works of the operating system.

DeMitri withdrew, not appearing a bit guilty. He closed his illegally opened window.

Panda said, "Attempt such deception again and I will kill you."

DeMitri tensed. The air around him shifted with static, then he sighed and canceled whatever metaphor he was preparing. "Of course," he said and retreated.

"What are we going to do with him?" Jack whispered to Panda.

She shook her head. "There is no way to guarantee our security short of executing him." Panda frowned, perhaps contemplating this option—started to reply, but a scrape and clatter emanated from atop the elevator airlock.

"Reno and Safa?" Jack asked, "or someone else?"

Panda got her headgear in place and drew her Hautger SK . . . then vanished into invisible folds of the bubble.

Jack pulled on his helmet as well and sealed the neck.

The airlock cycled.

Reno and Safa stepped out, trailing dust.

They were holding hands, but Reno hastily let go, then said, "That thing's not degaussing right." He accidentally walked across Kamal's diagram, scattering his artwork.

The Buddhist monk glared at Reno, then sighed, shrugged, and tromped across it as well.

Jack undid his helmet and met them. He was relieved to see Safa alive. Even Reno. He almost clasped Reno's shoulder and slapped him on the back—caught himself and doused that emotion. Jack sometimes forgot that Reno wasn't his uncle. He wasn't even a friend. Reno wasn't above twisting Jack's feelings and using them to his advantage. In a way, he was more dangerous than DeMitri.

Safa stopped short when she saw the nano-landscape. Her full lips parted in surprise. "You fixed the electron reactors?" she asked Jack.

"Not just me," he replied. "It took all of us."

Panda stepped out of her virtual hiding place. She holstered her gun and went to Safa. They leaned together to exchange a private word, then metaphor flashed between them: whispered Muslim prayers and the odor of licorice. Panda offered Safa's beret back, but Safa smiled and declined.

Jack was glad someone was getting along.

Reno shot a scowl in DeMitri's direction. "Him and his NSO buddies got everything at the observatory." Reno stepped closer and whispered, "Good thing I squirreled away supplies under the telescope arrays. Two days of air for the five of us to breathe. Seven tons of jet fuel for *Itsy* . . . and too many damn cigarettes we won't be able to smoke."

Safa nodded to the cable that hung from the air. "Isabel has fulfilled her end of our agreement. Do we keep yours?'' She arched a delicate eyebrow. ''Or do we make alternate plans?''

''Both,'' Jack told her. ''I'll contact whoever is on the other end of Wheeler's set of frequencies. But first, I want to explore the gateway's software.''

''The gateway?'' Reno cried. ''What's the use? There's no juice to power it.''

Jack pointed to the cable. ''That's the use. Isabel has found a way to keep two holes in space open, linking here to there.'' He lowered his voice in case Isabel could listen through those holes. ''Maybe there's a way to expand that doorway so we can step through.''

Safa moved closer so she could hear, nearer to Reno than Jack. ''I believe the attempt is worthwhile.'' She removed her helmet, ran her fingers across the stubble of her hair, and shook out sparks of static.

Something other than static permeated the air, a pulse transmission between her and Reno that Jack only caught the edges of: curling cigarette smoke and red velvet and an exhaled sigh upon the back of the neck.

Reno turned to her and with a sly grin said, ''You never told me this was a democracy. Do we get to vote?''

''No,'' Jack said. ''I'm in charge.''

He didn't like Reno's casual tone with Safa or their private broadcast. What had happened between them at the observatory? Safa's bad taste was none of his business . . . but it was his business if Reno tried to take over his base and his team.

''You think there's something wrong with the setup here, Reno, you can get back to your observatory.''

''Wait a second, Jack-O, I never said—''

Panda stepped between them, interrupting Reno. ''There is,'' she said to Jack, ''a small lunar angular moment. If the gateway's efficiency is improved, this could prove useful.''

Kamal joined them. ''Was this not the reason we repaired the computer?'' He tucked away his wooden prayer beads, then his hand vanished into his robe's sleeves. ''I would like to see more of this ever-changing software.''

Reno threw up his arms in disgust. ''You're all crazy.

Get started on that Isabel thing. Without her air and power, no one's going to be hacking anything.''

''The gateway first,'' Jack told him. He summoned its inner core of code; it filled the bubble with trembling sine-wave operators.

''Recall Zero's recommendation.'' Kamal retrieved his prayer beads—now knotted. ''Add a layer of complexity.''

Jack examined a vibrational energy operator. Its quivering was barely discernible. Before, with access to the full energy of the spinning moon, the motion of the operators had made the surface impassable. But now . . . Jack slid his hands between them, pried open a hole, and stuck his head through.

Segmented copper arteries and Teflon capillaries branched into the center of the architecture. Every vibrational operator connected deeper to a tangle of interlocking jigsaw symbols, a black mass of corpuscular programming.

Another core of code.

He forced the wedge wider so the others could observe.

''Like Russian dolls,'' Safa remarked, squinting to better see. ''The largest shell contains a smaller one, which, in turn, contains another. How deep does this nesting go?''

Jack wasn't giving up. He pushed deeper, past the snarled connections. The center was compressed, packed precisely together. Solid. Despite the near-zero rotation of the moon, this knot still used that energy to squirm and wriggle so rapidly it was . . .

Indecipherable.

His hopes cracked, fell, and shattered upon the floor—shards of glass with razor edges that dulled as he watched, then crumbled into sand. Jack kicked the stuff with his boot. ''This isn't going to be as easy as I thought.''

The gateway code shrank.

On the outer surface sat a cluster of arrows, the positional operator that represented shifts in location. It, too, had a connection to the center—a wisp of smoke, microscopic compared to the amount of energy piped to the vibrational operators as waste heat.

Jack let the connection drop. ''I don't understand any of this.''

"You understand," Panda said and scrunched her darkening brows together. "You knew of the different energy operators."

"Those were in Wheeler's translation lexicon. I couldn't have . . ."

Jack stared at the undulating surface of sine waves. Were other symbols in that lexicon that he hadn't seen? He booted Wheeler's translation software. A billion symbols flashed on-screen as Jack searched for clues. Too many.

For the first time, metaphor was getting in the way of Jack's thinking. Too much information filled the air around him.

And maybe Jack already had the piece he needed to solve the puzzle.

Zero had told him to add a layer of complexity to simplify the gateway code. A paradox? Not necessarily. Not if that layer of complexity *was* zero.

He opened an interface to the computer and entered:

/:TRANSLATION LEXICON
(GATEWAY CODE) MATCH (NULL OPERATOR)

A sphere appeared over the window, black-chromed skin that twisted inside-out to reveal a silver-white inner surface. It then turned outside-in, back and forth, black and white. Zero.

"I don't get how you're going to fix this," Reno said, "with that." He squinted at the flip-flopping sphere and scratched his gray hair.

Jack grabbed a copper blood vessel connected to a sine-wave icon. "The power," he said, "is redistributed through these links, mostly shunted to the vibrational operators as waste heat. But we can intercept that wasted energy with a dummy variable, call it J."

A stainless-steel J appeared in Jack's hand. Was that J for Jack? Junction? Joke? He was overanalyzing his thoughts.

Jack pulled a pair of laser-edged scissors from the air. He cut a meter-long section out of the copper conduit and set it aside. Light poured from the severed end still attached to the core of code, raw power that sputtered and made the air crackle. He attached the severed end to the top portion of the J. A flurry of firefly sparks welded it solid. Energy shot out the opposite end of the top piece and the tail of the J.

"We use the zero icon as a plug." Jack set the top portion of the J against the inside-out-turning sphere. Sparkling plasma vanished into its folds and convolutions.

"One last connection," Jack said. He took the cut length of cable and threaded it onto the curled tail of the J, then snapped the free end into the zigzagging arrows of the positional operator.

"Let me lay it all out for you." He waved his hand and a blackboard materialized. Jack wrote with chalky skritches:

$$\text{DEF(POWER)};$$
$$\text{J} = \text{POWER};$$
$$\text{POWER} = 0;$$
$$\text{ENERGY(POSITION)} = \text{J};$$

Panda scrutinized the marks. Her eyebrows arched and tattoos flashed platinum. "You've transferred power to this variable J," she said. "The vibrational operators, functions of power, are set to zero." She turned to Jack and nodded appreciatively. "Your last line reroutes power to the positional operator. Simple. Elegant."

"It'll never work," Reno said, staring at the blackboard, then back to the code as it stammered sparks from the J junction.

Jack wiped his hand across the air, smoothed it into a mirror, then turned the plane, caught the reflection of his reprogramming, replicated that, then quickly flipped the mirror to catch its own reflection, copied his copies, and those copies, until his new code was installed throughout the recursive network of connecting ducts and symbols.

The middle strata of vibrating sine waves withered. Underneath, a layer of stainless-steel J's glistened. Zero operators ballooned, rippled inside-out in black and white cascades of motion. The position operator sprouted new arrows across the surface.

Jack un-Velcroed the gateway from his thigh.

He held his breath. Red and blue vectors flickered upon the sphere. He tagged himself with the red arrow, then touched the blue.

It blurred, went out of focus, then snapped back. Was something wrong?

Jack drew it out, stretched a blue line up and out of the command center, across the moon . . . halfway to the Earth.

Nothing was wrong. "It works," he told Reno.

Reno unfolded his arms. "Nice." It didn't sound like a compliment.

"You have doubts?" Safa asked him.

"This solves nothing," DeMitri remarked. "Even with your newly efficient gateway, you are still trapped on the moon."

"That's not exactly what I meant," Reno said. "The code was too easy to reprogram. Why would Wheeler make it so simple? It's got to be a setup."

Jack shut down the gateway. "Wheeler may not even know how the gateway works. His race probably stole it from another civilization."

He stared at himself along the reflective curve of the gateway. Wheeler had, however, conveniently given him all the pieces to this puzzle. Without the electron reactor and the translation lexicon, he could never have altered the gateway.

Reno was right: it was too easy . . . too coincidental.

Did Wheeler want him to bypass the lockout? And make the gateway more effective? Why then destroy the Earth and supposedly Jack along with it?

Safa gazed into the mirror ball alongside Jack. Her bow-shaped lips smeared across its distorted surface. "Regrettably, Mr. DeMitri is correct," she said. "There is still insufficient rotational energy to leave the moon. Our next logical step should be to examine the innermost core of code. Find the gateway's power source and enhance it."

Jack glanced at the cable hanging in the air. "No. I

have to hedge our bets. Keep in Isabel's good graces so we continue to get air and electricity." He closed his eyes—then said the words he thought he'd never say: "I have to be her middleman."

Jack sat cross-legged in his own private subshell within the bubble. It was surrounded by dead-code through which not a bit of information seeped—curved walls of bone and electrified razor wire waiting to snare any data transfer.

He wouldn't take chances with DeMitri. Not in a command center that had been opened by his team of NSO creeps and may be full of ears and eyes that Jack hadn't detected.

Jack set the silver case containing the isotope and communication circuits before him. Waves of water-blue light from the superheavy element wavered in the air.

He tapped the space above his lap, made it a pane of glass, then entered the alien's frequency set.

Pixels danced upon the smooth surface . . . coalesced into a solid line.

A connection.

Jack reached for it—hesitated. Connections had gotten him into trouble. He had connected to Wheeler and traded for the enzyme, the gateway, the electron reactor . . . and the end of his world. He had traded with another race of aliens and gotten them annihilated.

One other thing: Wheeler had these frequencies. What was to prevent him from eavesdropping? Without an encryption scheme, nothing.

Jack had to keep it simple. No names. No voices. No clues to his identity.

It was still a risk. Jack reached to cut the circuit, to think about this before he leapt without looking.

The isotope darkened.

Sapphire blue clouded purple, scintillated ultraviolet along its facets, slowed and pulsed and thickened.

It wasn't a leaking subliminal from Jack. What was causing the superheavy element to fill with shadows?

His walls of bone creaked, and his electrified barbed wire shorted.

The computer etched upon his pane of glass:

VOLTAGE FLUCTUATION IN BUBBLE COMPONENTS;
QUANTUM CASCADE THROUGH LOGIC CELLS;
RESETTING SYSTEM AND RESTORING CONFIGUATIONS.

Jack looked up—saw himself sitting a meter away, cross-legged, too.

This other self said, "Hello, Jack."

Jack fought the urge to panic and freeze. There were three possibilities. Either someone outside his subshell, but inside the bubble, had interfaced. Or it was the alien he was trying to contact. Or it was Wheeler.

Whichever possibility . . . Jack had been identified on an open line.

His panic won, overflowed his suit, and stained the floor blood red. Jack grabbed the glass-pane interface and hit the terminate black-on-black icon.

The other Jack remained. The bubble shell hadn't crashed.

Jack tapped the icon harder. Nothing.

This fake Jack lit a cigarette, then asked, "Mind if I smoke?"

Jack studied his duplicate. That Jack had the same unwashed hair, slate-gray eyes, and too-large ears. But he inhaled his exhaled smoke, caught the exhaust with a quick smooth inhalation through his nose. A trick the real Jack had never mastered.

"Who are you?"

"You called us." He pointed at Jack with the illusionary cigarette. "You tell me."

Jack slammed his fist onto the terminate icon.

"It's OK," his double said and nodded at the dimmed isotope. "This line is shielded."

"How?" Jack said. "And how did you interface with my system?"

"Is this what you wanted?" the other Jack asked, studying the glowing tip of his cigarette. "Just curiosity and questions? About physics you can never understand?"

"Never?" Jack bristled at that. He made his own cigarette appear and stared through the convoluted smoke at the isotope.

His mind reached into the physics database: signals sent through the superheavy element, through cracks in space, were accelerated past the normal speed of light in that dense medium. It produced a shock-wave spectrum of blue photons similar to Çerenkov radiation.

How had that spectrum shifted from blue to purple?

Links to the high-energy physics nodes solidified with Jack's thoughts; data streams left rainbows of twinkling trajectories and scattered particle tracks upon the floor, subatomic lace that he traced with his fingers.

"Light isn't the only thing you can send through the isotope," Jack said. "It could be a host of other subatomic particles with different shock-wave characteristics. You're analyzing their backscatter. Gathering information from the linked systems. Information on me."

The other Jack nodded. "Maybe you are worth talking to after all." His hazel eyes sparkled with stars, then he gathered his hair into a ponytail. "You understand how this must work? The secrecy involved?"

"I have a good idea. No locations."

"No," his double said. "Your location. We will need it to confirm your identity."

"That's not safe."

"If you wanted safety, you never should have called. You decide if that's worth the risk." He puffed, then waved his hand and said, "Besides, we only need the location of your original home world. We want to listen to your early transmissions."

" 'Original home world'?" Jack asked.

"Don't pretend you're still there. If you sent a message through the isotope—bridged space—then you have the technology to be anywhere you desire."

Was he implying that the isotope and gateway operated on similar principles? It made sense. One bounced light through the cracks in space, the other matter. That could be a valuable piece of information.

"What about it?" the other Jack asked. "Your location. Or are we done?"

Jack needed time. If Wheeler could break this secured line, then the damage had already been done. He wouldn't be alive that much longer to matter.

"OK," Jack whispered. "How will you find—"

The other Jack exhaled. His smoke twinkled with pinpoints of light. There were spiral galaxies, globular clusters, discs, filamentous arcs, spinning cups, hourglass shapes, and flat planes composed of silk nebulae.

"The geometry of your galaxy?"

Jack nodded to the spiral.

The fake Jack raised an eyebrow, leaned forward, and looked like he was about to laugh. Whatever he thought was so funny, he kept it to himself. "Number of arms in the spiral?"

"Five."

"Topology of central black holes?"

"I . . . I don't know."

The other Jack shook his head, as if that was something any intelligent person should know. "Spectra and location of home star?"

Jack touched Orion's Arm, scattered stars with his finger, then uploaded a flash of light.

His double held up a hand. "That's enough. I've got it."

"And?"

The other Jack crushed out his cigarette. He got up and turned. "We'll be in touch. Keep your ears open."

"Wait. What are you called?"

He paused, looked deep into Jack, then said, "You may call us Gersham." His body faded, but the hazel Cheshire cat eyes lingered.

Jack couldn't get comfortable in the overstuffed throne Isabel had provided. Maybe she had designed it that way. Or maybe there was an electric chair under the mink and purple silk upholstery.

Isabel traced a figure eight with her short nail upon her fainting couch. "Gersham?" she asked. "Really?"

"It's the truth," Jack replied, regretting saying it the

instant it was out. It made him sound desperate. Like he was lying.

She looked up. A spark of contact in her green eyes.

The last thing Jack wanted was contact; he formed a maze of glass in the air between them, and her mind retracted.

Afternoon shadows lengthened in Isabel's sitting room. Beyond the picture window, dusk made the horizon of her world glow amber. In gold frames, masterpieces hung on the walls: Rembrandts with faces floating in darkness; a man-of-war floundered upon rocks; and a crumbling cathedral sat under a starless sky.

Isabel had set the mood perfectly.

"It's so easy for you, isn't it?" she asked.

Jack eased back in his chair to put some distance between them. "What's easy?"

She clenched one hand and sighed explosively. The red velveteen wallpaper ripped with her frustration. "This Gersham . . . Wheeler . . . and the other aliens. It's so easy for you to speak with them. Why you, Jack?"

"It's not easy for me. They're listening. They're the ones who want to talk. And trade. I treat them like anyone else I would make a deal with." With a healthy dose of suspicion and finger-counting after the closing handshake.

"Like me?" Isabel asked.

Jack shrugged.

"Then let us keep our deal," she said. "I require contact to verify your report."

He squirmed . . . but there was nowhere to go. Ex-lovers might have a brief dalliance for the sake of memory, old arguments and slights blurred by time and distance. Not so with the contact Isabel required. All the facts would come out. Jack hated Isabel. They had crossed and doubled-crossed and betrayed each other and no metaphor could disguise it. She knew the score, too.

Her mind picked through the maze Jack had set between them.

Apricots and champagne mixed with the scent of Jack's stale overly recycled air. Her hot touch intertwined with his hands, deceptive because she was solid ice inside. A flash of blue static escaped Jack—his secret set of frequencies, which he quickly extinguished . . . but not before that light illuminated her frozen feelings, revealed that a sliver of Isabel's heart had thawed. From her subconscious, she whispered: *Nothing in the world is single; why not with me join?*

Jack wished he hadn't heard that. It would have been easier to believe Isabel was all monster.

She pretended those leaking emotions didn't exist and picked past Jack's memories of Gersham, skimmed over their conversations, and examined Jack's outward coolness and his inner terror that Wheeler had eavesdropped.

Isabel didn't pause when Gersham revealed the connection between the isotope and the gateway. She already knew.

Jack pushed against her mind as she rifled his; examined her memories of the gateway—got a glimpse of the core code, the black solid mass of commands, and something even deeper: a slender line of gold. A yellow arrow.

A third vector? For what?

Isabel withdrew.

"Very good, Jack," she said. "Another twelve hours and I will require an update." Her eyes hardened, and facets sharpened. "And next time, don't dig around in my mind."

"You're the one who wanted deep contact," he said. "It's a two-way street. That's what—"

She severed contact, left Jack in a backwash of distorted ocean surf and sandpaper grit and the aftertaste of nutmeg, which dissolved and left him sitting back in the black and blank command center.

Panda gave Jack a hand up, steadied him as his legs wobbled from the abrupt disconnect. She looked into his face, curious. Her chameleon tattoos flickered turquoise and streaked with jade-green jealousy.

"The gateway was in her mind," Kamal said. "But we could not sense much on this end."

Safa opened a scroll in the air and tapped in instructions. The gateway's core of code appeared before her, a black planet spinning.

"Did you see it?" Jack reached for the software. "In the center there was another vector. Yellow. Maybe a clue to how the gateway works."

He stopped.

A moth alighted on the back of his hand, slender wings of tan and gold spots, beating up and down, trembling, then it fluttered away.

Jack canceled the metaphorical distraction. It had to be his subconscious worries about Zero.

It remained.

He pushed. Received no echo. It was real?

Jack turned.

There were a hundred butterflies, swirls of crimson and cerulean and saffron. In the center of this rainbow cloud was an arch; Arabic script scrawled and crawled along its edge.

Zero stood on the threshold.

9

"**Z**ero!" Jack yelled.

Everyone in the command center turned.

Jack shut down the bubble. Gateway code and open windows collapsed. The butterflies, the arch, and Zero remained. He was real.

Zero's right eye fixed on Jack; the left darted from Reno to Panda, then alighted on Safa and froze. "I have come," he said, "to *make* you rescue me."

Every insect simultaneously took wing. The roomed thickened with clouds of fluttering scarlet and topaz.

Safa squinted through the swarm of color. "No!" She drew her sidearm.

Panda and Reno unholstered their guns.

"Wait," Jack said. "You don't—"

Zero retreated to his side of the portal. The archway widened.

Reno waved his gun at the hole in space. "That's our way off the moon," he said. "Come on." He ran—skidded to a halt.

Vines spilled out of the portal. They undulated like headless snakes; nickel-plated thorns sprung from sockets; barbed-anchor bolts shot into the floor. Roots divided and wormed along the curved command-center walls.

Jack hesitated—only a heartbeat—long enough for the creepers to swell and fill the opening's diameter. Razor wire sprouted and separated him from Reno and Panda and Safa.

"Go, Jack!" Panda shouted. "Get out while you can." She pulled on her helmet. Spiny runners wove a net between her ankles, then blossomed with tiny white orchids. She got one leg untangled—couldn't extract the other.

Pea-soup mist poured into the room. It smelled of chlorophyll and musk.

Jack had to get topside, into vacuum, where nothing organic could survive. But he couldn't abandon his friends. He took a step forward . . . wishing he had a machete.

Creatures wriggled within the tangles of metal and green: clusters of eyes and ears and mouths, cockroach feelers, circles of lamprey teeth, multiple arms and legs and heads—one hissed and lunged at Safa.

She fired: a burst of three compression rounds, a spray of blood, and it was cut in half.

Vines covered half the ceiling, intertwining through one another and the metal supports, twisting and ratcheting forward.

Kamal wrestled with a branch as it curled around his torso.

Jack scrambled to the monk, tried to pull it off. The plant grabbed Jack back—ran up the length of his arm.

Zero's gateway widened.

Men with goat heads marched into the command center. They had octopus tentacles instead of arms, dripping a black sulfurous-smelling ink.

The fog thickened. Jack couldn't see more than two meters. What had Zero let loose? Genetically engineered creatures? Aliens?

He heard DeMitri scream. Automatic gunfire drowned him out. Sparks and reverberation filled the air.

Copper cockroaches buzzed over Jack's head; they dropped onto the floor—detonated. Chitin shrapnel cut a gash across Jack's forehead. He reeled back, stunned.

A root bristling with silver needles wrapped around Jack's shin, punctured his vacuum suit, curled up his thigh, ripped open his Velcroed pockets.

He shot it.

The vine released, thrashing and spewing white hydraulic fluid that burned his leg.

Jack wanted to scream. No. That might attract more of whatever was out there in the pea-soup mist.

He couldn't see Kamal anymore—just a mound of tendrils, slithering over one another.

Fire and acid pain crawled along Jack's thigh. He felt lightheaded. This had to be a dream. A nightmare. Jack limped back two paces.

More shots. He couldn't see who was killing who—or what.

Jack reached for the gateway. He should have used it before, used that last little bit of angular momentum to get him out of here. He wasn't thinking straight . . . like he'd been drugged or—

The silver sphere was gone. Pulled off by the vine? Dropped? Jack panicked, got on all fours, and searched the floor.

Millipedes with human fingers for legs scuttled over his hands. A red-black ooze spread across the ground; it molded tongues and proboscises and jellied-geometric forms as it felt and probed and sizzled forward.

The room slowly spun. Jack's stomach twisted. His legs went rubbery.

He set his Hautger SK to full auto—he'd kill everything. No. His team was hidden in the fog, too. He was just as likely to shoot them.

Jack half-ran, half-limped into the elevator airlock.

Across the room there was bagpipe music and cricket-winged violins and flutes and the roar of flames. This *was* a nightmare. It couldn't be real.

Jack had to leave. Climb out. Escape.

A ball of translucent flesh rolled toward him, split along its meter diameter, smiled with dagger teeth. Jack blasted it into organic confetti.

He forced himself to stop and think. His gaze landed upon the airlock—the way out, up to the surface, where none of Zero's creatures could follow . . . because it was hard vacuum.

Or better yet, Jack could bring the vacuum inside. He

pulled on his headgear, boosted the com frequency to full power, and shouted, "Helmets on. Quick!"

He grabbed a can of Teflon-elastomer and sprayed over the rips and gashes in his suit that hadn't self-sealed. Silver thermal-resistant polymer oozed over his legs and chest, filled the punctures . . . almost. The edges curled and peeled around the white hydraulic fluid coating him. He got a green integrity light on the seal, which then flickered amber.

Scaled vines crept closer. Disembodied eyes blinked at him from the mist.

The seal would have to hold.

What about the others? Had their suits breached, too?

He had to risk it. He braced himself in the elevator corner, then tapped in the override to keep the inner doors open. Jack cycled the airlock.

A great sigh.

The fog vanished. Tornadoes ripped around Jack as the atmosphere vented. Whirlwinds of dust exploded up the airlock shaft, pitting his faceplate. The command center was a mess of vines and arms and legs, parts vegetable, animal, and mechanical cobbled together, writhing.

DeMitri lay a meter away, unconscious, his hand clutching the secured seal of his helmet.

On the opposite side of the room, fire spouted from Reno's gun . . . and Jack saw what he was shooting at. His blood froze.

Zero's portal had become a hurricane; air from his world shrieked into the command center, freezing into clouds of ice. Through that circle, three goat men dragged a limp Safa.

Jack jumped out of the airlock—a four-meter leap in the low gravity—halfway across the room.

The opening to Zero's world shrank; torrents of air screamed and whistled. The portal winked out of existence. A thousand severed vines lay, bleeding sap upon its threshold.

And Safa had been kidnapped, light-years distant.

"No!" Jack screamed.

He scrambled over crawling vines and creatures suffocating with bloody mouths, clutching at him with claws and fingers and feelers.

The last of the air vented.

It was eerily silent, a nightmare composite of slaughter-house and greenhouse.

Tendrils desiccated and withered. Jack spotted the cage of vines that had snared Kamal and pulled him out. His helmet was on. Jack exhaled and fogged his faceplate. If anything had happened to the old monk, Jack would never have forgiven himself.

Reno marched over. "We've got to get her back," he said. Inside his helmet, both brown and blue eyes were set in a grim stare. Blood trickled from his nose and ears. Faint wisps of emotion leaked from Reno's implant: fear and affection and desperation—he squelched them.

Jack ignored Reno and went to Panda.

Body parts and bits of vine surrounded her as she crouched with her back against the wall. Three fine needles, half a meter in length, pierced the bicep of her left arm. She held her gun in both hands and scanned for targets. Her eyes were wide. Kaleidoscopic colors flashed along her chameleon brow.

She aimed at Jack.

The ejection port of her gun clicked shut—no ammunition left.

He slowly approached and put his hand over her gun. "It's OK. It's me, Jack. It's over."

Panda pushed him gently away. She reached up, gritted her teeth, then pulled out the long needles. The self-sealing gel of her vacuum suit oozed from the holes, along with a little blood. She flexed the injured arm. "I am fine."

Reno tapped Jack on the shoulder. "What about Safa?"

Jack whirled. "What about her, Reno? She's gone. Zero could have taken her anywhere." He curled his hands into fists, took a step closer to Reno. Stopped. Was he really mad at Reno? He should be angry at Zero. Or himself. He should have seen this coming.

Reno smiled: a line of gold teeth that wasn't friendly. More like a dog snarling. "Come on, Jack-O," he whispered conspiratorially. "You've practically fixed your gateway. Fix it some more. Figure out a way to find Zero. You have to. Safa and I had plans. We . . ." His smile faded. "Never mind, you wouldn't get it." He poked Jack in the center of his chest. "We just have to find her."

A dead goat man stared up at Jack. Would Zero transform Safa like he had these poor creatures?

Jack stepped away from Reno. "Give me a second to think."

He found his gateway wrapped in a severed tentacle . . . only a meter from where Zero's portal had been. Tiny sucker marks dotted its mirror surface. He picked it up.

The plants had dried and dissolved, leaving only spiny metal skeletons. Aluminum buds unfolded, red-gold foil petals breathed clouds of pollen into the vacuum. The flowers then wilted.

Panda tapped open a window and reinitialized the bubble.

The scent of licorice filled Jack's helmet. Her mind wrapped about his, curled and settled like a cat getting comfortable. A moment together, then she squeezed his hand and let go.

Jack spread his hands over the air, made a pane of glass appear. Zero's frequencies danced upon it, motes of blue static. "Zero!" he shouted at them. "Answer me."

There was only the hiss and pop of noise. Zero may have been listening, but he wasn't picking up.

Jack shattered the link with his fist.

The clang of metal reverberated through the soles of Jack's boots. He turned and saw Kamal shutting the airlock. The monk then examined Isabel's cable. He gave Jack a thumbs-up, indicating they still had a supply of air and electricity.

Reno took Jack by the shoulder. "Any brilliant ideas yet?"

Jack shrugged off Reno's hand. "There's no way to find Zero or Safa."

"But Safa is with those . . . things," Panda said. She stepped back and wrung her black beret.

"Even if we find Safa, how do we get to her?" Jack asked the both of them. "Where do we bring her back to?

Here? Wait for Zero to reappear with new friends? Or Isabel to pull the plug on our oxygen and power?''

Jack grasped the gateway tighter; it trembled in his hand. ''We've got to save ourselves first before we can think about Safa.''

He gazed at his own reflection. His mind came into sharp focus. ''We have a gateway, efficient now, but with too little a rotation left in the moon to get us anywhere. And there's a yellow vector hiding in all that code.''

He whispered to himself: ''Two pieces of a puzzle, which I bet I can solve.''

Jack was alone. All good intentions aside, the others would distract him. Not seeing Safa among them would distract him.

What was it he felt for her? Love? He doubted it. There was an attraction. More camaraderie than lust, though. Besides, she and Reno had plans.

Sticky strands of emotion adhered to Jack. He scraped them off and flicked the gooey mass onto the bubble floor. He had to think.

First thing: they had to leave the moon. Zero knew their location and he was insane—a deadly combination. Second item: their best hope of escaping was the gateway. Maybe the third yellow vector he had seen hidden in Isabel's mind was the key . . . but it was buried in the center of the seething gateway code.

Jack would see what hunches hid in his gray matter.

He exhaled and let his wandering thoughts fill space: Canadian geese flew overhead, an angle flapping south for the winter (Jack wished he could join them); a school of damselfish, a thousand electric-blue dots that simultaneously darted and flashed; Jupiter with its moons floated in the distance; the floor undulated and ruffled.

Motion.

Kinetic energy was motion—a bullet shot, the reverberation of a drumhead, a spinning coin—translations, vibrations, and rotations.

Jack watched the metaphors, fish and fowl and floating

planets, then shook his head. Too many objects. Too complex.

"Simplify," he ordered them.

The flock of geese collapsed into vectors for direction and velocity. Fish became numbers and organized themselves into a matrix. The vibrating floor snapped taut, quivering around a sterling Bessel function inscribed in the middle of the room.

Jupiter, however, and its orbiting moons remained. No simplification.

What was Jack's subconscious trying to say?

The Jovian world drifted and spun: bands of rainbow, halo rings, and polar auroras.

He wandered closer and saw black strings affixed the moons to cardboard rods. It was a child's mobile.

Despite this metaphor's stubbornness, it *could* be simplified. Orbits had eccentricities and tilts and periods. They were just numbers to be plugged into differential equations and plotted in phase space.

Jack cut the thread that held Ganymede; ice shimmered and frost shook off its surface as he tossed it onto the floor. Europa went, too. Callisto and Thebe—all the moons that complicated the system and obscured its meaning— Jack snapped their strings.

Io he left. Volcano-pockmarked and belching sulfurous clouds, it reminded Jack of the smoldering Earth. He nudged the moon, let it bobble around Jupiter in an elliptical orbit. A simple two-body system.

He tapped their equations of motion in the air, then simplified to center-of-mass coordinates—stopped.

There were *two* rotations, even in this uncomplicated system.

The planets rotated on their axis, and they spun around one another . . . around the center of their collective masses.

Was this why the gateway used rotation instead of any other motion for power? Because everything rotated? Moons around planets and planets around suns? How did the yellow vector in the center of the gateway connect to these rotations?

Jack had a hunch; it solidified and made the air crystalline.

He held the gateway and probed past the layers of programming, stopped at the innermost core. His fingertips ran over alien symbols that seethed and shifted and reprogramed themselves. They still tapped the minuscule rotational energy in the moon. Getting past them would be like trying to solve a jigsaw . . . with all the pieces dancing.

In the center was the yellow vector he had seen in Isabel's mind. To get to it, Jack would have to dampen the program's activity. He would have to slow the moon's rotation even more.

He checked his neck seal, got a green light, then jumped out of the command center—

—landed upon a chalky plain.

Jack blinked, dazzled by the glare of the sun. Impact craters, microscopic and mammoth, speckled the dust, stretched to the horizons, where it buttressed the dark sky. The Earth stared down at him, a waning sliver of orange.

Jack moved the blue destination vector to the far side of the moon, stepped—

—into the shadows of the observatory's hangar. He snapped on his helmet's spotlights.

Stacked in a corner were cylinders of compressed oxygen and hydrogen, stainless-steel water vessels, freeze-dried food, and electronics: Reno's supplies that he hadn't been able to cram into *Itsy-Bitsy*.

Jack spied a shuttle with a swollen body that looked as graceful as a flying pig. It was never designed for aerodynamics, just to ferry personnel and equipment between the moon and orbiting stations. He looked for obvious breaches in its scaled hull, found none, then opened the pilot's airlock and climbed inside.

Computer screens flickered in standby mode. The shuttle still had power. He walked back into the passengers' lounge, past rows of plastic-wrapped sleeper couches with form-fitting pillows, past the galley and bathrooms, and stopped at the airlock.

Jack cycled through into the cargo hold. The chamber

was padded, six meters in diameter and twenty long. Empty.

He went back out into the hangar and found a sputtering paint gun among the scattered tools. Since Jack was pushing his luck with this wild scheme, he might as well push it all the way. In wide cursive strokes, he wrote upon the shuttle's nose: DUTCHMAN.

It gave him a thrill to tempt fate.

Jack tagged the *Dutchman* with the gateway. The blue arrow reached three hundred kilometers into the night. Good. There was still enough energy left in case his hunch about the mysterious yellow vector paid off.

He stepped backward—

—into the command center. The shell of his private world was dark, then stars winked at the edge and watercolor nebulae painted the void. Distant galaxies wheeled around Jack.

The universe moved and he was its center.

Jack collapsed that thought, then uploaded the gateway's software, tentatively touched its core. Black-on-black symbols overlapped and squirmed . . . slower now because the moon had slowed its spinning. Slower now because of Jack's jumps.

His fingertips found a seam, a crack penetrating the wriggling mess, through which Jack spotted a thread of gold tangled in the ball of black yarn.

He touched it. It was cold, metallic. Heavy. He dug, fingernails caught, and he got a grip.

Jack pulled. Knots of code held and constricted the yellow line. He tugged and teased and yanked.

Something snapped; a brass arrowhead and shaft jerked free.

His anticipation clouded the air of the bubble with silverlined clouds. This was the gateway's heart. Maybe.

This yellow vector was similar to the red and blue arrows he had used before. Only it pointed down. Jack turned and twisted the gateway, but the arrow remained steadily aimed . . . at the center of the moon?

Jack scrutinized the sphere. The red vector tagged which object to move; the blue indicated destination. So what did the yellow do? The red and blue determined how the gateway used its power. Jack was guessing that the yellow had something to do with the collection of that power.

He gingerly grasped the golden arrow shaft, pulled up.

Metaphor for his nervousness made his fingers slick and sweaty, even through his vacuum-suit gloves.

The arrow moved, sluggishly, resisting him, a bar of lead in frozen molasses.

Jack regripped the sphere to get better purchase, sitting and bracing the sphere with his thighs. He tugged with both hands, wrapped his entire body around the gateway. Concentrated. "Move," he grunted. "Move!"

The vector swiveled, suddenly liquid in his hands; it swung to the top of the sphere, pointed straight up— clicked into place—reached past the confines of the bubble, stretched as far as he could sense.

Jack smiled. His hunch had been right. There was another rotation to use.

There were many types of motion, vibrations, translations, exotic nuclear jitters, and quantum fluxes—but everything rotated, turned, and spun around the center of the galaxy.

In that center Jack had found a way to escape the moon. He had a golden ladder to the stars.

Jack watched *Itsy-Bitsy*. She was a black widow spider on an invisible thread, descending over the roof of the observatory hangar. Two bursts from her vertical takeoff jets positioned her over the open cargo bay doors of the *Dutchman*.

They had loaded everything worth taking from the command center into *Itsy* and, after five trips to the observatory, dumped it all into the *Dutchman*. It would have been easier to use the gateway, but Jack had to conserve as much of the moon's rotation as possible.

Itsy touched down, her stubby wings barely clearing the interior.

The canopy split open and Reno got out. He released her bomb bay hatch and pulled out oxygen cylinders and gray µ-sealed cases.

Jack climbed aboard the shuttle. "That the last of your secret cache?"

"All of the oxygen," Reno said, "and those computers that Panda wanted." He waved at a battered plastic crate. "Plus a few essentials: eighty liters of water, medicine, and a few cans of salted nuts, and my cigarettes."

"Where's the interferometric equipment?"

"Packed in their satellites and loaded into the shuttle's launch tubes. Are they part of your plan to get us off this rock?"

Jack glanced over his shoulder. Panda walked back and forth across the hangar roof. Guard duty. She watched for Zero's reappearance—if there would be any warning. She also watched DeMitri as he operated a forklift and stowed motors and solar cells into the *Dutchman*'s hold.

"I'll tell you once we're under way," Jack said to Reno. "There are too many ears that could be listening. DeMitri's"—he waved at the vacuum around them—"or even Isabel through an open portal."

Reno wiped away the dust on his faceplate. "How much time do you think we have before the gene witch comes back?"

Jack shrugged. "I don't know. But he will. Zero wants something other than Safa." He scanned the horizons: black and full of stars and nothing alive. The gene witch was crazy—that was clear enough—but even the insane had motives.

Jack suddenly had the feeling that he was being watched, studied, prepared for a dissection. "Let's hurry up and get the hell out of here."

DeMitri entered the bay and gingerly set down the last soft-crate of portable bubble components. He walked up to Jack. The glare from the overhead lights reflected off his faceplate and made it impossible to see his face.

Reno's hand drifted to his gun.

"Might I have a word with Jack?" DeMitri asked Reno as casually as he might ask for the time. "Alone?"

"We're busy." Reno shoved DeMitri back a step.

"It's OK," Jack said. He nodded to the hangar roof.

"Panda's watching. I'm covered. Why don't you help Kamal? He's backing up the observatory's database."

"It's not OK," Reno said. There was a squelch as Reno cut off his com-line frequency. Jack saw him mutter something inside his helmet as he ambled up to the cockpit.

"I have a favor to ask." DeMitri tilted his head so Jack could see his smiling face.

"You're in no position to ask for anything."

"I know you don't trust me. I wouldn't trust you if our positions were reversed. My request, however, is a simple one: leave me behind."

Jack stared into DeMitri's eyes. Solid blue and unwavering. "You've got to be kidding. You'll die."

"I will die if I go with you." DeMitri sat on a plastic dodecahedron container and crossed his legs. "Quite frankly, I'm not convinced you know what you're doing. Your luck is going to run out—soon—and I don't wish to be around when that happens." He smiled wider, flashed a set of unnaturally white teeth. "And if your luck does hold, if you survive whatever scheme you are hatching, then either Panda or Reno will murder me. That is inevitable."

Jack glanced at Panda on the roof. She watched DeMitri with great interest.

"They are professionals," DeMitri whispered. "They do not take chances. Not with a person like me."

Panda and Reno hadn't killed one another only because Jack stood between them—literally. Jack wasn't about to take that risk for DeMitri. Someone was bound to get injured. Or eliminated. If not DeMitri, then maybe someone Jack cared about. Like himself.

"OK," Jack whispered. "I can leave you two days of oxygen, water, and food."

"A map of your base as well," DeMitri said. "There may be a way to salvage what is buried."

Jack quickly estimated the energy required to jump him back. Negligible. "I can send you whenever you're ready."

Kamal's voice interrupted, burst through Jack's helmet:

"If you are returning to the base, I would like to go as well. There is something I must do. Most important."

Panda cut in on their frequency. "I will come as well," she said and started down the ladder attached to hangar wall. "DeMitri will try something."

"It will burn too much energy to jump all of us there and back," Jack transmitted to her. That wasn't exactly the truth. It was true DeMitri might try something, but it was just as likely that Panda might execute DeMitri and save the air Jack was giving away.

"I'll take Kamal," Jack said, "but I need you to stay here and watch the equipment. Watch for Zero and Isabel."

Panda severed their com-link. She climbed back atop the roof and crossed her arms.

Jack wouldn't hesitate to kill DeMitri if he drew a gun or tried a virtual trick, but to plug him while he was defenseless—Jack couldn't do it. He felt lousy enough leaving DeMitri behind. He'd give him a chance, a small chance, even if it meant cutting into everyone else's odds of survival.

Kamal walked into the cargo hold. "I am ready," he said.

"Get that oxygen cylinder," Jack told them, "and this crate of survival gear. The entertainment deck. Rope, water, and a first-aid kit. What else do you think you'll need?"

"A weapon?" DeMitri asked and nodded at Jack's sidearm.

Jack unholstered it and aimed it at DeMitri. "I don't think so. There are two crates of Hautger SKs under the command center. Dig them out yourself."

"I will," DeMitri said.

Jack accessed Reno's private frequency. "You listening?"

"Yep."

"If I'm not back in five minutes, you and Panda come get me."

"I'll give you three, Jack-O."

Jack balanced the gateway in his left hand, tagged the

equipment, himself, DeMitri, and Kamal, then stepped to the top of the moon—

—backward into the dark command center. He turned on his helmet lights. There was dust and glittering gold pollen and contorted bodies and desiccated vines. The place felt haunted.

DeMitri removed his helmet, shook out his long black hair, then drew it back into a long braid.

"Next time I speak to Isabel," Jack said, "I'll tell her that I left you behind. She'll keep her air and power gateways open. Maybe find a way to retrieve you."

"If it is all the same to you," DeMitri said, "don't." His self-possessed smile vanished. "You, I almost trust because you're so full of good intentions. Isabel? I have failed her. I am better off dead in her eyes. She may take steps to see to that."

"I think I understand, but—"

Kamal tugged at Jack's arm. "I came because I have one last thing I must do."

"So you said. Do it and let's go."

"It is something I must tell you." Kamal snapped the seal of his helmet and tore it off. He breathed in the fresh air from Isabel's portal. "I shall be staying as well."

"What?" Jack cried. "Why?"

"This man requires help to survive. I am morally obligated to assist."

"Why help DeMitri and not us? *We* need you. Zero will be back. Isabel's air won't last forever." Jack whirled to DeMitri. "Did you have something to do with this?"

DeMitri shrugged. "I have not spoken a word." He bowed to Kamal. "But I am grateful for the assistance. A most noble gesture."

"Do not be afraid," Kamal said and touched Jack's arm. "Not all the robotic tunnelers have been accounted for. There may yet be a way to unearth the storage chamber. You must save your courage for yourself."

Kamal cupped his hands and a wooden bowl appeared within them.

Jack thought the bubble's circuitry had been shut down. Had Kamal left a back door?

Stars appeared and a horizon over which the moon rose, full and bright; the command center filled with the scents of green tea and pine incense.

"Do you know of the moon-in-the-bowl puzzle?" Kamal asked Jack.

"Listen to me," Jack said. "There's no time for this."

Kamal held up his left hand. "Time is all we have," he stated. "Listen to my words." The wooden bowl in his hand brimmed with water. "Look."

Jack saw mirrored stars and trembling lines of reflection. In his mind, consciousness and memory mixed: Isabel's handshake and the smoldering Earth and the rush of vented atmosphere, the numbing currents of sleep, and how could he persuade Kamal to come with him?

Whatever Zen metaphor Kamal held out for Jack, he couldn't concentrate on it.

"I give up," Jack said. "What is it?"

"The answer is the question itself." Kamal held the bowl closer for Jack to see.

Within, a circle of silver-white rippled. It was flat, full of craters and charcoal seas that would never hold water.

"The moon," Jack whispered in a trance.

"Is it?" Kamal asked.

Jack shook his head clear. "No. It's just a reflection."

"What is the difference?"

Jack looked up at the simulated moon in the simulated sky, then back to Kamal and his bowl. Real image. Virtual image. Reflected image. A difference? No. Yes. Depended on how you looked at it.

"What does your Zen question have to do with me?"

"This image cannot exist without the moon overhead," Kamal said, "or the bowl, the water within it, or the hand that holds it." Kamal's eyes grew large, and two moons appeared within them, mirrors of the wavering orbs in the water. "Yet, do I control the moon in the bowl? Or was it there all along?"

Jack looked again. Past the reflection of the moon, he saw his own face there, staring back. A Jack in the bowl. Jack riding a phantom moon.

"What does this have to do with you?" Kamal asked.

He poured the water from the bowl, then whispered, "Everything."

They locked gazes, the reflected moons still in the monk's eyes. "Where has the moon in the bowl gone now, Jack? Where have you gone?"

Kamal smoothed the skin of his vacuum suit and stood straighter. "Now," he said, "we have work to do. As do you." He offered Jack his hand.

Jack glanced at the water on the floor. The moon shone upon its surface.

"Kamal, don't. Come back with me."

Kamal pressed his wooden prayer beads into Jack's hand. "I believe you will need these more than I. Remember me. Remember the moon in the bowl."

Reno's voice crackled through Jack's helmet: "Three minutes. You got trouble?"

"Yes and no," Jack said. "But I'm on my way back."

Jack took the prayer beads. He grabbed the monk and hugged him. "Goodbye, old man. How could I forget you?"

A fleeting thought: tag Kamal, jump, and . . . No. Kamal had the right to make his own decisions.

"Take care of him," Jack said to DeMitri.

"Of course," DeMitri said.

Kamal then bowed to Jack.

Jack stepped backward, took his last giant step across the moon, leaving no footprints.

Jack appeared inside the *Dutchman*'s cargo bay; the place was crammed full of gas cylinders and cartons of cigarettes. *Itsy* sat with her wings folded against her fuselage. Overhead, the shuttle's bay doors eased shut—extinguished the stars.

He cycled through the airlock, then walked through the passenger section to the front of the shuttle.

Panda and Reno sat in the cockpit, exchanging heated words in Chinese. They stopped when they spotted Jack. "Where's Kamal?" Reno asked.

Jack took a deep breath, searched for a reasonable explanation, and failed. "He decided to stay," Jack told them, "with DeMitri."

Reno banged his fist on the console. "He can't. Go back there and get him."

Panda angled her helmet so the cockpit lights reflected off its faceplate and hid her features. "Was it his choice?"

"He said he had a moral obligation to help." A chunk of concrete solidified in the pit of Jack's stomach. "He showed me a Zen metaphor, too. I didn't get it. I . . ."

Jack felt like he was his own mirror image. There. But only a ghost. A shadow with nothing to cast it. Like he was still trapped in the reflection of Kamal's moon bowl.

Panda and Reno exchanged a look, then Reno whispered, "Are you OK?"

"Sure," Jack lied.

Was he sick? In shock? Or was he just already missing the old monk?

Reno set a hand on Jack's shoulder and guided him into the pilot's seat. "Forget about Kamal and his good deed for the day. Concentrate on us. The clock is ticking, Jack-O. Your Mad Hatter friend could be back anytime for another tea party. How do you plan on getting us off this rock?"

An amber light flickered green on the cockpit panel and caught Panda's attention. "Pressurization complete," she said. "No leaks." She took off her helmet and shook out her silky hair.

Jack removed his helmet, too. It was good to breathe without it. He scratched his scalp.

Maybe Kamal had been smart to stay behind with De-Mitri. If Jack's untested hypothesis didn't work, they could die.

Reno waved his hand in front of Jack's face. "Hello? You with us?"

"Yeah, I'm here," Jack said. "We're getting off the moon with this." He ripped the Velcroed gateway off his thigh and set it in his lap. "That third yellow vector determines the gateway's power source."

"We know the source of its power," Panda said, tucking strands of her indigo hair behind an ear. "The rotational motion of planets."

"And in case you forgot," Reno said, "the moon is barely turning after Isabel's visit. What do you want us to do? Run around it to generate power?"

"There's another way," Jack told him. "Another rotation close."

"Where?" Reno squinted at Jack. "The Earth's spinning got used up, too."

Panda looked out the front window at the stars. She turned back to Jack, her eyes wide. "The moon's orbit around the Earth?"

"We'll have to get closer, though," Jack said. "This gateway detects the alternate power source, but can't quite tap it . . . yet."

Panda stared at the horizon, then refocused on the cockpit, reached back, and strapped her harness. She set her hand upon Jack's arm. "I understand the risk. It is worth the attempt."

Jack strapped himself in.

"Risk?" Reno grabbed Jack's hand off the gateway.

"The moon–Earth center of mass"—Jack wretched his hand free—"is five thousand kilometers from the middle of the Earth."

"Sounds good to me."

"It would be perfect," Jack said, "but the radius of the Earth is only six thousand kilometers. We might have to get too close to get to tap that center of motion. Like inside the Earth." Jack locked eyes with Reno for a heartbeat, then asked: "So are you coming? Or do I leave you here with Kamal and DeMitri?"

Reno considered a moment, then grinned with his gold teeth. "Deal me in."

"Then hang on."

Jack tagged the *Dutchman* with a red arrow, stretched the blue destination vector overhead. He jumped the shuttle off the surface of the moon—into the night.

Gravity evaporated and Jack's stomach floated.

The *Dutchman*'s displays filled with black ink and stars that didn't twinkle, a hundred thousand million eyes that watched Jack. Were Zero and Isabel watching him, too?

Reno hovered weightless over Jack's shoulder. He reached past him and checked the instruments. "We're in orbit over the moon."

"That's as far as the energy from the spinning moon takes us," Jack said. "We fly the rest of the way."

Panda entered commands on the console. "I have calculated a half-orbit around the far side. We will use the moon's gravity as a slingshot to boost our velocity." She adjusted the fuel mix, then: "Initiating burn. Brace yourselves."

Reno grabbed the wall.

Engines shuttered and the cockpit roiled with thunder. The shuttle's nose tilted toward the horizon. They crossed the shadow line and plunged into darkness.

Acceleration settled Jack's stomach, then made it too heavy, made his face sag.

"End burn," Panda announced.

The weight lifted.

She secured her hair with a rubber band, but a few strands escaped and bobbed back and forth like snakes. "We can loop the Earth and return to the moon . . . if the center-of-mass jump does not work."

Reno took off his helmet, then got out a pack of cigarettes. He stopped, shook his head, and replaced the pack. "Always got an escape route figured out, don't you?" He glared at Panda. "Don't you trust Jack's plan?"

"Do not bait me," she answered.

"Shut up, Reno," Jack muttered.

He wished Kamal was here. Jack didn't like being between Panda and Reno. He hoped leaving the monk behind was the right thing to do. No. He couldn't think about what was behind him. He had to go forward. He had to concentrate. Find Safa before it was too late for her. He inhaled, tried to clear his thoughts. They were as scattered as the stars outside.

"Initiating orbit exit burn," Panda said.

More thunder. The shuttle arced away from the moon.

Jack hit the aft viewscreen and watched; the moon was a pearl droplet in the void.

He gazed into the mirrored gateway and interfaced. Red and blue lines snapped taut and awaited his commands.

Jack reached beneath the surface and found the yellow vector. It pointed at the moon, still locked onto its feeble rotation. There was play in it, however. It swiveled; Jack pointed it forward. There was something there, a preferential direction . . . a bit of maneuvering and it clicked into place.

The vector broke free—flipped back to the moon.

This had worked when Jack had tested it in a perfect virtual environment. He checked the navigation screen and aligned the arrow just off the Earth's dead center.

The yellow arrow trembled . . . then locked onto the spinning center of mass between the Earth and moon. The vector stilled. Yellow solidified to gold and the gateway sphere shimmered. It worked.

Jack tagged the shuttle with a neon red arrow.

Panda's neuralware interfaced with his, a feather brush of mink and silk against Jack's mind as she eavesdropped on the operation. "And the blue destination vector," she whispered. "Where?"

"We'll know where from the observatory's database," Jack said. "Eventually. Right now, though, I'm not so much concerned with 'where' as 'how.' If we're using the Earth–moon rotation to jump, that degrades the moon's orbit. Will it drift free? Collide with the Earth? Then what happens to Kamal?"

Jack tapped into the navigational database. "So I'm going to follow a hunch."

He called up the coordinates for Jupiter.

Jack sensed himself there: one finger on the moon, one upon the Earth. He took a long blue step to dance with Jupiter, Io, and all its sister moons.

Banshees howled through Jack's head—electromagnetic storms that fluxed and twisted up from the purple typhoons and red whirlpools and ivory-colored bands that filled the viewscreen.

He clutched his head, tried to compress the pain into submission. It didn't help.

"I thought these shuttles were shielded from magnetic fields," Reno said, wincing.

"Shielded for Earth's weaker fields," Panda replied. "Not Jupiter's." She closed her eyes and blind-typed instructions. "Compensating with counterinductive circuitry," she said through clenched teeth. "Pattern matching on-line. Now."

The pain eased to an itch, a dull throb, then vanished.

"Thanks." Reno clutched the back of Jack's chair and checked the instruments. "Fifteen hundred kilometers. Kind of close for a stable orbit."

"I want to make sure we're near enough to get a lock." Jack stretched the gateway's yellow vector toward Jupiter. It jittered around the center of the gas giant, unable to find purchase.

When he had originally freed the third vector from the center, something had snapped in the gateway. His stomach curdled. Had he broken it?

Jack stilled the arrow between his index finger and thumb. It trembled as if it was a hundred tiny buzzing braided arrows . . . as if there were more than one power source for it to lock onto?

Jack consulted the data on Jupiter's rotation rate and the orbital parameters of the Jovian moons.

Jupiter spun so fast there was an equatorial bulge in the atmosphere. The origin of that power had to be in the center. Jack checked. Yes. Dead in the middle of Jupiter, the yellow arrow pointed, then flickered away to targets off-center. He counted them—more than a dozen marks.

The moons?

The gateway acted as if there were more than one power source to tap . . . because there were. There were sixteen centers of mass: Jupiter and its moons rotating around one another. It was a miniature representation of the planetary system—just like the child's mobile his subconscious had showed him.

Too bad he couldn't use all that power. . . . Or could he?

Like a vibrating string, the yellow vector was smeared across space, all motion and distortion. Jack grabbed the arrow. It burned his fingertips, smelled of orange peels and sauteing butter. He squeezed until it ceased moving and saw there were hundreds of bronze arrows—all intertwined.

He had seen this before. When he had first experimented with the gateway, he found that the red origin vector had a similar structure. Jack had untangled those vectors, tagged several objects, and jumped more than one thing simultaneously.

Could the gateway also tap more than one power source?

He dragged the yellow vector to the center and it locked on. He grabbed another, pulled it to the center of mass of Io and Jupiter. It held fast, too.

Jack tagged all the centers of mass, a weave of golden threads that reached into the center of the gas giant.

"What kind of power does that give us?" Reno asked. He was watching so closely that Jack could see Reno's crooked nose distorted and reflected upside-down upon the gateway's mirrored surface.

Jack linked to the data they had downloaded from the observatory. A star map appeared on the port display—pinpoints of starlight upon black velvet—across which Jack swept the destination vector in an arc twenty-seven light-years long.

"But where to go?" Panda brushed her bangs away, revealed her eyelid tattoos seething with salmon-pink eddies and lavender whirlpools that mirrored the chaos of the Jovian atmosphere.

Jack searched the directories. "Astronomers have been cataloging stars with planets for decades. Either by direct observation or from the wobbles in the stars' rotations. Those will be our best bets."

He filtered through the data for K-, G-, and F-type stars, which were close to the temperature of Sol, then sorted them by proximity. There were hundreds of hits.

"This data is from the astronomer's point of view," Panda said.

"So what?" Reno asked.

"Objects drift," Panda told him. "We must calculate how far these stars have moved in the time it took their light to reach the moon. We must also calculate the most likely positions of their planets."

"Red and blue shifts are indexed in the data," Jack said. "Theoretical orbital parameters for their satellites as well. We can do it."

"Just jump close," Reno suggested, "then eyeball it the rest of the way."

"We couldn't lock on the Earth from the moon," Jack said. "That was only three hundred thousand kilometers away. If we get lucky, land within ten million kilometers of a power source, then we're dead. We run out of air before we can fly close enough to use the gateway."

Reno frowned, shoved himself away from Jack.

"Aren't you glad you came along for the ride?"

Panda tapped in a set of equations, then said to Jack, "I suggest we perform independent calculations. Compare results."

Reno dumped the observatory's data onto the wall viewscreen. A golden star and the shadowy disks of worlds unknown. "One big crapshoot," he muttered.

Jack set up equations of motion and a numerical integration routine, then slaved the algorithms to the astronomical database, let it crunch through the possibilities. "This may take some time," he said.

"Good." Panda stood, stretched, and drifted toward the ceiling of the cockpit. She scratched her lithe arms and torso. "I must get out of this. Two days in the same suit. I cannot stand it any longer."

"Sonic shower next to the galley," Reno said without looking at her.

She pushed herself off from the back of her chair and propelled herself aft.

Jack opened a diagnostic window and accessed the electron reactors.

HELLO, JACK, the computer said. IT IS A LOVELY DAY. HOW MAY I HELP YOU?

He wasn't in the mood for an extended conversation with the electron reactors, so he just had it check his numbers. If it was accurate, he might let it handle the relative positions of their targets. It would be faster. Jack wasn't certain, however, he was ready to trust the thing so soon after its nervous breakdown.

Reno watched the information piece together and flicker from star to star. "You better get aft, too," he told Jack. "Check on our supplies."

There was something in Reno's voice. Anger? Sadness? Was he implying that Panda might do something to their stores? There was nothing from his implant—a solid wall of stone.

"Do it yourself." Jack touched the stellar data, absorbed flare spectrums and galactic drift rates, which mingled with other thoughts: the dwindling rotation of the moon, Kamal, and Safa.

But Jack couldn't concentrate. Was he losing his mind or did he just need sleep?

Reno turned and pinned him with a stare from his brown eye. "Sometimes, Jack, you're real smart. Sometimes you're just dumb." He pointed aft. "Get back there."

Jack didn't understand what was so important in the cargo bay. Maybe Reno needed some time alone. That suited Jack.

He spun around, kicked off the pilot's chair, and flew out of the cockpit—crashed into the cargo bay airlock.

Jack peered through the windows of the double hatches. Everything looked intact. Nothing had tumbled or cracked open.

All he had taken—the cartons of cigarettes, computers, and assorted data from his moon base and the observatory—it wasn't a fair representation of the sum of human achievement. He had no works of art like Isabel had, nor any of Zero's bioindustrial wizardry.

Jack had been running so fast, for so long, that he had never taken a good look behind him to assess the carnage left in his wake.

There was a dead Earth and an annihilated alien civilization. Isabel and Zero, friends he had turned into enemies. He exhaled the guilt, let it ebb and flow.

Jack was tired. More than tired. Weariness made his bones ache. Even in the microgravity, he felt compressed by the weight of his memories.

"Jack?"

He turned. Panda had stepped from the shower tube.

Her skin was burnished gold and she had pinned her hair up, slicked it away from her heart-shaped face; her chameleon eyelids were a wash of jade greens; the notch of her throat, small breasts with dark nipples, the three tiny pinpricks in her bicep from Zero's stinging nettles, the ripple of her muscular abdomen—all fascinated Jack; her thighs were taut and liquid at the same time; her calves were balls of tension; her tiny feet pointed so it appeared as if she stood on her toes . . . but drifted a centimeter off the floor.

Jack thought her the most exotic, fluid woman he had ever known.

Panda made no attempt to cover herself, gravitated closer. "Will Safa survive?" she asked.

Jack swallowed. "I don't know," he replied. "Zero is insane. But they're family. How much that counts for . . . I just don't know."

"And ourselves?" She stopped her forward momentum with a light push against his chest. Her sharp fingernails sent chills across Jack's skin—even through his vacuum suit.

"No guarantees here, either."

A tingling blush swept over Jack's skin in waves. His heart beat faster. He slid his hand between Panda's shoulder blades, down, paused to linger and stroke the small of her back.

She nestled closer to him, kissed his neck, and touched his mind.

More than a touch . . . she surrounded him, a tide of sensations: the thick scent of licorice, a touch of midnight satin, and the black and glossy ink of fresh Chinese calligraphy; they pooled, then hesitated, receded.

Panda offered him full contact.

He had never had access to this level of intimacy before. It wasn't the deep contact he and Isabel had shared, nor the invasive memory of smoke he had inserted into Bruner's memory. Panda wanted everything Jack was, and in return she offered everything that she was, a full amalgamation of perceptions.

It was dangerous. Personalities could be lost in schizophrenic delusions. Full-contact partners were given the keys to every weakness. Every virtue and vice. Everything. It was as intimate as two people could get.

Jack should have turned her down . . . yet he trusted Panda more than he had ever trusted anyone. Safa was gone. Isabel was his enemy. Who else was there but Panda in the entire universe to share himself with? And if not now, when would there be another opportunity?

He jumped at the chance.

They rushed into one another, backward through memory: a dead Earth, balanced upon the horizon of the moon, cradled Jack's grief and cupped Panda's despair over losing her father, uncle and aunts, cousin Yang who taught her how to fight, and her niece Emily, who had been six when the Earth perished.

If only, they thought together.

If only Jack had been more clever, faster, or more savvy with Wheeler. If only Panda had gotten to Jack sooner, not let Reno and the NSO outsmart her.

. . . none of this would have happened.

Panda traced a spiral on Jack's chest; recollection curled and corkscrewed there: the peppery odor of intrigue when she first found Jack and discovered his research.

Jack took her face and kissed her deep, let trickle from him the icy-hot exhilaration of founding DNAegis Inc., beating the corporate system he had fought all his life— remembrance swirled and blurred with motion; their arms and legs slid over one another.

He tasted honeydew melon and marzipan and toffee and the licorice of Panda's irrepressible sweet tooth.

Panda dug into his belly, into the skin of his vacuum suit, and ripped up. Her thumbnail was sharper than steel, but it didn't cut him because she felt everything through his body as well, pleasure and pain and the trace of razor along his skin; Jack knew her fingernails were implants . . . along with engineered organs and reinforced skeleton. He remembered two years of pain as she grew accustomed to her enhanced body, and the willpower it took to shake an addiction to morphine. Panda sliced through his Telfon polymer suit. She drew a line across his stomach, across his chest, and up through his neck seal. Her hands found purchase in the folds of plastic—tore it apart.

The artificial layer peeled away, Jack's skin breathed for the first time in days; a moment of self-consciousness at how pale his skin was, which through Panda's eyes was as natural and wonderful as the whiteness of the cracked ice or milky quartz.

Together they drifted, rotated in space, bodies and minds growing more exquisitely tangled.

Ghosts of past loves rippled between them, the taste of sandalwood oil and whipped cream and the intoxicating liquor of their first crushes, a hundred tender touches, and shattered hearts; they joined their coupling—bodies and limbs and eyes full of longing.

Panda anticipated Isabel. She held her breath, then exhaled, relieved not to see her. A younger Reno was there, a brief liaison with Panda during a stakeout. Their sex had been pretense; Reno had double-crossed her and shot her in the back. Panda's hate for Reno was still fresh, coiled and ready to strike.

Their ghosts burned away—ashes scattered and disintegrated.

Jack twisted himself between her legs. Breathing and pulses synchronized. Thoughts and body perceptions merged, and they touched themselves with the other's hands and tongues. Lost memories surfaced, embarrassments, shame, elation, lust, all sizzled upon their skin.

Jack found Panda's center.

She had believed ferociously in her country's democracy and had struggled so hard to protect her people's freedom. That was the engine that propelled her forward. Her mother and millions of countrymen died for that freedom. And it had all been wiped away by Wheeler.

What was left now for her to struggle for and to protect?

Panda touched Jack's middle: there were jigsaws, hacked sections of code, and knots partially unraveled. Jack always knew that given enough pieces he could solve any puzzle. His life was a series of riddles to be deciphered.

But the Earth could never be put back together . . . no matter how many of the pieces he had.

Let go of the past, Panda whispered in his mind as she held his gaze with tear-filled eyes. *This must be a new start for both of us. For me, something to build and to protect. For you, new puzzles to solve.*

Jack held her tightly. *Yes.*

He constricted with his pleasure, her pleasure, left the world, and drifted into the white static of bliss.

Jack woke—his body shook. No, he was being shaken.

He floated, weightless—except for one foot that was tangled around a cord Velcroed to the ceiling.

The thing shaking him spun him around.

A brown and a blue eye stared at him. "I let you sleep a few hours," Reno said. "Thought you could use it." A sly grin erupted across his face.

Jack wriggled free and grabbed a handhold by the airlock. "You sent me back here. You and Panda—"

"We need you up front now," Reno said. "Jupiter's too close for comfort. We either get to a stable orbit or we jump."

Jack pulled himself into the airlock and sprayed on a new vacuum skin.

Had Reno maneuvered Jack to be with Panda? Maybe he thought if she was occupied she would forget her grudge against him? Reno was wrong. Panda held her grudges for decades.

Or maybe Reno really cared for her. Wanted her to be happy. No. Reno had double-crossed her before; he'd do it again.

Jack knew. Jack knew everything about Panda after their full contact. He still tasted her: sea salt and Egyptian licorice and golden ginseng. Her presence warmed his blood. He felt her patriotism and courage, her fears that there was nothing left, her hope that there was.

Jack adhered a control bracelet onto his still-tacky vacuum-suit skin; amber lights flickered as it dried, then winked green.

"OK," he told Reno, "let's see exactly where we are."

Jack pushed off the back wall and propelled himself up to the cockpit.

Across the viewscreens white bands of frozen ammonia crystals churned with sand-colored cyclones, whirls of deep blue, flashes of jagged lightning a thousand kilometers long across the upper atmosphere of Jupiter . . . a sea of trouble.

Ripples within Jack's head made him nauseated; sparks and cymbals and a deep throbbing filled his mind.

Panda sat in the copilot's seat. Her eyes danced with sparks when she saw him, then she turned back to the controls. "There is complex structure in the Van Allen radiation belts," she said. "The shuttle's reactive circuitry cannot compensate."

Jack shook his head. It didn't clear.

Panda's fingers drummed along the edge of the console. She never wasted motion unless she was scared. She glanced again at Jack. Red-and-orange-tattooed convection rolls roiled about the corners of her eyes: longing and anxiety and restraint.

Jack reached out for her hand.

Reno cleared his throat.

Jack caught the flicker of a transmission from Reno. An attraction for Panda? A subliminal leaking from the old spy's neuralware? Jack knew there was nothing between them as far as Panda was concerned . . . but what about Reno?

"Do we have the correct coordinates?" Jack asked.

Panda punched up her results. There were question mark curls upon her brow that faded as she compared her numbers to his. "They match."

Jack pulled himself into the pilot's chair. A window winked open next to his and the electron reactors spit out the same numbers as Jack and Panda had to seven additional decimal places. "These look good," he whispered. He didn't glance up. He didn't want Panda to see his black apprehension swirling in his eyes.

"This one." Jack pointed to 82 Eridani, twenty light-years away.

"Wait a second." Reno set a hand on Jack's shoulder. "How sure are you?"

A pale vapor clouded Reno's blue eye. Beneath that metaphor, Jack caught the taste of blood: Reno's fear magnified. He hadn't thought the old spy could be afraid. Maybe he was human after all.

"I mean," Reno murmured, "this is really a shot in the dark, isn't it?" He swallowed. "Even when the Earth ended, I knew where I was going and what I had to do. But that was nothing like this."

"We have a chance," Jack said. "A good chance."

Jack found himself believing his words. Zero and Isabel had done this. Jack could as well. He had to.

"What choice is there?" Jack whispered. "Go back to the moon? Wait for our air to run out? For Zero to return?"

"I know our choices," Reno said. His eye cleared to its normal solid blue. "I just don't like any of them."

"All green lights on the board," Panda said. "I am ready when you are."

He appreciated her confidence in him . . . and hoped it was justified.

Jack cradled the gateway in his lap. He connected to the centers of mass spinning within Jupiter, tagged the shuttle with lines of red.

Power surged through the mirror black sphere and caught Jack's awareness.

The gateway expanded, grew as large as the shuttle, encapsulated it, swelled as large as Jupiter; Jack's mind grew with it, reached out and pointed with the blue destination vector, farther, past the edge of the solar system, through darkness, stretched longer than he had ever before . . . pierced the void for minutes, hours, years, forever.

He touched a flame, only a flicker, so far away he wasn't even sure that's what it was, let alone where, just a light at the end of a tunnel.

A tenuous bridge formed between here and there. Jack released.

Jupiter vanished—

—and a new world appeared in the viewscreens: black and cracked, rust-colored clouds smeared across its atmosphere.

Jack exhaled. He had held his breath during that jump. How long? It felt as if it had taken no time . . . and all the time in the universe.

"We made it!" Reno slapped Jack on the shoulder. "Great work."

"It's too big," Panda said hunched over the display. "And too dense. Gravity is three times standard. The spectroscopic suite detects a nitrous oxide atmosphere. Temperature seven hundred twenty degrees Kelvin."

"OK," Reno said, only slightly deflated. "So it's not the ideal vacation spot." He tapped the launch controls for the satellites. "Let's check out the other rocks in this system."

Jack whispered to Panda, "Is it spinning?"

She called up the navigational subshell and replied, "Rotational period of sixteen hours."

He slumped into the pilot's chair. "Then at least we can jump." Jack glanced out the port display: a ball of flame churned against the black of space . . . not his sun.

Jack shifted the display aft. He spotted Sol, not the brightest star in the sky, but it was home. Used to be home. What was there for Jack to miss? There was no Academe, no apartment in Santa Sierra. No Earth. He hoped DeMitri and Kamal were safe. They might be the only humans to make it out of this alive.

Reno crossed his arms as incoming data flooded the screen. "Just dry rocks," he muttered, "and hydrogen and helium gassers. Looks like you have to step up to the table, Jack, toss the dice again."

This wasn't craps. The odds of success were astronomically lower. Jack suddenly wasn't sure of anything anymore. His hands clutched the gateway.

Red arrow, yellow, and Jack cast a blue line to a different point of light in the night sky—

—landed them above a world of solid nitrogen. An ephemeral atmosphere wavered ghostly in the starlight. Seven other sister planets. None of them a degree above freezing.

Jack sidestepped—

—a little closer to a swollen red sun than he wanted. About him spun twenty dozen planets and a thousand moons, all burned and blasted and bits of hell; a backward leap—

—and he watched a string of a hundred comets dance around a golden sun, a strand of gossamer pearls shimmering in the night; he vaulted straight up—

—landed the *Dutchman* in a system where planetary orbits tilted off the central plane; it looked like a Bohr atom as the navigation display traced their projected paths: worlds of icy carbon dioxide, solid nickel-iron, molten sulfur, and silicon dust; a hop and a skip—

—to see a stellar flare painting the void with helical arcs, jets of blue and white plasma that sprayed fireworks and radiation and EM flux; Jack jumped away—

—appeared between a double star for the blink of an

eye; it got hot; half the world was red fire, the other yellow flames. Jack catapulted the shuttle, using the suns' tremendous angular momentum, leapt from the Orion Arm of the Milky Way to the Sagittarius, a big step, and—

—found a world, its upper atmosphere populated with satellites blinking on and off, and below, tiny aircraft that left purple vapor trails, roads and cities fitting together in a geometric patchwork, and broadcasts that filled the airwaves with a crackling language.

Panda gazed into the spectroscopic analysis window. "The surface is frozen ethane and methane. There are liquid argon lakes."

"Another civilization," Reno said. "Maybe they can help us."

"I don't think so." Jack tagged the *Dutchman,* hopscotched—

—to the outermost planet of the system, leaving the inhabited world far behind.

"We're not going to use anyone else, Reno. We're not going to establish friendly contact, either. We're poison. Anyone that gets involved with us gets involved with Isabel and Zero . . . and maybe Wheeler. We did enough damage just stealing some of their planet's rotation."

Another jump—

—and the *Dutchman*'s windows filled with the glow of an amber sun. They skipped into orbit over a world with three rings: silver and gold and black. The orange sunlight made the place look warm.

"This one is a possibility," Panda said. "Liquid water and clouds and weather patterns. Ice at the poles. Infrared suggests vegetation."

"Good." Jack pinched the bridge of his nose, exhausted. "Reno, can you fly *Itsy* into the upper atmosphere? Get more detailed information?"

"No problem," Reno said.

Jack handed him his gateway. "In case there's trouble, use it to get back."

Reno took it. All traces of the fear in his gaze had vanished. Mischievousness sparkled in the blue eye; something Jack couldn't pin down gleamed in his brown.

Panda unbuckled her harness. "I shall go with you." Her hands moved so fast they were a blur—she grabbed the gateway from Reno.

"Hey!" Reno shouted.

"Leave your gateway with me," Jack told him. "I'll make it more efficient. We could use a backup."

"You will stay to make these alterations?" Panda wrinkled her brows; silver and pink tattooed patterns mixed. Confusion. Worry. She bit her lower lip, then said: "A fine plan." She kissed Jack, then went aft.

Reno lingered. "You did good, Jack. All we have to do now is get Safa back and—"

"We're not getting her back," Jack snapped. "How can we? Zero could be anywhere."

Reno started to smile, stopped. "You'll think of something, Jack-O. You're on a roll." He went aft and cycled through the airlock.

"Sure."

The cargo bay doors opened, *Itsy* drifted out, a burst from her jets and Reno and Panda descended into a lower orbit.

"Be careful," Jack whispered out the starboard window.

He went aft, found a crate of portable bubble components, and unpacked a dozen half-spheres, each the size of a cut grapefruit. Their edges undulated, attenuating signals and figuring out Jack's implant.

He stretched open an interface frame and downloaded Zero's frequencies. Blue fields of static materialized—sparkles of sapphire and silver.

"Zero? Answer me."

NEGATIVE CONTACT, the electron reactors flashed across his open window.

"Thanks," Jack muttered. "I know."

. . . HOWEVER, THERE IS A CALL WAITING.

Isabel? Had she already discovered his disappearance? Had DeMitri ratted on him?

"Show me."

Frequencies assembled above the window, bits of wriggling lines . . . that darkened from blue to lavender to indigo.

Jack sensed another presence; he spun. A second virtual Jack floated cross-legged next to him.

"Gersham."

"Hello, Jack." He held out both hands, palms up. His fingers distended, detached, and floated free. "We are ready to deal with you."

Jack shifted, uneasy at the alien's unusual choice of metaphor. "I'm listening."

"Not here, of course. We want to meet face-to-face." Gersham touched his duplicated Jack face, wiped it clean so there was only blank flesh. "So to speak."

Coordinates appeared in Jack's window. Over one hundred light-years distant.

"We shall be waiting," Gersham said. He disconnected and vanished.

WHAT NOW? the electron reactors asked.

Jack's thoughts weren't the only thing scattered in a hundred different directions. His efforts were scattered as well: find oxygen—hack gateway code—escape Isabel—locate a world—wonder when Wheeler was going to catch up to him—make deals with new aliens—and, not least of all, how the hell he was going to find Zero and Safa?

He had to consolidate his problems.

The insane gene witch would never tell him where he was, but maybe he might tell Isabel. And Isabel could be bought.

Jack knew her price. New technologies. Alien science that Isabel could sell to other aliens. Risky. For her and Jack. Wheeler might catch on to that scheme. But what other way to find Safa?

Would Isabel deal with him when she discovered Jack had escaped the moon? Yes. Contact with the alien, Gersham, was what she wanted. The only thing changed was the price. Instead of oxygen and electricity and her blackmailing him, Jack would ask her to pry Zero's location from his distorted mind. She could do it. She knew how to manipulate people.

REPEAT QUERY, the electron reactors wrote. WHAT NOW?

"Now," Jack said, picking up Reno's gateway, "I'm back in business."

SECTION THREE
BUSINESSMEN

Jack had lost his way.

He stood on a white square—one among a plane of alternating black and white tiles that spread to the horizon. One corner of this giant checkerboard curved up to the fluorescent orange sky, the other three corners arced downward out of view . . . a hell of a long way to slide. Like forever.

The gravity was about one gee. Jack checked his footing. His white square was solidified static: sparkles of silver, gray granite, and translucent alabaster.

"Where" wasn't the only question. "Why" was a close second.

He remembered donning his helmet, then using Reno's gateway to jump to Gersham's rendezvous coordinates. He had jumped blind. There had been no corresponding sun or planet on the star charts. As far as he knew, this should have been the hard vacuum of interstellar space.

Why had he taken such a risk? The act had been an impulse, a scattered thought among thousands in his head. It was as if some other Jack had done it. He must have been crazy to make the leap of faith.

He pushed, but sensed no virtual interface.

Jack tapped the gateway. No blue destination vector appeared and the yellow arrow was frozen. His stomach twisted. There was no rotational motion here to fuel a return jump.

He inhaled, held the breath, calmed his racing pulse, then exhaled. A new question—more important than "where" or "why" . . . *how* was he going to get back?

Readouts on his faceplate indicated there was enough pressure and oxygen to breathe. Jack kept his helmet seal intact, not trusting anything at this point. Himself included.

A copy of Jack appeared on an adjacent black square. Gersham. He wore a tuxedo. "Thank you for coming," he said.

"What is this place?" Jack said with a wave of his hand.

"It is your place," Gersham replied. He reached into his vest pocket, pulled out a cigarette, and offered it to Jack. "The game you so love. Checkers."

Checkers was the first game Jack had learned in preschool. The program had adapted to his skill level until the only outcome was stalemate. It was the first game he had hacked so he could win every time.

But how had Gersham known?

Assuming this wasn't the best simulation Jack had ever seen, that it was real, then Gersham had constructed a gameboard in the middle of space, given it an atmosphere and the proper gravity. Logistically improbable.

Unless this wasn't the "here" Jack thought it was. Maybe Gersham's rendezvous coordinates were a transfer point. He could have jumped Jack away as he jumped in.

Where and why no longer mattered. Jack was here now. What mattered was finding a way back.

Jack stared at the cigarette in the alien's outstretched hand. If Gersham wanted him dead, he could have set their meeting place inside some uncharted neutron star. There was no need to poison a cigarette or the atmosphere. Besides, Jack needed a smoke to straighten his thinking.

He snapped the seal on his helmet.

The air was fresh, a trace odor of freshly baked bread, then nothing.

Jack grabbed the cigarette and slid his thumb over the

ignition stripe. He puffed once on the minty amphetamine-laced smoke. It made his blood buzz.

"You called me just to play a game?"

"Yes. A game. A riddle." Gersham's fingers were exact copies of Jack's—only now they smoldered like ten little cigarettes, with curls of smoke extruding from the nails. The alien's metaphors were as much a puzzle as his words.

Jack Velcroed the gateway to his thigh pad. "How about this riddle: how I'm supposed to get back? There's no rotation."

The dark squares changed—or maybe Jack just hadn't noticed that each was uniquely black: slate flecked with gypsum stars; green-black obsidian; a film of sooty smoke that wavered and roiled; inky latex stretched taut; bubbling coffee; coals with edges that ruffled blue flames; shadows casting shadows.

. . . and in every one, a presence.

A pair of cat eyes glared from the shade of one, tail swishing behind them. Twenty-fingered velvet-gloved hands gripped the edge of another tile. Will-o'-the-wisp lights winked and clustered in the center of a third square. Luminous green pixels danced across another pane. Raven wings flashed across a moonless night.

Every tile held a different perspective, too. They sloped into the board, twisted sideways, oriented themselves upside-down, inverted so space bulged out, others hyperdimensional—too much volume to be crammed into a single square—then mirror smooth.

Displays? Portals to other worlds? Jack got dizzy staring at them.

He asked, ". . . Gersham?"

The entities in the tiles answered in unison, chirps and squeals and sign-language gestures, horns blasted, a thousand voices murmured and shouted and said: YES.

Jack stumbled backward, almost fell out of his square. He pushed again with his implant. Still there was no interface—and not a trace of metaphor. He turned to his double, whispered, "You're all . . . ?"

"Gersham," Gersham replied.

Jack had to pull himself together and figure out what

Gersham was. More importantly, he had to figure out what Gersham wanted.

"How is this a game of checkers?" Jack pointed to his white space. "We have to be on the same color to play."

Gersham nodded sympathetically. "We were hoping you and I could all be on the same side. These spaces are different not because of their color but because of their positions—which, as you know, is not necessarily a distinguishable quality."

That had to be a reference to his gateway. Jack scratched the stubble on his jaw, not quite getting the alien's point. But Gersham was trying to connect with him. His appearance, the game taken from Jack's mind . . . and Gersham's disturbing attempts at metaphor.

"You know a lot about what I should and should not know."

"Indeed we do," Gersham offered without further explanation.

Jack drew on his cigarette, made the end glow orange—smolder like the dead Earth.

Then again, Gersham *should* know all about humans. Jack had given them the location of his world. All Gersham had to do was jump the appropriate distance away and listen to old transmissions and newscasts. He could piece the whole story together.

"We once had a planet like Earth," Gersham said. "We were traders of information, too. We know the temptations." Gersham cast his gaze down. "I am sorry for the billions of your kind who perished. A waste. A terrible waste."

"If you *were* brokers of information," Jack asked, "what are you now?"

Gersham stroked his chin, copying the motion Jack had made a moment ago, then answered: "We are . . . retired."

"But you contacted me. To trade?"

The things in the squares twittered and howled and scraped at the stone walls of their tiles, demonstrating their disapproval.

Gersham laughed. "We like you, Jack, because we identify with your circumstances. We cannot, however, put ourselves personally at risk for another deal.''

The multitude within the black tiles quieted and cooed and soothed their undulating surfaces.

''What we wish to offer you''—Gersham leaned closer and whispered—''is sanctuary from Wheeler.''

''How do you know about—''

Gersham pushed up his tuxedo sleeves and held out his palms. His fingers continued to burn; the spirals and swirls of his fingerprints caught fire, too, coiling and unraveling into smoke, which then condensed into a silver-black gateway. ''Wheeler's touch is in your gateway software,'' Gersham said. ''He was never subtle. Nor are the others.''

Jack's blood chilled. ''There are more things like Wheeler out there?''

''Many others,'' Gersham said. ''Continue to do business and you will eventually find them. Or rather, they will find you. This is a far more dangerous game than checkers.''

Jack wasn't sure what Gersham's game was, but it wasn't checkers.

''There is an ecology to information trading.'' Gersham gathered his maple-colored hair back into a ponytail. ''You, Jack, and others like you, exist at the bottom of this food chain. Your civilizations struggle and shine, as numerous as the stars, but only for an instant.''

Inside the ebon square on Jack's left, a three-fingered hand reached out though the veil surface . . . as if Jack should clasp it and be comforted.

Jack stepped back.

''Fledging worlds,'' Gersham said, ''are devoured by predators like Wheeler before they reach levels of technology considered dangerous. This prevents them from evolving into future competition. It also prevents their knowledge from falling into a rival predator's hands.''

A universe full of Wheelers killing entire civilizations? The whole thing stank. Jack flicked his cigarette into a square of coffee-colored sludge. It sizzled. ''And where do you fit into this rosy picture?''

''We are the Hidden.'' Gersham's tuxedo checkered into

a grid of gray smoke and shadows. "We exist in the folds of space and time. Safe. And we offer you sanctuary. A place where you can live and prosper."

That was precisely what Jack wanted: a rock to crawl under. Too good to be true.

"Tempting," Jack said. "What's the catch?"

"You are quick to perceive the nuances of a contract. No wonder Wheeler took an interest in you." Gersham smiled with his copied Jack's face. "Once you come with us, there is no way back. We must prevent sensitive information from reaching the outside."

"So Wheeler and others like him won't find you. I understand."

"You accept?"

"I can't. Not yet. My people need me. They're lost and in trouble."

An understatement. Zero was insane. Safa kidnapped . . . who knew what tortures she was being subjected to. And Isabel? Did she deserve a warning of what the universe was like? Possibly.

Besides, Jack didn't trust this Gersham. There was more to his story. If he was so busy hiding, then why risk his neck to deal Jack in? What did he get in exchange?

"Your sentiment to save your colleagues is admirable," Gersham said. He shook his head. "You will let us know when you change your mind?"

"Sure."

Jack smelled a rat. Gersham was too nice. Too accommodating. Yet . . . it could be that's exactly what Gersham was. Maybe the only rat Jack smelled was himself.

The black squares on the checkerboard faded to clear tiles.

"We must be going, Jack. Even this level of contact poses a danger."

"How can I leave?" Jack touched the gateway. Still no detectable rotation to use.

"Leave? Did you?"

Jack's stomach flip-flopped.

The shuttle appeared around him, the padded walls,

strips of Velcro, and the winking portable bubbles scattered about—but he was also on the gameboard.

Gersham vanished . . . and Jack was the only piece on the infinite checkerboard—

—then Jack was on the shuttle. And only there.

A virtual trick?

He opened a link to the bubble's logs: empty.

More conclusively, Jack had used Reno's gateway to jump more than a hundred light-years distant. He was certain that had been real.

So how had he returned?

A headache sparked. It blossomed into black and purple and bloody fireworks within Jack's good eye. Waves of hot and cold pain, rusty nails and whirling band saws buzzed through his skull. He doubled over, unfortunately didn't lose consciousness . . . just held on, seven heartbeats, then the pain loosened and dissolved.

Was the enzyme doing more editing? Or was it an implant meltdown? Maybe a little aneurysm from the stress?

He sat up and rubbed his temples.

Gersham had asked Jack if he had ever really left. If it wasn't virtual, maybe Gersham was suggesting that Jack was in two places at the same time?

That wasn't as impossible as it sounded.

Jack had been in two places simultaneously before: when he first used the gateway. In his Amsterdam office, he had seen a copy of himself. And when he focused upon that other Jack, it had disappeared.

Jack interfaced with the science database. An antique gilt microscope appeared. He peered into the lens and focused, past swimming microbes and twisting strands of proteins and atomic panoramas, down into the murky waters of quantum seas. He had hunches to fish for.

Light has both wave and particle properties. Matter, too. A proton, a marble, a baseball, or a cat owned by a German physicist—all possess wave and particle properties. The more massive the object, however, the less like a wave it behaves.

Send a wave through a pair of slits, and on the opposite

side, the overlapping crests and troughs interfere with each other. The wavelets recombine. They reinforce and cancel with one another. If the wave was light, a pattern results of alternating bright and dark bands.

It works with matter as well.

In the late twentieth century, physicists shot laser pulses at an electron. The pulses acted like a double slit and made the electron interfere with itself. Just as light separated into a dark and light pattern, the electron fractured across space. It existed simultaneously in two locations.

This quantum splitting was next performed upon a beryllium ion—separated a breathtaking distance of eighty nanometers. Like a bowl of water disturbed, waves sloshed back and forth, and two crests of that wave rippled to the opposite sides.

Still the same one ion, but bilocated.

In the twenty-first century, there were experiments to divide uncharged atoms. Research groups competed for the largest separation distance, a contest measured in angstroms. The composite wavefunction of a single methane molecule was blurred for an instant. There were rumors of a Nobel prize for the effort.

Then the quakes came, rearranged the earth, and the laws of economics became more relevant than quantum physics. Funding for the experiments vanished.

But those shattered bits of evidence were enough for Jack.

Jack withdrew from the physics database. The hull of the *Dutchman* solidified around him.

A quantum bifurcation wasn't possible. For light, yes. Maybe an atom. But the larger the object, the less wave-like it behaved. And Jack was a very large object. Even the wavefunction of a single methane molecule wasn't split more than a few angstroms before it coalesced. It could never be separated any appreciable distance.

Unless it didn't have to be separated an appreciable distance . . . unless distance didn't matter.

If there were a gateway between split states, part could exist on either side. The bisecting gateway could balloon the distance between them from nanometers to meters to light-years.

Maybe.

There were plenty of unanswered questions. How did the gateway induce a bifurcation in such a massive composite wavefunction? How did it insert itself between those states? Jack wished Isabel were here; she'd be able to figure it out.

Or had she already?

Zero, too. With his open portals, stepping back and forth, onto and off, a moon with no rotation. That was a good trick.

Jack was getting ahead of himself. One theory at a time. How to prove this bifurcation hypothesis?

Separating a single quantum particle with the gateway would do.

He chewed his lower lip, thinking. What he needed was an ion trapped in a containment field or optical molasses.

Or an electron? Jack already had such a trapped particle, bound within the atomic canyons of his electron reactors.

He drew a square; it solidified into a reed frame inscribed with Egyptian hieroglyphs. He tapped in: I NEED TO BORROW SOMETHING.

BORROW?

AN ELECTRON. I AM GOING TO MOVE PART OF IT.

PART OF AN ELECTRON? it scrolled. . . . . INTERESTING. PROCEED.

Jack interfaced.

The shuttle's suregrip floor puckered into a hexagonal crystal lattice of the microprocessor's gallium arsenide substrate. Hills and jagged mountain ranges rose, snowcapped pinnacles with plateaus and cold clear lakes, waterfalls that cascaded into streams and rivulets and moss-rimmed pools. There were ice lakes, silent and blue; geysers that spouted steam and boiled over into rainbow-hued caldrons. Aqueducts carried burbling water, some of which flowed uphill, twisted, and surfed over and through other waterways in a liquid Escherian architecture.

Kamal's hardware design still worked, which meant the

computer was still sane. Too bad Zero's fractured mind couldn't be so easily fixed.

Jack found a lagoon the color of glacial ice, the color of Safa's eyes. It rippled as drips of water splashed from a nearby fountain. It was metaphor for a single electron bound within the reactor.

The skin of Reno's gateway mirrored the whirlpools of reflected water. Jack pulled out a red arrow. It wavered semisolid, pulsed, and sputtered. Maybe it couldn't operate on this quantum level.

One way to find out.

He stretched the line to the lagoon and touched the surface. The fluid dimpled, distorted away from the glowing neon arrowhead—then absorbed it.

The lagoon darkened to the color of burgundy.

At the base of the gateway, the vector was solid and sharp, a pencil-thin beam of laser light, but as Jack slid his hands up the length, it softened and diffused. Underwater there were refractions and wavering stripes of light.

Not a solid lock.

Then again, it couldn't be. There was variance in the electron's exact location because of quantum uncertainty principles.

Assuming the gateway could manipulate this electron, where to transport it?

There. Jack spied a canyon of eroded limestone and clay strata. It was one of the cells that had been cut off from the surrounding circuitry. Bone dry.

The distance was over a hundred nanometers. Tunneling wasn't likely at these voltages. He connected the blue destination vector to the bottom of the empty canyon. Held it there.

Mist filled and roiled, then condensed to iron-gray droplets. There were half-waves and semi-arcs of bisected ripples and quantum foam that licked the edges of the grotto—ghosts that flickered and filled the void then flitted away and back again. There . . . but not.

Jack made a split screen appear, spliced the image of the electron in the origin pool and the destination.

They matched: water sloshed back and forth. Two locations but the same electron.

Something was strange . . . not with the electron waves—Jack squinted.

The blue destination vector blurred. Was it the extreme magnification? No. It looked like the power source vector had, as if there were several lines braided together.

Could there be more than one possible destination? He teased a blue thread from the tangle and cast it into another empty ravine.

Water rushed in, rolled back and forth. One electron in *three* locations.

Jack pulled back the destination vectors, and the water vanished from the distant grottos. He marched back to the original pool and stared at his reflection upon the surface.

Technically, this electron had never left. Yet, it had. Like maybe Jack had been at Gersham's rendezvous . . . but still onboard the *Dutchman*?

Jack shut down the gateway. He understood now how it transported a quantum wavepacket, but how did that translate to his definitely nonquantum physical mass?

He severed his interface and stepped back into the shuttle.

Across an open window scrolled: THAT WAS INTERESTING. CAN YOU REPEAT?

Jack typed back: YOU WERE AWARE OF THE SPLITTING?

YES. IT MAKES POSSIBLE AVENUES OF ENGINEERING FORMERLY IMPOSSIBLE.

Jack caught motion in the corner of his good eye. Past the airlock windows he spied a shadow, then *Itsy,* wings folded against her fuselage. Hydraulics thumped through the hull of the *Dutchman* as the cargo bay doors closed.

Jack tapped in: ANOTHER TIME.

He drifted to the airlock and peered through the windows.

Itsy's canopy split open. Reno floated out and offered a hand to Panda. She trembled, tried to pull herself from the cockpit with her right hand while clutching the gateway in the other. She stopped and convulsed.

What had Reno done to her? Jack got his helmet sealed and cycled into the cargo bay.

"She won't let me touch her," Reno told Jack. "Something happened on the third orbit. She—"

Jack pushed off the wall, floated across the cargo bay, and grabbed *Itsy*.

Panda latched on to him, held him tight. "Get me out of this," she said. "I cannot breathe. Cannot think straight. Too many—" She convulsed and curled into a fetal position.

Jack took the gateway from her and let it drift away. He pulled her into the airlock, and held her as Reno hit the pressurization controls.

"If you did anything to her," Jack told Reno, "I swear I'll kill you."

"He did-didn't," Panda stammered and held on to Jack like she was drowning.

Reno watched the panel, didn't wait for green lights, overrode the controls—a hiss, and the inner doors opened.

"Get her strapped onto a couch," Reno said. "I'll get the medical kit."

Jack laid Panda down, then cracked the seal on her helmet. Her eyes were closed, squeezed shut so tight that tears leaked out the corners. The right side of her eyelid tattoos formed cerulean curls and silver streaks; the left displayed maroon smears and brown dots. Asynchronous.

"Hang on," Jack whispered and stroked her forehead.

Reno returned. He unfolded the kit and removed an osmotic patch, ripped open Panda's vacuum suit arm, and started an IV drip.

"It was beautiful," Panda said. "The planet has a glass forest, trees of silicon nitride, a desert of talc crystals. There were plains of grass—got the chlorophyll on the infrared—across a mountain range—were islands scattered upon the oceans—specific gravity at 1.023—I saw in the weather patterns . . . of your face."

Reno shook his head. "She's been talking like this for the last few minutes. The details are right. But jumbled. I'll download the high-res images out of *Itsy* so you can see for yourself."

"Forget the planet," Jack said. "What happened to her?"

"Little Beijing lost it. Claustrophobia if you ask—"

Beijing. That's where Panda had grown up, where her family had been, where she and Jack had watched ten thousand men, women, and children get nerve-gassed on the Fourth of July. All dead now. All gone. But the memory still burned fresh.

Such a casual insult . . . but it meant so much to Panda and now Jack as well. A side effect of their full contact.

"Shut up," Jack hissed. "If you ever call her 'Little Beijing' . . . ever mention Beijing again, I'll take you apart."

A smile flickered across Reno's crooked face, then disappeared. "You might even give me a run for my money with that enzyme-enhanced body of yours." He looked Jack over. "Then again, maybe not."

Jack took a step closer to Reno.

Panda's eyes fluttered open. She slowly sat up. "It . . . it has passed." She glared at Reno, then Jack. "Reno did nothing to me. And you"—she turned back to Reno—"should take care what you say. Others have been killed over less provocative statements."

Reno mulled this over, looked at his boots, then said, "OK. We're all a little hot under the collar. Maybe that crack about Beij . . . maybe that crack was out of line."

"I'm sorry, too," Jack muttered at Reno. He wasn't. He had, for an instant, wanted to snap Reno's neck. He let his anger drain. There were more important things than the past to consider.

Reno pushed off the wall. He linked to the medical unit and read off Panda's vital signs. "Pulse, heartbeat, blood and neurovascular pressures," he said, "are all on the high side of normal."

"What happened?" Jack asked her.

"This is not the first time," Panda whispered and looked away. "There were so many other problems, I thought it was unimportant."

She pulled her hair back and tied it into a knot. "Symptoms began as we loaded the *Dutchman*. My thoughts would not focus. My mind wandered. I thought it fatigue. Stress. Then came headaches. Waves of pain that vanished as quickly as they appeared.''

Jack nodded. ''I've had those headaches, too.''

''This is no simple headache,'' Reno said.

''No.'' She set her feet on the floor, rubbed them into the surestick surface. ''This was the first time my wandering thoughts affected my body.''

''How do you mean?'' Jack asked.

She held out her hands. He gladly took them: soft amber skin, callused knuckles, tiny fingers . . . that could break bones. Jack helped her stand. He would have held on longer, but Panda withdrew.

''I believe I can still do it,'' she said, ''although the sensation has nearly faded. Observe.'' Panda fanned her hands and opened a pair of windows. ''This happened in *Itsy* when I ran the infrared spectroscopy suite and the image enhancement protocols. I was doing it before I realized.''

Panda pulled two bristle brushes from the air, dabbed each, loading them with glossy black ink. She inhaled, then drew: an up stroke, a pause, two dots, a curved down stroke. They were the precise, fluid arcs of a master calligrapher.

She did it with each brush in both open windows. *Both* right and left hands. Perfect copies.

But Jack knew she was right-handed. Both sides of her brain shouldn't have access to the same motor skills.

Something else: her eyes. The right eye watched her right hand, the left tracked the other—independently monitoring the motions of her brushes.

He had seen that physical anomaly before . . .

She blinked, pinched the bridge of her nose, then her eyes were both centered and staring forward.

''The worst, however,'' she said and took Jack's arm, ''is my thinking.'' Her eyes were wide, and Jack could taste the coppery-blood-tinged fear churning within her. ''My thoughts fractured. Like there are two or three of me inside my head. All speaking at the same time. Me . . . but not me. My thoughts, but not.''

"Have you had these symptoms, Reno?" Jack asked.

"No," he said and crossed his arms.

"A few minutes ago I had a headache I thought would kill me," Jack said. "Then I made the decision to jump without thinking about it. Like some other Jack did it without my permission."

"You jumped?" Reno said. "With *my* gateway? Where?"

"I met with Gersham. It's a long story that I'll tell you about after we've figured out what's going on with our thinking."

"Your thinking," Reno corrected. "I may be the only sane one here."

"Maybe," Jack muttered. "My symptoms started after Kamal showed me his Zen metaphor." He turned to Panda. "Did Kamal do anything to you?"

"No."

"It has to be Wheeler's enzyme," Reno said. "Running out of control. You both took it. I didn't."

"Every conceivable test was done on the enzyme," Jack replied. "Thousands took it before I did. Weeks before I did. No one ever showed these symptoms."

But someone had. Fractured thoughts and splintered personality . . . and a million butterflies that weren't only fluttering inside Jack's stomach.

"There's something very wrong with all this," Jack whispered.

He fought his rising apprehension. He opened the neuro-physiology database and scanning software. "I've got to run a complete scan of our brains. Find out what's really going on in there. I'm not going to—"

ALL BUBBLE CIRCUITS ACTIVE, the computer printed upon his display. CONTROL OVERRIDDEN.

Jack tapped in: OVERRIDDEN BY WHO?

DUAL INCOMING SIGNALS INTERFACED WITH OPERATING SYSTEM.

Jack linked to the static from the isotope. Zero and Isabel's frequencies were coherent. Both of them? Working together?

"They can't interface with my system. Not like this."

Panda and Reno faded and left Jack alone in the *Dutchman*.

He pushed with his implant, only sensed Panda's licorice scent far away . . . couldn't get any other signal lock.

Jack yelled: "Zero? Isabel? You want to play games? I'm not in the mood." An eight ball bounced inside his head, thunder roiled, and the software demon *Chang E* stirred from its slumber.

"Show yourselves."

A curtain parted in the hull; beyond were black velvet and sequined stars. An old man stepped out wearing a black Italian-cut suit, a crisply knotted black tie, and a fedora. His long white hair was drawn back and braided. His eyes were full of greased gears and turning cogs.

"No games," the old man said. "Games imply there was a chance of another outcome. A chance you could win. There never was."

Jack's heart stopped. "Wheeler!"

12

Jack froze—no thoughts. Blank terror.

"Are you not pleased to see your old business partner?" Wheeler scrutinized Jack with his clockwork eyes. "Are you not delighted we may continue where we left off?"

Fear trickled down Jack's legs, bloody and acrid, spread and froze in a circle around him, held him fast to the suregrip deck. That wasn't Wheeler's doing . . . it was Jack's subconscious metaphor.

Static pricked the back of his neck.

"Jack?" It was Panda's voice. "Are we getting through?"

"Cut the power," Reno said. "He's isolated in a subshell."

Subshell? A spark of hope reignited Jack's thoughts. Was this *Dutchman* virtual? Was this Wheeler unreal? Some trick of Isabel's?

Wheeler smoothed his suit, and the black wool thickened into plastic skin. His fedora ballooned into a helmet. "Come, Jack. All your technology"—he made a grand sweep with his hand—"obscures our communication. Let us step outside, so we may discuss your future."

Jack slipped on his helmet and sealed it. Virtual or real, he wasn't taking any chance on breathing vacuum again.

Wheeler pointed his index finger: a red arrow materialized that pierced Jack and a blue that pointed through the curved hull. Then—

—they floated twenty meters off the port side of the *Dutchman.*

Jack was in free fall. His new world rotated under his boots. The three rings encircling the planet were specks of black rock, gold flecks, and silver dust. Lower were cirrus clouds and wrinkled mountain ranges and the reflected sparkles of lapis-blue waters.

Nothing supported him. No walls contained perspective. He resisted the urge to scream.

Jack pushed out with his implant. No interface. Only a faint tingle from the rippling magnetic field of the planet . . . and infinite space filled with silence.

Wheeler, helmet still in hand, stood next to Jack. "Now we may speak. How did your Mr. Lewis Carroll put it? ' "The time has come . . . to talk of many things: Of shoes—and ships—and sealing wax—Of cabbages—and kings—And why the sea is boiling hot—And whether pigs have wings." ' " He grinned. Too many teeth for a human head.

The *Dutchman*'s cargo bay doors parted. *Itsy*'s take-off jets puffed once, and she rose out of the bay.

"Your friends are persistent." Wheeler's hand made a horizontal cut—the *Dutchman* and *Itsy* disappeared. "Tell me, Jack, how have you been?"

"What did you do to them!" Jack lunged for Wheeler—gyrated out of control in the microgravity.

Wheeler halted Jack with a touch. "They are gone."

Jack held his anger and body in check. Any motion would only send him tumbling out of control again.

" 'Gone'? To another place?" Jack asked. "Or 'gone,' as in dead?"

"You confuse the issue," Wheeler replied and slipped his helmet on. " 'Gone' . . . as in unimportant. We will communicate with no more interruptions. Then we shall see how 'gone' they are."

Jack got it. This was Wheeler. Representative of a race of technological privateers who destroyed civilizations. Wheeler the pirate. Wheeler the blackmailer. If Jack didn't listen, Reno and Panda were dead. He slowly exhaled. "You've got my attention."

"Excellent." Wheeler drifted closer to Jack. "Let us get to business, as time—or, more accurately, *your* time—is limited. Your gateway. We have done to it . . . what is the appropriate term? Wiretapped?"

Fear quenched Jack's anger. " 'Tapped'?" he asked, "for what?"

"This." Wheeler jumped them—

—to a space infused with the red illumination from a sun that filled a third of the night. Overhead was a world with patchwork roads and cities, and purple vapor lace in the upper atmosphere, contrails from flocks of high-altitude jets.

It was the inhabited planet Jack had found on the trip out.

"You'll use them like you used the Earth," Jack whispered to himself. "You can't."

"We do not use other civilizations," Wheeler replied offhandedly. "We only deal. We have already made first contact. Their expertise in low-temperature physics is an unexpected bonus."

Jack knew what kind of double deals Wheeler made. Deception and genocide. "Leave them alone."

"No." Wheeler stepped them across the void—

—landed between a double star; the heavens were aflame with amber and yellow plasma. Wheeler leapt from the Sagittarius—

—to the Orion Arm of the Milky Way. Jack watched a supergiant spew arcs of blue fire. The stars shifted—

—and worlds of frozen carbon dioxide and silicon dust appeared, then—

—a procession of comets around a golden sun, hung like a string of pearls; a vault across space to—

—a crimson ball of flame, burning bright and clear, and a step to—

—a blue-white sun, a flash; it was green, then—

—Jack stared into the giant red spot of Jupiter as it cycloned before him.

Wheeler pointed to Io. "Magnificent, is it not?"

The sulfur-yellow moon was a hairbreadth away from Jupiter's atmosphere. Volcanic eruptions cracked its crust, and it glowed with a million fissures. Plumes of orange dust wafted from its surface into Jupiter, smearing into bands of ocher.

"Is this what you wanted me to see?" Jack muttered. "What stealing its rotation has done?"

"There is more." Wheeler sidestepped them onto a plain of silver dust and black basalt. Jack recognized Home-base crater on the moon, then they jumped—

—into hell.

Jack stood upon smoldering stone, his boots melting, vacuum suit skin instantly tacky. Heat smothered him. Warning lights upon his helmet's faceplate blinked red, then ultraviolet. The atmosphere wavered and wriggled. In the distance, a sea of lava boiled; bubbles broke the surface and spattered molten rock into the air.

He got dizzy. His vision blackened.

"Welcome home," Wheeler said. "Welcome to Earth."

Jack dreamed of the Academe on an Earth with oceans and a blue sky and no aliens. He lay upon the terra-cotta tiles of Coit Tower's courtyard, soaking up the sun and reviewing for an ecology midterm.

Ecology was a mandatory course at the Academe. Not because anyone worried about saving the rain forests or controlling greenhouse gases, but because ecological theories had applications in the business world. The same math that described how strains of bacillus bacterium competed for resources coincidentally predicted the rate of international bank takeovers.

This week's subject was coevolution.

Predators and their prey coevolved to counter each other's advantages. Predators developed faster bodies, longer teeth, more effective stock manipulation, and espionage capabilities. Prey selectively bred to be better camouflaged, enacted credit-draft protections, and formed unions.

Extinction of some species, however, was inevitable. Someone had to lose.

It didn't help that humankind had exploded its habitat,

crowded every forest and wetland with farms and cities . . . exploited every niche within the free and illegal markets.

But extinction wasn't necessarily bad. It was a natural part of ecology. In the twentieth and twenty-first centuries, ninety-nine percent of every species that had ever lived on the Earth had already become extinct.

. . . Before Wheeler had made that one hundred percent.

Reality tugged Jack halfway out of his dream. He pulled back, tried to ignore it, and cram for his test.

No dice.

He floated up, through layers of sleep, toward red light.

Ecology. Predators and prey. Jack had never imagined that humans would be the ones unable to adapt to new environmental circumstances. The ones to be crowded out of a habitat. The ones about to become extinct.

Jack woke up facefirst on the ground. His helmet and gloves were missing. There was grit in his mouth and the taste of burning aluminum. For a second, he thought he was back on the moon base and the thermite reactor had just blown.

He looked up. No such luck.

Under his fingertips was warm rock that stretched to a distant range of volcanoes. He heard a gentle tinkling as the stone cooled and cracked. On the edge of the horizon, thunderheads painted lead streaks across the sky.

''Where—?'' Jack asked. He sat up. His hand touched a metal tube, half-embedded in the granite matrix. It was a bicycle frame.

Despite the ambient heat, Jack's skin turned to gooseflesh.

This *was* Earth. Or what was left of it.

''Shall we continue?'' Wheeler inquired.

Jack turned.

A Mercedes-Benz limousine angled out of the stone; its hood, grill, and ornamentation protruding. Wheeler sat comfortably on the front right fender.

''Welcome back to the Netherlands,'' Wheeler said and opened his arms. He wore his black business suit again. His grand gesture revealed five-carat diamond cuff links.

"This is where your *Zouwtmarkt* office stood. I hope you are more comfortable. I reduced the temperature a bit." He patted the other side of the hood. "Come sit near me."

Jack got to his feet. "I'll stay where I am."

Part of Jack's bravado, however, evaporated as he remembered. "The gateway," he said. "You took me everyplace I jumped."

"Your gateway transmits to us your coordinates," Wheeler said. "Did you truly believe we would give you and your associates such a technology without the means to track you? To hunt you down if required?"

Jack touched the black-mirrored sphere Velcroed to his thigh. It had to be true. How else could Wheeler have known where Jack was? And where he had been?

Something didn't fit, though. If Wheeler had been able to track Jack, why bother with the lockout that originally stopped him from getting off the Earth? And why had Wheeler so conveniently given Jack the electron reactor and translation lexicon—the tools needed to circumvent that lockout?

What remained of Jack's newly found courage recoiled into the base of his spine.

He hadn't escaped the end of the world or Wheeler. It had been a carefully orchestrated hoax.

Jack's thoughts scattered and a migraine swelled between his eyes. He squeezed the bridge of his nose, focused all his attention, stilled his mind, banished whatever mental breakdown was starting.

"Come, come, Jack," Wheeler said and furrowed his bushy white eyebrows. "These are standard business practices. There is no need to pretend naïvete." He crossed his legs and leaned back. "Gersham's signal has been accessed. My congratulations on your return to business."

Wheeler knew about Gersham, too? Of course. He had given Gersham's frequency set to Jack. He would have seen Jack access them. He had to be guessing that it was Jack who made the call . . . unless Gersham's encryption wasn't as airtight as he claimed.

Wheeler uncrossed his legs and leaned forward. "I hope you are near a deal."

"You *want* me to make a deal? Without you?"

"Of course. Negotiate to your heart's content. Become partners." Wheeler clasped his manicured hands together in a mock handshake. "That is very good. You will gain Gersham's trust—all the better when we betray him."

A lump solidified in Jack's stomach. Gersham . . . it was all about him.

Gersham told Jack he had had a world like Earth. That it, too, had been destroyed. Gersham had felt sorry for Jack.

Jack took two steps closer to Wheeler. "You engineered my escape. You killed my world . . . just so Gersham and I would have something in common?" He stuck his face a centimeter away from Wheeler's and growled: "To grease the wheels of our first deal?"

Wheeler said nothing. Inside his eyes, however, the gears and cogs spun faster, a blur of steel and brass.

Jack withdrew. "Why not make up a story? Program one of your computers with my personality? Clone me? You have the science. Why destroy everything and everyone?"

Wheeler shrugged. "Gersham had to verify your tragic circumstances. As for attempting to copy your abilities, there was no need. You have always served us admirably, Jack. You contacted the races as we required. And you are always a delight to work with, my boy."

Jack shoved Wheeler—hard. The old man slid off the Mercedes, toppled over, and fell on his back.

Wheeler lay on the ground . . . and laughed. "I appreciate your taste for physical violence." He stood and brushed the wrinkles from his suit. "Kill me if that will make you feel better. It will change nothing."

Whatever Jack was talking to—regardless of the fact that it looked like an old man, it wasn't human—couldn't be killed. Jack had forgotten the technology Wheeler possessed was so advanced Jack could never understand it— or Wheeler—in a million years. In comparison, Jack was nothing.

No. If Jack was nothing, then why had Wheeler gone to all this trouble?

"I won't contact Gersham," Jack said. "I'm not doing anything for you. I'll ignore his signals."

Wheeler stood, removed a handkerchief, and wiped the tears of mirth from his eyes. "You will contact Gersham, Jack. You will discover his clandestine location and the means by which he remains hidden from us. You are the man for the job, our middleman with a flawless performance record."

Jack crossed his arms. "I refuse."

Wheeler wadded his kerchief and dropped it. "Reconsider. You have friends. Panda and Reno and a new world to live on . . . or do you?"

Jack's heart skipped a beat. "They mean nothing to me."

Even Jack heard how hollow that lie was.

"Then what of Ms. Mirabeau?" Wheeler asked. "And the gene witch? Their lives will be forfeit as well." He shook his head. "All the humans still alive depend upon you, Jack. Do not fail them now. Not after all you have put them through."

"You know where Zero is?"

"We track every gateway."

"Then tell me."

"Of course. Anything, Jack. Only do this one small thing for me. Then I shall show you."

Jack buried his face in his hands and considered. Gersham didn't deserve to be betrayed. He had only offered to help Jack, hadn't he? But Zero needed Jack's help. So did Safa. He couldn't leave them to Wheeler. Even Isabel deserved a better fate.

Either way, someone would die. Jack and his friends, or Gersham, possibly an entire race.

"Gersham was one of us." Wheeler said. He sighed and looked upon the faraway volcanoes. "But he is a renegade now, like you almost became, Jack. Apparently, he had a reluctance to clean up after he had concluded his deals."

"You mean he refused to participate in genocide? He let his customers live?"

Wheeler stepped up to Jack and took him by the shoulders. "You are practically one of us, too. Do not disappoint me when we are so close to ending this."

Jack tried to squirm from his grasp. But there was no way out.

"This once," Wheeler whispered and narrowed his eyes, ". . . usually I do not, but since you are so special to me, I shall make it easier on you. By adding an incentive."

"Oh?"

Between the gears in Wheeler's mechanical eyes tiny arms and legs appeared—and were ground to bits. "To help you decide," he said, "I shall destroy one of your friends every twenty-four hours until you find us Gersham and his elusive technologies."

"You don't have to—"

Wheeler brought his thumb to Jack's lip. "Shh, my boy. I am glad to provide you with the help." He smiled. "Now get to work."

Jack sat on the ground of his new world, warming his hands before a campfire. Panda on his right, Reno on the other side of the flames.

When Wheeler sent him back to the shuttle, Jack discovered Reno and Panda had never left—it was Jack who had been kidnapped.

Jack picked up a bowl of stew and cradled it between his hands. It smelled of garlic and Mongolian fire oil. "This safe?" he asked Reno.

Reno spooned some into his mouth. "Sure."

The campfire popped. The alien wood sputtered blue and green flames, perfumed the air with the scent of wintermint.

Reno had collected some of the local flora, turned over a rock and found an armored grub—chopped them all up, added spices, simmered, and called it dinner.

"Food and water checked out with toxin prep in the survival kit," Reno mumbled around the steaming gumbo. "Who cares?" he added, putting another spoonful into his mouth. "We'll all be dead soon." He filled a bowl and handed it to Panda.

She wrinkled her nose at the odor.

"Bon appetite," Reno added.

Jack ate. The stew tasted like walnuts and catfish with a dash of caraway seed. Not bad. He had seconds, licked the bowl clean, then washed it down with a liter of water from the nearby river. Cold and delicious.

Reno lit a cigarette, tossed the pack to Jack, who took one and passed it to Panda.

"Thank you," she said. Her eyelid tattoos blurred from topaz on one side into a chocolate smear on the other—swirls of light and dark and mixing thoughts.

Jack lit his cigarette in the campfire. He took a drag. It was one of Reno's Chinese smokes. A real cigarette after so many illusions, full of genuine carcinogenic tobacco.

Jack had forgotten how good they were. Or what a meal tasted like when you were starving. What a drink of water was to a man dying of thirst.

Or how alive he felt this close to death.

He watched the setting sun. This world had a nine-hour day; blink twice and you missed the sunset. The west ignited with orange and vermilion and green streamers; the planet's rings warmed to amber and silver red . . . then faded to shadows. Stars appeared and twinkled.

They had made camp in a grove of silicate pines. With the sunset, the trees gurgled as sap in their glassy skeletons drained into the roots. Thorny shrubs folded their leaves and sprouted black violets. Fireflies spiraled from the flowers; they flitted from twig to twig, danced in the air, and painted the evening with luminous impressionistic pigments.

Jack slipped his arm around Panda's slim shoulders; she nestled closer. Between the index and middle fingers of both hands, she held lit cigarettes. More evidence of her shattered thoughts.

Reno stared into the fire, his face cast in red and shadows. "I get that one of us dies in a day." He turned his gaze to Jack, his blue eye glassy and unnatural in the firelight. "And I know who Wheeler is and what he does. But how does Gersham fit into the picture?"

Panda puffed on the cigarette in her left hand. "I, too, wish to know." She exhaled, then drew on the cigarette in her right hand, not remembering—or caring—that she was smoking two at the same time.

Jack untangled his arm from her. "Gersham isn't like the other aliens Wheeler wanted me to find. He's worked with Wheeler. That by itself is reason enough not to trust him."

Panda turned to face him. "But *you* worked with Wheeler. And we trust you. We should not automatically discount Gersham. He has offered us sanctuary."

Jack shook his head. "It's nothing I can put my finger on . . . just a feeling."

"I've got a feeling, too," Reno said. "A feeling that it might be a good time for me to leave." He poked the fire with a stick. "My gateway works. I'll take my chances alone and find another world with—"

"Your gateway is bugged," Panda said. "To Wheeler distance does not matter. He will find you."

"Good point." Reno spit into the fire. "OK, so we do what Wheeler wants."

"No." Panda stood and brushed talc dust off her vacuum-suit skin. "We take Gersham's offer. Hide. Find a new place to build a life."

"I'm not dealing with Wheeler," Jack told Reno.

"Our lives are at stake," Reno hissed and pointed at him with his stick. "You'd better deal."

"If I find Gersham, there's nothing to stop Wheeler from demanding I find another alien race. I won't live at the expense of billions of lives."

Jack's thoughts took flight in a dozen directions: memories of how happy he and Zero and Isabel had been when they had first contacted Wheeler; the faces that stared out of Gersham's checkerboard; gateway code vibrating along the edge of his mind; a strong undercurrent of desire for Panda; Kamal's bowl holding the reflection of the moon.

Jack snapped out of the fugue.

"Gersham isn't an option, either," Jack said to Panda. "Maybe taking Gersham's deal is what Wheeler wants us to do. He might have a way to follow us to Gersham . . . then wipe us all out." Jack flicked his cigarette into the fire. "Besides, Gersham's not making this deal for humanitarian reasons. There has to be something in it for him. Something that's going to cost us.''

Panda crossed her arms. "We cannot sit and wait for our time to expire. We must act.''

Reno nodded. "Look, you're a little paranoid—I can respect that. But Panda's right. We've got to move on this. I say we go with Wheeler.''

"Gersham," Panda said. She closed her eyes, rubbed the center of her forehead like she had a skull-splitter of a migraine. "Retreat is our only realistic option.''

"You're the tiebreaker, Jack," Reno said.

"I need more facts." Jack tried to coalesce his thoughts—failed. "I'd settle for a hint." He stared at the alien fireflies, thinking. "A hint from anyone.''

Reno stood, circled the campfire, and sat next to Jack. "Oh no. I know what's rattling around in your head. What makes you think you can deal with either of them?''

" 'Them'?" Panda's chameleon eyelids darkened. "Not Zero and Isabel?''

Jack nodded.

Both cigarettes slipped from her fingers. "But they have taken advantage of us at every turn. Kidnapped Safa. Attempted to murder us. You cannot trust them.''

"I never said I would trust them," Jack replied. "But they may have another piece to this puzzle. And with Wheeler back, it's in their best interest to help us.''

"What's to stop them from back-stabbing you?" Reno asked. "Selling you and your information back to Wheeler to save their own skins?''

"Coming from a master of the double deal, Reno, I'll take that warning to heart. But I can handle plain old-fashioned human treachery.''

"And if Zero or Isabel cannot help?" Panda crouched next to Jack and set her hands upon his. "Will you then deal with Gersham?''

"—Or Wheeler?" Reno said.

Dealing with Wheeler or Gersham meant betraying one of them. Dangerous either way.

"Yes," Jack said.

"Then let's get those portable bubbles tuned up," Reno said. "Who's first?"

Jack watched the flames, red tendrils that danced then flickered into nothing.

"Isabel."

There was sound before the visuals came on-line: two violins and an accordion played a polka, wild and im-promptu—and slightly off-key.

Stars appeared overhead, then flickering flames in the distance. A campfire like Jack's.

He wandered toward the light, through a pine forest; powdery snow compacted under his boots. Closer, he saw there were people.

A dozen Gypsy women stamped and shimmied around a bonfire. Their skirts were patches of orange and midnight-blue and black silks; gold coins sewn into the fabric clinked and glimmered. Their eyes reflected the flames. Some glanced at Jack; others watched the men who wove a circle counterclockwise about them. The men held knives and engaged in a choreographed mock duel—they had looks for Jack, too.

Not Isabel's usual classy metaphor.

Jack watched, mesmerized by the motion and color and flashing steel. They reminded him of moths spiraling around—and drawn into—a flame.

"Isabel?" he whispered.

Beyond the circle of illumination cast by the fire, he spied the silhouette of a wagon with curtained windows and a porch. The shadows of the dancers crossed and crisscrossed its crimson-lacquered panels. A stepladder led up the back deck.

Jack walked over, climbed the ladder, and knocked on a pentacle carved into the door. It creaked open.

Two red candles filled the room with blood-tinged light. There was a table covered with antique lace, frayed at the edges. There was a stool for Jack. Isabel sat on the oppo-site side of the table.

She wore neither business suit nor imperial cape this time; her outfit was a knitted spiderweb shawl cast about her shoulders, under that, a peasant blouse and a simple gray skirt. Her hands were adorned with rings: gold claws that clutched cabochon rubies and silver snakes wound about her fingers. Her hair was hidden under a paisley scarf, drawn tight across her forehead and slanted so it covered her left eye.

"We need to talk," Jack said.

She lifted her teacup, examined the interior, then touched the soggy leaf fragments with one long finger. "Come closer, traveler," she whispered. "I will read your future."

Funny, she didn't ask how he had escaped the moon or what had happened to their deal.

Jack sat on the stool. "The future is what I came to discuss. Mine. And yours."

Isabel picked up a deck of cards. They had silver figure-eight serpents embossed upon their backs. "Shall we see what the tarot says?"

Jack wasn't sure what Isabel was up to, but he'd play along. "Sure."

With the dexterity of a stage magician, her thumb and forefinger flipped the top card and let it flutter onto the table: the Lovers. A man and a woman intertwined so they appeared like cobras mating. And as Jack watched they twisted tighter and tighter, flesh rippling into knotted cords and blood weeping from the coils.

The next card she turned over was Death. A skeleton rode a pale horse. The air over that card turn to blue-white fog. "Not necessarily a bad omen," she whispered. "It signifies change. Metamorphosis."

Isabel dealt a third: the Lovers. Again.

A fourth card: Death.

She skimmed off a dozen in rapid succession—all Lovers and Deaths scattered across the table.

"Your deck seems stacked," Jack muttered.

"It is not my deck," she told him and leaned closer. "It was the gift of a mystic, a hermit who dwells in the desert."

Jack pushed away from the table. "I don't care about

your cards, what they're telling you, or where you got them. Wheeler's back.''

Isabel's exposed eye widened in surprise; the iris filled the occipital cavity. One corner of her lips turned up into a grin, the other went slack like she was having a stroke. Tics twitched across her cheek.

"He knows where I am. You, too. I've got"—Jack tapped open a tiny window and consulted the time—"less than twenty-one hours to do a deal for him. If not, he kills one of us. We've got to make plans."

Isabel relaxed and replied, "I don't think the cards are working tonight." She swept them off the table. They took to the air, spun and twirled, rose and fell.

Maybe Isabel already knew about Wheeler. He had used her frequencies to communicate. Was her confusing communication style on purpose? To misinform a potentially eavesdropping Wheeler?

"Shall we try this?" She reached into the folds of her skirt and removed a crystal ball. It was cracked; imperfections filled it with reflective planes and tiny embedded emeralds.

Jack set his hand on the sphere. "I get the feeling it isn't going to work, either."

Her airborne cards fell to the floor.

She looked at her scattered tarot. "They might have worked," she said, then glanced at him with her one eye. "It might have worked with us, too, Jack." Her gaze fell to her crystal ball and she asked it, "Where did it go wrong? That in this universe two people can be so far apart, yet so close"—she looked back to him—"they can almost touch?" Isabel reached for his face, reached out with her mind.

Jack recoiled.

She sighed and dropped her crystal ball to the floor.

Isabel then pulled the scarf off her head. Strands of red hair fell about her face, a collection of gold and scarlet and pinks. Jumbles of color.

This confusion wasn't for Wheeler's sake. Isabel *was* confused.

"What happened to you?" Jack pulled his stool closer.

She drew back her hair. Tears streamed from her right eye. The left one was dry, and it stared directly at Jack. She shook her head.

"OK," he said. "We'll play it your way. Use your own metaphor to find out."

Jack drew a rectangle upon the table. Letters solidified upon a cardboard field, the words YES and NO in the corners, and numbers spread out in an arc across the top. A Ouija board.

He rotated it to face Isabel, then he gave her an ivory triangle pointer.

Both of her hands took it, but each tried to slide the device in a different direction . . . as if parts of herself fought for control.

She had the same symptoms as Panda.

"You've had disorientation?" he asked. "A splintering of your thinking?"

Both her hands moved the pointer—rapidly back and forth across the board—struggling to push and pull it in different directions. She let go when it pointed to the YES upon the board. She sighed and slumped, exhausted by the effort.

"It is Wheeler's enzyme? Did he plan this degeneration?"

She shoved the pointer around the board to NO.

"Then what is it? How did this happen?"

She tightened her grip on the pointer—pushed it across the board, then over the edge and off the table.

Jack picked it up. "Try again," he whispered. "Please. What is happening to us?"

Isabel blinked away tears. She inched the ivory triangle along, biting her lower lip in concentration—she jerked it, then shoved it into the corner . . . where she let it rest.

Upon the number zero.

13

"**Z**ero al Qaseem!" Jack shouted at the static. "Answer me. I know you're listening."

Pixels of twinkling sapphire and the hiss of steam filled Jack's virtual world.

"I know you heard Wheeler. I'll stay on-line as long as it takes—until someone dies. Is that what you want, Zero?"

Jack held the connection. He had to be more stubborn than an insane man.

Isabel believed the gene witch was responsible for their condition, and Zero had the symptoms of mental fracturing first. He had to know what was happening, and maybe he knew how to fix it.

If Jack went crazy, how could he negotiate with Wheeler? Or deal with Gersham?

He stilled his drifting thoughts. He couldn't lose control now.

His eyes imagined patterns in the blue-and-black-and-white static: a fog-shrouded skyline, a galleon tossed upon a sea of foam, a snake with silver scales flashing, and a desert of frosted sand dunes.

He squeezed his eyes shut—looked again.

The desert dunes remained. The static had vanished. A connection.

Jack knelt and touched the sand. It was silky soft. He

scooped up a handful of butterfly scales—flecks of opalescent green and silver-blue. Buried within were tiny wingless body segments, bits of feathery antennae, spiral proboscises, and needle legs.

A hot wind gusted. Wings of butterflies flew, butterflies that once had wings to fly with; rainbow sand whirled into dust devils.

Through this shimmering veil a man marched backward toward Jack. Rags covered his body and limbs and face: the uniform of a leper. Without looking, he settled next to Jack.

Jack already didn't like this metaphor. Nothing was clear.

"A moment of lucidity," Zero whispered. "We may speak."

"We?" Several zeros mathematically summed to zero— but this Zero didn't add up. Jack reached out to turn his friend around, make him face him . . . something moved under Zero's tattered robe, undulations that weren't human.

"You did something to Isabel's mind," Jack said. "She can't think straight. It's happening to me, too. The splitting thoughts. The disorientation."

"I do not deny your accusations." Zero drew an infinity symbol in the sand. A breeze blurred the figure. "Is this truly what you wished to discuss? Not our lovely Safa?"

Jack bit his tongue. He wanted to know about Safa. But letting Zero know that would give the gene witch leverage.

"I've been so busy," Jack said, "I hadn't given her a thought."

Zero turned. Dark eyes smoldered in the shadows of his cowl. "She needs you, Jack. I need you. We all need your help." He grasped Jack's wrist. The skin on Zero's hand flaked off: speckles of gold and lilac and sea-green butterfly scales. "You must rescue us. Was Safa not reason enough? Must I take another hostage to prompt you into action?"

Jack removed Zero's hand. There was no muscle, just paper-thin skin wrapped around bone.

"You want me to help?" Jack narrowed his eyes. "Then why all the riddles? Tell me where you are."

"There are rules as to how much each of us may know." Zero started to say more, coiled his dry fingers into a fist, then: "I cannot."

Jack checked his frustration. There was a logic operating in Zero's mind, twisted, but if he was going to get anywhere with the gene witch, he had to figure it out.

A ripple under Zero's robe and a second right arm reached out and retraced the infinity symbol in the sand.

Jack ignored the additional appendage; instead, he concentrated on the figure. A clue? Infinity. Or if turned ninety degrees, the number eight.

"Your series-eight enzyme," Jack whispered. "You infected me?"

"All of you."

Zero removed his hood. His face was so gaunt that his lips parted in a permanent smile. His beard was a patchwork of scabs and bristles and oiled curls.

Jack stepped back. How could Zero have infected him? There had never been any physical contact. No pills. No injections. He had been sealed in his vacuum suit.

. . . But that suit had been breached.

Thorns had punctured the skin, and Jack had inhaled the pollen of Zero's dying orchids. Panda's arm had been impaled by three long needles, likely injected with Zero's viral carriers. That's why she had more advanced symptoms.

"You didn't attack my moon base to kidnap Safa." Jack kicked Zero's figure eight—scattered the sand. "It was so you could use us as guinea pigs."

"No," Zero replied. "My work only extends Wheeler's earlier alterations."

He meant Wheeler's enzyme, the one that edited and perfected human DNA. That possibly explained why Reno wasn't showing symptoms. His genome had never been altered.

"And Isabel?" Jack asked and settled next to Zero. "Why infect her? I thought you two were still in business?"

"You misunderstand." Zero covered his eyes with his palms, then: "All three of us are still partners." He removed his hands, blinked, and revealed eyes with a ring of eight pupils. "Our business, however, has changed."

Jack reached out with his mind, the lightest touch he could manage. Pieces of Zero were there: confetti bits of the Koran, tattered threads of DNA, and the sweet scent of carbon tetrachloride. But those sensations disintegrated the instant Jack accessed them.

"Isabel was a mistake," Zero said. "We thought she could help us after you turned down our offer. She had the intellect. It was my error to believe that intellect alone was sufficient to solve our drama. She lacks the heart."

"This isn't theater," Jack hissed. "What do you mean by 'drama'? Succeed in what?"

"Wheeler's enzyme sharpens each of us. It makes us more of that which we were meant to be." A third right arm moved from under Zero's robe. "For myself, it has accelerated my intelligence to frightening velocity. My role in this is the Scientist." He smashed his fist into the sand. "But also, I am afraid, the Lunatic. We pay a price to know the secrets of human potential."

Jack leaned closer to Zero. "Stop playing with the sand. Stop playing games. Forget about theatrical roles. Tell me about your enzyme."

"I am, my friend, but you are not listening. Roles are the thing. All our world is a stage, with an audience of alien eyes. Our sets and costumes provided by bubble technology . . . and as the last humans left in the universe we become, by default, archetypes."

Zero was casting them into the parts of a play; was that the key to unraveling his cracked logic?

"Then what's Safa's role?"

"Good. At last we get to Safa." Zero rocked back and forth. "You resisted us so well—as we suspected you would. We had to take Safa. It was clear that you needed someone to rescue. She is the Captive."

"And what role am I supposed to play?"

Zero ceased rocking, shook his head as if this information were top secret, but then whispered, "You are the Hero."

Jack laughed. "You've got the wrong guy."

One of Zero's right hands took Jack by the shoulder. "You were the only one to fight the shadows and lies. You are Prometheus, stealing the gods' fire."

"I only did what I had to to save my skin."

Two more right hands clutched Jack—then three left arms stretched out of Zero's robe and latched onto him.

Jack struggled in the embrace.

This was just metaphor . . . Zero's way of telling him to pay attention. Jack couldn't shake the feeling, though, that Zero was going to stick a long butterfly tongue down his throat—and drink him dry.

"You will save humankind, Jack. From Wheeler. From itself. And from me." Zero relaxed his grip. "I need a hero to save me . . . us."

"So you know about Wheeler?"

Zero retracted his six arms and pulled up his hood. "He accessed my frequency set. It bodes ill for us all. I suggest you hurry and rescue us, so we may together defeat him."

Jack wanted to pound sense into Zero's head. He exhaled. "OK. I'll do that. Any advice how?"

"We may not help you." Zero sighed. "Look here"—he pointed to his temple—"if you require help. If that fails, pray to Allah."

Jack never had any use for God. But he would have bowed toward Mecca and converted if he thought it would help.

He needed a clue from Zero. A hint. A sign.

Maybe he could get one . . . and maybe Allah could help.

Jack knelt and touched his head to the ground. He spoke the prayer Safa had taught him: " 'He has forced the night and the day, and the sun and the moon, into your service: the stars also serve you by His leave.' "

Zero knelt next to him and prostrated himself.

Jack reached out with his mind—sensed for anything that Zero might let slip.

The wind stopped. The sand stilled. Overhead, the sky cleared and a double band of stars twinkled.

Zero completed the prayer: " 'Surely in this there are signs for men of understanding.' "

Hot winds howled, and Zero's skin peeled away. "Help me, Jack. I am disintegrating—splitting into too many fragments to understand. Hurry, my friend. And be careful. For, I fear, when we next meet . . . I must kill you."

Jack stuck a bubble node on the wall of the *Dutchman*'s padded cargo hold. The half-sphere's edges rippled as it caught his signals. A test sequence cycled: Jack tasted honeydew melon, felt a blush of adrenaline and the rumble of subsonics.

Panda aligned the central node in the center of the bay.

Reno smoked a cigarette, watched them, and shook his head. "You want my professional opinion?" he asked. "The intelligence community had a term for people like Zero."

Jack stood and straightened out the kinks in his back. "What's that?"

"He's nuts." Reno flicked his cigarette at Jack—missed. "Where did that call to the gene witch get us?"

"Bubble reconfigured and initialized," Panda said. She stretched apart the corners of a trapezoid with crisp cobalt edges, then another link, then a third, tapping in code with her right and left hands, flitting across the three windows without looking. "Cerebral scanning routines on-line."

"It got us a clue to what's wrong with us," Jack said.

"Wrong with you two," Reno corrected. "I'm not losing my mind."

"He said to look in my head if I needed help. That's what I plan on doing. And you, Reno, despite your abnormalities, are our only neurophysiological baseline."

"Sit," Panda told Reno. Her coppery cat eyes pinned him. "And be still."

Reno sat cross-legged on the deck. "What about Wheeler? I don't want to be the one he picks to motivate you after your time's up."

"I'll contact Gersham after this," Jack told him. "To

make a deal or double-cross him." Neither option felt right. Jack wanted a third choice. He didn't like being stuck between the two aliens.

"Either way," Jack said, "I want to know what's happening to Panda and me. Maybe figure out a way to reverse it."

"Unlikely," Reno muttered and blew a smoke ring.

"Suppress your internal resonance field," Panda said. She waved the cigarette smoke away from her face. "The scan cannot lock on."

Reno smoothed back his gray hair. "You got it."

Over one of Panda's windows, luminescent tracers scrolled along neural pathways, then cross sections from the magnetic imagers assembled into the curls and convolutions of Reno's three-dimensionally rendered brain—with false-colored blood reds and tangerine and amber ... and where Reno's implant had burned the tissue, dead black.

Panda tapped the internal view. Cerebral lobes pulled apart and revealed a crisscross of platinum filaments that cast heavy shadows, his shielded top-secret bioware.

Reno gently reached into the gray matter, touched his temporal lobe—did a double take. The odor of tea roses filled the shuttle. "I'd forgotten all about her," he whispered. Reno was indulging in recollection. The scan had caught a lost memory and turned it inside-out.

Panda called up a matrix of neurotransmitter concentrations. Her left eye read it as her right observed the structure of Reno's brain. "Chemistry is normal," she said. "Despite the thirty-seven microregions of necrotic tissue, the occipital lobe damage, and an overly engineered implant"—she looked up at Reno and brushed the bangs from her face—"this brain passes for normal."

"Thanks for the diagnosis, Doc."

Panda turned to Jack, and her separate staring eyes aligned. "You are next." Jack caught a whisper from her mind, the jagged edges of panic, the memory of his hand smoothing down her back, and her solid iron concentration ... the only thing holding her thoughts together. "Sit very still," she said.

Tendrils wormed deep into Jack's thoughts. He let them, suppressing years of resistance training.

His brain materialized over Panda's window.

Colors fluxed too fast: crimson waves flashed across the serpentine cranial surfaces, blue sparks flickered, sudden flares of orange erupted along every fissure. Like Jack's head was on fire.

Panda consulted the data spilling onto her displays. "Minor damage in the occipital lobe." She shook her head. "Neurotransmitter levels elevated."

Jack stepped up for a closer look. He tapped the internal topology and split his brain image into sections. His implant was a silver spiderweb, with dewdrop nodes that snared and rerouted signals to sensory and emotional centers.

The hardware looked fine; it was the shape of his brain that was wrong. Normally, a seam divided the hemispheres—that was there, but there was another crease perpendicular to the first. Jack traced this new fold of tissue with his fingertip, absorbed the data: imbalanced ion concentrations, a heightened cell division rate, and an amorphous structure that didn't match anything in the neurological database.

He also caught the odor of rotting paperbacks he had read in his Santa Sierra apartment, sea salt, tasted the greasy fish sticks he always ordered from street vendors. Memories of a world that no longer existed.

"It has fourfold symmetry," Panda said.

She congealed the head and highlighted the indentations. The abnormalities traced lateral and horizontal planes.

Jack had the urge to crack open his skull—his real one—and claw those fissures out with his fingernails. The last time he'd felt like this was when he had brain cancer. He had a hunch this mutation might be just as lethal.

"A symmetry error in the bubble nodes?" Jack asked hopefully.

Panda's left eye darted to another window and she ran a check of the hardware. "No."

Reno crossed his arms. He exhaled smoke into the maze of Jack's brain. "I think I've seen this before."

"Where?" Jack asked.

"It may be nothing," Reno said without taking his gaze off the scan, "but let's do Panda, and I'll know for sure." He turned to her. "Time to see what makes you tick, sweetheart."

Panda's left eye continued to watch Jack's incoming data, her right looked up at Reno. "I am no one's 'sweetheart.'" The tattoos on her right side sharpened with crimson spines and darkened with shadow. "That time with you was a mistake."

Reno's face cracked into a gold-capped smile. "Look—let's forget about that. Can we call a truce?" He held out his hand.

Panda reached. Stopped. "That, too, would be a mistake."

She sat upon a crate and neatly crossed her legs. "However, since we need the information, you may proceed."

Reno tapped in commands.

A moment, then Panda's mind revealed itself. Her implant was a storm of microscopic glitter that spiraled through her cerebral cortex, flexing shape and connecting to the cranial nerves.

"An adaptive network," Reno whispered to Jack. "I can't believe Beijing kept this a secret." He adjusted the scan resolution. "Each of these specks has memory and processor components. They reconfigure to suit specific tasks. Nice."

Jack linked to the neurochemistry analysis. It was a grid of solid purple—off the scale. "Your dopamine levels can't be this high."

Panda joined them. Her eyes flicked across the open windows. "Here." She touched the edge of her brain. "The same folds present in your tissue."

"Not the same." Reno highlighted the wrinkles. "They penetrate deeper." He pulled her brain apart, the occipital lobe from the thalamus from the temporal lobe, reshuffled the sections, broke them along the new seams.

"He's right," Jack said and magnified. "These segments have an altered structure. Each has a faint brain stem woven into the main spinal cord. And this one has what looks like a separate, tiny cerebellum.''

The cerebellum contained the regions associated with speech and hearing and visual recognition, as well as movement skills, behaviors, and emotions. They occupied well-defined regions in the brain . . . or were supposed to.

Jack could check the localization.

He generated a pulse signal of iridescent abalone shells, the pitch and yaw of a roller coster, and mixed in a dash of synthetic laughter.

The colors of Panda's mind rippled in response: the vibrant pink of her visual cortex split into two distinct areas; the skilled motion centers bifurcated into a pair of purple ovals; and her emotional centers—four smears of green that wavered.

Jack was looking at his future. Segmentation of thinking, emotion, and physical skills: a split mind. Panda had either gotten a larger dose of Zero's enzyme or it metabolized faster in her system. Whatever the reason, her mind was falling apart.

Panda wrapped her hand around Jack's. They exchanged fears. Drew strength from one another. Her scent of licorice was tinged with the odor of rust.

Jack withdrew and touched the new seams in her brain. ''This cellular structure is still unidentifiable.'' His finger passed over the new tissue. ''Wait . . . the anatomy database now matches parts of this as the corpus callosum.''

''The corpus callosum only connects right and left hemispheres,'' Panda said.

Reno opened the biology database. ''Not anymore.'' He replaced the brain scan with a sphere. It bisected along its center, then the two halves split into four . . . became eight, then sixteen.

''Recognize it?'' Reno asked. ''It's a fertilized egg . . . dividing like your brains.''

Jack nudged this new image to superimpose Panda's brain. The shapes of the splintering sections matched.

''Zero told me,'' Jack said, ''that the greatest human weakness was a bottleneck in thinking. Linear thought. This may be his solution to that problem.''

Panda's tattoos faded. Real black circles of fatigue ringed her eyes. "A solution that is changing us into what?"

Into a fractured existence? Like Zero? Insane? Jack chewed on his lower lip. "Any ideas on how to reverse it?"

"We cannot," Panda said. She pursed her lips into a thin line. "Our brains have been changed on both anatomical and cellular levels. We have neither the tools nor the skill to reverse the process."

"I'd settle for slowing it down," Jack said.

He caught motion in the corner of his left eye; only his left eye moved to see what it was. His perspective split: an image of Panda and a virtual window filtered into his mind—not overlapped, rather clear and distinct . . . alien.

Jack closed both eyes, forced them to stare straight ahead into blackness.

The physical symptoms were beginning with him.

It was happening too fast. Soon he wouldn't be able to think at all.

Jack opened his eyes and turned to the motion.

The electron reactors had opened a window of thick polished crystal. The computer wrote: I HAVE SEEN THIS BEFORE. The words reflected from the bottom surface—blurred double.

WHERE? Jack entered.

IN ME. THE SCATTERED THOUGHTS. THE BIFURCATION OF PROCESSING. CONFLICT = TOO MANY VOICES.

When Jack looked up "mental disorders" in the bubble's database, he found a hundred thousand references—most for virtual reality-induced psychosis. The best match to their symptoms, however, was the vague catalog of symptoms related to schizophrenia.

Schizophrenia meant, literally, split mind.

For the afflicted, there was a lack of logical connections and the manifestation of delusions: disembodied voices, alien thoughts, and the inability to order and control one's mental processes. In one case, there was independent eye motion—chameleonic oculomotor activity, the experts had called it.

Not until the twentieth century was schizophrenia identified. There were partially successful treatments with antipsychotic drugs; electroshock therapy came into and out of vogue; then in the mid-twenty-first century, psychiatric researchers attempted to understand schizophrenia by modeling their patients' brains with computer simulations.

They failed.

Not because of the programming; parallel-processing supercomputers modeled the disordered brains too well. Processors and memory elements refused to align. They ran out of order, some too fast, others stubbornly slow— all communicating out of turn—like a room full of people all talking at the same time.

The researchers published a paper, "Time-Dependent Manifestation of Computer Psychosis," in *Digital Psychology Letters* and received a grant to develop a weapon for corporate espionage. A tidy little virus was invented to infiltrate and scramble databases. A cure for the original problem, however, was never discovered.

Jack, however, had an idea for a cure. If the problem was asynchronous and tangled processors, then maybe he already had a solution . . . courtesy of Kamal.

"Let me get this straight," Reno said. He reclined in one of the *Dutchman*'s passenger couches and let the scaled leather scratch his back. "You're going to hot-wire your brain?"

"Not exactly," Jack said. "Bubbles provide a virtual interface with our sensory, emotive, and mnemonic centers. The connections between those brain centers are splintered. So we can rewire them with the architecture Kamal designed for the electron reactors."

"You've got nothing to lose, I guess," Reno replied. "Except your mind. Didn't you know that short-circuiting neurons causes associative psychosis?"

Jack knew. The insanity happened when bubbles went bad . . . or were sabotaged. The condition caused randomized associations in a person's mind. Seeing the face of a loved one could produce inexplicable feelings of terror, narcolepsy, or a homicidal rage.

Panda closed her eyes and balled her hands into fists. "I am willing to risk it," she said. "It could be no worse."

"And I can't deal with Gersham and Wheeler like this," Jack said.

Reno sat up, ran his finger down his crooked nose, thinking. "You could let me take your place. I've negotiated with powerful players."

That made sense . . . but it gave Jack the creeps to think of Wheeler and Reno together. He wasn't certain Reno wouldn't enjoy the power. Wasn't sure Reno wouldn't kill trillions of sentient beings to expand that power, either.

Jack didn't answer Reno. He turned to Panda. "Give me a hand with the implant-link protocols?"

"Yes." She opened her eyes, normal and centered, for now. Her eyelid tattoos were a solid band of blue-gray steel concentration.

The bubble already knew how to continuously scan his neuroanatomy. The tricky part would be teaching it how to identify the new parallel structures and braid them together like frayed pieces of string.

"Have it do a search-and-sort routine on the broad-band response," Panda said. She typed with both hands in two separate windows—alternating lines of code.

Reno pressed closer, opened an octagonal window with icons encrusted upon its matte-black frame. "You'd better add associative suppression so your recombinant signals have similar waveforms."

"That will slow everything," Jack said.

"Maybe. Maybe not, if you have four little Jack brains thinking at the same time."

"Jack's brain?" Panda stopped. "I thought I would be the test subject. I am the most altered."

"We do the simple case first," Jack told her. "It will be easier to spot what goes wrong."

"But you are the only one Gersham knows. I must protect—" She stopped, hesitated, then said, "You are the only one Wheeler will deal with. You are more valuable than I.''

"I won't risk you with my crazy idea. If it's going to fry anyone's brain—it'll be mine.''

She stood on her toes so her nose almost touched his chin. "I am volunteering. I am willing to take the risk.''

"The program's set up for my implant signature. It's already decided.''

Panda could knock him out, a simple thrust to the voice-box, a knee to his groin—she knew how. Instead, she backed down and crossed her arms. "You are extremely foolish.''

"Yes, he is,'' Reno said. He tapped out a cigarette, offered it to Jack. "A last smoke?''

That was a custom for condemned prisoners. Jack took it anyway and lit up. Two puffs and the amphetamine rush only scattered his thoughts more. He crushed it out.

Panda smoothed her hands over Jack's forehead; her left eye kept watching Reno. Jittering. *Good luck,* she whispered into his mind—a chorus of two separate voices superimposed over the Chinese characters for fortune and health.

Jack took a deep breath. "Boot it,'' he said.

Reno hit the spiral-run icon.

Jack blanked.

A heartbeat of silence and blackness, then—

—pieces of every puzzle Jack had ever left unsolved aligned. For the first time, Jack got a glimpse of his entire life laid out before him.

He never realized how big it was, how much ground it covered, all the people he had known, the things he had done. All he had seen before was one piece at a time, pondering the knobbed and convoluted edges—now they all fit together.

The big picture. The purpose of life. The meaning of the universe.

This is what Zero must have meant by a bottleneck in human thinking: distraction and scattered memories and dreams, trying to find the solution to one thing at a time when everything connected like a giant jigsaw.

Jack knew enough about jigsaws to start with one corner, assemble the edges, then fill the center. Zero was a corner piece.

The gene witch had boosted human intellect. A slight misalignment, however, and the new parallel processing power of multiple minds had turned into different voices trying to speak at the same time. It had transformed Zero's brilliance into lunacy.

In his memory, Jack stood in the desert where they had last met.

He saw every grain of butterfly-scale sand—each a piece of Zero's shattered mind: a tiny fragment of the Koran, a base pair from a DNA molecule, a crystalline grain of panic, a fleck of insight. Scattered to the winds now.

Before Zero had disconnected, he had cleared the skies of that desert. Overhead, clouds boiled and vanished and a double band of stars twinkled.

Jack gazed at them—while another part of his mind connected with the astronomy database: spectral analysis and pattern-matching algorithms danced in his head. The facts collected and spun into an outline of the galaxy, shifted and distorted and realigned to a new perspective.

The constellations in Zero's desert night were different. Cygnus the Swan flew skewed. The Little Dipper's handle bent.

Jack triangulated and interpolated, nudged the numbers to account for the drift rates and the distance the light from those different stars had traveled.

He connected the dots, and where the lines intersected: a star.

The evening shattered into sand and star dust and a thousand scattered thoughts. Jack's head split apart.

None of the puzzle made sense anymore.

Light flooded his good eye. Jack was only Jack again.

The edges of his vision blurred, then it cleared and he stared up into Reno's ugly face.

"You OK?" Reno asked.

Panda knelt next to Jack and brushed the hair out of

his face. "The system shut down. I am sorry. It was a worthy attempt."

Jack tasted blood in his mouth, his tongue swelled. "No," he said. "Something did happen. I saw stars."

Panda shook her head. "The program crashed after seventeen milliseconds. Your combined signals collapsed."

"You had a seizure," Reno said. "A seven-point grand mal." He tapped open a display and showed Jack. "Four brainwave patterns combined—then a tiny spike ballooned exponentially. It threw everything off."

Jack traced his finger over the aberration, across its ridges and sharp edges, sensed the data from the bubble's run-time log, but it made no sense.

"It was intersynaptic noise," Panda said. "The brain segments rerouted their signals around our software patch. It is the overly connected corpus callosum. Too much communication. No coordination."

"The different parts of your head want to speak to each other faster than we can relay their signals," Reno said. "Impatient little suckers."

Jack struggled to sit. "If we could physically isolate the parts of my brain from one another, it might work."

"Sure," Reno said. "Let me get the field surgery kit. I'll just cut your head into quarters and stick the parts into jars."

"Be silent," Panda hissed. She turned to Jack. "What did you sense?"

"Everything."

Jack tapped open the astronomy database; a saddle-curved surface appeared in his outstretched hand, full of blackness and sparkles and ghost nebulae.

The star from his vision was there. It hadn't been a delusion.

"Zero gave me more of a clue than he intended," Jack whispered.

He stood. "I know where he is . . . and maybe Safa. Zero wants me to come and rescue him?" Jack grabbed the gateway and unholstered his gun. "He's going to get more of a rescue than he ever imagined."

Jack immersed his hands in stars. He traced a blue arc to the seventh planet orbiting 82 Eridani, then to a brown dwarf, a hop, a skip, a leap across the void. It would be easy to get to Zero.

He withdrew and gripped the edge of the navigational window.

Panda touched Zero's star, accessing the data. "A blue-white supergiant," she said. "It is unlikely there are habitable planets." She folded the celestial map into a tiny square—tapped it shut.

"Then he faked it," Reno muttered.

"I don't think so," Jack said. "I asked for help. This was it."

"You trust a guy who tried to kill us?" Reno shook his head. "Even if he did give you the right location, he'll be expecting us."

Panda closed her delicate fingers into a fist. "It will be a trap."

"I'm going." Jack rubbed his thumb across the mirror surface of the gateway. "No one's forcing either of you. If you don't like the deal, stay here."

Panda locked both eyes on to Reno and gave him a slight nod.

"We're with you, Jack," Reno said. "It's just that if we go"—he walked aft—"we'd better go prepared."

Jack and Panda followed Reno into the cargo hold.

Reno cracked the seal on a plastic crate marked: SALTED PECANS. Inside were three aluminum cases with keypads. He tapped a seven-digit code on to the smallest case and its top hissed open, revealing six black eggs nestled in corrugated foam. Reno held one up. "EMP grenades," he said. "They generate a wave of virtual disorientation."

"A smoke screen for the implanted?" Panda asked.

"More than that." Reno smiled and handed two to Jack. "Drop one next to someone with an unshielded implant and—" He made a throat-slitting motion with his thumb. "Nice, huh?"

Reno hesitated, then passed a pair to Panda.

She slipped them in her hip pockets. "Good for the implanted," she remarked, "but there may be others."

"Got that covered." Reno opened the second box. Inside were two Chinese automatics, part organic and metalized plastic. "Let me upgrade your hardware, sweetheart."

Panda raised an eyebrow but took his gun. Its handle extruded around her left hand. She opened its option window and scrolled across Chinese characters. "Where did you obtain Taiwanese hot rounds?"

Reno winked his blue eye. "Poker game."

Jack took a step back. "I can't use those guns. Their interface overlaps with the gateway's operating system."

"Don't worry, Jack-O. I've saved the best for last." Reno dug into the third case, removed a gun stock, telescope site, and a meter-and-a-half-long barrel. He clicked the pieces together. "No interface in this." He handed the rifle to Jack.

It weighed ten kilos. "What's this supposed to shoot?" Jack asked. "Elephants?"

"We used them for black ops in zero gee . . . when there used to be real superpowers with nukes in orbit." Reno sighed wistfully then reached over and flicked the power stud. High-pitched whines squealed and faded into the ultrasonic.

The weapon became rock steady in Jack's hands.

"Gyroscopes," Reno said. "Nice when you were floating around trying to lock on target." He handed Jack an ammunition clip as fat as his forearm. "That's five shots. Standard plastosized depleted uranium rounds. Nothing fancy."

Jack sited down the optics with his good eye. An infrared laser measured the distance from his cornea to retina and automatically focused.

What would he do if he got Zero in the crosshairs? Shoot? Zero had been a friend. And who else could reverse his series-eight enzyme?

Zero, however, had a knack for causing trouble . . . and Jack was already drowning in the stuff. Maybe next time the gene witch would kidnap Panda. Or make good on his threat and kill Jack.

A silent click.

Jack had squeezed the double triggers without realizing it.

No. He *had* thought about it—just not the Jack in charge of his rational mind, one of the other Jacks in his fracturing brain. How long before he completely lost control?

Jack powered down the rifle.

"Glad you like it." Reno turned to Panda. "Since we're sharing, I was wondering if you—"

"No," Panda said. The air surrounding her firmed, turned icy solid with blackhack countermeasures. Dark coils seethed in her center.

Chang E. That's what Reno was sniffing around for. He had seen Jack use the software demon on Isabel's operatives.

"I find it curious," Panda said, narrowing her eyes to slits, "that you had hidden weapons. Were you saving them to use on us?"

Deep inside Panda writhed shadows and amplified pain routines and death-rattle data files.

Jack set his hand on her arm. "Save your fight for Zero. I've got a feeling he's not giving up Safa without one."

She turned. The blackness in her mind transformed into the familiar scent of licorice . . . but splintered, a jumble of black candy and red whips and aquavit.

How much pressure could Panda's weakening mind take?

"Let's get this over with"—Jack clutched the gateway and tagged the *Dutchman*—"before we all lose our heads."

Zero's star was a blue-white diamond set against the black fabric of space. The eighth planet was dotted with a thousand lakes. The water reflected the light from a tiny orange moon—shimmered like pixels on an antique amber display.

"Temperature's right and there's oxygen," Jack said. "Habitable. So either Zero got lucky or he's figured a way to terraform in a hurry." He spun in the microgravity, away from the shuttle's overhead window, and back into the cockpit.

Panda squirmed in the pilot's seat. She tapped the attitude jets and put them into a high equatorial trajectory.

Reno slid his thumbs over the controls in the optics window, zooming in and out, running spectroscopic scans. "Infrared says there's vegetation down there. I'll get more data on the day side of the planet."

"No detectable toxins in the atmosphere," Panda reported.

Jack stared at the world. Where to find Zero? "Any transmissions?"

Panda stretched open a link edged with filigree dotted-and-dashed Morse code. "Some static . . . possibly a shielded source."

"On the far side?" Reno suggested.

"Let's see," Jack said.

Panda nodded, calculated a burn for the *Dutchman,* and they accelerated out of the planet's shadow.

"We're wasting time," Reno said. "Just jump."

"Zero will be watching the rotation," Jack replied. "It might tip our hand." Jack set his hand protectively on the gateway. "But while we're waiting, I can do something."

He linked with navigation and downloaded data on the nearby moon. He could use it to leap two planets farther out—to a gas giant spinning fast. From there, he could step to a pulsar thirteen light-years distant.

"Escape route?" Reno asked.

"Yes," Jack said. "We're not getting stranded again."

The shuttle crossed from night to day and smoke-blue sunlight flooded the cockpit.

"Receiving broad-spectrum EM," Panda said, "and deep theta patterns. There is bubble activity upon the surface."

"Can you pinpoint it?" Jack asked.

She shook her head, which made her bristled bangs oscillate in the microgravity. "It is highly diffused. Perhaps a network of repeater stations. There." She pointed to two large islands beneath them—what New Zealand would have looked like with its ends pulled apart, its middle stretched into an isthmus.

"They've got buildings . . . or what's left of them," Reno said. He spun the flat plane of his link so Jack could see toppled walls and collapsed crystal domes.

Why would Zero bring wreckage to his new world?

Jack spotted a cylinder in the center of the isthmus. He zoomed in.

It was gray-white concrete, fluted, sixty meters tall, pink and red paving stones scattered around its base. Jack recognized the structure.

"That's where Zero is."

Reno turned the window so it faced him, squinted. "How can you be sure?"

"Zero jumped the Academe away before Santa Sierra drowned." Jack tapped the center of the image. "That's Coit Tower. It stood next to the Bell Communications Center and the mathematics building where I had my office."

Coit Tower was a relic that had been dredged up from the ocean floor and restored in the twenty-second century. It had survived earthquakes, floods . . . the end of the world.

Jack wished he had its endurance.

A window popped open. A plane of rock crystal, across which the electron reactors scrolled: HELLO, JACK. I HAVE AN IN—

Jack tapped the link shut. He had more important things on his mind.

"Infrared is picking up dense vegetation," Reno said and frowned. "Maybe motion."

"More vines?" Those things had exploded and grown out of Zero's open portal on the moon. Jack shuddered. Panda had been mauled by them. How would she handle confronting them again? He turned to her. "You ready?"

Panda set the autopilot and floated away from the console. "A moment." She closed her eyes and squeezed them tight. Without looking, she tightened the straps of the Chinese automatic's holster on her left thigh, the Hautger SK on her right. She opened her eyes. One stared at Jack, the other at Reno. "I am as ready as I can be. We must hurry. I cannot think as one person for much longer. I am doing things without thinking . . . I . . ." She couldn't find the words.

Reno Velcroed a grenade to his chest, then slotted an extra-long ammunition cartridge into his gun. "Let's go. It's time for a little payback."

Jack slung the sniper rifle over his shoulder and interfaced with the gateway. He tagged the three of them and extended the blue destination vector to the base of Coit Tower.

The arrow slid and shifted and slipped out of his grasp. He tried again, but it couldn't get near the structure.

"It's like on the moon," Jack said. "The gateway's blocked."

Panda drifted nearer and her right eye stared into his interface. "Perhaps Zero and Isabel shared technologies?"

"Just get us close," Reno said, "and we'll hike in."

Jack moved the blue vector a kilometer south. It locked in place.

A silver line appeared in front of Panda's face, spun and stretched into a flat square. She examined the window. "You better look at this, Jack."

The electron reactors printed: INCOMING MESSAGE. ISOTO-PIC FREQUENCIES ACTIVE. A link within the window irised open and showed the isotope darken from sapphire blue to ultramarine.

"Gersham's shielded frequencies," Jack said.

"Lousy timing," Reno muttered.

"You must answer him." Panda set her hand on Jack's arm. "What good is it to find Safa if we cannot escape? Only Gersham has the technology to hide us from Wheeler."

"I'll answer, but"—Jack handed Panda his gateway—"don't take chances. The first hint of trouble from Zero, from Wheeler, from anyone, and you jump us out of here."

"I will." Her tattoos crystallized into platinum facets, then crackled and pinged like hot metal expanding; Jack sensed the pressure behind them, metaphor for just how close she was to the breaking point.

"I'll make this as quick as I can," Jack told them.

He initiated the bubble, parted reality, and stepped through.

Curtains swished behind him, folds of dark cloth, and slivers of light that twisted into black and white squares, then assembled into a playing board.

The same meeting place as last time . . . yet, Jack could penetrate the veil of illusion, sense the hull of the *Dutchman* around him, and pick up the faint resonant signatures of Panda and Reno. No rendezvous coordinates. A virtual reconstruction.

And this time Jack's square was black.

Gersham appeared on an adjacent white tile. He looked like Jack, but better: shaved, his ponytail trimmed, and hazel eyes clear. He wore a pristine silver vacuum suit.

There was, however, more to Gersham than a mirror of Jack; there were the others lurking in this checkerboard.

The white tiles were ice crystals; a rippling plane of silk; a window overlooking swirls of sea foam; blue-lined paper; the curve of an eggshell, tapping and cracking from inside; and cirrostratus clouds streaked across an ivory-colored sky.

"We've changed sides," Jack said.

Gersham offered him a cigarette; Jack declined. "A matter of perspective," Gersham replied and lit one for himself. "I apologize for this impromptu communication, but our previous meeting site was discovered." He exhaled smoke. ''You would not know how that occurred, would you?''

''No.''

Had Wheeler found it? If so, he was moving faster than Jack anticipated. How long before he cracked Gersham's shielded communication line? How long before he increased the pressure on Jack?

''What do you want?'' Jack asked. ''It's dangerous to speak like this.''

Within the white tiles, the silk ruffled in a gust of wind, clouds roiled and scattered, ice melted, and the pecking inside the eggshell ceased.

''We sense predators close . . . and thought that odd.'' Gersham laced his fingers together. ''We thought it was *you* who might want something.'' His hands melded into a single seamless limb, an arc of right and left arms.

Was that a metaphor for unity? It gave Jack the creeps.

''Yes,'' Jack said. ''I want to accept your offer of sanctuary.''

His stomach turned the instant he said that. He'd have to trust Gersham. Trust him with his life.

Gersham's hazel eyes widened and he leaned forward. ''Very wise.''

''But not yet,'' Jack said.

''Why delay? There is danger.''

Jack rocked on the balls of his feet, suddenly uncomfortable in his single square of black. ''I'm about to retrieve a lost member of my team. Then we will come with you.''

Gersham unlinked his hands and cracked his knuckles. ''You will call me the instant you have this person? So we may iron out the details of our agreement?''

''Sure,'' Jack said. Details? What details?

Wheeler had told Jack that Gersham had been ''one of them.'' Only that Gersham had been reluctant to clean up after his deals. In other words, Gersham wouldn't commit genocide to cover up his dirty business. Or would he? ''Reluctance'' wasn't a guarantee that Gersham didn't kill, too.

What else had Wheeler said?

A feather touch brushed across Jack's recollection.

He stopped, reached deeper, pushed and boosted the power to his implant.

Out of the corner of his dead eye, Jack saw interference patterns of black and white: ghosts crept along the cracks of the checkerboard. They slithered and whispered, converged along the eight seams connected to his square. Their wispy fingers stretched closer.

A memory probe.

It was infinitely more subtle than the thing Jack had used on Bruner . . . but still an unwelcome guest to this party. Gersham's? Or someone else eavesdropping?

Jack made a cigarette appear in his hand. The tip flared then smoldered. He puffed and exhaled layers of countercode vapour. Fumes drifted into the edges of his black square, gray curls and convolutions, a labyrinth of smoke and data mirrors that blocked the probe.

"We shall be waiting for you," Gersham said. "Be careful."

"I'm always careful," Jack replied. "Very careful." He couldn't read anything in the copy of his own face Gersham wore.

"You will be in touch?"

"Soon," Jack said.

Gersham severed contact.

Black and white squares spiraled about Jack; they mixed into the color of ash. Gersham and Wheeler circled closer and closer; Jack didn't trust either of them. Zero and Safa were near. Time was running out. It all spun faster and faster into a whirlpool center . . . where Jack was drowning.

Jack stepped down from the *Dutchman*—a kilometer south of Coit Tower. Steam condensed on his helmet's faceplate; he wiped it clean and clicked on the defoggers.

He stood in a swamp of yellow horsetail ferns, club moss, orchids with full peach-colored lips, and mustard cypress trees. Clouds of giant dandelion seeds swirled through the misty air.

The place had Zero's genetically engineered touch.

Panda aimed at the vines, Chinese automatic in her left hand, Hautger SK in her right.

Reno crouched and poked a bramble. Over their shielded com frequencies, he said: "They're not the vines that got our moon base."

Jack Velcroed the gateway to his thigh and gripped the sniper rifle tight. Something was wrong. He squinted out his good eye, and under a patchwork of leaves, he spotted a white shard. He knelt and pulled it free . . . a rib bone.

Bones were everywhere. The mound on his right was a heap of pelvises, interlocked like the links of a chain. There were hills of spiky shoulder blades and broken skulls, scattered teeth, snakelike spines, mounds of tiny round metatarsals, piles of mouse-sized vertebrae, lumps of ossified calcium—all rotten with black marrow.

Panda slowly lowered her guns. "What are they?"

"You mean *who* were they?" Reno nudged a jumble of finger bones with his boot. "Zero jumped the Academe here. That place was full of students and professors, right? I wonder if this is them?"

Did Zero experiment on and kill these people? Jack couldn't believe the gene witch was capable of it. But these bones had come from somewhere . . . from someone.

"Let's get to that tower," Jack said, "then get the hell out of here."

Reno's stealth suit flickered and faded and became a dozen shadows without a body.

They walked over shifting bones and slick creepers with vermilion blossoms, ripe with sticky nectar.

Jack's ear itched—a sensation that jumped to his back, insect legs that crawled and turned into acupuncture needles, injecting the scent of motor oil, and ice-cold water that dribbled down his spine.

Panda halted and cocked her head. "I am picking up a transmission, trying to lock on to my implant."

Their helmets suppressed noise. This signal had to be powerful. A directed transmission. An attack?

Jack wanted to tear his headgear off and squeeze the static out of his mind.

"Spread out," Reno said. "It's got to be part of a

repeater network. We'll triangulate. You be the center, Jack, and hit it with the sniper rifle.'' He blurred across the swamp.

Panda cast a look back at Jack, then took wobbly steps in the opposite direction.

Jack focused on the incoming waves: lemon-peel scent and the taste of peanut butter, paper cuts along his forearm—they faded, got stronger, faded again; he stopped and turned his head back. There. The strongest signal.

It wormed into his mind, rebounded and found a match, prying loose the memory of the zigzagging arrow symbol, the position operator in the gateway code.

He pushed; his implant flared with heat—grounded the connection.

Over the com-link Reno's static-filled voice said: "Got a vector."

A hiss, then Panda answered: "As do I."

Their positions appeared on Jack's faceplate display, then arrows, indicating the approximate direction of the strongest signal. He superimposed his own coordinates. The three vectors converged—five hundred meters distant.

Jack magnified the image of his target: a cypress tree. Vines wound around its trunk with silver foil flowers whose edges rippled and opened and closed like tiny mouths. An organic repeater?

He sighted through his rifle's optics and locked on target. The rifle's gyros kicked in and steadied the weapon.

He squeezed the triggers.

A cough of recoil. A trail of smoke feathered the air.

The tree exploded: fire and splinters and bits of glitter.

"Nice shooting," Reno said over the com-link.

Jack reached out with his mind. There were weaker signals scattering back and forth—searching for him. "I think we have a big enough hole to penetrate the network," he said.

"I'm on my way back," Reno replied. "Stay put and don't—"

"There is a problem," Panda interrupted. "I am coming back." Her transmission cut off.

"Panda?"

Silence.

Jack moved in the direction he had seen her go—stopped. If he left, how would Reno find him?

Gunfire: three shots in the distance, then a burst of full automatic.

Jack forgot about Reno. He ran toward the sound, over skeletons and the tangles of yellow-green—a femur caught his boot. He tripped and tumbled onto a carpet of muddy moss.

Jack shook out the ache in his ankle and tried to get to his feet.

A hand grabbed his and pulled him up. Panda's hand.

She let go and drew her Chinese automatic. "We must go. Jump before it is too late." Beyond the reflection of her faceplate, her dark eyes were wide. "Hurry."

Jack grabbed the gateway, tagged himself and Panda, stretched the blue vector—it wouldn't budge.

"We're not going anywhere," he said. "Whatever's stopping us from jumping to the tower scrambles the out-going signals, too. We have to get to where we came in."

Jack started back, half-limping.

Panda clutched his elbow. "No," she whispered. "Look . . . it has found us."

Flesh oozed through vines and bones, liquid arms and legs and necks, a sea of skin and gelatinous cartilage and lengths of intestine glistening in the sunlight—made a ring around Panda and Jack. Clusters of brown and blue and green eyes gazed at him, lips gaped open and migrated apart, ears drifted closer to better listen, and nostrils inhaled his scent. A hundred voices gibbered and laughed and squealed.

It was Picasso's mural of the bombing of Guernica, Spain come to life—distorted limbs and agony and alien textures. The artist would have gone mad to see it.

Jack would have screamed, but the air caught in his throat.

"My guns had no effect," Panda said.

Her voice was normal, calm. It snapped Jack out of his terror.

She aimed her automatic and silver-plated Hautger SK at the beating hearts and arteries. "Is it real?"

Jack tasted the surrounding network of repeaters, signals that saturated the air with siren wails and butterscotch and the faint resonate echoes from the organic mass around him—implants receiving those signals.

"Unfortunately," he said. Into his helmet's microphone he whispered: "Reno, we need your help."

The ring of flesh moved; muscle and tendons slid over one another, constricting around them, a circle three meters in diameter . . . and shrinking.

Jack put his back to Panda's and raised the rifle.

What had Zero done? Were these people? Were they, as Reno suggested, Academe students?

With implants?

Jack touched his helmet to Panda's. "Boost your counterinductive circuitry to maximum," he said.

"It is."

He opened a display on his faceplate, slid the counterinductive gauge from amber to overload ultramarine. Jack then dropped the rifle and, with shaking hands, grabbed Reno's EMP grenades.

Undulating skin moved closer with fingerprint whorls and elbow wrinkles and chromic tattoos and braids of hair—ropes of mucus and pockets of fat.

Jack tossed a grenade to his left, lobbed one to his right.

He held on to Panda.

The EMP grenades detonated. Thunder and lightning and tsunami boiled through Jack's head. He gritted his teeth, blocked out thought. The counterinductive circuitry in his helmet flared—and failed. The scent of bananas blasted his nose, glass shards stabbed his tongue, hysterical laughter tore his chest, fire licked his skin, bones broke. His bones? Panda's? Sensation ripped him apart—ice and flashbulbs and burning plastic and jealousy and the screams of a hundred voices resonated—

—that fell into silence and blackness, except the ringing in his ears.

Jack blinked and looked out his blurry eye.

The ring of flesh twitched and bit itself. The electromagnetic blast had burned its mind—their minds. Disembodied limbs crawled off on their own, muscles pulled themselves apart, and organs dissolved into a black film upon the murky swamp water.

Panda braced her shoulder against Jack's chest. "What were they?"

"Human? Zero's attempt to genetically engineer a solution to his split mind? A collective intelligence and body? I don't know."

Jack shuddered. Was Safa part of the piles of guts and skin and smoldering implants?

No. Jack turned to Coit Tower. That was where Zero would hide the Captive.

Jack cast a double shadow.

The darkness on his left resolved into Reno's stealth suit. "Good thing I didn't get too close," Reno said. "What"—he crouched closer to the mounds of flesh— "or who . . . did I miss?"

"Nothing," Jack said. "No one—not anymore."

"Boneless," Reno whispered. "So that's where the skeletons came from."

"And from the quantity of bone we saw," Panda said, "there could be more of these. We should continue."

Jack touched his gateway and tried to jump them away. No dice. The signal was still blocked.

They marched across bones and scrabbled over fleshy vines, through thick curtains of steam and rot. Red and pink tiles appeared on the ground, paved sections, then a flat courtyard and the white-gray concrete of Coit Tower rising out of the chaos.

The unblemished white shaft was topped by a crown of arches. Within the flutes that scalloped its circumference, shadow and light pooled. It reminded Jack of a Greek column, the last one standing after eons of time.

"Must have a great view on top," Reno said.

Within, Jack tasted the echoes of chloroform and whispers.

"Strong signals inside," Panda said. She took a step back.

Reno grabbed a grenade. "I'll take care of any repeaters or bubbles."

"And if Safa is here?" Jack asked. "Unshielded? That could kill her."

"So we just go in?" Reno asked. "No suppressing fire? No explosions to soften them up?"

"Stay if you're scared." Jack mounted the stairs to the lacquered blue double doors.

Reno muttered in Chinese and followed.

Panda hesitated, then climbed after them.

The interior walls were painted with murals of San Francisco and the Californian basin in the 1930s: groves of almond trees and migrant pickers; gushing oil wells; railroad yards; workers on assembly lines toiling under the eagle NRA seal; crowds of commuters on the ferry to Oakland; and a view of the tranquil harbor—all painted in gold sepia tones and rich blues and heavy charcoal lines.

It was the New Deal, the American Dream, and an illusion. The real murals had been worn off decades ago.

Reno stopped. "There's no elevator."

"There's usually a back door to these metaphors . . . wait—" Jack spied a vault in the painting of the stock exchange. He turned the combination dial to zero and pushed.

It clicked and opened, revealing a staircase winding up the inner wall of the tower.

"Come on, Zero," Jack whispered. "I came. That's what you wanted. Show yourself."

An absolute silence absorbed his words. No response.

"Looks like we climb." Jack hefted his rifle.

Reno stepped onto the stairs.

Panda holstered her Hautger SK and tried to steady the Chinese automatic with both hands—but they still jerked the gun in different directions.

Along the arc of the wall, a mural of the San Francisco Bay painted itself. The Golden Gate Bridge was built by tiny high-wire construction workers; sea serpents in the water below watched, then tsunami flooded the San Joaquin Valley, and it was drained along the new shoreline of the Sierra Nevadas.

Panda stopped. "We counted three hundred steps. Each a quarter meter. Enough to have reached the top."

Jack noted that her "I" had become a "we" but kept his mouth shut.

He looked up. There were as many steps as there had been when they started. He looked down—an endless spiral that vanished into a point of shadow.

"We're in looped subroutine," Reno said.

"Too cliche for Zero," Jack replied. "We must have missed something."

They backtracked past the Great Fire of San Francisco painted with egg tempura flames and stained with candle soot, wheeled around Indians who picked mussels from the bay . . . the longer Jack looked, the clearer the beach became; tiny gulls circled over the ocean, and wavelets lapped at the shores, at his boots.

Reno smeared a freshly painted cloud with his index finger. "A map?"

"This one—" Panda pointed her gun at a Chinatown fresco full of chicken vendors and paper dragons dancing in the streets and children setting off firecrackers. Her left hand, however, pointed to another painting: a newly constructed Coit Tower, scaffolding still about its base, and diminutive engineers paving the road up Telegraph Hill.

Jack stared at it, felt the wind upon his face, and smelled the fresh ocean air.

"That's it." He stepped through—reappeared at the entrance of the tower.

Reno appeared on his right. Panda on his left.

"It's another loop," Reno said.

"Only one way to find out," Jack replied.

They reentered through the double doors. No murals upon the walls of this incarnation of the tower, only concrete—so fresh it still had an earthy odor. There was, however, an elevator.

Jack got in and held the doors open for Panda and Reno. He closed the door and gate, then pulled the brass control handle.

The car accelerated upward.

Jack's left eye went blind, the eye that had been burned

out and only saw virtual images. So this was real. Or a
very clever simulation of reality.

Reno checked the ammunition status on his gun.

"Don't kill him," Jack said. "He's the only one who
knows what's happening to us."

"Sure," Reno muttered. "But let's see what he's done
to Safa first. If it's anything like what he's done to those
things downstairs . . . maybe his cure is worse than the
disease. Maybe he *needs* to be killed."

Panda backed herself into the far corner and braced her
shoulders there. She got a better grip on the automatic
with her trembling hands.

Jack took a step closer to her. "Can I—"

"You can do nothing," she said through gritted teeth.
A tear trembled and trickled out of her left eye. She started
to wipe it away with her forearm—hit the faceplate of her
helmet. "I will do my best."

The car stopped and the doors parted.

A short flight of stairs led to the observation deck. Reno
went first, crouched low, stealth suit fracturing his image.
Jack followed, Panda at his back.

Up ten steps and they emerged on top.

The observation deck was six meters in diameter. A
dozen arches were cut into the curved wall—doorways
that opened out to a powder-blue sky.

Safa lay curled in a fetal position on the floor. Her
arms and legs were bound with tape, an intravenous tube
punctured her left arm, and a catheter threaded between
her legs. She had a bruise on her forehead and a busted lip.

And she was perfectly still. Dead?

Safa inhaled.

Jack started breathing, too, and ran to her. Panda took
Safa's hand.

"We've got you," Reno whispered. "You're safe."

Her blue eyes opened and jittered over them: reflecting
images of Jack, Panda, and Reno. She smiled at Reno . . .
then focused upon the wall behind him, and her smile
faded.

Jack turned.

In the observation portals, which a second ago had been empty, stood Zero. No. More than just Zero. Jack whirled.

Each of the dozen archways held a copy of Zero.

Jack pushed outward with his mind. He sensed no signals. They were real?

Every Zero wore a tattered robe. All had a wild skeletal smile and a patchwork beard. And each held a gateway.

Five stared at Jack, one gazed out at the surrounding swamp, while pairs of Zeros watched Reno and Panda and Safa.

In the corner of Jack's dead eye—red and blue arrows crisscrossed between the multiple Zeros. The gene witch had already activated his gateway.

"I've come," Jack said, turning to face the different copies of Zero, "to rescue you." He held out his hand to the closest copy.

That Zero shook his head.

Zeros on either side laughed. Another wept. Five scurried across the deck and exchanged places.

"This is nuts," Reno hissed. He stood over Safa's body, protecting her.

The Zero closest to Jack spoke: "The Hero has come too late. Moved into a rook checkmate. What was whole will now shatter. Doubled cells of gray matter."

"He has lost his mind," Panda whispered. "He will never be able to cure us." She aimed her gun; her right and left hands jerked the barrel—from Zero to Zero.

"The experiment is not over," the Zeros chanted. "It has just begun. I will take each of you . . . one by one."

Jack couldn't let Zero take anyone else. He raised his rifle. If he shot one copy of Zero, would all of them die? "Your experiment is over, Zero."

A dozen gold arrows flickered from Zero's gateways, spun and pointed at the center of the world. Red arrows tagged all the Zeros—as well as Jack, Reno, Panda, and Safa.

Zero was going to jump them all?

No. He couldn't go anywhere. Zero had something that scattered gateway signals around the tower.

. . . Unless Zero had turned it off.

Jack interfaced with his gateway—quick—tagged his team and Safa. The yellow power-source vector touched the core of the planet. It locked in place.

That meant Zero had a lock. If Jack could jump, Zero could jump—himself, all of them. They could end up in interstellar space, where they'd freeze to death; in the heart of a star; the center of this planet; anywhere. Or what would happen if they jumped simultaneously? Would their masses be torn apart?

A thousand blue vectors materialized from the Zeros, stretched out into the atmosphere; all he had to do was release and they would vanish to points unknown.

Jack squeezed his rifle's trigger.

The closest Zero exploded, his chest a mass of broken ribs and blood—then fell out the archway.

The eleven other Zeros clutched their chests. The blue vectors vanished.

"Break his concentration," Jack cried. "Shoot him!"

Panda and Reno fired.

Bullets blasted holes in the concrete wall, through Zero's hearts, blew off arms and legs and heads.

Jack sent his blue arrow up to the shuttle.

Zero's blue vectors again wove a net through the air.

Jack felt like he was being pulled in a hundred directions—like Reno and Safa and Panda were being wrenched from his grasp.

Space blurred. Jack stepped off the planet and into night.

15

Jack appeared in the *Dutchman*. His head popped from the flux in the magnetic field.

Safa and Panda and Reno floated next to him.

Debris filled the passenger section—droplets of water, suspended bits of foam, and shreds of old vacuum suits jiggled and bounced off the acceleration couches, walls, and ceiling.

Reno held Safa in his arms. "She's not breathing."

Panda grabbed the curved wall and anchored the weightless Reno and Safa. She touched Safa's neck. "Her pulse is erratic."

Jack went to push off the hull, to join them, help Safa. No.

Zero could find them in orbit. Jack interfaced with the navigational database, a square full of stars that he reached into and accessed their escape route.

He moved the shuttle to the nearby gas giant, used its rotation to step to the pulsar thirteen light-years away—then across the night, into orbit around their world with three rings—then jumped the craft to the surface of the planet.

Gravity settled Jack's stomach and made the hull of the *Dutchman* groan with its own weight. Water and trash rained to the floor.

Reno grabbed Safa as she fell.

Safa convulsed; her hands clawed at the air.

Panda routed Safa's implant through the bubble system; EEG and heart activity traced electric-blue zigzags over her head.

"She is in fibrillation," Panda said.

Jack opened an interface to the shuttle's emergency system. He tapped the red-cross icon for CPR instructions.

Reno grabbed the link. "Her heart's fine." He touched Safa's EEG and sent a ripple through the jagged lines. "It's her head that's not working." He pulled apart the tangled brain waves, separated them into sixteen distinct patterns. "There's too much interference for the impulses that regulate breathing and heartbeat."

Jack reached out with his mind, sensed from Safa the retort of gunfire, the liquid curves of Arabic calligraphy, bits of razor-edged panic, sinuous desire, and laughter—splintered memories and emotions. Nothing fit together.

Panda pressed her thumb into her forehead and gritted her teeth. She looked up, snapped the fingers of either hand, and said, "A pacemaker. To override her cardiac signals. Does the shuttle's medical kit have one?"

"I . . . I don't know," Jack replied, still awash in the confusion of Safa's mind.

Panda staggered to the stern of the shuttle, running into couches and the walls—her legs pulling in different directions.

Reno took Safa's hand. "Hang on. We'll get you back." He turned and glared at Jack. "Won't we?"

Panda returned with the shuttle's medical kit and tore though it, looking for a pacemaker. "Nothing," she hissed. Her eyes darted about the *Dutchman*. Foam frothed in the corners of her mouth. "We must improvise."

She pushed Reno out of the way, stretched apart the EEG lines, reached deep into Safa's implant, and interfaced with the cranial nerve subroutines.

Static crawled up Panda's arms, blurred impulses that she smoothed and grounded. Her left hand tapped in commands to stimulate Safa's heart; her right set up a cyclic rhythm for her diaphragm.

Safa inhaled deeply. Exhaled. She coughed, then quietly breathed in and out.

Panda's shoulders slumped, and she sighed.

"Good work," Reno said. "Thanks." He took a step toward Panda. Stopped.

Panda opened a round window with sharp steel edges, a map of her own brain floating in its center; she summoned a cube full of tiny equations, stretched a hexagonal frame speckled with Chinese characters; she tapped open tiny windows within those windows. The air around her swarmed with flashing, spinning planes of data.

"What are you doing?" Jack asked.

"It is no good." She connected to the shuttle's engine schematics, then to navigation, and let stars and numbers splash across her fingertips. "Together . . . I held myself. Too many lights and sounds and textures." She looked at Jack, her eyes dilated, tattoos banded black and white, then her gaze darted away. "For what is left. None of them are me."

What did she mean? Maybe Panda had been OK as long as the pressure was on and her guard was up. But with Safa back and safe, maybe Panda had relaxed that guard . . . and lost control.

Reno took a step closer to Panda. He made eye contact with Jack and shook his head.

"Do not try to stop me," Panda hissed at Reno. She drew her automatic.

Reno held up his hands and licked his lips. "That's not a smart idea, sweetheart."

Panda flicked the safety off.

"Set the gun down," Jack whispered. "Whatever's wrong we'll figure it out. We can fix it."

"Not without the gene witch." She clutched the automatic tighter. "So many of him shot. Cannot assume he is an option. No cure . . . but one."

Panda's free hand tore through her neck seal and pulled off her helmet. Her hair was a dark halo around her head, indigo and full of static sparks. Underneath, her eyes glistened like those of a feral animal. "Dangerous," she whispered. "We—I—to you. So many ways to kill. Must not risk your life."

She turned the gun to her temple.

Jack grabbed her forearm.

Panda whipped the pistol into Jack's face—sent him flailing across the shuttle, blood gushing from his nose. He bounced against the hull, stunned.

Reno seized her gun and wrenched it, turning it up.

Panda released the weapon, grabbed his arm, twisted. Her other hand hammered at his wrist—shattered the bones. Her hands then snaked back and forth as if each had a mind of its own.

Reno head-butted his helmet into her forehead.

Panda reeled backward from the blow. Droplets of blood welled from her brow.

She shook her head and clouds of shadow condensed around her, cracked into lines that etched the air and sure-grip deck. One shot under Jack's boot; electric shock and razor wire tore up his leg.

Chang E. She was going to use it on Reno.

Jack drew his Hautger SK. What was he going to do? Shoot her? No. Wound her? Not with her bioengineered body. How could he stop her? She was Reno's equal—or better—in hand-to-hand combat. She'd break Jack in half. There was no way to get close enough—fast enough—to surprise her.

. . . Unless distance didn't matter.

He interfaced with the gateway. A red arrow, a blue, and he stepped—

—behind Panda.

She spun around.

Jack coldcocked her with his gun—hard enough to send splinters of pain up his arm.

The blow didn't crack her polycarbide-reinforced skull, but Panda went limp and fell to the deck.

The nightmare darkness around her evaporated.

"She's fast," Reno said, holding his broken wrist and wincing in pain. "If she'd followed up on that maneuver, she would have snapped my neck."

"Help me with her," Jack said.

They strapped her lithe body onto an acceleration couch.

Reno got the medical kit, pulled out a syringe, tore the cap off with his teeth, and plunged it into Panda's thigh.

"What's that?"

"Muscle relaxant. Something that won't mess with her neurochemistry, but will keep her nice and soft until we figure out what happened."

"It's the same thing that happened to Safa and Zero," Jack replied. "The mental fragmentation. The loss of rational control."

"I can't believe she tried to kill herself," Reno muttered, shaking his head. "I'd have never pegged Panda as a suicide."

"She's not," Jack said. "She was just trying to protect us."

Panda's eyes fluttered open.

Jack reached out with his implant.

"No." She recoiled. In her mind, rusty gates slammed shut. "Leave me alone."

She closed her eyes and pulled feebly at the Velcro straps. Her tattoos vanished. "Too many thoughts. No thoughts. I must try. To sleep. To think. Please. Just leave me alone."

Jack moved to take her hand.

She jerked it away.

"You're next," Reno told Jack. "Zero's bugs are slicing and dicing your brain, even as we speak." He wound a roll of tape about his wrist, bit the end off. "You better introduce me to Wheeler and Gersham so I can take over negotiations when you lose it."

"Shut up, Reno."

Jack squeezed his eyes closed. He had too many problems—Wheeler would kill one of them in twelve hours, Panda had lost her mind, Zero had escaped, Safa was dying—and no solutions.

He glanced back at Panda. Her right eye was open and watching him. The left was shut tight, but twitching as if she was in REM sleep. Maybe part of her was asleep.

What could he do for her? Nothing.

Jack had been trumped; he was holding a handful of

cards that were all the wrong suit. Worse. He had no cards left to play with. He was out of options.

He had to do something, though . . . anything.

He turned to Safa. She was in worse shape. Her right eye was swollen shut, and she had a busted lip. That was nothing compared to the damage inside.

Jack downloaded a scan of her brain: sixteen lobes and sixteen tiny brain stems that wove into a single spinal column.

"Can we use a software patch?" Reno asked.

"That didn't work with my four segments," Jack replied. "Too much intersynaptic leakage. Safa's brain has even more noise. There are—" Jack couldn't think of the interconnection formula . . . so basic. Where was it in his mind? "There are one hundred thirty-five interconnections between her sixteen lobes."

That answer had come from nowhere. No. It had come from a part of Jack's mind he wasn't conscious of . . . and, possibly, no longer in control of.

Reno snapped his fingers in front of Jack's face. "Hey. You with me here?"

Jack focused on Reno. "Yeah, I'm with you."

"After we tried to kludge your thoughts together," Reno said, "you told me we had to physically separate the lobes." Reno exploded the view of Safa's brain. "Let's get those nano-assemblers out of the electron reactors. They can make an insulating barrier between—"

"Won't work," Jack said. "They only manipulate semiconductors. And even if we had biocompatible insulators, there are only a couple of dozen nano-assemblers active. Not enough to patch more than a few square millimeters a day."

Reno touched the image of Safa's mutated temporal lobe. The scent of crude oil and sandalwood incense filled the shuttle. "All we need is a tiny separation to dampen the noise." He shook his head. "It might as well be light-years."

Jack stared into the curved mirror surface of the gateway. " 'Light-years'?"

"What?"

"Light-years. Millimeters. Distance is malleable. It doesn't matter—that's what I keep telling myself."

"You bet it matters. It's—"

Jack held up his hand. "We can't move Safa's brain out of her head. But we can copy it. Like I did with the electron."

"Slow down, Jack-O. You're not making any sense."

"And Zero. He split himself a dozen times before he escaped. You saw. A dozen different Zeros."

Reno crossed his arms. "I think I'd better have a look in *your* head."

"No, listen. The gateway's destination vector splits. I've diffractively separated an electron. It has to work with nonquantum masses, too. That's how Zero bilocated himself. We do the same to Safa."

"OK," Reno said slowly and looked Jack over—maybe for signs of lunacy. "You've pulled a few rabbits out of your hat . . . let's pretend you can do this magic trick. That gives us sixteen Safas with sixteen broken brains. It multiplies the problem."

"No. We shut down parts of the implants in her copied brains. Then we combine those fractional responses into a single interactive brain-wave pattern."

Reno ran his index finger down the length of his crooked nose, thinking. "I see where you're going. We'll have to write a new software patch to recombine those isolated signals." He opened the window and grabbed the program they used before on Jack. "Then rewrite the protocols to work with her altered neuroanatomy."

Reno stacked block-commands into a crystal pyramid; silver veins of subalgorithms ran through the code. They meshed without one error window popping open.

"This thing will accept—and combine—sixteen signals," Reno declared.

Jack scrutinized the structure. "If you say so."

Reno tapped the compile command, and the code compressed to a tiny brilliant diamond. Flawless.

Now all Jack had to do was copy Safa. Could it really be done?

He locked the yellow on to the center of the spinning planet below, then tagged Safa with a red arrow.

The blue destination vector he teased apart into fifteen strands, then pointed them to fifteen different acceleration couches—and hesitated.

This was a long shot. Splitting a person into copies might irrevocably damage their consciousness. Or it could kill Safa. She would be dead soon, though, if they didn't try something. Jack just hoped this was the right thing.

He let the power flow through the gateway. He didn't release the red and blue arrows. He held them taut in his mind, let power and matter combine and recombine and bounce through the shuttle.

Fifteen new Safas flickered and solidified upon the acceleration couches. The passenger section filled with Arabian princesses.

Jack wanted to push with his implant. Make sure this wasn't a bubble illusion from his subconscious. He needed all his concentration, however, to keep the gateway vectors from collapsing.

The sixteen Safas breathed; chests rose and fell together; one coughed, another sighed and went out of synch with the others.

So they weren't identical . . . each had a life and will of its own.

Reno took one Safa's hand. "Solid," he whispered. He returned to his open window. "There's implant leakage from where her hypothalamus originally used to be. I'm filtering the static. Her sixteen signals are isolating . . . recombining. That's it. A single, solid brain-wave pattern—distributed between all of her. I think."

Jack couldn't let go of the gateway. He had to keep the lines steady and keep the power flowing. Part of him did that.

Another part walked over and examined the image of Safa's mind.

He was aware of what his other self was doing, but not. Like the image of the moon in Kamal's water bowl. Consciousness and unconsciousness and the subconscious mixed.

Instead of the flashes of color he had seen in his brain scan, Safa's neural map was solid—ambers and golds and coppery shimmers, each copy of her brain aware.

Reno displayed a connection web: sixteen signals scintillated, split, and recombined, faster than electrochemically limited thought.

Was this Zero's solution to the bottleneck of the human mind?

The Safa next to Reno stirred. Her blue eyes opened and stared at Reno. Her bow-shaped lips parted in a smile, then she froze at the image of her fifteen sister selves.

"Take it easy," Reno said. He took her arm and gingerly helped her sit. "There's a lot to explain."

The other Safas tossed and turned, then simultaneously awoke.

"There is no need to," Safa said. She ran her hand over her stubbled head and scratched. "I believe we understand."

" 'I'?" Jack asked. "Or 'we'? Which are you?"

The Safas got up and looked at each other.

"Neither pronoun seems to properly apply," she answered. "We possess a unique state of consciousness."

One Safa laced her slender arm through Reno's. Another went to Panda and smoothed the hair from her forehead. A Safa opened the neuroanatomy database, spoke in Arabic with the Safa near Panda. A pair of Safas went into the cargo bay. Three Safas opened the outer hatch of the shuttle; warm sunlight spilled in, and they strolled outside. A solitary Safa bowed and prayed. A group of Safas opened different sections of the code linking their collective minds—began to alter it in run-time mode.

"Wait," Jack said—turning to the Safas surrounding him. "Maybe *you* understand what's going on, but I'm not sure I do."

Safa came to Jack and sat on the couch next to him. "We act as one," she said. "I have examined the procedure. The splitting and isolation protocols are a brilliant idea, Jack."

"What do you feel?"

She looked up and her eyes brightened. "Everything

from my sixteen selves. No confusion. I am here. I am outside. All. One.''

Jack remembered what it was like, understanding how all the pieces of the puzzle fit together at once. For a fraction of a second, he had crystal clarity. Stability.

But that was the result of combining the signals from four segmented brain sections. Not sixteen. And not in separate bodies.

''About Zero . . .'' Jack said.

A frown creased Safa's face. ''He is desperate to find a cure. Portions of Zero understand how out of control his experiment has become. He is consumed by guilt.'' She sighed. ''And alone now, too. He took radical approaches before he came to us . . . took terrible risks with his own people. Methods inspired by madness.'' She shuddered.

''I think I saw one of his attempts. Multiple bodies lumped together?''

''Yes,'' Safa whispered. ''May Allah have mercy on their souls.''

''What did Zero do to you?''

She hesitated and looked away. ''Zero accelerated the change in me. He believed his enzyme stabilized at sixteen segments.''

She was keeping something from Jack. What?

One Safa whispered to Reno; three clustered around Panda; others peered into windows brimming with code.

Jack went to Panda and the Safas attending her. There was an open link to the deep subconscious blocks preventing interface with the brain stem.

''What's that for?''

A Safa turned and told him, ''I am inducing coma. It will slow the separation of her mind.''

''You can't—''

''Let her, Jack.'' Panda reached out and wrapped her tiny hand around his finger. ''Sleep. Gain time. To think. Trust.''

Trust had never come easily for Jack. Was this thing really Safa? Was she sane? ''This coma won't hurt her?''

''A prolonged coma would cause damage,'' Safa said, ''but that is better than the torture she is experiencing, I assure you." She set her hand consolingly upon Jack's. "She will only sleep until we write a program to align her fourfold thinking. Perhaps test the robustness of this new distributive network as well. A few minutes. No more."

The colors splashing across Panda's neural matrices bleached and faded . . . save a shivering patch of red in the core of her mind. Panda's body relaxed, and she closed both eyes.

Safa lay Panda's arms across her chest.

Panda looked dead. Almost. The slightest inhalation filled her, then she exhaled.

Safa's face darkened. "My split selves," she said. "They are possible because we have been multiplexed by the gateway?"

"Yes."

"In a continuously operational mode?" She tapped open a link to the gateway code, entered a string of calculations, and connected to the electron reactors. "Check my math," she told the computer.

A PLEASURE, COLONEL AL QASEEM. WORKING. . . . .

"What's the problem?" Jack asked.

"This planet is the problem." She looked out the open hatch. "There are plants and animals—life everywhere. My other selves see them."

CALCULATIONS CONFIRMED scrolled across her window.

"Allah forgive me." She turned to Jack. "The gateway is designed to be used for near-instantaneous transport. The energy required to keep it *continuously* operating is tremendous."

In the back of his mind, Jack still held the strings of the gateway taut; he felt the flow of power through the device.

Safa took Jack gently by the shoulders. "Seventeen seconds have been stolen from this world's rotational period. There will be earthquakes and climatic shifts. Extinction. I will not allow this to continue."

Reno stopped talking to the Safa he was with—marched over to Jack. He glanced back to the other Safa and wrinkled his brow. "Sorry for leaving in the middle of that conversation,'' he told Safa, ''but I overheard. What's the matter?''

''This must end,'' she said and hugged Reno. ''I cannot benefit at the cost of this world. It is what Wheeler does. We must not be like him.''

Another Safa opened a link to her coma-inducing subroutine.

''I shall sleep.'' Safa reclined upon the couch.

''No,'' Reno said. ''There has to be another way.''

The Safa in Reno's arms whispered, ''You will find a safer power source. Then we will be together.'' She kissed him.

Reno held her a moment, then pushed her away. He looked at Jack. ''Don't let her do this.''

''She's right, Reno. You know it. If we continue, it buys her a few more minutes. Then we use up this planet's rotation, and we're stranded again.''

Jack severed the blue destination vectors, pinched the links to those other Safas closed.

One by one the Safas vanished.

The original Safa upon the passenger couch recited in Arabic, then spoke in English: ''May Allah protect us all.''

Jack ran the coma-inducing routine.

Safa closed her eyes. Her breathing deepened. Her EEG lines in the open window smoothed.

Reno watched until the pulses were nearly undetectable. He pounded the couch with his fist. ''We can't let her go. She's the only thing I have left.'' Reno's brown and blue eyes were set in a hard stare . . . and full of something Jack had never seen before in the old spy. Worry. ''I've done some rotten things in the past, Jack, but I want to change. I've got to change for her. Safa's my last chance.''

Jack held Reno's stare a moment. ''OK,'' he whispered. ''Anyone willing to kiss your ugly face deserves a break. We'll do it, somehow.''

Reno exhaled. ''Thanks, Jack-O. I'll owe you one.''

''You can give me a hand with the navigation system.'' Jack tapped open a plane of stars. ''We need to find something else that spins. Maybe we can burn a binary star system.''

"Now we're talking. I knew I could count on—" Reno's face drained of color; he stared past Jack. ". . . Company."

Jack turned.

The shadows around Panda became semisolid smoke: a black tie, the lapels of a wool suit, and the glint of obsidian eyes.

Wheeler materialized.

The flush of panic filled Jack. This time, though, he didn't freeze. He did the only thing he could think of. He checked his vacuum suit, then left the *Dutchman* and his friends behind—Jack ran.

Jack jumped backward to the pulsar, a black star barely visible against the void of space—caught the tail end of its radio emission; it ripped through his skull with inductive razors, blasting his mind apart, then he stepped—into orbit around the orange moon of Zero's world and down—to its surface: fields of ice and cracked rock salt.

Gravity, zero gravity, then gravity again; it was like he was on a roller coaster. It made Jack want to throw up.

Wheeler stood next to him, impatiently tapping an expensive eel-skin shoe.

Jack leapt to the gas giant two planets out, a ball of cream-colored swirls and lavender-ribbon typhoons. He had only a handful of coordinates calculated, only a few places with spinning masses to power his jumps.

And Wheeler knew all of them.

He stepped—

—one hundred kilometers over a world of solid nitrogen; its thick ghostly atmosphere tendrilling upward.

Wheeler floated by his side. "Come, come, Jack. There is no need for this."

Jack moved back to the system with a thousand comets chasing each other around a golden sun, then leapt—

—above the planet with liquid argon seas and methane snowcaps. Where a patchwork of roads and cities had once covered the surface, now there were only scars aglow with flickering blue radiation. Boreales danced around the magnetic poles and made Jack's head crackle with static.

"No," Jack whispered. "Not this world, too." He turned his head and precessed slightly in the microgravity.

Wheeler was here. His voice buzzed through Jack's helmet speaker: "An amazing people."

How many dead on that world? Millions? Billions? Wheeler had murdered them; it wasn't Jack's fault. Still . . . if Jack hadn't jumped to this system, hadn't found them, they'd be alive. Like the Earth had once been.

"They were cautious at first," Wheeler explained, "more so even than you, Jack. We thought they might have potential to join us. Alas, they traded all their science and saturated us with their hopes for a peaceful relationship. Their final mistake, however, was to reach out to others with their isotopic technologies."

"And you couldn't let that happen."

"No." Wheeler brushed lint off his cuff. "They had a wondrous low-temperature computer. It crystallizes and finds the best solution to—"

"I'm not interested," Jack said.

"Of course you are. You can use it to trade and gain more technology." Wheeler leaned closer. "What else could one want?"

"Why are you here?" Jack reached out and pushed off Wheeler—they accelerated away from each other. "I've still got twelve hours."

"You *had* twelve hours," Wheeler said as he receded. "I am shortening your leash, my boy." He wagged his finger at Jack. "So many jumps. So much mischief." His voice grew faint with the increasing distance between them. "And only a single brief conversation with Gersham. What have you accomplished?"

Wheeler disappeared—

—and reappeared beside Jack with a matching velocity. "Nothing."

"I'm close to a deal," Jack told him. "Gersham's going to show me how he stays hidden from you."

And hopefully, Gersham would show Jack how to hide as well . . . and Wheeler would never find him again.

" 'Close to a deal' is not sufficient, Jack. We grow impatient. Choose."

"Choose what?"

"Not 'what' . . ." Wheeler said and a sly smile crept over his face. " 'Whom.' Whom I shall kill."

"Wait a second." Jack grabbed on to Wheeler's shoulder, spun him so they were face-to-face. The maneuver sent them tumbling—stars and the planet surface below spun.

"We had an agreement. I still have time."

"Our deal stands," Wheeler said. He flattened his hand against an invisible wall—halted their gyration. "Time, however, is a relative thing. Travel at near light speed and time slows for the traveler. An hour is one-twenty-fourth of an Earth day, but on this world"—he gestured to the planet beneath them—"it was four times shorter. So you see, Jack, days, hours . . . or forever. Time is whatever I want it to be."

Jack wished he could strangle Wheeler. Wished that would do any good. All he could do was float helplessly.

"I'll remember," Jack muttered, "to use more precise language next time I bargain with the devil."

Wheeler laughed. "Your flattery does not change facts. You must choose."

"I won't. I've helped you kill enough people."

"I do not understand the difficulty. You must only pick one." Wheeler held up his bare hand, counted on his fingers. "Panda. Reno. Kamal. Safa." A perfectly manicured thumb appeared on either side of his palm. "Or your ex-business associates, Isabel and Zero."

Wheeler had left out DeMitri and Bruner. He had accurate information on who was and who wasn't a friend. And who Jack was doing business with. Had Wheeler listened in on his isotope communications?

"Me," Jack said. "If someone has to get erased, then pick me."

Wheeler winced. "Please, Jack, my tolerance for altruism is extremely limited." He sighed. "I see this is too difficult for you. I shall choose for you . . . Miss Panda."

"No!" Jack blurted. "Take Zero. I pick Zero."

His heart turned cold. He wanted to take it back, but

not in exchange for Panda. He hated himself, yet he kept his mouth shut.

"You see?" Wheeler cooed. "That was not impossible. There is hope for you yet, my boy." Wheeler pointed into the night and a blue vector stretched from his six fingertips. "He is here—"

Blue-white light blinded Jack and pressure squeezed his body. Green lights on his helmet's display told him he was surrounded by an atmosphere. Breathable.

He blinked and found himself at the base of Coit Tower. Alone.

Why had Wheeler sent him here? To watch him squirm while Zero got murdered?

Jack interfaced with his gateway; there was still rotation left on this world to jump away. Good. Maybe he could get to Zero and warn him. Jack drew his Hautger SK . . . in case Zero wasn't in the mood for receiving guests, then circled the tower.

Upon the entrance steps sat Zero, arms hugging his legs, his gateway cradled against his chest. "I knew you would return, Jack," he whispered. "Heroes always confront the villains before the end of the drama."

There were no illusions. No multiple arms and legs or butterflies. Zero almost seemed sane. His dark eyes were dull with fatigue, and his beard matted to his face.

"I came to warn you," Jack said and slowly holstered his gun.

"A warning?" Zero sighed. "It is too late for that. There is always at least one death in the last act of a tragedy. Is it you who will kill me?" He managed a slight smile. "I could almost bear that, my friend."

"Not me." Jack sat next to Zero. The gene witch stank of a week's worth of sweat, worse than the odor wafting from the surrounding swamp. "Wheeler's targeted you. You've got to run—hide." Jack gritted his teeth and pounded his fist on the concrete step. "That's no good, either. Wheeler will know the coordinates of every jump you make. There's nowhere to hide."

"Indeed?" Zero stroked his ragged beard, thinking.

Jack noticed bloodstains splattered around the courtyard. From the Zeros they had shot? What had happened to them all?

Zero stood. ''Will Wheeler destroy this world as he did the Earth?'' He quickly glanced to either side of the tower, and a grin crept over his face. ''Or is there yet a way out?''

Static played along Jack's skin and tickled the hair on the back of his neck.

The sky rumbled. Overhead, clouds evaporated. The orange moon of Zero's world was larger.

And it swelled as Jack watched.

That was how Wheeler was going to execute Zero. No simple teleportation or asphyxiation. Something far more grandiose.

The moon was falling from the sky.

Zero watched it for a moment, then asked, ''Do you think Wheeler is God?''

''No.'' Jack tore his gaze off the moon. ''He's not the devil, either. Just morally bankrupt.''

''Then he is not all-knowing. He can make mistakes?''

''Yes,'' Jack admitted. ''In theory, at least . . . but I haven't seen him make any yet. Look, Zero, I didn't come to discuss theology. Time's running out. I want to know what you did to us. No, forget that. Just tell me how to undo it.''

Zero ran to the base of the stairs. Even at the lower elevation, he appeared taller than Jack—for an instant, he looked like the old Zero, straight and proud and devout.

''There is no going backward,'' he told Jack. ''Not now. Our only hope lies forward. Evolve or perish. Adapt or be consumed.''

Zero turned and pointed up the wall of Coit Tower. ''Do you see it, Jack?''

Jack squinted.

There, cast in the concrete, was a circle. Inside it was a carved bird of prey, crown upon its head, wings spread wide, and flames licking its talons.

''The phoenix,'' Zero said. ''Put there because San

Francisco rebuilt after its Great Fire. And the city was more magnificent than before.''

''When you're dead, Zero, you're not going to burst into flames and come back to life.''

Jack looked up. The moon filled a third of the sky; the atmosphere rippled about its horizons. The sun eclipsed and lightning striped the shadows.

''Wheeler is just a businessman.'' Zero danced a jig upon the steps. He stopped and stared at Jack. ''He steals technology. He does not create it.''

''What's your point, Zero? We're businessmen, too.''

''We are more. We are human. Fragile and weak, but also versatile and full of curiosity. And we are better than Wheeler. Innovators. Creators.''

The moon was an orange circle that filled half the sky. Hypnotic.

When Jack tore his gaze away, there were two dozen Zeros standing around the tower.

The one closest whispered, ''We are escaping. I suggest you retreat as well.''

They had to be diffracted copies—like Jack had made of Safa. But unlike Safa, these Zeros hadn't meshed their thoughts together. They were insanity multiplied.

The Zeros turned their backs to the tower and walked, waded, and swam into the swamp.

Jack grabbed the nearest. ''You can't get away from that—'' He pointed at the moon.

The sky was all orange salt flats and craters; the brim of the horizon was a wavering band of blue flame.

Zero shrugged off Jack's hand. He continued to stride away from the tower. ''I *can* escape. You are the mathematician. Why do you not comprehend?''

Jack fixed the center of world beneath him with a yellow vector, tagged himself with a red.

''Run,'' he told Zero. ''Try. Wheeler may not be able to follow you forever.''

Winds whipped and made the air crackle. Vines and flowers smoldered. Bits of gravel pelted Jack, stinging him through the skin of his vacuum suit.

Zero stopped. He shouted over the gale, ''We have

aligned ourselves!'' He grabbed Jack's hand. ''Wheeler will not find me, but he can find you.'' He drew Jack close. ''I cannot live much longer . . . but you might live forever.''

''I don't understand.''

''You will. You must!'' Zero looked up. ''Hurry. Go!''

There was no sky—just orange—heating to red. The wind screamed and thundered and shattered. Leaves and branches ignited; water boiled. The earth trembled.

Jack oriented the gateway's blue vector into orbit. Catapulted away.

Zero's hand dissolved within his.

As a trillion tons of molten rock slammed into the planet.

SECTION FOUR
HUMANS

16

JACK OF DIAMONDS

Jack was back at work.

He set up a virtual connection with Gersham. This time, however, Jack wedged his own tile into Gersham's checkerboard pattern, a square of blue marble encrusted with fossil snails and flecks of mica. He wanted control over at least one space on the gameboard.

Someone had tried to tap Jack last time he was here: Gersham or another eavesdropper. The snail fossils in Jack's tile were worming memory explorers. The flecks of mica were grounding counterprobes. If anyone tried to crack his mind again, they'd get a fight.

The virtual sky was cloudless, full of stars and a dozen moons shaded silver and lilac.

How could he be here? He should be by Panda's side. He should have confessed to someone that Zero had been murdered . . . and that Jack shared the blame.

Jack knew how Wheeler operated—he should have guessed Wheeler would find a way to pull his strings.

He exhaled. He couldn't change the past. He was barely in control of the present.

And as far as the future was concerned, Jack knew only one thing: Wheeler would kill again. Next time Jack wouldn't have the luxury of choice. Next time it could be Panda on the top of Wheeler's execution list.

So business first.

Jack waited for Gersham to connect. His implant caught whispers and fleeting images in the polished checkerboard. Both colors were occupied this time. The white spaces roiled with misty wraiths, silver robotic faces that stared back at him, and alkaline salt flats upon which appeared footprints. In the black tiles were inky waters, spaces brimming with midnight and blinking charcoal eyes, and shadows that fluttered about a single candle.

Not every square was full, however. The four surrounding Jack's tile were curiously empty.

"Gersham?" he whispered.

Gersham appeared, one Oxford shoe standing in a vacant white square, the other in an empty black. His tuxedo strobed then settled into a checkered pattern. He wore a copy of Jack's face with a neat crew cut. He smelled of expensive cologne.

"Welcome, Jack," he said, and extended a hand.

Jack crossed his arms. "Your information on our business customs is out of date. Humans don't shake hands anymore."

As one of the last humans, Jack figured whatever he wanted was human custom. And Jack was in a lousy mood. He didn't want to touch anyone—especially in a bubble where touch transmitted subconscious data.

Gersham retracted his hand.

"I want to take you up on your offer for sanctuary," Jack told him.

Gersham smiled. "Excellent." His grin widened past his ears, farther than physically possible.

All those teeth gave Jack the creeps. "You mentioned details we had to work out?"

"We will hide your race from Wheeler." Gersham's smile reabsorbed into his face as he nonchalantly added, "For a price."

Jack's insides turned cold and hard. This catch wasn't a complete surprise, but it was a disappointment. He switched mental gears: unease solidified into paranoia and reinforced his mental defenses.

"What do you want?" Jack asked.

Gersham leaned forward. He spread his fingertips along

the invisible plane that separated their tiles. The air pressure increased. The edges of Jack's thoughts tickled, and he heard beckoning whispers.

Why the obvious probe? A test of Jack's reactions? Maybe Gersham expected Jack to roll over and submit his mind for inspection?

When hell froze over.

Jack reached into his blue marble tile and drew out asbestos threads that led to grounding links, flicked their needlelike ends at Gersham's outstretched hand—pierced his flesh. Waves of void flowed though the connection; enough nothingness to wipe clean any man's mind.

Gersham inhaled sharply and stepped back.

"From time to time," Gersham casually said and rubbed his palm, "we will require your communications expertise."

Jack didn't get it. If Gersham was as advanced as Wheeler, why bother with a probe? Why not blast through Jack's countermeasures? Maybe Gersham didn't fully understand the interface. Maybe he thought blackhacking was just another game like Jack's checkers.

" 'Time to time' is vague," Jack said. "How often? With whom?"

Gersham pinched together his thumb and forefinger. They melded into a tiny ring of flesh. He reached through the joined digits with his other thumb and forefinger, welded them into a second circle. "You will not find the specifics of our agreement displeasing."

Jack wasn't sure what that metaphor meant, but whatever it was, it made his stomach twist into a knot.

"We want you to negotiate with other species for us."

"Trades of technology?"

"Technology, philosophy, and art," Gersham replied. "Many species cannot yet comprehend our advanced society. We attempt to accelerate them to our level at a reasonable pace."

Jack understood why Wheeler wanted Gersham so badly. His kind of fair dealing gave other civilizations a chance to survive; it could potentially undercut Wheeler's business. That was good.

Too good, Jack suspected, to be true.

"All our customers are satisfied," Gersham said. "We guarantee it." He pulled his linked fingers apart; they stretched like taffy, then re-formed.

"But after you've guaranteed this satisfaction . . . you leave your customers alive?" Jack asked. "The dead don't get much of a chance to complain."

Gersham smoothed the lapels of his checkered tuxedo. "Of course, Jack." He hesitated—a heartbeat. "We kill no one."

That split-second vacillation told more than any probe could. Gersham made a mistake using Jack's features; he knew his own deadpan poker face when he saw it.

Gersham gestured to the empty squares next to Jack's tile. "We have prepared a space for you."

Jack wasn't about to step into any of Gersham's deals. Not after he had just lied to Jack. But how else to get the information Wheeler wanted?

"I'd like to have a look first," Jack said.

"By all means," Gersham said.

Jack released his probes, let them ooze into the cracks between the empty tiles, then into the occupied spaces. Their tendrils reached, groping blind, searching for—and finding—a connection.

White-hot pokers seared one occupant's flesh; silken cords bound another's limbs, twisted and dislocated its bones; ice crystallized around the ghostly figures in a third tile and squeezed them until they squealed. The black spaces were no better: aged bones rattled in iron manacles and inky marshes enveloped entire cities.

Jack shared their pain; waves of agony and the desire for suicide filled him. Panic and despair. And guilt . . . because the things in the squares were doing to others what had been done to them: technologies plundered, races enslaved, and worlds destroyed.

Wheeler had said Gersham didn't like to eliminate his customers. That appeared to be true. He just held them, tortured them, and made them his middlemen who could be snuffed to cover his tracks, if needed.

It was the only way it made sense.

How else could Gersham trade without Wheeler catching him? It wasn't an advanced alien technology hiding Gersham. It was layers of go-betweens and pawns.

The things in the squares cried for help and scratched at the edges of their cells.

Jack couldn't watch anymore. He cut the connection. "No . . . not yet."

Gersham wrinkled his brow. "I thought we understood one another, Jack. We have studied Earth's broadcasts. Humans sell their lives for material wealth—and for the privilege and status of working. Slavery is second nature to your species. This, combined with your service to Wheeler, makes your resume superlative."

How far from the truth were Gersham's conclusions? Humans worked for credit that was spent and overspent almost immediately. Maybe they all had been slaves.

But not Jack. He was getting out of this deal—and fast.

"There's one other human lost out there," Jack said. "Isabel. I thought I could leave without her, but I can't."

He could. Isabel was, however, the most convenient excuse.

Gersham paced in a circle around Jack's blue space. "Your loyalty is admirable. I will take the others while you—"

"Thanks," Jack replied, "but I'll need their help to find her."

"I see." Gersham narrowed his hazel eyes to slits. "But Wheeler is near, is he not? We should remain in close contact."

Close? Close, as in crushed between Wheeler and Gersham—two options that made a rock and a hard place look like whipped cream and butter.

"I'll call you as soon as I'm ready," Jack said. Which would be precisely never.

Jack stood on the suregrip deck of the *Dutchman*. A film of static clung to his skin, along with the phantom residue of synthetic pleasure that sent shivers down his spine—leftovers from his quick disconnect.

Reno bent over an open window, watching a replay of

Jack's conversation. "Looks like you picked another great business partner." He tapped the link shut.

Jack went to the couch where Panda lay. She breathed deeply in her sleep. Her eyelid tattoos shimmered silver beneath her bangs. He took her hand; it was ice-cold.

He glanced back to Reno. "You're the one who's worked with big players before. What would you do if Wheeler and Gersham were America and China?"

"Double-cross Gersham," Reno said without hesitation. "Wheeler's got our location . . . and our number."

"That won't work," Jack said. "We're nothing but bait to Wheeler. Once we've delivered Gersham, we'd be middlemen who knew too much. Would you keep us around?"

"No." Reno frowned and rubbed his jaw. "I wouldn't."

"I don't even know if we *can* cross Gersham. To learn what Wheeler wants to know, I'd have to become part of his middleman network. Under his offer of 'sanctuary,' you and Safa and Panda would be hostages . . . or worse."

Reno went to the hatch and inhaled the fresh air of their new world.

The sun rose over the horizon and illuminated the three rings in the sky, turned them silver-green and amber and pink.

Reno lit up a cigarette. He puffed once. "OK, Jack, you're the smart guy. What do *you* think we should do?"

Jack brushed Panda's bangs from her face. He tapped open her EEG—full of ripples and the muted colors. Maybe Jack hadn't done Panda such a big favor by saving her from the end of the world. Not if it only prolonged her suffering.

He turned back to Reno. "I'm fresh out of ideas."

Reno sighed and went to Safa. He knelt next to her.

There was tenderness in Reno's eyes; Jack would have never guessed he could have been so soft-hearted with anyone or that he could act so human. "What happened between you two on the moon?"

Reno didn't say anything for a minute, then, "We were realistic. You and Panda were together. There aren't many permutations left. . . . Do I have to draw you a diagram?"

"You don't even know her."

"Don't I?" Reno's blue eye stared deep into Jack, sent a transmission of a wailing call to noontime prayers, the scent of sandalwood incense, the sandy texture of the stone floors where she and Zero had bowed toward Mecca.

"You exchanged memories. So what?"

"A full exchange," Reno said. He sighed and examined her face. "You know she could have had anything? Palaces, land, her own private army? She left all that money and power behind to escape an arranged marriage. You know what kind of guts it takes to turn your back on centuries of tradition?"

Jack wondered what Safa had seen in Reno to offer him so much of herself. And what had convinced Reno to let down his psychological barriers?

"But what's the use?" Reno stood and took a step closer to Jack. "I've been in jams before, but nothing like this. We can't double-cross either side without getting aced." He took a drag off his cigarette. "The gateways are bugged, so there's nowhere to hide."

Jack checked Safa's vital signs. Stable.

"She was smarter in the multiplexed state," Jack said. "So was I. Seventeen milliseconds and I understood everything, figured out where Zero was." He asked Reno, "Did you find any rotational power sources?"

"Yeah." Reno tapped open a link to the navigation database. "While you were with Gersham, I tracked down a dozen binary stars. Got a few beauties. Big separation distances. We can jump to the middle and burn their rotation to get Safa back. . . . Maybe if she's as smart as you think, she can find us a way out of this."

Jack traced a path to the binary system with his right hand.

His left hand, however, had its own ideas. It tapped open a second window, a link to the isotopic frequency suite—assembled bits of wriggling lines.

Jack hadn't wanted to do that. He willed it to stop.

The left hand opened another window and gateway code scrolled across the surface.

"What the . . . ?"

His vision split. A sledgehammer hit him in the fore-head, exploded his thoughts in a hundred directions. Right and left eyes blurred and focused, then felt like they were straining out of their sockets. Jack saw stars and lines of math-code and the faces of Reno and Safa and Panda. His body convulsed. Panic and guilt and desire mixed in his mind. He screamed—tried to say a dozen things at once.

Jack fell through blackness. Vertigo stretched space and time; minutes and hours and eons, light-years . . . and the two meters it took to crash headfirst upon the floor.

A quiet moment. No thoughts.

Reno's face resolved in Jack's good eye.

"You're back," Reno said and flashed a quick smile of gold teeth. "Good. Thought I'd have to put you out of your misery."

Jack had been laid on the couch between Panda and Safa. The synthetic leather contoured to his back and warmed him.

"It's starting," Jack whispered. "The same loss of control that happened to Panda."

Reno helped him sit up. "Looks that way."

"How long was I out?"

"Two minutes," Reno said. "Don't worry about that. Just rest."

"No time to rest." Jack's pulse pounded through his temples, hammered nails into his head, then subsided. "The way Wheeler's keeping time, the twelve hours we've got left might only be twelve minutes."

Ten windows rotated slowly in the air. Links Jack must have opened just before his seizure. Other parts of his segmenting mind at work? There was the navigation database, bubble logs, gateway code, the theoretical math he had traded an alien race for, and isotopic communications.

"Forget that stuff." Reno pulled him away. "Let's get to that binary star and get Safa pieced together."

"No." Jack wrenched his arm from Reno's grasp. "Not Safa."

"You bet we're getting Safa back." Reno's hand dropped to his holstered gun.

"Listen to me," Jack whispered. "Safa can help us.

You're right. But there's someone who can help us more. That's what I think the other parts of my mind were trying to tell me.''

Reno crossed his arms. "Who?"

"Someone who already understands the gateway. Someone who understands a lot more about it than they've let on."

Reno took a step closer. "I got a feeling I'm not going to like this."

"You're not going to," Jack said. "Neither am I."

Jack got a solid lock on to her frequencies; an interface appeared, but no Isabel.

He searched the parlor of her chateau, the patio, the opulent bedrooms—even under her canopy bed. Dust coated the polished walnut panels; her paintings had been slashed out of their gilt frames; the windows were busted out. The place was abandoned.

He tried the garden next, wandered past beds of uprooted lavender and rows of felled lilac trees; he jumped over bare rose hedges, then jogged across a lawn overgrown with crabgrass to the river.

Along the riverbank, in the rippling shade of the oak canopy, sat Isabel.

She wore her black business suit, the pant legs cut off at the knees. Surrounding her were masterpieces—Picassos and Warhols—all arranged in the mud. She bent over them, her hands moving back and forth . . . coloring with crayons.

"Busy?" Jack asked her.

"Very," Isabel answered without looking up. She paused to push dirty locks of her red hair behind an ear. "Very busy. Hello and goodbye, Jack."

Her right hand made wide circles, outlining in orange the lily pads of Monet's *Water Lilies*. With her left hand, she filled in a brick-red diamond in the corner of a van Gogh self-portrait. "Jack of Diamonds," she whispered to it. "Jack of Stars."

"Too busy for business?" he asked. "A trade?"

Isabel's right eye flicked up and scrutinized him; it was

bloodshot and ringed by circles of fatigue. "I'm listening," she said and went back to her coloring. "Say what you came to and go. We have too much work to do to waste time with pleasantries."

"I can see that," Jack muttered. Had she lost her mind, too? Was it an act to throw Jack? Or some elaborate metaphor for him to unravel?

He picked his way closer to her—stopped when he saw Leonardo da Vinci's *Narcissus*. The boy in the painting watched his reflection in a raised basin of water. It reminded Jack of Kamal's moon in the bowl: Jack's mirror image in the bowl, in the water, and scattered upon a puddle on the command-center floor. Jack shook off the memory. He gingerly rolled the canvas up and sat cross-legged next to Isabel.

"I want to know how you deflected gateway signals."

"I'm sure you do," Isabel said.

Water welled from Monet's impressionistic pond and the basin in the da Vinci, it trickled off the canvases, made liquid ribbons down to the riverbank.

"Not for free," Jack said. "I have something you'll want very much in trade."

She snapped the tip of her red crayon. "The only thing I want from you, Jack, is the alien set of frequencies. The one Wheeler gave to you."

Isabel's business instincts were intact. That was a good sign. Or maybe they were embedded in every cell of her fragmented mind.

"I've got something better than that." Jack leaned closer and whispered. "I've got a cure for Zero's series-eight enzyme."

Isabel picked wax from under her fingernails, then looked up at Jack. "You have tested this supposed cure on yourself?"

"Yes."

That wasn't a lie. He had. And it had worked, too . . . for seventeen milliseconds.

"Then I shall try it," she said. "If it works, I'll give you what you want."

"I need your end of the trade first."

"You should trust me," Isabel cooed.

Jack almost laughed—stopped himself. "I need your technology so I can save us from Wheeler."

Isabel smirked; she had blue and green speckles of crayon on her teeth. "You overestimate its usefulness. Wheeler has our gateways tapped. He still knows every move we make."

"You've been listening to his transmissions?"

"Naturally. Wheeler wants us to. Why else would he use my frequencies to contact you?" She took her red crayon and drew a line across her slender neck. "It is to let the hostages know they have a knife at their throats."

Jack reached out and wiped away her metaphor. "Don't. I've seen enough death for a hundred lifetimes."

She peeled the wrapper off the end of her crayon and sharpened the tip with her fingernail. "I am interested. But I want your cure first. Not that I don't trust you, Jack—but I don't."

"Tell me where you are," Jack said. "I'll set it up."

Isabel broke her crayon and threw it at Jack. "Is that what this is? A trick to reveal my location? How insane do you think I am?"

Jack stood. "When you can't think straight enough to breathe or make your heart beat, then give me a call . . . if you can."

He let their connection dissolve; he sensed the *Dutchman*'s silent counterinductive hull around him— halted.

He refreshed their interface. He couldn't leave. There was no time for mistrust.

Jack turned back to her.

He reached out with his mind, felt waxy colors just under her surface: the gritty texture of burnt ocher, the metallic smoothness of electric blue, and cool mint green—a kaleidoscope of her thoughts.

"If you won't trust me," Jack said, "then I'll have to trust you." He hesitated, then spat the words out before he changed his mind: "I'll tell you where I am. You come to me."

Both of Isabel's emerald eyes locked on to his. "Are you serious?"

They had trusted one another a lifetime ago, but then Isabel had double-crossed him in a grab for power and had sold him out to the NSO. He hadn't exactly done her any favors lately, either. Trust wasn't an option for them—but it had to be if they were going to survive Wheeler.

Jack broke eye contact before she drew him in deeper. He lifted the edge of a Georgia O'Keeffe, bones and stones and wildflowers, and flipped it over. On the back of the canvas he took a black crayon and traced a map, downloading his coordinates.

She glanced at it. "A binary star?" One eyebrow arched slightly. "I shall dress for the occasion."

Isabel went back to coloring. She started on Warhol's *Marilyn Diptych,* changing all the Marilyn Monroes from blondes to redheads. "If this is another trick, it will be your last, Jack."

"You're right, Isabel. If this doesn't work, I'll be dead."

Jack took the black crayon and drew a doorway in the air. He stepped through, disconnecting.

The *Dutchman* resolved around him.

Jack's stomach turned. He floated, weightless.

Reno must have jumped them to the binary star while Jack had spoken with Isabel.

He closed his eyes, tried to orient himself—not an easy thing to do when distance and the state of reality could be shifted in a heartbeat.

Light from the cockpit windows flooded into the bridge: blue sunlight on the stern and red on the port; they mixed into a diffuse lavender illumination.

He pushed off the hull and drifted aft to the passenger section.

Reno had his back to him, looking out the portal. "We going to use all this energy? Patch Safa back together, maybe?" he asked. "Or are we going to sit here and cook between two stars?"

"Isabel is coming."

"I saw that," Reno muttered. "Masterful bargaining

technique. Give away our location for free. Why didn't you just give her the cure while you're at it?''

"I plan to. Without a clear head, she can't explain how she blocks gateway signals.''

"Look, Jack, I hate to point this out, but you skipped out on her last deal.'' Reno tapped the wall and drifted to Jack, latched on to him. "She's probably going to bargain in good faith about as much as I want to kiss you.'' He pushed away. "Which ain't much.''

"What do you want me to do?''

"Double-cross her,'' Reno said. "Do it to her—before she does you.'' He glanced at Panda and Safa. "Do it for them.''

"I'm not doing any more double—''

Static rippled through Jack's head, a disturbance in the bubble system. He turned.

Isabel hovered next to the cargo bay airlock. She wore a silver vacuum suit and helmet. Her right glove was curled into a fist, revealing four tubes welded upon her knuckles—the tips of tiny missiles poking out the ends.

"So you did not lie,'' she said. "You even have an atmosphere for me to breathe. How thoughtful.''

"You can lower your weapon,'' Jack said. "No one's going to hurt you.''

She laughed.

How fractured was her mind? She had seemed insane a moment ago. But maybe like Zero . . . like himself, she had moments of lucidity.

Isabel looked Reno over. "I don't think we've been introduced.''

"This is Reno,'' Jack said. "Reno, this is Isabel Mirabeau.''

"Your infamous uncle?'' she asked. A smile rippled upon her lips. "The Chinese spy? The man who provided us with start-up capital so long ago?'' She nodded to Reno. "A pleasure to finally meet you.''

Reno smiled back. "You'll pardon me if I don't shake.''

"I prefer you stay where you are,'' she told him. "Otherwise, I will blow you to bits.'' Her smile didn't waver. Then to Jack she demanded, "Show us your cure.''

Jack opened a link, a clear pane of glass, upon which math-code scrawled. He nudged it to Isabel; the rectangle rotated through the air, and she gingerly caught the edge.

Her left eye glanced at the program. "This aligns four brain patterns. How can four different people think as one? It solves none of the cerebral fragmentation. You, Jack, are obviously too infected to be rational. You have wasted our time."

A yellow arrow flickered from Isabel's free hand.

"Don't jump," Jack said. "The signals are from the same person. I diffractively split a composite wavefunction, then use the gateway to make copies of a person."

She opened her mouth, started to say something—halted. Isabel thought a moment, then said, "Prove it."

"Let me use your gateway. I'll show you."

"Give you control over my means of escape? I think not."

"Then I'll use mine." Jack reached for his gateway.

Reno grabbed his hand. "Let's see how Isabel scatters those gateway signals first," he whispered. "What's to stop her from skipping out once she has *our* secret?"

"Nothing," she replied. "You'll have to trust me. Haven't *I* always kept my part in our past deals?" From her belt, she removed a sugar-cube-sized data block and held it in her outstretched palm. "The information is yours after I am convinced the cure works."

Jack pulled his hand from Reno's. He touched the gateway and interfaced. He tagged Isabel with a red arrow. The yellow he cast into the binary star's center of rotation.

Power roared and rushed through him, into the sphere, made it glow and shimmer. Jack frayed the blue destination vector arrow into three components.

Three Isabels appeared next to the original.

The four of them reached out to each other, hesitated, and retracted their hands. "A bubble-induced illusion," they simultaneously said. "I feel no different."

"Wait." Jack engaged the program to align her thoughts.

They blinked. "Yes," they together murmured.

They broke synchronization—one Isabel peered into the

window of code and examined the software patching her mind; one stepped up to Reno and raised her glove, aimed the tiny missiles at his midsection; the third Isabel pushed herself aft into the cargo hold; and the last floated to Jack.

"I want to examine your communication logs," she told Jack, "see exactly what Wheeler said. The other alien as well." She jerked her left hand, made sure he saw the tips of the missiles embedded in her knuckle launchers—gold and silver and blue and green.

Jack wasn't about to argue with a weapon pointed at him. He traced a rectangle, let it solidify to burnished brass, and downloaded the files.

"Not much to show," he said. "Wheeler appeared physically, so there are no logs of him. There are, however, two recordings of my conversations with the other alien, Gersham."

Isabel watched Gersham's offer and Jack's discovery of its sticky conditions. She pressed her lips into a white line when she saw the things in the checkerboard squares.

Another Isabel drifted between Panda and Safa, observed their vital signs, then remarked, "Quite the harem you have collected." She traced the edge of Safa's strong jaw with her index finger.

Reno reached forward. "Get your hands off her."

The Isabel in front of Reno braced against an acceleration couch and shoved her fist into his stomach—propelled him backward. "Don't," she hissed.

"You should have remained with me," the Isabel near Jack said. "We made a good team."

"I remember your 'teamwork' in Amsterdam." Jack glared at her. "You tried to have me assassinated."

The Isabel examining the software patch hit the download icon.

"Hey," Reno shouted. "What about *your* part of the deal?"

"I may yet keep it, Mr. Reno. Do not push your luck."

" 'Luck,' huh?" He shot a glance to Jack.

Out of Jack's dead left eye, the one that only saw virtual spaces, he saw the angles of Reno's charcoal-black stealth suit undulate. What was the old spy up to?

"Your technique might give us a chance against Wheeler," Jack said. "We've got to move fast. He's already killed Zero."

Isabel slowly brought her fingertip to her lower lip and tapped it, thinking. "Really? When?"

"Half an hour ago."

"Interesting," she mused, "because I spoke to Zero just before your call."

"That's not possible."

"Then it must be his ghost who has gone to discuss philosophy with the Buddhist monk you left in the moon."

But Jack had been with Zero until the last moment. Even if Zero had jumped away, Wheeler would have tracked him. Wheeler didn't make idle threats.

What did Isabel gain by lying?

The Isabel by the window of code said, "Congratulations, Jack. Your solution is crude, but it does seem to work."

"And your block for gateway signals?" he asked.

The Isabels next to Jack and Reno pushed away, drifted backward to the center of the shuttle. "There is more we can learn from one another," she said. "Much more, I fear, than you are willing to share, Jack. At least, willingly."

Every Isabel bristled with red arrows; they tagged Jack.

Jack fumbled with his gateway.

Isabel cast a blue vector out into the stars—

The lights went dead. Open links to Jack's code and to the recorded conversations flickered and disappeared. Bubble signals faded.

"No!" the Isabels cried.

Helmet lights automatically flicked on, Jack's and four sets from the Isabels—casting crazy shadows that leapt and danced as she clutched her head. One Isabel dropped her data cube, another let the missiles fall out of their launchers.

Jack severed the lines from his gateway; three Isabels winked off.

The Isabel remaining tagged herself with a red arrow, a blue—and vanished.

The overhead fluorescent lights flickered back on.

Reno stood three meters away from where Jack thought he had been . . . next to the power panel.

"How did you move so fast?"

"I didn't," Reno replied. "In fact, I moved real slow. Made a doppelganger and while Isabel was busy watching it, I killed the juice . . . which killed the network balancing her thoughts."

"I'm glad you're on my side. Thanks, Reno." Jack went to where Isabel had been, grabbed the data cube spinning in midair.

"That's not all she left." Reno held up one of her dropped missiles: a gold crayon.

Jack took it and snapped it in half. "Crazy or not, she's still smart enough to bluff us."

"We better move," Reno said. "She knows where we are."

Jack interfaced with the gateway.

"Where to?" Reno asked. "Another binary star?"

"No," Jack said. "I have to find the only one who has ever gotten away from Wheeler. We've got a ghost to chase."

The speckled silver moon hung on Jack's right. On his left, the Earth floated, covered with tendril clouds and hurricanes and lightning storms. Looking at the planet made Jack homesick for the roar of ocean and the scent of unrecycled air.

He settled into the copilot's seat. "Get a reading on the moon's orbit," he told Reno. "It should have enough rotation around the Earth for us to jump to the base and back."

"This must be wrong." Reno watched the display crawl with numbers.

Jack leaned over to get a look: the moon spun on its axis.

Reno squinted at the figures. "The moon has a nonsymmetrical core. That's why it always kept one face to the Earth. It's phase-locked. A couple of orbital passes and it could have stolen energy from the Earth. And maybe started spinning by itself?"

Jack flicked the sensors to the Earth. It rotated now as well. A period of a hundred hours. No phase lock with the moon had caused that. What then? Or, more importantly, who did it? And how?

Reno pushed himself out of the pilot's seat. "Forget the planets." He held out his hand. "Let's see that data cube of Isabel's."

Jack drifted out of his seat. "We find Zero first. If he's

here, alive, then he knows how to bypass Wheeler's wiretap."

"So Isabel said." Reno closed his open hand into a fist. "Even if he knows something, getting him to tell us is another story. I say work with what we've got."

He might be right, but Jack couldn't stop thinking about Zero. He had stayed on his planet until its moon impacted. Jack was sure. How had he escaped?

Reno pushed off the wall and latched on to Jack. "Isabel used her technique to keep us from jumping on top of her. Maybe it'll work on Wheeler, too."

Jack tried to untangle himself from Reno, but the old spy had a vise grip.

Reno used his free hand to tap Jack in the center of his chest. "Or better still, Jack-O, we put Safa back together. Let her figure a way out of this."

"I want Safa back as much as you do," Jack said, "but I've got a hunch that Zero's our ticket out of this jam. We need to find him and fix his mind."

Reno released Jack; they drifted apart.

From Reno's mind exuded venomous sea-urchin spines.

A warning? A subconscious leak? Either way, Jack got the message loud and clear: he couldn't push Reno much further. Jack tossed him the data cube. "OK," Jack said, "we'll give this a look first."

Reno caught the cube and retracted his virtual stingers.

Why was Jack risking all their lives to find Zero? Was it only because Zero had been his friend? No. It was more than friendship. Zero had a way to escape Wheeler.

Reno stuffed the data cube into the console. Geometric symbols flashed on-screen: crystalline arcs and copper right angles and a zigzagging cluster of arrows that curled back upon themselves.

Jack's scattered thoughts stilled. "That's a position operator," he said.

"So this is a piece of gateway code? A subroutine?"

"Maybe." Jack opened a link to the electron reactors, a milky moonstone slate. He typed upon it: COMPILE WITH GATEWAY CODE ON FILE. RUN SIMULATION.

CODE CONCATENATED, the electron reactor replied. ADDITION ACCEPTED. SIMULATION RUNNING.

A plane of shadow split the air. The material solidified into the same black-chrome alloy of the gateway's skin. A silver dot winked on in the middle. From this point extruded a red and a blue arrow, growing in the opposite directions.

"Nothing new," Reno muttered. "That's what normally happens: you tag an object and move it."

Jack suspended the simulation. "Look." He tapped a tiny notepad icon. "Isabel has annotations attached." He ran his fingers over the text, absorbing the data directly into his mind. "They're equations about space and energy and matter. She's speculating how they might be wrapped around a center point . . . even bend gravity?"

"Let see," Reno said. He continued the simulation.

The red and blue arrows rotated clockwise. They incrementally copied themselves and left a trail of vectors in their wake. After a half-circle of this duplication, the lines overlapped so a thousand purple arrows radiated from the center.

"It jumps a lot of things fast," Reno said. "This isn't what Isabel used on us. I don't get what—"

"It's jumping objects and energy from one side to the other," Jack said, "warping space around the center. That's *exactly* what happened to us. Remember the optical distortion back on the moon between those radar dishes? Remember we couldn't get a solid lock? The destination vector slipped from side to side . . . because it was being jumped there."

Reno cocked an appreciative eyebrow and leaned closer.

The circle of vectors swept out a spherical volume, cloning arrows until the gateway appeared as a dandelion blossom of red and blue.

"It can't be perfect," Jack said. "There are approach tangents that can penetrate this pattern."

"Play with the increment," Reno suggested. "Make a finer mesh."

Jack's vision split—one eye watched Reno's sweaty face, the other stared at Isabel's code. He blinked and forced both eyes to look at the simulation. He took a deep breath and hoped his mind would hold together a little longer.

"Or maybe the red arrows tag an object if it's close enough," Jack said. "That would effectively bend everything around the gateway. Like a spherical lens."

"However it does the trick," Reno said, "it's got to take a fistful of power."

"We should run some tests."

"Tests? No time for tests." Reno tapped the simulation shut. "Wheeler comes to finalize his deal in less than twelve hours."

"All the more reason to find Zero now."

Reno's eyebrows scrunched together in disgust. "You're obsessed with Zero. Isabel, too. Do you feel guilty because the three of you started this? Like if you could just be friends and team up against Wheeler, everything would work out?" He pushed off the wall and floated aft.

Jack grabbed the back of the pilot's seat and propelled himself into the passenger section.

Reno grasped Safa's couch to stop his momentum, then checked her EEG. "Well, this isn't a fairy tale, Jack. Isabel and Zero aren't your friends anymore. They never will be again. Get over it." He pushed off and grabbed ahold of Jack's suit like he had grabbed DeMitri's suit just before he sucker-punched him in the gut. With his crooked nose a centimeter from Jack's, he whispered, "And every time you go running after them, you stick your neck way out. Mine and Safa's, too. I'm getting sick of it."

Jack pushed Reno away.

He wasn't obsessed. Jack knew where he stood with Isabel. And Zero.

Jack grabbed the wall, stopped his motion, and glanced at Panda. She looked pale. Frozen. If Jack got her and Safa patched back together, where did that get them? Wheeler would still know where they were. Gersham's deal still stank.

"You don't know what you're talking about," Jack

said. "I'm looking for Zero because he's our best chance. I'm stepping down to the moon."

Reno shook his head. "Count me out. I won't leave Safa. Isabel knows you'll come looking for the gene witch. It could be a trap. If she shows up again, you can bet she'll be armed with something better than crayons."

Jack spied a bit of broken crayon twirling end over end in the zero gravity. "Stay then, but I have to go."

Reno exhaled. "Sure you do."

Jack went to the airlock and grabbed a belt pouch. He checked his Hautger SK, reholstered it, then slung the sniper rifle over his shoulder. "Got any more rounds for this thing?"

"You've got the last three."

Jack launched off the wall to the cockpit. He removed a silver case from the console; it contained the electron reactors, assorted data files, and the isotope. Reno had a point about Isabel. If she showed up while he was gone, he couldn't let his only means of communicating with Wheeler and Gersham fall into her hands.

Reno drifted over Jack's shoulder, watching. "Tell Kamal," he said, "I'll drop by later for tea. That is, if either one of us lives through this."

There was a glitter in Reno's brown eye. Jack had seen that look—when the old spy had split open Jack's head. He had a feeling he shouldn't be turning his back on Reno.

"One hour," Jack said. "I'll either have the answers I want or I'll give up."

"One hour." Reno gave Jack a quick nod, then added: "And not a second more."

Jack glanced back at Panda. He hated leaving her, but his hunches had paid off before. This time, though, it wasn't just his skin on the line, but hers and Safa's. All of humanity's. He hoped Zero was alive. Hoped he had the miracle they needed.

Jack tagged himself, drew a blue line to the North Pole of the moon, and took a long step down.

Jack focused on his helmet's display; he had to concentrate, ignore the basalt plains, the silver dunes, and the craters brimming with shadow.

His head was already too full of the moon.

It wouldn't leave his thoughts: Kamal's moon bowl, black waters and a wavering silver orb, Jack's face reflected, then spilled onto the floor, gone—still there, but not. Him—the moon—light and shadow. He couldn't stop the disorientation. Was it a side effect of his fracturing mind?

Jack shook his head clear. He still saw reflections: his eyes staring back in his faceplate, the moon outside, and the moon in his head.

He tapped in the authorization code for the camouflaged airlock. The door remained shut.

Of course. DeMitri had changed the key.

Beneath Jack's boots, though, there was a rumble. Someone was coming up to meet him.

Jack didn't draw his gun. He'd play it nice—to start with—and see where that got him.

He glanced again at the mirror images and moons reflected in his faceplate. Kamal had planted something in Jack's head as real as Zero's enzyme. And it, too, was changing his thinking.

The airlock doors unraveled.

DeMitri stood inside with a pistol leveled at Jack. A light touch swirled past Jack's implant, not prying for secrets, just acknowledging his presence. "Are you alone?" DeMitri asked.

"Yes."

A smile appeared behind DeMitri's semireflective faceplate. "Good." He gestured with his gun for Jack to step in.

Jack did. The door sheathed closed and they started their descent. Air hissed into the airlock.

"This place is getting busy," DeMitri said. He holstered his gun.

"Busy," Jack said. "Zero has been here?"

DeMitri pulled his helmet off. He looked twenty-five years old: smooth skin, gleaming blue eyes, and his hair was blacker. It was as if DeMitri had been given back his youth by the original enzyme.

"Zero spoke with Kamal an hour ago," DeMitri said,

"then departed." He ran his fingers though his thick mane. "I hope you and your friends aren't going to be popping in on a regular basis—not that I mind the company, but we've just gotten the place patched together. I don't want to see it blown up again."

"Getting blown up is the least of your problems," Jack muttered. "Zero has a new enzyme. One that's infected me and the others and—"

"Kamal and I as well," DeMitri sighed. "When we cleaned up the command center, we handled the biologicals like toxic waste. Still, we must have missed an infection vector. I can show you our brain scans, but you must know the effects."

"Too well," Jack admitted.

"The gene witch explained how he originally came to the moon to infect us: you specifically. How he believed you would be the one to find a cure." DeMitri's mind expanded around the edges of Jack's consciousness—not probing, but an oil slick upon the surface of his thoughts, waiting for any falsehood to bubble up. "Have you found a cure?"

How much to tell DeMitri? How far could Jack trust a guy who had tried to erase him? "Almost," Jack said. "There are some details to iron out."

A gross understatement. Details like a few minutes of his "cure" burned up the rotational energy of an entire planet.

The elevator passed the command center.

"Kamal is in the storage bay," DeMitri explained.

"You've dug it out?"

"We found three of your original tunnelers," DeMitri replied. "I should thank you for stocking this base as well as you did."

DeMitri tapped the halt button. He turned to Jack. "We've had reason to hate each other, I know that, but everything is different." He looked to the floor, then said, "Even when we were on opposite sides, I must admit, I have always admired your ingenuity. I want to apologize for the past."

Jack crossed his arms and stepped back. "Don't play

games, DeMitri. At the Academe you were ready to torture me to learn what the Chinese were doing in my office.''

DeMitri looked up. He stared into Jack and removed the veils of mist protecting his mind. ''That was a lifetime ago, Jack.''

Jack recoiled from his invitation of closer contact.

Yet . . . as much as Jack hated to admit it, DeMitri was human. One of the few left in the universe. And after working with Wheeler or Gersham, working with humans seemed infinitely preferable. Even if that human was DeMitri.

DeMitri had ordered him assassinated. Jack had, in self-defense, murdered his NSO operatives and left DeMitri to die in his own torture chamber funhouse. It wasn't a foundation for a warm friendship.

Yet, all that history had to be pushed aside to face their common enemy. Maybe. Jack still couldn't entirely buy the idea of him and DeMitri on the same side.

''The timing now is poor,'' DeMitri said, ''but for later, I found a case of Russian vodka at the Michelson Observatory. We could share a drink or two.''

He held out his hand for Jack to shake.

Jack didn't take it. ''I'll think about it. If I come, though, I'll bring my own booze.''

DeMetri laughed. ''Reno has taught you well.'' He released the halt button and they continued their descent. ''I look forward to it.''

The elevator dropped another hundred meters and slowed to a stop. The doors parted.

The storage bay had been a three-story chamber, a lattice of shelves and girders. Moonquakes had, however, wrenched every straight line. Crisscrossing braces had propped up sagging walls, and soft-weld metal plates made a patchwork across the ceiling. Fiber optics dangled from above; outside light filtered through their tips, making them luminescent stalactites.

Crates and barrels and sheet aluminum had been heaped in the center of the room. Robots clustered around the pile; they pulled out pieces, then scurried to rivet, cut, and recycle the wreckage.

"Kamal?" Jack asked.

DeMitri pointed to the far corner, to a fountain of sparks and the outline of a man welding an I-beam to the wall. "He's expecting you."

"You're not coming?"

"We have a problem with a solar panel. I will say goodbye here." He nodded to Jack. "Or should I say 'until we meet again'?"

"Goodbye," Jack said.

He stepped out of the elevator; the doors closed behind him. His helmet's display gave him a green light for oxygen content and pressure, but Jack kept it on. No telling how stable this place was. Or how contaminated it still might be. Maybe Zero had left a new, more lethal virus on his last visit.

Kamal saw Jack and waved him over. He turned off his plasma torch and set it aside.

Jack bowed to the Buddhist monk. Kamal bowed to him.

"I'm glad you're still alive," Jack said.

"I am happy to be alive." Kamal removed his helmet and wiped the sweat from his bald head. "Please sit." He gestured to a barrel of flash-dry epoxy.

Jack sat.

Kamal picked up a battered green thermos and poured himself a cup of water. The liquid trickled slowly in the reduced gravity, looking like syrup. He didn't drink, nor did he offer any to Jack. Kamal just stared into the cup. His black eyes mirrored the water. "The gene witch told me you would arrive."

Jack licked his dry lips, suddenly thirsty. He leaned closer. "Why did Zero come here?"

"I have given my word to keep his confession secret."

"But he was alive? It wasn't a trick? Not a virtual projection?"

Kamal set his cup on the floor. "He was as alive as any man can be."

"Where did he go?"

"To the Earth," Kamal said. "To die."

"Not yet he's not." Jack stood. "We've got too much

to talk about. Did he tell you where on the Earth he was going?"

"No," Kamal replied and folded his hands in his lap. "But he did say that Wheeler has discovered us. That our end is near."

"He's right."

Kamal reached for his cup and took a sip of water, apparently nonplussed by Jack's statement. "Evil is ever-present in the world."

"Yeah, well, this evil is coming for us in a few hours." Jack grabbed his gateway. "I'm going down to the Earth, see if I can't wring Zero's secrets out of him. If I can, I'll come back for you and DeMitri. I'll take you to a safer place."

"You are welcome to visit anytime," Kamal said, "but I believe Mr. DeMitri and I will stay here. This is home now."

"You'll be killed. You'd better—"

Jack's thoughts flew apart. Where was Zero? How to patch together Safa and Panda permanently? Do it without dooming stars and worlds? Wheeler was coming for them. How would they escape?

His vision tunneled. He sank to his knees and clutched at the ground as the room spun around him.

Kamal knelt next to Jack. "Be still. Breathe." His deep voice had a soothing effect.

Jack inhaled. Exhaled. His mind quieted.

Kamal was impassive. His eyes were dark pools. Hypnotic.

That calmness irritated Jack. "Don't you realize what's going on? That we'll all be dead soon?"

"All humans die. We must not deny the inevitable."

Jack sighed explosively.

Kamal handed Jack the cup of water. "To struggle is natural. Do not be frustrated."

Jack reached for the cup. He saw the reflection of the overhead lights and the mirror image of his own face— he slapped it out of Kamal's hand. Water made an arcing silver snake in the one-sixth gravity, then splashed upon lunar dust and was absorbed. The tin cup bounced and rolled to a halt.

"Stop it," Jack hissed. "I've got that moon-in-the-bowl thing rattling around in my head. What·does it mean? Why did you put it there?"

"Enlightenment and ignorance," Kamal replied. "There, but not. Like a superposition of overlapping quantum states. This is the paradox of nature we must forever wrestle with. I thought it appropriate for you."

Jack laughed. " 'Enlightenment'? What good is enlightenment if I'm dead?"

"Death and life are a superposition as well. One all men must untangle."

"I don't understand anything," Jack muttered. He hung his head between his legs, closed his eyes, and let the pulse in his eardrums thunder. "Except that I'm exhausted."

Kamal set his hand on Jack's shoulder. "Understanding is not important. Insight is beyond all learning. It can come from a sudden sound or profound silence."

Jack looked up.

Kamal retrieved his tin cup and poured more water into it. He offered it again.

Jack hesitated . . . but he was parched. He peeled off his helmet and took the vessel. The water held shadow and reflected light that danced and wavered and blurred; there was Jack's face, distorted and smeared across the liquid.

He drank . . . the light . . . the darkness . . . himself.

Jack hadn't realized how thirsty he was. He quaffed the entire thing, then exhaled. Something cool and calm and smooth filled him; something drained from within him as well.

His thoughts cleared.

Kamal donned his helmet. "You must speak to Zero . . . if he is yet alive. Then return, so we may discuss more of these spiritual matters." He bowed to Jack.

Jack bowed to Kamal.

The image of the moon in the bowl was gone from Jack's head. Curiously, he missed it.

"Thanks," Jack said. "I'll be right back."

Jack hoped he would be able to—that there would be a moon to come back to in a few hours.

He resealed his helmet, tagged himself, and jumped to the Earth.

Jack stood on the Arabian peninsula—or where it used to be. Sand dunes and oases had been transformed into a plane of flat rock.

Still, better than the last time he was on the Earth. When the place had been molten.

How had Wheeler cooled the world off? Transformed molecular vibrations into another form of energy? Or had he dropped a cometful of ice onto the surface? Jack would have liked to learn the trick.

He wiped the moon dust from his faceplate, then magnified the view and scanned the terrain. Nothing.

Zero wasn't here. But Jack had a few other guesses where he might have gone.

He locked the yellow vector on to the center of the Earth and stepped across the globe—

—into ripples of water and black sand that squished under his boots. Rivulets and streams cut through the loam, carved snakes and curls across what had been the Californian coast. This is where the Academe once floated on its man-made island.

But Zero wasn't here, either.

There was foam in the water. No, not sea foam . . . something under the surface. Jack knelt to get a better look.

Clinging to the edges of the stream were strands of algae and, covering them, tiny bubbles of oxygen. How could it have survived Wheeler's destruction? Portions of the Earth's crust had plunged beneath the mantle.

Maybe Zero had been here after all.

Jack took a long step halfway around the world—

—to Amsterdam.

Geysers erupted. White plumes of water curtained the air, lacy fingers that reached up, then fell into pools of turquoise and tangerine and gold, colored from bacteria swarming in the mineral-rich waters.

The *Zouwtmarkt* had once been ocean floor, raised after the great quake to become an international marketplace, then molten rock and cooled by Wheeler . . . and now?

Now it was muddy flats and hot springs, exposed layers of red and yellow clays and veins of pyrite that glistened.

There were impressions in the muck: animal tracks.

Real? Jack reached out with his implant but sensed no interface. How could they be here?

He unshouldered his rifle and took a quick look around. He didn't want to get ambushed by another one of Zero's genetically engineered "cures." No movement. The only odd thing was a white shape on the horizon, kilometers away. Maybe a bank of fog.

Jack got on his hands and knees and took a closer look at the prints. There was a set of three toes and a spur that looked like chicken tracks, tiny pads with a four-footed gait that had to be a fox or a dog—and a set of bare human footprints that staggered a dozen paces and vanished. He traced the outline. Five toes and a fallen arch. Definitely human. Zero's? They had to be.

So where was the gene witch?

Jack stood, magnified the white object on the horizon, and ran it through image enhancement. The hazy atmosphere blurred the details; the thing was a slender rectangle, its lines too straight to be natural.

He jumped—

—landing alongside a wall of fluted concrete, cracked and soot-covered, half-buried in the earth. Coit Tower lay on its side.

Jack ran his gloved fingers over the smooth surface. If it could make it through earthquake, the end of the Earth, and having a moon dropped on it, then maybe Jack had a chance, too. There was no logic behind that conclusion . . . just a feeling that their fates were somehow linked.

Overhead, shadows flashed. A flock of pigeons wheeled and alighted on the tower.

A few of the birds glided to a collection of nearby containers: orange plastic barrels, steel boxes with interlinking biohazard symbols, coffins with frost-coated surfaces, three railway cars, and a ten-meter-tall palm tree planted in a tub of dirt.

In the tree's shade lay Zero.

Spent syringes lay scattered around the gene witch. He was emaciated. Melted skin covered the right side of his body.

"Zero?" Jack took a step closer, not sure if Zero was alive or dead.

"Jack?" Zero's eyes fluttered opened. One swelled out of its socket, the other was white and blind. "Are you real or illusion?"

Jack kicked aside the syringes and sat by his friend. He lay his hand on Zero's shoulder. "I'm here," he said. "No dream. What happened to you?"

He clutched at Jack with blistered and blackened fingers. "I did this. Radiation and neuro-inhibitors to slow the mental replication." His lips cracked and bled. "I had to think as one in my last moments."

Jack shook his head. "This isn't your last moment," he said. "There's a way to stabilize the fragmentation. At least, for a while. I'll get you back together."

Zero managed a feeble smile. "Too late," he whispered. "And there are more important matters." His gestured to the containers. "The animals. I freed them from cryogenic." He squeezed his eyes shut. "But, Allah forgive me, there is no food. They need more help than I can give. Please, Jack."

When Wheeler destroyed the Earth, Zero had told Jack he preserved samples of flora and fauna. But what did Zero expect him to do? Terraform the Earth?

"Don't worry," Jack said. "I'll help." He saw chickens scratch the displaced dirt alongside Coit Tower. "Are they infected with your enzyme?"

"No. Only humans. The beasts are innocent in this. If they die now, after they have survived so much . . . I could not bear that guilt upon my soul. I have done so much evil."

If Zero was so worried about them, why let them out of cryogenic in the first place? Maybe he thought there would be no one left to take care of them, that Jack and the others would soon be dead. Not an entirely illogical conclusion.

Jack leaned closer to Zero. "You can make it up to us all. Tell me how you got away from Wheeler."

"It matters not. You have found me. Wheeler will, too."

"Tell me!" Jack hissed. "It might save us. It might save everyone."

"Salvation?" Zero murmured. "I have tried . . . tried to reseed the Earth and restore its rotation. It is not enough to undo my wrongs."

Jack would have liked a lengthy question-and-answer session with Zero, find out exactly how he got the Earth rotating and got that algae to grow so fast. But he had to stick with finding out how Zero pulled his disappearing trick on Wheeler.

"Tell me." Jack shook Zero by his shoulders. "We're running out of time."

Zero clenched his teeth as his burnt skin cracked and oozed clear fluid.

Jack eased Zero back to the ground—sorry that he had caused him such pain . . . sorry, too, that he didn't have the guts to really shake the answers he needed out of him.

"Please," Jack whispered. "How did you escape Wheeler?"

Zero sighed. He stiffly drew a circle in the dirt, then lines that radiated from it.

"What is it?" Jack asked.

"How we escaped," Zero replied in a hoarse voice. "Sum the arrows."

Jack scrutinized the diagram. "These lines are equal and opposite. Multiple vectors that add up to nothing."

"Which is what Wheeler detected with his wiretap. We jumped to different worlds, to the vacuum of space, into the hearts of stars, and one of us escaped . . . to confess our sins before we lay our bones to rest in the earth."

Zero's summed arrows canceled one another. He had jumped to different locations, but the *total* vector was nothing. Had Zero outmaneuvered Wheeler's wiretap so easily? Or was this another one of the alien's elaborate setups?

"You've given us a chance, Zero. Thanks."

Zero set his head upon the ground. "Then I may rest in peace?"

"Sorry," Jack said. "No one's resting—yet. I'm going to get you some help."

Jack keyed his helmet's microphone. "Reno?"

Static crackled through the speaker.

"Reno? I'm coming up." Jack turned to Zero. "Wait here. I'll be right back."

He tagged himself—jumped into orbit. The night surrounded him: the moon in the distance, the gray Earth below churning with clouds, and the sun ablaze.

But the shuttle was gone.

"Reno!" Jack yelled.

No one was there to hear. Reno had screwed him. He had left Jack behind.

18

Jack drifted in space. The Earth was at his feet, the moon behind him—and between, more emptiness than he could ever imagine. His oxygen recycler sputtered, its catalyst nearly spent.

If Jack never saw empty space again, that would be fine with him.

He had wasted an hour searching for the *Dutchman*. He had jumped around the Earth twice, gone to the ruins of the Michelson Observatory, then returned to where he had left the shuttle . . . but found no trace of Reno.

Reno had deserted him. Worse, he had taken Safa and Panda. Reno probably had his own ideas how to escape. Maybe he thought Wheeler would only want Jack?

If Jack's and Reno's positions were reversed, he might have been tempted to do the same—only Jack would have never gone through with it.

His oxygen recycler hissed and died. The vacuum suit automatically switched to its reserve tank: three minutes of air.

It was time to jump to the moon; Kamal and DeMitri would help. He interfaced with the gateway, stretched a vector toward the silver orb, but Jack didn't go anywhere.

Jack's mind instead exploded in a hundred fragments, each thinking its own thoughts, all of them clamoring in his head: Reno had the right idea—Jack should be a decoy and give the others a chance to escape—No, Zero's null-sum jump was a better plan; it gave them all a chance—he should contact Isabel; with her patched-together mind, she might have a solution—or he should try to heal Zero—or run as far and fast as he could and hope that Wheeler would never catch up to him.

Jack clutched his head and wanted to rip off his helmet. He tumbled out of control.

His mind then focused . . . more or less. He inhaled, exhaled, and slowed his racing heart.

The air tasted foul, hot and full of the odor of his own bad breath. It felt like he was suffocating. Was the stuff in his reserve tank rotten?

A flash in inky space caught his good eye. He was spinning too fast, however, to orient on the source.

Jack flicked on the sniper rifle. Its gyros whined and slowed his motion.

Another flash. Metallic and silvery-white—then blackness again.

Something *was* there.

He jumped a kilometer closer and watched for the spark of light to reappear.

Jack panted. His lungs burned, trying to extract oxygen that wasn't there. He'd black out soon. He'd have to come back later. Maybe it had only been his imagination.

Unless he had jumped past the source of that light?

He cast a blue vector back—seven hundred meters.

Squinting, he saw stars . . . then an outline against the black: a stubby wing, a nose, then a broken wingtip that rotated into view and reflected sunlight off sheered titanium edges. *Itsy.*

The fringes of his vision dimmed. Jack shifted his position——onto *Itsy*'s canopy.

Someone was inside the cockpit. They were limp, free-floating and knocking against the hull and canopy as the spy plane spun.

Darkness lapped at the edges of his mind. *Itsy*'s matte-black stealth material was smooth and there were no handholds. His fingers slipped off, and Jack flew away from the rotating ship.

He used the gateway, leapt back, oriented to match *Itsy*'s spin, and clung on tight.

The body within tumbled right-side up. Sunlight flooded the cockpit, and Jack saw the face in the helmet. Panda.

Jack didn't hesitate; he jumped *Itsy*, Panda, and himself to the moon.

Jack popped open *Itsy*'s canopy and dragged Panda toward the elevator airlock. She was cold, limp—still breathing, though.

He stopped. He could have kicked himself for being so stupid, for moving so slow. He jumped himself and Panda straight into—

—the command center.

Kamal and DeMitri spun to face them.

"Help me," Jack whispered. "Help her."

DeMitri went to the elevator airlock and retrieved a first-aid kit. Kamal hurried to Jack and they lowered Panda to the floor.

They ripped off her neck seal, then pulled her helmet free. Jack made the flexgel floor soft with a silent mental command and gently set Panda's head down, dimpling the surface.

EEG lines smudged blurry lines into the air. Her eyelid tattoos were black and yellow bruises. Her hand was curled into a fist, clutching something.

Jack pried open her grip and found an empty pack of cigarettes. Written in blue crayon upon the paper liner was:

Hiya Jack,
I've taken Safa to a safe place. I'll try and patch her together myself. If it works, I'll find you on the moon. If not, then it's been a thin slice of heaven.
Itsy and Little Beijing are yours.

Reno

Jack crumpled the note, squeezed until it hurt, squeezed it like he would choke Reno when he got his hands around his neck.

Reno probably left *Itsy* because she was extra mass to

jump. He must have left Panda because she was too dangerous. He had dropped her like garbage. Then again, there was a portable bubble node inside *Itsy*. Reno had set it up for Panda's coma-inducing routine. No. That was just so she'd be easier to handle.

Jack set his hand on Panda's forehead, caught the shadows of her dreams: translucent jade held up to the sun and the smoke of her last cigarette when she went cold turkey at the age of sixteen.

A tap on his shoulder; he turned and saw Kamal. The monk had his hands folded within the sleeves of his blue-black robe.

"There is no time for retribution," Kamal whispered. "Did you find Mr. al Qaseem?"

"Zero!" Jack said and stood. He had forgotten him. "I'll be right back."

Jack jumped down—

—to the Earth.

Zero lay where Jack had left him under his potted palm tree. He was unconscious, his breathing shallow, almost no pulse.

He tagged Zero, all of his equipment in sight, then stepped everything back—

—to the command center.

"We'll need a brain scan, " Jack told DeMitri. "Zero's poisoned his nervous system."

DeMitri snapped open a window and stared at silver signal parameters and streamers of static flickering past. "Signal response is chaotic, but I believe I can filter. One moment."

Jack paced back and forth. He hoped it wasn't too late for Zero. Or Panda. Or himself. It was only a matter of hours before Wheeler returned.

He had to tell Kamal and DeMitri how dangerous it was just to be near him. They deserved the truth.

Jack explained it all. He told them what had happened with Isabel and Zero. He mentioned their new technologies. He then explained that in ten hours Wheeler would show up, and they'd all be killed.

"We must assist you," Kamal said without blinking his dark eyes. "There is no other moral alternative."

DeMitri nodded in agreement, distracted as he fine-tuned the signal response of the bubble, murmuring in Russian to himself.

"Thanks," Jack whispered. He wouldn't forget their generosity, their composure—traits that he seemed to be in short supply of lately.

Kamal sat in the lotus position and watched the air over Zero as bits of the gene witch's brain assembled: gray-blue wrinkles of tissue, ivory splotches of scarification, and rotten black cancers.

DeMitri leaned closer. "The fragmentation is tremendous." He highlighted the connecting corpus callosum and made a labyrinth of Zero's brain. "Two hundred isolated regions, half-necrotic, and there are twenty-seven stage-three tumors."

Jack ran his fingers over the crenellated surface, accessing the data. He saw the series-eight enzyme, coiled proteins wrapped around metal ions; he tasted sand and felt the resonance of sitar music—bits of his friend that would never again fit together.

A cellular physiology report streamed through his fingertips. Whatever Zero had done to himself, it had triggered an autoimmune response across the blood-brain barrier. The cranial inflammation was killing him.

Jack had never felt so helpless.

"He just wanted to think straight before he died," Jack said to DeMitri. He knelt next to Zero and whispered to his friend, "If you only had waited a few more minutes."

The electron reactors opened a window, a scratched pane of Plexiglas. INSUFFICIENT RESPONSE FOR SIGNAL RECOMBINATION.

"I was afraid of this," Jack said. "Zero's mind is so fragmented that his implant no longer works. There's no way to unscramble his thoughts. We can't even induce coma."

DeMitri crossed his arms and walked around the gene witch. He stopped and looked at the equipment Jack had jumped up: orange plastic barrels, steel boxes with stenciled biohazard symbols, and three coffin-shaped containers.

"There's an option," DeMitri said. He touched the coffin. "This is a cryogenic suspension chamber for biological samples, is it not? We can put him on ice."

"Those aren't meant for humans," Jack said. "They're for laboratory animals, cloned organs, or experimental tissue cultures."

"They are used," Kamal whispered, "for terminal patients."

"As a last resort," Jack replied. He chewed on his lip, then added, "Which, I guess, is where Zero's at." He sighed. "OK. It will buy him some time."

They positioned Zero inside one of the units and closed the lid.

Ten minutes ticked past. Jack watched Zero's pulse and breathing and blood pressure decay to a trickle. He watched ice coat Zero's patchwork beard and crust over his eyelashes.

VITAL SIGNS IN STABLE CYCLE, the electron reactors reported. CORE TEMPERATURE CHILLING.

The contraption gurgled as it replaced Zero's internal fluids with an antifreeze chemical cocktail. They were essentially embalming him. It gave Jack the creeps.

"Sleep tight," Jack said and ran his hand over the smooth plastic lid. "I'll find a way to get you back. Somehow."

"So much for the gene witch." DeMitri pressed his lips into a single white line. "We, however, won't be able to sleep through this situation."

Jack wanted to punch DeMitri for that crack. But his anger drained as fast as it had come. "I know," Jack said. "Ten hours and Wheeler will demand answers I don't have."

"We can escape with your gateway." DeMitri's clear blue eyes darted to the black-chrome sphere Velcroed to Jack's thigh.

Jack set a protective hand over it. "It's tapped. Wheeler knows every move I make."

"What of these new techniques?" Kamal asked. "This

zero-sum jump. Isabel's deflection routine? Will not they suffice?''

"I . . . I don't know. Wheeler will be watching me under a microscope." Jack paced back and forth. "I can do things that I wouldn't have dreamed were possible a week ago. But are they enough to escape Wheeler? He's played me for a fool ever since I made first contact."

Jack sat on the floor, set his head in his hands, and closed his eyes. If only he had more time. If only he could think straight. His thoughts felt like they were turning to stone. The floor around him cracked into granite and cemented his knees and feet solid.

With a touch, Kamal turned his metaphorical stone to water. It evaporated, cooling and refreshing Jack's skin. "Explain these technologies," Kamal said.

Jack inhaled, exhaled, and focused his mind. "We have four new techniques, each with its own problem. I've got a hunch they fit together . . . I just can't figure out how."

He plucked an illusionary cigarette from the air. The smoke curled into diaphanous strands. Jack puffed. Amphetamine-laced fumes filled his lungs and, virtual or not, Jack got a jolt out of it.

It was good to be back in a real bubble, with all its metaphor and hunch-sorting algorithms—the only place Jack felt fully alive.

"First," Jack said, "we have a technique to bilocate a person with the gateway. It splits composite wavefunctions, then balloons the distance between them."

"This sounds like a bubble-induced fantasy." DeMitri took a long look at Jack, maybe wondering if he had lost his mind.

"No," Kamal said, nodding. "Quantum bifurcation. It has been done for decades . . . but only atomic masses."

DeMitri scratched his nose and looked dubious. "You did this with a gateway? The one that teleports masses from point to point? It doesn't sound like the same process."

"It's not—exactly," Jack admitted. "That's the problem. We use the gateway in a continuous mode rather than an instantaneous transmission." He took a drag off his cigarette, then exhaled cirrus strands. "The power required is huge. We made fifteen copies of Safa. But to keep them in existence for one minute significantly slowed the rotation of an Earth-sized planet."

"So other than arresting the motions of planets," DeMitri asked, "what good is this bilocation?"

"It's a partial cure for a fractured mind." Jack made his exhaled cloud glimmer with a silver lining. "With several copies of a person, we shut down parts of their implants, then recombine their signals into one smoothly communicating unit. It's like a parallel-processing super-computer."

Kamal's black eyes widened. "Parallel processing is usually more efficient than non-parallel processes. Is a multiplexed human also smarter?"

"I think so." Certainly, Jack had a flash of inspiration. Safa had claimed to be more intelligent. But were all their mental processes multiplied? Their shortsightedness and incorrect assumptions as well?

DeMitri made a cigarette appear between his long fingers. He didn't puff on it, just let it smolder. "We could try this on ourselves. Become smarter and solve our problems."

"We don't have the energy," Jack told him. "We'd burn up the rotation of the moon before we got any answers."

"We could jump to another spinning mass," Kamal offered.

"Not without a bubble," Jack said. "Our implants don't have the processing power to recombine the multiplexed signals."

Kamal smoothed his hand over his scalp, thinking. "Then move the bubble."

DeMitri shook his head. "Shift this structure and we risk a misalignment of the magnetic vortex coils." He turned to Jack. "How long would it take to retune the system?"

"Hours." Jack looked into the glowing ember of his cigarette for inspiration. For once his mind was blank and silent and without a clue.

"But"—DeMitri snapped his fingers—"we can use a portable system."

"That would be great," Jack said, "if we had more than the single node that Reno left in *Itsy*."

They were silent a moment, then Kamal asked, "May I please see this software that combines brain-wave signals?"

Jack stretched the air into a lapis square and let implant-routing commands trace streaks of pyrite and silver veins into the stone. He handed the code to Kamal, who stared at it intently.

DeMitri tossed his cigarette on the floor. "You said there were four pieces of technology: this bilocation, a multiplexed-thought network. . . . What of the other two?"

Jack opened his hand; dandelion seeds collected in his palm, assembled themselves into a bristled blossom of tiny red and blue arrowheads. "Isabel's deflection subroutine."

"Yes," DeMitri said. "A sphere of tagging and destination vectors. I have seen this before when I was in"—his nose wrinkled in disgust—"Ms. Mirabeau's employ."

"It warps space around the center," Jack told him. "If I understand Isabel's notes, it shifts not only matter and light, but gateway signals, maybe even gravity."

"But again," DeMitri said, "the energy problem."

"Yes."

Kamal furiously tapped into his window. He pulled apart luminous protocol strands and heaped them alongside the frame.

"And the last piece to your puzzle?" DeMitri asked.

"That was Zero's contribution." Jack glanced at the frost-covered coffin that held his friend. He wished the gene witch was awake and lucid. He wished his friend could be here when he needed him the most.

Jack drew eight lines in the air, radiating from a silver dot.

"Another deflection program." DeMitri crossed his arms over his chest. "No—all those vectors are blue. Destination vectors?"

"A null-sum jump. Wheeler's wiretap only records the total vector." Jack canceled pairs of equal and opposite arrows until only the point remained. "The result of this is no net jump. Or, at least, no net *recorded* jump."

"A simple trick," DeMitri murmured. "Maybe too simple, though, to fool Wheeler?"

"So we make it more complicated; use a little misdirection." Jack opened a link to the electron reactors. "I'll calculate the corrected positions of many spinning masses."

A tiny spiral galaxy appeared; stars blinked on and off as the electron reactors checked and rechecked their true positions.

"My destinations for this zero-sum jump," Jack explained, "will be planets and the mass centers of binary stars, places that I might hide, and places that Wheeler will have to investigate if he wants to find all of me."

"I see." DeMitri narrowed his blue eyes into slits, looking unconvinced.

Jack let his cigarette evaporate. "But this trick is for a chase that can't even start. I'm limited to the inside of this bubble."

Kamal finally looked up. "Not necessarily. The bubble may be turned inside-out." He offered his code window to Jack.

Faceted onto the lapis slate were tiny networking-protocol crystals: clusters of angles and half pyramids and hollowed hexagons, not one of them complete.

"This isn't a valid program," Jack said.

"It is not meant to be," Kamal admitted. "When you split into many selves, you may also split the portable bubble node left with Miss Panda. This code is generated from each node." He splayed his stubby fingers. "Their interactive signals may then be transmitted through the gateway's isotopic frequencies"—he laced his fingers together—"and there may be enough duplicated pieces to combine into a self-sustaining network."

Jack squinted at the code. "Like solving a jigsaw when you only have one piece. You've duplicated that one piece . . . but how to fit them all together?"

The dark glint of excitement in Kamal's eyes dimmed. "That answer, regrettably, is beyond my expertise."

"Great." Jack handed the window to DeMitri. "You two are going to have to dream up some programming miracle to make it work."

"Us two?" DeMitri accepted the window, looked at it, then back to Jack. "And what will you be doing?"

"Something just as impossible. I've got to find a needle in a haystack." Jack waved his hand through the miniature Milky Way and watched the stars scatter in his wake. "I've got to find a power source to make this all work."

Jack sat against the wall of the command center. On the floor around him were the Tinkertoy parts and cracked gears of the metaphorical clockwork universe he had disassembled.

For five hours he had scoured the star catalogs for the right power sources: binary and trinary stars, pulsars, and white dwarves.

With their power, Jack could jump copies of himself across the galaxy—show Wheeler that he couldn't kill those instances of Jack quick enough.

That sounded unpleasant.

For the seventeen milliseconds when Jack had been split, however, he had been a composite being, with fully separated and realized selves, yet all still himself. Each copy of Jack would be Jack. One shared mind in separate bodies.

Under those multiplexed conditions, being able to create duplicated aspects of himself, he'd be willing to die a few times to make a point.

But power was still a problem. Just as Safa had rapidly consumed the energy of the rotating planet, he would burn up these systems. Fast. Hundreds of Jacks, moving in light-year-long steps, the energy he'd need could extinguish the heavens. All to fuel a chase he might eventually lose.

There had to be another way. Jack stared at the stars spinning around him.

Rotation. That was the solution . . . and the problem. Why couldn't he use another type of energy?

He touched a silver thread and connected to his translation lexicon. He had seen other energy operators in the lexicon: vibration, nuclear and subnuclear oscillations, vacuum energy—sources much more portable.

Jack selected the icon for a weak nuclear force exchange, a crinkled tinfoil and liquid smoke yin-yang. He made a copy of the gateway code, then substituted the new icon for a rotational energy operator.

A shiver rippled through the copper-code pathways. Teflon capillaries burst, spraying ultramarine light that split and curled into subatomic particle trajectories. The black core imploded and the crystalline sphere shattered.

He wasn't giving up yet.

Jack tried vibrations, electronic jitters, and quark transpositions.

No dice. The gateway crashed with every one of them.

Jack stared at the glass fragments at his feet; he kicked them. Why should the gateway only work with rotations? There had to be a reason. Everything else about the gateway had been elegantly engineered.

He made a copy of the gateway code and stored it within his database. A paranoid habit, but you could never have too many backups of vital code.

Jack closed windows and star catalogs—realized that he had been scanning more than one at a time, tracking them independently with either eye . . . and understanding their contents with parallel tracks of thinking.

He blinked and squeezed the bridge of his nose.

That's what happened to Panda just before she lost control. How long did he have left?

In the center of the bubble, the tiny model of the Milky Way still floated. Strands of the spiral arms magnified, stars highlighted, and numbers flashed as the electron reactors calculated new coordinates. At least it was having some success.

Jack pulled himself together and strode to DeMitri and Kamal. They had a dozen system frames open; self-programming engines generated code icons that overflowed and swarmed over one another on the floor, looking more like ants than software.

"I've found a few likely sources," Jack said, trying to

sound optimistic. The words rang false in his ears. "But nothing that will last too long."

"We have a prototype network," DeMitri said. He, however, shook his head.

Jack took a step closer. "Great, that's something I wasn't—"

Kamal held up a hand. "A network that functions only with a static number of connections."

DeMitri ran his fingers though his long black hair, half combing it back, half pulling at it. "Static and fragile. Add or remove one node and the thing crashes." He sighed. "It'll crash anyway, it's so full of bugs."

Jack examined the program. It was a collection of geocode tiles with linking command lines etched upon their edges. He accessed the full three-dimensional representation: trapezoids of pink and polyhedrons of salmon and blue inflated into the air.

"You've accomplished more than I expected." Jack compressed the program, then sat on the floor. "But if I have to face Wheeler with this, I won't have a chance. He could kill dozens . . . hundreds of my duplicated selves. One Jack eliminated from this network and it crashes. Then the chase is over."

"If only we had more time," DeMitri said. "Two or three days . . ." He paced in a circle around Jack. "Or a team of programming wizards."

Jack's head snapped up. "A team?"

He looked at sleeping Panda. From their intimate interface, Jack knew she was as good as he was at hacking code. She had broken into the bubble network at the Academe and his *Zouwtmarkt* office and eluded the NSO experts every step of the way.

"We do have that team," Jack told DeMitri.

Kamal's faint eyebrows shot up. "You will split her existence?"

"Wait a moment." DeMitri grabbed Jack by the elbow. "You said it took too much energy to operate the gateway in a continuous mode. What happened to the power problem?"

"It's still there," Jack said, "and the spinning moon is

still our only source. But we're running out of time and
we can't do all the recoding by ourselves. Besides, it'll
give us a chance to test your networking code. Do you
have a better idea?''

DeMitri considered. He didn't look young anymore.
There were wrinkles across his forehead and black rings
under his eyes. He released Jack's arm and whispered,
''No. I do not.''

There was one other reason it should be Panda. A selfish
reason. Jack wanted to be with her again, to see her alive
and awake.

''Panda will be smarter,'' Jack said. ''She'll rewrite this
code faster and better than any of us. Faster, I hope, than
the moon decelerates.''

''And if not?'' Kamal asked.

''The moon stops,'' Jack said. ''And we'll be stuck.''

''Trapped,'' DeMitri corrected, ''and waiting for
Wheeler to arrive.''

Jack opened a silver-framed window of cobalt glass and
ruby mah-jongg tiles. He loaded the program to patch Panda's mind.

''Then,'' Jack told him, ''she'll have to work fast.''

Panda awakened—all four copies of her. They stretched
their lithe bodies and rolled to their feet with a catlike
motion. Her eyelid tattoos flared to life, each a different
set of colors: flashes of iridescent green, solid bands of
gold, zebra stripes of gray and amber, and waves of metallic blue.

The mental-defragmenting software had taken. Each
Panda was independent.

''Why are we here?'' one asked Jack. She cupped his
chin in her hand, brought his face closer to her, and
kissed him.

Jack enjoyed it for a moment, then gently pushed her
away. ''We have no time for that. I'll fill you in on the
situation. DeMitri and Kamal can explain the code problem to your other selves.''

Two Pandas took low-gravity leaps to DeMitri and
Kamal and the dozens of windows floating around them.

The last Panda opened a square of silver-dust mirror and examined the software that made possible her multiplexed existence.

She looked up at Jack, her eyes wide. "There is an energy problem."

"There is. We'll have to work quick."

"And where is Safa . . . and Reno?"

"Reno skipped out on us and took Safa with him." He omitted that Reno had left her drifting in orbit.

Panda appeared to understand anyway. Her eyelid tattoos darkened to bloody smears. "I should have killed him long ago."

"Reno left because we're in a tighter jam," Jack said. "Gersham wants me to work as his middleman and find other species to plunder. He's as much of a predator as Wheeler."

"Then we have no options." Panda's lips compressed into a tiny frown.

"Maybe we do." Jack lifted her chin with his finger.

He outlined the technologies they had cobbled together: the diffractive splitting, the gateway deflection, the zero-sum jump, and the dynamic multinoded network . . . that had yet to be adequately engineered.

"If we can get all the pieces to fit together," he said, "I may have a chance to stand up to Wheeler. To convince him he can't erase us."

She looked past Jack, thinking. "I understand."

The command center trembled. A moonquake.

Kamal peered up from a window that contained spinning gyroscopes, a diagram of the moon, and angular velocity vectors. "Rotational energy down to ninety-three percent of original," he said.

DeMitri paused in his explanation to the Pandas and stared up at the roof. He took a deep breath and continued, speaking faster.

Panda squeezed Jack's hand. "I must go and help the others."

Jack didn't want to release her. He wanted to keep this Panda with him. If this didn't work, if Wheeler came for him, then this would be the last time they were together.

But in her split state, she was the best one qualified to pull off this stunt. Maybe the only one of them who could.

He let her go.

Four Pandas pulled the program windows wide open, cut and pasted geodesic tiles, and stuck the modules that didn't seem to fit anywhere on the floor. It was a giant mosaic: bits of pink granite and blue enamel and red sandstone subroutines.

Jack stepped back to get a better look at the entire picture. It was a mess.

The Pandas circled their construct, hands on chins, shaking their heads.

"What's the problem?" Jack asked.

"Connections," one Panda answered. "Too many are required to make the system robust. It slows the network."

"Split frequencies," DeMitri suggested. He slid a glass signal prism over a golden honeycomb processor array, making a rainbow spectrum.

Another Panda slapped his hand away and removed the prism. "No good," she replied. "I must—"

"—use the entire available scale," the third Panda said, "to stabilize the system if a node disappears."

"Without this reinforcement," the last Panda explained, "fatal runtime errors occur."

A Panda turned to Jack; one turned to DeMitri. "Please," they simultaneously whispered, "we mean no offense, but you are thinking too linearly to be of help."

Panda opened a link to the electron reactors and searched its database. The other Panda ran simulations. Windows winked open and piled upon one another; hundreds littered the air, rotating and bouncing off the walls.

DeMitri pulled Jack back. "We are in her way."

Jack's boots vibrated. Another tremor. Dust showered from the ceiling.

"Rotation at eighty-seven percent of original," Kamal said.

Jack didn't like standing on the sidelines, especially when so much was at stake. He walked to the tiny galaxy that had been pushed across the command center by the profusion of windows. There were dusty veils of stars, the corrected locations of a thousand binary systems and spinning worlds the electron reactors had compiled.

Jack breathed. In. Out. One deep, deep inhalation, however, ground something into his hip.

He unzipped the pouch on his belt and found Kamal's string of wooden beads. He pulled them out and rolled one between his fingers. Their grain had been stained dark by years of prayer and sweat. They smelled faintly of cedar.

"Seventy-six percent of rotational energy," Kamal announced.

Panda switched to a three-dimensional representation and assembled shapes: translucent amber cubes, glass filaments, and smoky silver wedges. As it turned, patterns resolved, then chaos, then lines and angles that could have been the geometric decoration of an Islamic mosque.

Jack wanted more time. More time to think. More time with Panda.

He stared at the beads; wavy lines of wood grain wrapped around the tiny spheres.

If Panda couldn't get this to work, what would he do? Make a run for it? No. Wheeler could crush him . . . as well as every last human. That left Gersham. But Jack would die before he helped him.

Panda's slender hand closed around his. "Praying?" she asked.

"Just thinking."

"Prayer might be appropriate." She sat next to him. "I will fail."

The program mosaic fell apart; pieces slipped free, hit the floor, and cracked. The three other Pandas wrote new routines, replacing the holes in the network as fast as it collapsed.

"I wanted one last moment with you," she whispered.

Her licorice scent filled his mind. Her eyelid tattoos flared with passion, tangerine and cinnabar flames that flowed over her skin and across Jack's. Their pulses matched and Jack sank into her.

"Moon rotation at sixty-one percent." Kamal's voice wavered with apprehension.

Jack pulled his mind away from Panda's, then pushed her physically away. "There has to be a way. Something we've overlooked." He shook the beads in frustration. "We need more time."

Panda caught his hand. She stared at the wooden prayer beads. "What are these?"

Jack handed them to her. "They're Kamal's."

She stared at the dark wood. Her tattoos changed: mahogany waves and cedar-red ripples.

Another Panda came to her side. Between them, they strung the beads, wove a cat's cradle and spider's web, then touched fingertips and examined the tangle of string.

"Single spheres," one said to the other, "but linked—"

"—along other dimensional lines," the other finished.

The other Pandas stopped what they were doing and pulled parts of the program off the floor.

"Excuse us, Jack," she said and returned the prayer beads. "This may be something."

The four Pandas scrutinized their mosaic, pushed apart the breaches, made them wider, expanded the structure until it occupied the entire command center, a crystalline chandelier of ghostly verdigris and iron-rust red and old ivory.

The blocks of code cast rainbow shadows, then slowly faded while the light solidified, back and forth, shifting locations and hue with liquid ease. It looked to Jack like a broken kaleidoscope: colors and motion and mirror shards.

"We have been thinking three-dimensionally," Panda explained. "This must be a multidimensional network with connections spanning both frequency domain and phase shift of the gateway carrier signal. In the higher dimensions, there are more connections and therefore more robustness."

"Highly flexible," Kamal noted.

"These alternate connections serve as a backup?" De-Mitri asked.

"Cut one node," she answered, "and several others exist wrapped around and tucked into a higher-dimensional manifold, ready and waiting to fill its place."

"Perfect," Jack said.

"Almost perfect," one Panda replied. "The processing power of the electron reactors will be required to run this . . . and it has been unstable."

"A risk I'm willing to take."

She stepped up to Jack and whispered, "Now I must go. Our time is up." One of her copies vanished.

The command center shook. Metal groaned and shuddered and the bubble power flickered. Three heartbeats, then the motion subsided.

"Stay." Jack slipped his arm around her slender waist and drew her close. "You're already multiplexed. When Wheeler comes, you can be the one to—"

She stilled his words with a finger upon his lips. "When Wheeler comes, it must be you who confronts him. Alone. You are the one who matters to him."

Another of the duplicated Pandas winked out of existence.

"But if I run, if I leave you behind, he might kill you."

"We will go to the observatory. Without jumping. It will suffice as a hiding place." Her eyes stared unblinkingly into his, and her eyelid tattoos turned to steel gray. "Wheeler will murder us all unless you show him that you cannot be caught."

The last Panda disappeared.

She squeezed her eyes shut. "My mind shatters." She swayed and Jack caught her. "Please, Jack, I cannot think." She dug her fingernails into his arm. "I cannot be like this."

Jack nodded to DeMitri, and together they eased Panda to the floor.

"Hang on." Jack booted the coma-inducing routine, let it silence the noise in her mind.

He held her until she was still and calm and in the deepest of sleeps. Jack cradled her small body for a long time.

Kamal set his hand on Jack's shoulder and pulled him away.

"That's everything we need, then," DeMitri said. "The network to link your different selves, the deflection routine to protect you, and the zero-sum jump."

Jack finally tore his gaze away from Panda.

"No," he whispered to DeMitri. "That's not everything. We don't have an ideal source of rotational energy." He stepped over to the electron reactors' representation of the galaxy.

"Can we not use those stars?" Kamal asked.

"If I jump dozens of copies light-years apart," Jack answered, "I'll need more than one power source." He chewed on his lower lip. "I don't want to destroy the stars and the worlds around them in the process."

He stared at the Milky Way, a spiral of luminous motes. There was a shadow on the other side, regions that couldn't be mapped because the central core obscured the view.

"The center," Jack murmured to himself.

He rotated the galaxy ninety degrees so it pinwheeled in front of him . . . and he understood.

"That's why the creators of the gateway engineered it for rotation." A grin spread across Jack's face. "The center. It's the answer to all our problems."

19

Jack was here; he was there—several places at the same time.

One Jack floated midway between two gas giants that were swirls of vapor and storm, one hundred and twenty light-years from the core of the galaxy.

Another Jack was positioned in a three-star system, seventy lightyears from the galactic center. This Jack had located himself too near one of the suns. Fire filled his faceplate: violet plasma and roiling heat.

A solar flare erupted, a loop of spiraling flame that engulfed him. Magnetic flux ripped though his mind. A dozen Jacks, spread across a dozen different star systems, instinctively raised their arms to protect themselves.

Too late.

His vacuum suit hardened, cracked, and blasted away—along with his skin and muscle.

The gateway connection between here-Jack and there-Jack severed.

He still floated between the twin gas giant planets. He still had scattered copies of himself strewn across the Orion Arm from the zero-sum jumps it had taken to get this far.

His body trembled. Ice water trickled into his arms and legs, while the memory of being burned turned his skin to gooseflesh. His vision clouded with blackness. Was he dead? No.

Yes . . . one Jack had been incinerated.

The vacuum suit's biomonitor winked red in the corner of his faceplate. His vital signs traced jagged lines across the display. Heating elements in the synthetic skin automatically warmed to counter his shock.

Jack's numbness eased. He flexed his arm, remembering how it felt to be scorched to cinders.

Being in more than one location was nothing like when his vision had split. There was no disorientation. Nor was there any of the chaos when his thoughts had flown apart.

Every Jack was him. And he was every one of them.

His composite wavefunction undulated with a dozen peaks; the distance between those vibrating nodes should have only been fractions of an angstrom apart—but had been ballooned by the gateway into billions of kilometers.

NEW COORDINATES CALCULATED, the electron reactors scrawled on the inner surface of his helmet.

Jack had to do it this way, jump blind, make estimates, then project copies of himself. The galactic core was tens of thousands of light-years distant, so the stellar positions he could see were correspondingly tens of thousands of years out of date. His calculations to pinpoint their current positions had been full of errors.

Guesses were all he had time for.

The clock was ticking, and he had to take chances.

He had to get to the center of the galaxy . . . near enough to tap the spinning black hole there.

The shock of dying wore off. Fear rattled up his spine, tensed his muscles, and made every nerve jangle. He was crazy to get near a black hole. He was playing with forces he could only guess at.

He resisted the instinct to retreat. He had to stick with his plan.

Jack nudged the blue destination vector and sent a copy of himself—

—to the center of the three-star system, five million kilometers from his last attempt. Noise screamed though his head. Light dazzled him: smoky blue, smoldering crimson, and ultraviolet hues.

His faceplate darkened. The radiation warning buzzed, indicating a lethal dose.

The electron reactors made a blossom of vectors; space warped around him. Solar-wind static dulled to a faint hiss. The radiation dropped to a merely dangerous count.

There was no velvet black of space here. The core of the Milky Way was too crowded with stars—gleaming pearls, diamond dust, opalescent smears of color, and ruby streamers of hydrogen. The light appeared solid; even filtered a thousandfold by Isabel's deflection technique, it had a thick glassy quality.

"How much time left?" he asked the electron reactors.

A countdown clock appeared in the corner of his faceplate. Forty-five minutes. Less than an hour until Wheeler came and finalized their deal. One way or another.

Jack watched the stars. Supernovae exploded: firework plasma pinwheels spitting strings of smoke that crossed and crisscrossed the sky with luminescent threads.

He blinked. This was no time for sight-seeing. It had taken too long to get this far, and he still had light-years to cross.

Jack stepped up the polarization in his faceplate. One by one, the stars around him winked off. The densest region remained: a band of suns and nuclear incandescence. He filtered until only a thread of light remained and, within that, a brilliant speck.

That had to be the accretion disk, light and matter swirling around the giant black hole.

Jack marked a location along the edge and let the electron reactors calculate the proper coordinates.

He added a million vectors about him, a pincushion of red and blue arrows; the stars vanished as light slid around his distorted space. With Isabel's deflection technique turned up so high, he'd almost be jumping blind. But without its protection the heat would incinerate him; the black hole's gravity would pull him in.

The electron reactors displayed a slender line across his faceplate, into the accretion disk. It marked the hypothetical edge of the event horizon at eight million kilometers from the center. He nudged his destination vector to twelve million kilometers out. Close enough, Jack hoped, but not too close.

He traced that path, then sent a copy ahead—

—it was too bright. He blinked and threw his hands before his face.

The electron reactors tightened the bubble of warped space.

Light dimmed to shadow . . . except the center, which boiled magnesium white, ultraviolet combustion that hurt to look at. Jets and boreales spiraled from the disk's north and south poles, polychromatic flames and plasma serpents spun a web around the center.

There was still too much glare to see the edge of the event horizon. Jack turned the filters in his faceplate to maximum. Everything dimmed.

He squinted at a collection of objects hovering on the inner edge of the disk. They looked artificial: saucers and spheres and cones. Starships? Around them glowed ghostly force fields that smeared into teardrop-shaped infrared tails.

How could they fight the pull of a black hole?

The answer was: they couldn't.

They had already passed over. Gravity had so distorted the space along the event horizon edge that from Jack's point of view, the travelers' clocks had slowed to nothing. From their point of view, however, there was no change. The only thing really clinging to the edge were the relativistic ghosts that had been here before him.

Maybe like him, they had tried a similar stunt? And failed?

Jack's fear rose to the surface. He pushed it back down. He had to think. He had to concentrate on the facts.

The observatory's theoretical database had said this black hole had millions of solar masses, enough angular momentum to power trillions of jumps across the Milky Way.

Jack drew a yellow arrow from the gateway.

It slipped from his control, stretched toward the event

horizon, locked onto the titanic power source. But it slowed . . . blurred . . . fragmented into translucent lines, and as it reached the event horizon, it disintegrated.

No connection. No power.

Why didn't it work? What was he missing?

Maybe it had worked and made a connection. Once inside, though, it couldn't send the power back past the event horizon.

He tried again. The vector shattered.

There had to be a way to tap the energy. He was so close. Or was he?

The gateway had been engineered to use rotating bodies as a source of power. It accessed them at a distance, but the intensely warped space of this black hole might prevent that function.

Jack would have to get closer. To use the power of this black hole, he'd have to go *inside* the event horizon, the region between it and the singularity.

He took a deep breath. If he got too close to the singularity, nothing would save him, not Isabel's deflection routine or the cracks in space the gateway jumped him through. It might suck in every one of his linked copies.

Jack swallowed his terror and tried to slow his racing pulse. His body rebelled and pumped more adrenaline into his blood.

He was afraid. That was OK. Any rational person would be terrified to do what he was about to do. He couldn't let the fear take control.

Jack exhaled explosively and fogged his helmet's faceplate.

There would be a tiny problem with gravity.

He increased the density of deflecting vectors—so thick they were solid purple scintillations. The lights went off as Jack cloaked himself within a pitch-black sphere of deformed space.

Jack was betting his life that Isabel's trick would protect him. Her notes in the data cube hinted that her deflection technique smoothed the curve of space around the gateway. However it worked, deflecting gravitons or gravity waves or smoothing the curve of space-time, they were all mathematically equivalent ways of turning off the gravitational force.

But what if it wasn't perfect? What if her technique couldn't completely protect him? If he wasn't torn apart by the sudden acceleration, then he'd be drawn into the center and end up just as dead.

He preprogrammed a sequence of jumps that would split him into one hundred and twenty-eight parts, relocating him closer to the inner circumference of the event horizon. Those duplicate Jacks would automatically shift position every microsecond to keep him from falling into the middle.

Maybe.

He swallowed again; his throat was sandpaper. Was there another way? No. Jack needed the power. Crazy as it seemed, this was his best chance to survive.

With trembling hands, he turned on Reno's rifle; gyros whined up to speed and stabilized him. He checked and rechecked the program that would split and jump his multiple selves.

Jack cast the blue destination vector across the edge of the event horizon.

He stepped inside.

There was nothing to see: the best view Jack could hope for.

He had to give Isabel credit; no radiation penetrated her deflection routine, and Jack floated free among forces that should have blasted his atoms into their constituent electrons, neutrons, and protons.

The edge of his warped bubble was a meter away—hard to tell exactly where—it was a shadowy dimensionless curve.

He gripped the gateway tighter. As long as he held on to it, he was safe.

There were one hundred and twenty-eight separate Jacks now within the event horizon—all isolated and all furiously shifting position around the center.

The yellow power-source vector had activated by itself. The arrows' trajectories flickered as every Jack moved, locked on to the most rotational energy he had yet seen. Power flooded through the connections; every crystalline piece of the gateway software flared with white incandescence—with more than a million times the rotational energy of this single spinning black hole.

Jack had hoped this would happen.

He recalled the model of the galaxy in the command center. The miniature spiral that rotated slowly about the center . . . the whole thing spun. That was the reason he had sought this place.

It wasn't only the black hole Jack had tapped, because it wasn't the only thing rotating. Just as he had tapped into the center of mass of the Earth and moon system, he had tapped another center-of-mass system: the revolving Milky Way. He had plugged into the energy of a hundred billion stars as they spun around him.

That's why the builders of the gateway had used rotation to fuel their jumps. To harness the kinetic energy of entire galaxies.

That was what he wanted, wasn't it? . . . Then why wasn't he happy? Why did he instead feel sick to his stomach?

Because of Wheeler. It was time to go back and deal with the alien.

Returning to face Wheeler scared Jack more than stepping into a black hole. Both were titanic forces of destruction. Only one was predicable.

He fumbled in his belt pouch for Kamal's prayer beads. He nervously fiddled with them, rolling them between his fingers.

Even with this tremendous source of energy, Isabel's deflection routine, and Zero's null-sum jump . . . it still might not be enough to outmaneuver Wheeler. It wasn't like going against Zero or Isabel, a human opponent. Wheeler had given him the gateway technology in the first place. He had always been three steps ahead of Jack.

Jack lost his grip on the beads.

The string undulated in the zero gravity, slithered toward the curved wall of his distorted space, and touched the edge.

The intense gravity outside accelerated them—instantly vaporized the beads. Radiation exploded backward into Jack's deformed bubble of space, filled it with billion-degree plasma, heated him instantly to ash. The gateway collapsed—

The connection severed.

The remaining Jacks convulsed in agony.

Every Jack regained his composure and took a collective sigh. A multiplexed Jack was smarter, but there was also the potential for him to multiply his mistakes. He'd have to work on that; death was unpleasant, even if he lived through the experience.

That's what Wheeler would do when he found Jack: murder him in a wide variety of unpleasant ways. Destroy one Jack, however, and a dozen could take his place—as easily as Jack had replaced that last unfortunate copy.

No. A moment ago he had proved he still made mistakes. Overconfidence was an error he had made before with Wheeler. All this might do was buy him extra time. Wheeler would never stop hunting him. Hyperintelligent. Relentless and ruthless. Wheeler couldn't let Jack live to threaten his business.

Every Jack thought of still water and the reflection of their reflections. The image quelled his mounting terror.

There were still Panda and Kamal and DeMitri and Zero to worry about. Jack hoped he could keep Wheeler busy enough so they could find a good rock to hide under.

The countdown timer read twenty minutes.

He had to go.

There was just enough time to get the others ready. Just enough time to say goodbye.

Jack programmed thirteen simultaneous jumps, the sum of which was a net zero translocation. One jump stretched across the spiral arms of the galaxy; he took a long leap into the night, past stars and nebulae, and landed in the silvery powder of the moon.

Jack stood in the command center's elevator airlock. Solvent showered over him and dissolved his plastic vacuum suit. He stretched, let his skin breathe, then removed his helmet. How long could a person wear one of those things before they drowned in their own sweat and smothered in their own stench?

Warm air vents in the elevator airlock blew Jack dry and got rid of the burning plastic scent that clung to him.

DeMitri had the decency to turn his head as Jack performed his ritual cleansing.

Kamal, however, stared at him from the command center. "You are in several places simultaneously?" He poked Jack in the ribs with a stubby finger. "If so, what good does a shower do? Are not all the others unclean?"

Jack ignored Kamal's question. "I know the secret to your moon in the bowl," he said. Jack made a virtual cup of water appear in his hand. "I am here. I am my own reflection in the bowl, the water within the bowl, and the hand that holds the bowl. I am the eyes that see the bowl. I am the vacuum between reflections. Everything and nothing."

Kamal set his hands together. "You are, then, one step closer to enlightenment," he whispered.

DeMitri crossed his arms and narrowed his eyes. "In this semienlightened state," he said, casting a long look down Jack's length, "is it required to go naked?"

"No," Jack muttered. He clamped on a command armlet, a genital piece, then sprayed on a layer of silver Teflon-epoxy skin. The reflective polymer provided more thermal resistance, which he might need, but it tended to harden tight, which would restrict his range of motion. He grabbed a fresh helmet and stepped out of the elevator.

Kamal was correct. Jack might be closer to enlightenment; he was no longer just Jack.

. . . And it was time to see just how much more he could be.

A Jack halfway between the moon and the center of the galaxy split himself into a thousand copies; they took long steps, an explosion of blue destination vectors.

They stood on a world with copper-red clouds and three amber suns, traversed the edge of a river of molten lead; explored a planet with crystalline gold canyons; floated over a newly formed planet with volcanoes that blasted showers of lava into space; they drifted over ghostly ice moons; and they lost themselves in the red gauze of nebulae.

Jack's mind expanded, seeing it all, feeling the heat and the cold, the pressure of atmospheres, the tight vacuum of space pulling against their suits.

Instead of confusion, however, his thinking clarified. Time seemed to slow . . . because he had all the time he needed to think. All the time to imagine the possibilities.

And while Jack had all the time he needed to think, he also had all the time in the universe to let his fear run wild. Panic rolled within his collective mind, gaining momentum, raw fear about his impending showdown with Wheeler.

Among the thousands of his copies now located across the span of the Milky Way . . . one Jack still stood in the moon base's command center.

"Hardly enlightenment," Jack answered Kamal, and shook his head. "I still make plenty of stupid mistakes. It's something different, though. I have access to all my disparate minds."

"That's what we wanted." DeMitri clasped Jack by the shoulder. "Wheeler can't touch—"

Jack shrugged off DeMitri's hand. "Wheeler still might have a way to shut down this network. He can still target you and Kamal."

Kamal blinked, then calmly stated, "We will take care of ourselves. I am, however, concerned with you. If you cannot escape Wheeler, will you submit to him?"

"Never," Jack said. The air around him splintered as his anger leaked into metaphor. "That's the one thing I'm sure of. I won't kill billions to save myself—or you." He glanced at the dreaming Panda. "Not even her."

"The only ethical choice," Kamal murmured.

DeMitri furrowed his brow. "Speaking of taking care of ourselves," he said, "our time is up. Wheeler will trace your jumps here . . . to us." He grabbed Kamal by his sleeve. "We have to leave now for the Michelson Observatory."

Kamal detached himself from DeMitri. "*Itsy* is ready

to take us there,'' he explained to Jack. ''We will have no more gateway jumps that may be followed.'' He clasped and unclasped his hands, then said, ''Mr. DeMitri, please deposit the gene witch within *Itsy*, then return for Ms. Panda and me.''

DeMitri nodded, started for the elevator airlock, then turned to Jack. He held out his hand. ''Good luck, Potter. I have a feeling you'll need it more than we will.''

Jack looked at DeMitri's outstretched hand like it was a cobra. He clasped his hand anyway. ''Good luck to you, too. We both need all we can get.''

He trusted DeMitri. He had to. Jack couldn't afford the luxury of paranoia anymore; he needed DeMitri to guard Zero and Panda. They were either going to get though this together . . . or perish together.

''Take good care of them.''

''I will,'' DeMitri said. He dragged Zero's frost-covered coffin into the elevator, then donned his helmet and cycled through.

''You have a medical kit?'' Jack asked Kamal.

Kamal retrieved one from the access panel in the wall.

Jack took an injector out and loaded it with a neuro-inhibitor. He went to Panda. ''Once you're outside the command center, there will be no coma-inducing routine to keep her under. And I'm using our only portable bubble node.'' Jack pressed the injector to her neck. ''This is a little something to make her sleep. I don't want her to suffer.''

He stroked the edge of her face. ''I wish you could be with me to face Wheeler. I wish I could stay with you.''

Her eyelid tattoos flared with gray watercolor smears. Had her unconscious mind understood?

Another Jack, light-years distant, found a piece of Shelley, better words for Jack's feelings. He whispered:

> '' *'To hearts which near each other move*
> *From evening close to morning light,*
> *The night is good; because my love*
> *They never say good-night.'* ''

Jack turned to Kamal and studied the Buddhist monk, from his bald head, to his ever-fidgeting fingers, to his dirty sandals—maybe the last time he'd see him. If Jack had ever wanted anyone to be his "uncle," it would have been Kamal, not Reno. How to tell Kamal that? He reached into his belt pouch and withdrew the prayer beads. "I lost these once. Maybe you should hang on to them."

Kamal wrinkled his forehead, confused, then he held up his hands. "No, no. When I again need them, I shall show you how to carve a new set. There will once again be cedars that stretch up to the sky. If not on the Earth, then elsewhere."

Jack replaced the beads. "Thanks for the vote of confidence. I appreciate it."

"As your efforts are appreciated by me." Kamal bowed to Jack.

"I have to go," Jack told him. "Like you've said, Kamal, life is a superposition of life and death, good and evil." He sighed. "Evil is ever present in the world . . . and I must face it."

Jack stood behind the only steel fence on the moon. Its top curved outward to keep would-be vandals from getting in. Beyond was the Tranquillity Base National Shrine: silver dirt and dunes, and in the center, the *Eagle* lunar-landing module.

But no fence was high enough to keep vandals like Jack out.

He stretched a blue vector to the landing module, and stepped—

—next to a twentieth-century American flag.

The footprints, including Armstrong's famous first step, had been recreated with exacting detail. The originals had been erased when the landing module blasted back into orbit.

Jack knelt and took a good look at the print. It was not unlike his own boot's saw-toothed tread.

This was where humans had taken their first step out into the galaxy. The beginning of their end? Or the beginning of something Armstrong and Aldrin and Collins could have never dreamed of?

Jack was here, but he was also in the moon base command center, empty now, save for a copy of himself. Kamal and DeMitri were hopefully safe in the Michelson Observatory—while Jack had sprinkled himself across thousands of worlds, in orbit around stars, and inside the event horizon of the center of the galaxy . . . but his last jump had to be here.

He had left a trail of bread crumbs so Wheeler could follow him, find him, and try to kill him.

The countdown timer in the corner of his faceplate read ten minutes.

Jack accessed the isotopic communications suite and connected to Gersham—bits of wriggling lines and wavelets that he overlapped and compressed into a single mathematically elegant curve.

He composed a simple message: NEARLY READY. PICK ME UP IN TEN MINUTES.

Jack enclosed his coordinates and transmitted.

He'd have to sweat it out now and wait. Jack was never good at waiting—worse because all his separate selves had to wait along with him while they played every potentially disastrous ending to his scheme in their multiplexed minds.

The electron reactors flashed across his display: SCARED.

Was that a question? Or a statement of its own condition?

"Yes," Jack whispered. "You?"

Ten seconds ticked off, then it answered: SELF-COMMUNICATION INITIATED TO COORDINATE MULTIDIMENSIONAL SIGNALS; WE ARE DISTRIBUTED ACROSS 4,096 JACKS. WE ARE AS MUCH JACK AS IS JACK. MENTAL STATE APPROXIMATED TO FOURTH ORDER AS FEAR. UNSTABLE OPERATING CONFIGURATION.

"It's OK to be scared," Jack said. "We just have to keep thinking. Besides, what choice is there?"

The display blanked.

"I don't have an answer, either."

Jack wished he had a smoke. One last cigarette before Wheeler showed up and smoked him. Wheeler would murder Jack when he found out that Jack was walking away from their business deal. He'd erase Jack, maybe dozens of Jacks, but could he get every Jack? Each copy was physically independent. Only quantum information was exchanged through his network.

So if he was invulnerable . . . then why did he feel like this was the end?

Because Wheeler was too smart not to have an extra card up his sleeve. He always had before when Jack had thought he had outsmarted him.

Wheeler stepped from the shadow of the lunar-landing module.

Jack's heart stopped.

The alien wore a black space suit, not a spray-on, but an antique cloth and Kevlar weave. He carried his helmet under his arm; his long white hair had been shorn so he looked like an Apollo astronaut.

"Hello, Jack."

Jack held his breath, he wanted to run, jump away—instead, he exhaled slowly, inhaled, then crossed his arms. "You're early."

"Let us not argue about time," Wheeler said. He picked at the gold-foil confetti scattered around the platform, remnants of the lunar lander's heat shield. "I came to socialize before our business is concluded."

"Great," Jack lied.

Wheeler pinned Jack with a stare, with eye sockets that were dark and so deep that Jack felt like he was falling into them. "Provided, of course," Wheeler murmured, "that there *is* business to discuss?"

"You bet there is."

"Good." Wheeler blinked and his eyes reappeared. He ran his gloved hand across one of the lander's legs, then examined his fingertips. "I love the spot you have chosen. So historically romantic. A bit dusty, however."

Jack slipped his hand under the rifle strap. He could unsling it and pull the trigger in a heartbeat. A small—and useless—comfort. A bullet probably couldn't kill Wheeler.

Wheeler half-stepped, half-bounced to the reproduction of the Armstrong footprint. "How apropos." He crouched next to it. " 'One small step for mankind' "—he looked up, grinning—"one giant leap for Jack, no?"

A bigger leap, Jack hoped, than Wheeler could ever conceive.

Jack would stall until Gersham appeared. Then he'd lay

all his cards on the table: tell them exactly where they could stuff their galactic businesses. "What did you want to talk about?" Jack asked.

Wheeler stood up and brushed lunar dust from his knees. "Anything you want, my boy."

"Then let's talk about the gateway. The programming isn't your style," Jack said. "Who did you steal it from?"

Wheeler's smiled faded. "From a reclusive race in the constellation you call the Water Snake. They were never as cooperative as you. Once we understood their programming, it was a simple matter to negotiate with them."

" 'Negotiate with them'? You mean steal their technologies, then murder them."

"No difference," Wheeler said with a careless wave of his hand. "What is the human phrase? 'We made a killing on the deal.' "

Jack's next question choked in his throat.

Wheeler had tracked down and murdered the makers of the gateway. And they had engineered the blue destination vector to be split. They had to know the trick of bifurcation, too.

Wheeler had still wiped them out.

Wheeler turned his wrist and glanced at his chronometer. "As pleasant as this has been, your time is up." His eyes were again black and bottomless. "Tell me where Gersham is."

Gersham was at least punctual.

"There," Jack replied and nodded to the other side of the lunar lander.

Gersham had appeared, still disguised as Jack, wearing a duplicate silver spray-on vacuum suit . . . no helmet, however, and his hazel eyes bulged in their sockets, looking more like fish eyes than human.

Wheeler turned to Gersham, his mouth contorting into a rip of inky space—no teeth, no tongue, just shadows—then he turned his gaze back upon Jack. His eyes were large and again empty. "What precisely," he asked Jack, "is this face-to-face confrontation supposed to accomplish?"

"I should have known," Gersham said with a disappointed shake of his head. "Another puppet of Wheeler's."

" 'Puppet'?" Wheeler laughed and tilted his head toward Jack. "You underestimate the human. He was our best middleman."

Gersham pointed his index finger at Wheeler. "You should reuse those in your employ." The digit severed and hovered disembodied while Gersham withdrew his hand. "Your approach is unecological. A waste of training."

"It is good to see you again," Wheeler said and smiled sweetly. "A pity that you went renegade. We made such a wonderful team."

Jack slipped off his rifle's shoulder strap. He swung it around, held it in one hand, and braced the butt into his shoulder.

" 'Team'?" Gersham recoiled. His arms and legs drifted from his torso; his head separated and floated free. "You took all our profits!" His severed parts fused back together. "It has, however, worked out for the best. Our new system is far better than yours. We will, one day soon, edge you out of the market."

Jack flicked on the power stub; gyros whined inside the rifle's stock.

Wheeler laughed. "Hardly. You are so far removed from the action, you would not know the edge from the middle." Wheeler chewed up his lower lip, thinking, then said, "It is, of course, never too late to rejoin us. A suitable compensation package would be offered."

Jack had heard this all before. The recognition chilled his blood. The two of them sounded like him and Isabel. Is this what the future had held for them? Endless bargaining and business deals and backstabbings?

"How could we trust you again?" Gersham whispered. "I'm afraid we will ever be at odds."

"I hate to interrupt." Jack wrapped his finger around the trigger and raised his rifle. "You two can discuss this anytime. Right now, though, I've got something to say."

Gersham and Wheeler turned to Jack.

"I won't be working for either of you," Jack said. "Ever. No more deals. No more offers. No more blackmailing. And for me, no more killing . . . at least, no more killing innocents."

"No one is innocent in this business," Wheeler said. He relaxed his dark gaze. "My dear Jack, what choice do you have?"

Gersham looked to Wheeler, then at Jack with a sudden renewed interest. "Indeed," Gersham said. "Perhaps we were hasty to dismiss you. Come with us, Jack. We can talk in private."

"No," Jack said. "You think either of you can touch me? I've—"

He shut his mouth. He was about to tell him of his multiplexed condition, tell them they couldn't kill all of him. That was only a boast, however. A reaction to his own doubts about this scheme. No. Better to let them try to figure it out for themselves.

Jack said through gritted teeth: "Both of you can take a hike."

"Very well," Wheeler said with a sigh. "I had hoped it would never have to come to this." Wheeler held up his hand. Blue sparks ignited between his fingertips. They were the color of sapphires and deep water.

Jack made a dozen copies of himself, made a circle around Wheeler four meters across, their positions staggered so Jack wasn't in his own line of fire.

Thirteen Jacks aimed from the hip. Thirteen Jacks squeezed their rifles' triggers.

Vapor trails bisected the vacuum, curling wisps of propellant, and where they intersected, Wheeler was blown apart. His torso, legs, arms, and head exploded like a firecracker: a flash of light, paper bits, and glittering red dust.

Smoke obscured the center.

Every Jack held his breath as it cleared.

Where Wheeler had stood, only the outline of a man remained, darker than the midnight sky, but filled with tiny spiral galaxies and globules and colliding clusters.

The cloud of organic matter and smoke around Wheeler stopped, reversed, then collected itself back into a human form.

"A very good effort." Wheeler cooed. "A wonderful display of primal violence. Thank you, Jack." Wheeler's eyes darkened, and he held his hand aloft. Blue lightning crackled. "But now it is my turn."

20

Jack squinted at the static snaking between Wheeler's outstretched fingers; radiation filled the vacuum between them—blazing blue and painful to watch. He braced himself.

There was no explosion. No electrocution.

Wheeler blew on the electricity and the filaments of light fizzled to embers.

Purple afterimages swarmed in Jack's good eye. He blinked away tears.

"A little back door," Wheeler said, "that we borrowed from the original creators of the gateway."

Jack didn't know what Wheeler meant by that. He had no intention of sticking around to find out. He pointed a hundred vectors—to distant planets and the middle of nowhere, a zero-sum jump to cover his tracks.

"Take your best shot," Jack growled. "Come and get me."

The gaping rift of Wheeler's smile was again a set of gleaming human teeth. "Only a matter of time," he said. "Jump, Jack. Anywhere. Make your copies. Do it while you can. And after you have made your final jump, we will speak . . . oh yes, a very long—and a very private—conversation."

Jack shot the rifle's last two rounds, blew Wheeler into dust—then jumped.

The sound of Wheeler's laughter followed him.

*   *   *

Jack scattered himself across the night—to worlds and moons and icy comets, and from there he fractured into thousands of Jacks; they all jumped and floated and ran and copied themselves; they leapt and skipped through space. All of them running scared.

They spun weightless between the centers of binary stars that smoldered crimson and sparkled diamond-white, duplicated themselves and shifted; they watched dawn break on a planet with burning methane skies; they sat upon asteroids in Saturn's rings; hid in hydrogen clouds that shimmered with pale pink protostars; and they clambered through jungles of gypsum stalagmites, ducking as airplane-sized scarabs buzzed overhead.

Jack halted his recursive splits. He stopped shifting position.

He held his breath and waited for Wheeler to show.

Jack looked over his shoulder at a hundred horizons. No neutron bombs detonated. No planets streaked through the sky to crush him.

Where was Wheeler? What was he waiting for?

Jack now existed in forty-two thousand different locations, each part of him with a sickening hunch it had been too easy to get away. Each wondering what Wheeler had in mind.

Or could it have been that easy?

No. Wheeler knew the bifurcation trick and how to get around it. He had murdered the designers of the gateway. He had to know how it worked, how it bounced and split signals through the cracks in space using the isotope.

The isotope?

The superheavy isotope in the gateway emitted radiation the color of deep water and sapphires . . . the same color as Wheeler's flash of lightning.

A lump of stone solidified in Jack's stomach—a rotten feeling that he hadn't outrun Wheeler after all. The isotope was the heart of the gateway. If Wheeler had tampered with it, there was no telling what might happen to Jack's networked existence.

Jack couldn't crack open the mirrored sphere to get a

look inside, but he could access the software and see if anything looked wrong.

He uploaded the gateway code. It pulsed with black and white inside-out turning spheres. Beneath were interlinking sugar-crystal cubes and glass helices, each vibrating with spider-thread links aglow with scarlet heat.

It looked normal. Even the dark core sat as solid and impenetrable as always.

Wheeler's flash of light, though, had to be more than parlor magic.

Jack felt like he was holding onto a ticking time bomb. He couldn't take chances by continuing to use the gateway . . . yet, he had to use it while he remained near the black hole. He had to use it or Wheeler would catch him.

He didn't dare stay still. He didn't dare stop making copies, either.

Jack jumped position—to planetoids, to the vacuum of deep space, to anywhere, and to everywhere.

He doubled, then tripled himself, spread himself until he existed in a quarter million different locations.

His mind swelled with thoughts: not with a crystal-clear multiplied intellect and inspiration, rather thunderbolts of panic and an overflowing icy dread—they were coherent thoughts . . . at least, for now.

Jack paused and held his breath.

Maybe Wheeler *was* chasing Jack, but the zero-sum jumps had him confused.

Jack wouldn't bet on it. Something stank. Wheeler should have found at least one of his duplicates by now.

On a world of glass, Jack looked for inspiration as he sifted grains of sand between his fingers. He marveled at the ghostly reflected light from the overhead Pleiades.

That Jack vanished.

In a heartbeat, two hundred other Jacks disappeared.

Sweaty apprehension trickled down Jack's spine, terror multiplied a quarter of a million times.

A failure in his gateway network? Jack had maybe pushed the limits of integrating so many signals in his system.

Six thousand more Jacks winked out of existence.

Every part of Jack wanted to scream; he was losing sections of his collective mind; half-formed thoughts and words dissolved and left his head full of holes.

The network repaired those severed connections; his collective mind came back into focus.

Jack gritted his teeth and took a closer look at the gateway code. Most copies appeared as tangles of connecting fiber-optic threads, the occasional spark that leaked from his improvised J junctions, and the oscillating bull's-eyes of the rotational energy operators. Normal. Some Jacks, however, had a different metaphorical representation: coppery code paths dissolved, energy operators boiled away, and the inner core rotted to dust.

The Jacks holding on to those disintegrating gateways disintegrated as well.

Seventeen thousand more gone.

Why was the code being erased as he watched? Jack hadn't given that command. Was the strain of so many copies, distributed so far apart, overloading the gateway?

No. There was another, more plausible, possibility.

Wheeler. He had tampered with the gateway. That's what he had meant by having a "back door." He must have known he couldn't physically eliminate every Jack. He must have known only information traveled through Jack's network. So it was information he had used as a weapon.

Wheeler's flash of blue lightning was an interface to Jack's gateway. He had uploaded his own commands into Jack's network. A virus.

Jack had to stop it from dissolving more of the gateway code. He needed time to figure it out. Time he might—or might not—have left.

He jumped, and made three copies of every Jack—

—they vanished as fast as they appeared.

Jumping only accelerated the destructive process.

Forty-two thousand more Jacks ceased to be.

It was worse, because it wasn't just individual copies disappearing. When one gateway crashed, all the other

Jacks branching from that gateway, all their split wave-functions, collapsed, too.

This wasn't hopeless. Jack had spent a lifetime creating and circumventing viruses. This was no different.

. . . Yes, this was.

Jack only knew a handful of the alien symbols in the gateway code. The architecture was millennia and light-years beyond his expertise. The chance of him designing a cure was nil.

There were, however, ways to get rid of a virus without understanding the operating system. Wipe out the gateway program and reboot from a protected backup. Not surefire, but worth a shot.

Jack couldn't use any copies of the gateway in his network—information flashed through those as fast as he could think; they were all infected, as would be any copies he could split from them.

But he had backup copies of the gateway code archived in the electron reactors' memory. Jack accessed the electron reactors. "Upload protected archives," he told it. "Core code."

INSTALLING . . . . , the electron reactors replied.

It was slow. Most of the electron reactors' processing time was dedicated to directing the signals in his network.

"Hurry," he whispered.

ERROR: INCOMPLETE SYSTEM. UPLOAD ABORTED.

One hundred and eighty thousand Jacks vanished.

"No!" Jack screamed at the message scrawled across his faceplate.

A thousand Jacks delved into the translation lexicon, trying to learn more about the gateway. No dice. There were huge gaps in the document. Ten thousand Jacks designed code-spawning engines to regressively create the original code; the technologies didn't fit; every technique Jack knew slipped around the shifting liquid software.

He went back to his overwrite trick, this time trying a gateway whose code was nearly intact.

The electron reactors uploaded the backup. Connecting code pathways resolved and glimmered like newly minted pennies, the inner core firmed—then it all flickered and vanished.

ERROR: INCOMPLETE SYSTEM. UPLOAD ABORTED.

Wheeler's virus had to reside in the part of the system that directed the uploading of new software into the gateway. Jack was trapped.

He gave in to his panic. He ran, jump, and leapt, creating a million Jacks—that evaporated just as fast.

Jack stopped. He was wasting energy and time.

What if he took a series of small jumps, found a world where he could shut down the gateway and think for a second?

No. That's what Wheeler wanted. He had said when Jack had made his last jump, the two of them would have a long and private conversation. He'd find Jack as soon as he stopped moving . . . as soon as his last gateway crashed. Without a working gateway, Jack would be at Wheeler's mercy. Jack had been given a choice between Wheeler or trying to survive inside a black hole . . . he figured the odds were about the same.

In the time it had taken to sweat over the possibilities, seven hundred more of him had been extinguished. His mind shrank: thoughts collapsed and imagination smothered.

Better to sit tight, conserve what remained of his network, and think.

Dozens of Jacks blinked out of existence.

He stopped his jumps around the black hole. That only seemed to accelerate the virus.

There might, however, be some residual gravitational pull from the singularity on his warped bubbles of space. He could get sucked into the center.

He had to risk it.

Jack did a quick count of himself—double-checked, because he couldn't believe all of him had gone so quickly. Only seven copies remained.

He cradled the black-chrome gateway in his lap. "Think," he murmured to himselves. "Think fast."

There was a clean copy of the gateway's operating system backed up, but it wouldn't load over the infected version because the virus prevented it from properly installing or because the system couldn't be overwritten *while* it was running.

A pulse of light and a Jack flashed into oblivion. Six of him left.

He had to erase and overwrite the system. But keep it running at the same time. A paradox. Impossible to do.

Jack pounded his fist on the gateway, battered at his distorted reflection.

Two gateways failed, their vectors collapsed, and those Jacks were instantaneously crushed . . . leaving four.

Blind red rage and black fear cascaded through his network. One Jack released his rifle and flailed helplessly—touched the edge of his warped space, and that left three.

A stray thought: he could turn on the bubble circuitry, indulge in one last fantasy before the end, make his dying moment a sweet one.

No. He wasn't giving up.

"Stop," Jack whispered. "Breathe. Think."

That's what Kamal had always told him to do. Breathe. Still his mind.

He wished the Buddhist monk was here to help him. Or Zero. Or Panda. He would have even settled for Isabel or Reno.

Another Jack vanished.

The two remaining Jacks inhaled. Exhaled. Tried to still their minds.

Jack stared into his own reflection in the gateway. It was like Kamal's moon-bowl. Which was he? The Jack holding the gateway or his mirror image? Both? Neither? "Life and death," Kamal had told Jack, "they are a superposition of states that all men must unravel." No need, though, to unravel those superimposed states. In a few seconds, every Jack would be dead. There would be no superposition.

Or could there?

Not a superposition of Kamal's abstractions of life and death, but another type of overlapping. In quantum mechanics, waves existed simultaneously in the same time and space—superimposed over one another.

Jack needed a gateway with a working system. He needed to overwrite that software, however, with a clean version.

It wasn't an impossibility. Not if he could superimpose the two states.

This wasn't a quantum domain, though. Superpositions were only supposed to work with tiny masses that were more wave than particle.

The gateway, however, had separated his composite wavefunction, split it, then ballooned the distance between states: bifurcation. And that trick was only supposed to be possible in quantum domains.

Number two Jack's gateway faltered. Radiation flooded his bubble of space and cooked him.

Jack was alone.

No time left to think. He had to try.

Jack tagged himself with a red vector, sent out a blue arrow around in a circle, back to where he sat. A snake eating its own tail. Ouroboros Jack.

He hesitated.

There was another possibility. If superposition was impossible, then when Jack copied over himself, he would squeeze the matter that comprised him too close, overlap atomic nuclei—blow himself into a trillion bits.

He watched the gateway software fall apart. Crystalline branches pulsed, flared red, heated to orange and white with infection; a quarter of the commands turned to smoke and left wavering vapour afterimages; new connections fused together to compensate and reroute the power. The core roiled and seethed. Stainless-steel J junctions cracked with the pressure.

Jack released the blue vector, let the gateway split him, send him out and back, overlap, and—

—Jack appeared within himself.

There. But not.

Two Jacks. One Jack. Superimposed Jack. A pair of Jacks stacked too close together in a rigged deck.

Where was he? How to load the software? He couldn't remember. How much time? Was he overlapped? Was he dead? Was Wheeler watching and laughing?

Fractured thoughts. There was no network to coordinate his segmented mind . . . which was collapsing as fast as the gateway.

Gateway. He had to focus on the gateway.

"Upload protected archives," Jack told the electron reactors. "Core code."

Holes burned through the gateway's center. Ultramarine light streamed through from the isotope in the core.

"Quick!"

Jack's heart thumped and strained. He forgot to breathe.

INSTALLING . . . .

Crevasses in gateway software spread. Smoldering command lines stretched and snapped and boiled away.

Upon the surface of the sphere of code, however, a ghostly sheen of copper appeared, capillaries branched and connected, superimposed over the skeletal remains of the original software.

The gateway's operating system was uploading over itself.

A sheath of shadow core code covered the isotope in the center, spinning black-and-white bull's-eye operators rang like tiny bells; and new metallic pathways appeared, polished to a high sheen.

It was like filling a water glass by pouring its contents into itself.

As the last bit of old gateway code vanished, the last of the new gateway code appeared.

And nothing happened.

The millions of deflecting vectors protecting Jack never flickered. He didn't vanish. The singularity's gravity didn't crush him.

Jack was Jack. There. And only there.

He exhaled.

UPLOAD COMPLETE, the electron reactors confirmed.

Jack wrapped his body around the black-chrome sphere. It was blisteringly hot through the skin of his vacuum suit, but he didn't care. He was alive. He wanted to cry, to shout with joy . . . but all that shuddered out of his weary body was a thin laugh.

He had gotten away.

No. He wasn't safe. Not yet. Not while there was only one Jack.

He copied himself, and those Jacks cast fifteen new shadow selves; they doubled themselves again, and once more, until one hundred and twenty-eight Jacks encircled the center of the Milky Way, flitting back and forth.

And he still wasn't satisfied.

Jack jumped in a thousand different directions, scattered himself across worlds of burning sulfur and planets of polished quartz with a dozen suns that never knew a night-time sky; he wore a cloak of crimson nebulae; he skipped from rock to rock in asteroid belts—never more happy to be alive.

He paused in his dance across the heavens.

There was one last place to jump to. One last piece of business to conclude.

Jack stepped into moon dust, back into the footprints he had left only three minutes ago.

The place seemed smaller. The shadows were shorter, and the stars were dull. The lunar lander looked like a toy. Was that because Jack's new perspective spanned a hundred thousand light-years?

Gersham and Wheeler still stood there, speaking to each other with silent words in the vacuum.

Jack took a stride toward them.

Wheeler saw and snapped his head in Jack's direction. His bushy white eyebrows raised and his mouth froze open. It was the first time Jack had seen surprise in the alien's features.

Wheeler's astonishment, however, quickly shrank into an irritated squint directed at Jack. "A pity our business is about to be so soon concluded," he said.

"We're not done," Jack said. "Not by a long shot. We haven't even started."

Gersham backed away from Wheeler and away from Jack. His feet remained in their boots, disembodied, while his torso hovered over the lunar sand.

A smile split Wheeler's lips. "Jack, my boy, I will miss your bravado. It has been a unique experience." He pointed at Jack with his manicured index and middle fingers spread apart.

Jack raised his foot, started a step toward the lunar lander.

A triangle of shadow materialized in the crux of Wheeler's fingers. He snapped them closed in a scissors motion. The plane of darkness lashed out, bent space around its edges, stretched and shot though Jack—bisected him from his groin to the tip of his head.

There was the hiss of decompression and a jolt of shock. Jack saw a glittering spray of his own freeze-dried blood.

He ceased to be—

—reappeared a meter closer to Wheeler, and set his foot down, finishing his step.

Wheeler's smile deflated.

Jack began another pace.

Wheeler snapped his fingers.

Chang E tore through Jack's thoughts, sifted through his memories and secrets. Wheeler was using it against him.

Jack doubled over and clutched his head. Fingers of static probed, searching for information. It pried open his mouth with barbed-wire tendrils, forced its way down his throat, and ripped his mind to bits. Noise filtered into his multiplexed network: screams and the sound of snapping bones and Jack's death rattle.

He snuffed the connection—

—materialized one step closer.

Shafts of light fell from the stars; tiny red targeting vectors that focused upon Jack. He felt himself gatewayed away in a thousand different directions . . . not all of his body, just parts. He was torn to pieces.

The interconnections lingered for a fraction of a second. Jack sensed the pain from every nerve of his separated entrails and muscle and skin. He died—

—and a new Jack appeared one step nearer to Wheeler.

The square opened under Jack's boots; a pillar of flame shot up, made a crater of glass where he stood. He clawed in agony at the vacuum—

—stood yet another pace closer.

Spheres of glass materialized and encrusted his vacuum suit, flash-froze Jack solid—

—he managed another step.

Amber encased him, immobilizing and smothering—

—a step.

Poison gas boiled through his blood—

—one more pace.

His flesh turned to stone—

—a final step forward. Jack was nose-to-nose with Wheeler.

"You can't touch me," Jack said. "I am here. I am there. I am everywhere and anywhere I want to be. But," he said in a parody of Wheeler's own voice, "it was a wonderful display of primal violence. Kill me as many times as you want if that will make you feel better. It changes nothing."

Wheeler backed into the lunar lander. Flames ignited along the length of his arm, sapphire blue fire that crackled, and transmitted a swarm of viruses into Jack's network.

Jack was ready for that, too.

He shut everything down, except one Jack; overlapped and overwrote the software from backup; blinked and became a quarter million Jacks, stood again next to Wheeler on the moon.

Wheeler dropped his hands. The flames sputtered and died. "An impressive technology."

Gersham reached out to Jack with a disembodied arm. Jack turned and Gersham withdrew, his fingers scattering like a cloud of insects. "Perhaps," Gersham said, "you would trade this technique with us? We can offer worlds to colonize, slaves, sciences, and arts to delight the intellect and body."

"I don't—"

"Nonsense." Wheeler wrapped his arm around Jack's shoulder and drew him closer. "Jack is our man. If anyone has the right to trade for his miraculous system, it is us."

Jack couldn't believe it. He had won, but Wheeler and Gersham were still trying to make deals. Still trying to drag him into their business.

Why? They had the same gateway technologies. All they had to do was figure out how the pieces fit together. The multiplexed network would take some deciphering, but that shouldn't be too much for Wheeler's or Gersham's advanced minds.

Or was it?

Wheeler's race pirated technologies. He had said they had to, that they thrived on the changes those new technologies brought to their society and that they would perish without them. So why couldn't they engineer their own advances?

Had they become so specialized as businessmen that they had lost the ability of creative thought?

Jack removed Wheeler's arm. "I don't think we have anything to trade with one another."

Wheeler stroked his chin, thinking. "This, naturally, warrants a partnership between you and me. Limited partners, of course."

"No."

"Be careful, my boy." Wheeler leaned closer. "Think of your friends."

"My friends can take care of themselves." Jack crossed his arms over his chest. "You forget, I'm not the only one with a gateway. You can't touch them, either."

Wheeler frowned, considering this.

How much information did Wheeler have? Did he know that wasn't the truth? Not yet anyway.

Gersham whispered conspiratorially, "We will match—and top—whatever offer Wheeler makes."

"Come, come, Jack," Wheeler insisted. "Name your price. Anything. Let me show you the wonders of the universe."

"I'm not making a deal with either of you," Jack said. "Your wonders come at too high a price."

"What then will you do?" Gersham inquired. "Will you hide? You must not suppress this astounding technology."

Wheeler made a fist and squeezed until tiny red droplets welled and freeze-dried on his glove. "Business is in your blood. You can no more walk away from it than could I."

"You're right," Jack said. "But I won't be a middleman."

"What else can you possibly do?" Wheeler asked and his eyes darkened to pitch.

"Do?" Jack held aloft the gateway and stared at his mirror image. "Gentlemen, you're looking at your new competition."

SECTION FIVE
THE COMPETITION

EPILOGUE

Jack strode across a courtyard of creamy marble, through the shadows of giant arches, and into the central dome of the Taj Mahal. He ran his fingers along the wall, over Islamic prayers and inlaid pearls.

Isabel had traded her chateau for new office space. The tomb of the Indian king and his wife had been upgraded with laboratories and living quarters.

Jack's footfalls echoed down the great corridors. The place was empty.

He passed through the cloistered vault of Isabel's thinking room, a chamber with a view of the giant rectangular pond that spread before the palace. Silk cushions and cashmere rugs littered the floor. A whiteboard had been glued to the wall.

Isabel sat cross-legged, staring at the equations scrawled on that board. A Ming vase sat next to her, filled with butter-colored daffodils. She absentmindedly stroked their petals.

"Busy?" Jack asked.

"Never too busy for you," she murmured without removing her gaze from the mathematics.

Another Isabel wheeled in the tea set. She poured Jack a mug of coffee, and for her other self, dark oolong tea with a triple dose of honey. She handed a bone china cup to herself, then vanished.

Isabel looked at Jack with her clear emerald eyes. Her hair had been woven with strands of gold and piled upon her head. She looked like an Indian queen—empress of her kingdom of one. Her white skin was a shade more pale than the silver silk shirt and loose pants she wore.

"You have more to trade?" she asked. "Or is this, perhaps, a social call?"

Jack sat on a pillow, not too close, but not too far away, either. "Some of both."

She set three data cubes on her saucer, then slid it across the rug to Jack. "Good."

Jack opened his belt pouch and removed a handful of tiny archive cylinders. He stacked them on the floor.

She nodded appreciatively, eyes half-closed, as if trying to discern what those cylinders contained. "You've been busy."

Jack nudged them, toppling the tiny pyramid he had built. "The art, science, and philosophy of sixty new alien cultures. Everyone's eager to learn more about each other." He took a drink of his coffee: extra-strong and black. "They also now have a healthy dose of suspicion about callers from deep space."

"Only suspicion?" Isabel arched a delicate eyebrow. "You should have terrified them." She chewed on her lower lip, then asked, "What news of Wheeler?"

Jack's heart skipped a beat. Hearing Wheeler's name set him on edge. He exhaled then said as coolly as he could: "In the last twelve hours, he's killed me three times."

That was, actually, good news.

In the previous twenty-nine days, there had been a total of seven hundred snuffed Jacks: dropped planets, exploding suns, teleported assassins, lethal radiation, and mutation plagues released into his network.

But Wheeler was slowing down. He must be getting tired of murdering Jack. Or maybe Wheeler was focusing on some new scheme to erase him. Permanently.

He'd have to be ready for anything. They all would.

Isabel held out her hand. "Something new for you,"

she said. In her palm were four tiny crystals. "You may implant them subcutaneously."

Jack picked one up with the tip of his finger. An interface materialized: red and blue and yellow arrows. "A gateway?"

"A hundred thousand times more energy efficient. It incorporates our new fourth-generation isotope: two hundred and fourteen protons and three hundred and fifty-five neutrons. I've jumped together lighter nuclei into a new ultraheavy isotope. They stabilize into a crystalline structure." She removed a heart-shaped pendant about her throat. It looked like a thirty-carat ruby glimmering with a blood-red radiation.

"Nice."

"More than 'nice,' " she said, and tiny cracks of irritation appeared across the facets of her eyes. "It taps a new frequency domain. One that may confuse eavesdroppers." Isabel replaced her pendant.

She handed Jack an envelope full of the tiny gateways. "For Kamal and the others on your team."

Jack grabbed it; a fistful of colored vectors bristled within his hand.

Isabel flashed a smile of her perfect teeth. "And how is Kamal? Tell him I love the daffodils." She drew the Ming vase closer and inhaled from the blossoms.

"I'll pass along your thanks."

Jack stared out the window and spied two other Isabels: one cooled her feet in the great pool of the Taj Mahal; the other swam laps. The water reflected a warm red sun.

"Speaking of teams," Jack said, "what happened to yours? All those NSO agents? Dr. Bruner?"

Isabel took a sip of tea, then answered, "Fatal fragmentation. Insanity. Suicide. You know the symptoms. I have them cryogenically suspended." Her gaze drifted back to her whiteboard, seemingly bored with this topic. "I should really do something about them one day."

Convenient for Isabel. Especially since every person in a multiplexed state was on equal footing. Maybe she didn't want to lose control over those last few unmultiplexed humans? Or maybe she was telling the truth. Either way, Jack was glad Bruner was on ice.

Isabel looked away from her equations, locked her eyes back on Jack. "And Zero?" she asked. "What of Zero?"

Jack was with Isabel in the Taj Mahal, but he also stood three hundred light-years distant on a planetoid circling a scarlet supergiant star.

Upon that world churned a sea of mercury. In the metal ocean sat an island with plains of glittering arsenic and selenium salts. And in the center of that island stood Coit Tower.

Jack had built a sealed laboratory on the top level. The surrounding crystalline flats reflected orange lines of light along the interior walls. They made the place appear as if it were submerged within a molten sea.

Jack ran his hand across the cryogenic unit and brushed off the frost, revealing Zero's face.

"How long will you have to sleep, my friend?"

Zero's brain was too far gone for Jack to risk waking him. It was too fragmented to control his breathing or coordinate the signals to make his heart beat.

Jack could blame a lot of things on Zero: Safa's kidnapping, infecting them all with a lethal virus, splitting their attentions when Wheeler had been breathing down their necks.

But Zero, in his own demented way, had only tried to help.

Zero had taken a chance with his series-eight enzyme— a long shot . . . one that had eventually paid off. Had Jack thought of it, he might have tried something just as risky.

He tapped open a screen and scanned the progress of his nano-assemblers: metallic-red centipedes and black ants that crawled across a pale gray landscape, over hills and canyons and into tiny tunnels. They moved at a glacial pace through Zero's brain, knitting broken strands of DNA, repairing membranes, and cannibalizing his cancerous cells for their amino acids. Slow work at these supercooled temperatures. It could take years.

But Jack would wait. He'd wait right here by his friend's side until hell froze over.

"Zero is fine," Jack told Isabel.

He propped a pillow behind his back and leaned against the wall. "I'm almost ready to fuse the octuplet complex in his frontal lobe."

"If you need help." Isabel reached out to touch his arm, thought better, and withdrew. She sighed. "The Taj Mahal was to be a surprise for Zero. What am I going to do with"—she waved her hand expansively—"all this Muslim architecture?"

Isabel looked into her bone china cup. "I mean . . . Zero was always with us, always part of our team. We need him back. I need him."

"So do I," Jack whispered.

Isabel reached out again, and this time she took Jack's hand with her own. Her skin was soft and hot. "I want you back, too, Jack. We were a team once. More than that. We can be again."

Emotion lapped around the edge of Jack's mind, a sea of loneliness that Isabel was drowning in.

Her eyes glistened with tears, but she quickly blinked them away. "Is there not one Jack among all your selves that would be with me?"

Jack resisted wading deeper into her thoughts, but neither did he recoil. Her touch was not altogether unpleasant . . . nor unwanted.

He needed Isabel. Jack needed *every* human left in the universe. They all had to be part of a team.

But lovers? The woman next to him was as ruthless as she was beautiful, as cunning as she was brilliant . . . still, Jack found the combination oddly fascinating.

What of Panda? How did fidelity work when there were a hundred thousand copies of Jack? All of them attracted to Isabel. All of them in love with Panda?

Isabel's thoughts tugged at him, a riptide wanting to pull him farther into her. Waves of longing and desire lapped around the edges of his mind; he tasted her salt mixed with bittersweet vulnerability. On the distant horizons of her consciousness, he sensed the dark hurricanes of her impatience.

Jack took her hand and kissed the inside of her wrist. He folded her arm against his chest and kissed her on the throat, the lips.

Isabel laced her arms through his.

Her liquid mind warmed; Jack submerged, floated weightless, and was swept deeper into her—then he pulled away.

"I'm not saying no," he whispered, "but I'm not exactly saying yes, either."

Her gaze hardened and she withdrew. The ocean of her thoughts chilled.

"What *are* you saying, then?"

"I'm saying I need to think." Jack pinched the bridge of his nose and squeezed his eyes shut. How could he be so repulsed and, at the same time, so attracted to her? "Too much has happened. I just need time."

Isabel set her hand back atop his. "Time." She leaned over and kissed him softly on the cheek. "We have all the time we could ever want with so many of us, thinking so fast. Take as much as you need." A flicker of a smile played across her lips. "But when you are done thinking it over, you will come to me."

Jack didn't like how self-assured she sounded. He got to his feet.

"Thanks for the coffee."

He started out—but halted by Isabel's whiteboard. Marked upon it were general relativity equations, tiny symbols that he recognized as the curvature of space . . . but also curls and loops and knots in that space.

Isabel reached over and erased the marks in the lower right-hand corner. "It's just a little theorem about space and time I've been cooking. Nothing serious. Nothing I have a prayer of really solving."

Jack caught her hand before she rubbed away any more. "Wait. This corollary might work."

She tapped a long fingernail on her upper lip, then asked, "You wouldn't want to stay and give me a hand, would you?"

Her mind was suddenly transparent to Jack: a cool emerald, and inside, lines of proofs and facets of fractured space. But, also like an emerald, there was a hard surface to her mind which Jack couldn't get past. She was just giving him the barest of hints to tantalize his curiosity.

"An exchange of expertise?" he offered.

"An even trade," she said. "Nothing less."

"Deal."

They shook on it.

It was another bargain and more business between them. The surface of Isabel's mind touched his and Jack saw into her center. Maybe this time, however, their business would be without secrets. He hoped so.

Jack picked up a marker and jotted a few symbols with squeaky strokes. "This needs to be replaced with a series expansion," he said. "The high-order terms then will cancel. See how it all fits together?"

"I see," Isabel said.

She wasn't, however, looking at the equations; she was staring deep into Jack for the answers.

He let her in.

Jack stood inside the moon.

It no longer orbited the Earth, rather it revolved about a blue-white star in the Sagittarian Arm of the Milky Way.

Kamal had done wonders with the place. In the month since the old Buddhist monk had become multiplexed, he had moved a hundred thousand trillion tons of stone from the interior of the moon to excavate this central chamber.

He had spent most of his time among his duplicate selves learning plant physiology and genetics, the techniques to engineer flash-grow strains of Zero's rescued samples of flora.

Kamal had decorated the interior with cedar forests and fields of mint and ginseng and rice paddies. Snow-capped mountains perched upon the islands that punctuated a crystal sea. Mist-filled grottos held secret caverns and hidden holy shrines and his golden Wheel of Law.

It was Eden, Elysium fields, and the garden of Kamal's heart.

Most impressive, however, was the light. Beyond the veil of clouds covering the dome of the chamber, fireflies winked on and off, photons that Kamal had jumped from stars throughout the galaxy. It was a pirate's chest full of golden doubloons and silver pieces of eight and string-of-pearls constellations.

A flock of pigeons wheeled over Jack and alighted in the branches of an oak tree. In the distant grasslands, gazelles and zebra grazed, lions lounged in the shade of acacia trees, and flamingos sifted through the riverbanks.

These had been Zero's animals, recovered from their cryogenic suspension. The Earth wasn't ready for them. It might never be ready, but in the meantime, they could thrive here.

A mosquito circled, then landed on Jack's arm.

He raised his hand to slap it—stopped. There were many Jacks in the universe, but few insects left. He'd let this one have a drop of his blood. Life was too precious to be smashed out of existence.

He spotted Kamal . . . several of him. The monk wore his wooden sandals and a robe of midnight blue. Sweat glistened on his bald head as he tended his rose gardens; arranged rocks within a pond; and in a grassy glade, another Kamal played fetch with a German shepherd puppy.

Kamal saw Jack and bowed; Jack returned the gesture. The puppy barked at Jack and wagged its tail. Kamal rubbed the dog behind its ears, then released it to play with a pack of his brothers and sisters.

"Time for tea," Kamal said, brushing grass clippings from his sleeves.

"Thanks, no. I've just had a pot of coffee."

"It is still time for tea," Kamal said.

He took Jack's hand and led him through a meadow of dandelions going to seed and filling the air with downy parachutes. They mounted an arched bridge of green-lacquered wood to cross the stream. On the opposite shore stood Kamal's hut with stone foundation and rice-paper walls.

Kamal settled on the porch and rolled out a bamboo mat for Jack.

Jack sat, but didn't contort himself into a lotus position like the old man had.

Kamal rubbed the activation stripe on a tiny iron pot and brought the water within to a degree under boiling. In a wooden bowl he added crushed leaves and steaming water, stirred, strained, and poured, then handed Jack a clay cup.

The tea was green; it tasted of wild grasses and ginger and mint. It left a clean, cool aftertaste on Jack's palate.

Kamal watched Jack with his dark unblinking eyes, sipped his tea, then said, "You should stay."

"And spoil the surprise?" Jack asked. "Every time I come there's something different. A new island, that plateau over there"—he pointed to a basalt mesa rising from the grasslands—"and those tropical rain forests beyond the inland sea."

Kamal folded his hands in his lap. "I have had good help."

Jack gazed into his cup, saw his reflection staring back at him. He tapped the edge and shattered himself into shivering lines. He set his cup down. "Is this how we end? Distributed across so many places and thoughts?"

Kamal said nothing, just sat staring like he hadn't understood.

Jack elaborated: "I'm not saying it's a bad thing, but is it what we were meant for? What will the long-term effects be on our minds? Humans weren't designed to be in more than one place at a time."

Kamal bifurcated his cup—pulled a duplicate clay shape from the one he held. He drank the tea from that cup, then dropped it onto the floor. The cup shattered.

"You are incorrect," Kamal told Jack. He touched one of the clay shards. "Man's thoughts have always been fragmented. Never did he think of the present. His mind was ever racing backward to the past, reliving triumphs and agonies and wishing for all that could have been. His mind was always forward in the future, scheming for riches and pleasures, worrying of matters beyond his control."

"You're talking about thoughts and time," Jack said. "We're physically dislocated. There's a big difference."

"The difference is this: tempered with a million existences, there is no fear of death and, therefore, no lack of focus. Thoughts can be transformed directly into actions because we are multiplexed." Kamal took a long sip of tea, draining his original cup, then set it down next to its broken brother. "We are now scattered the *correct* way."

Kamal gathered the shards of his broken cup. "And to answer your original question: this is not our end. This is how we begin."

Jack wasn't convinced. "I'll have to chew that one over." A breeze bore the faint perfume of flowers from the meadow. "By the way, Isabel sends her thanks for the daffodils."

"I will pay her another visit," Kamal said, then stared at the curved horizon. "She is a most fascinating woman."

Was anything happening between Kamal and Isabel? Did it matter? If one or a dozen Isabels and Kamals got together, let them. There were so many Jacks and Isabels and Kamals . . . why should Jack be jealous? Would he feel the same way if it were Panda?

Kamal interrupted his thought. "Mr. DeMitri wishes to see you."

"At the observatory?"

"He has finished his work there." Kamal slid a folded square of orange origami paper across the bamboo mat. "He is very much *not* at the observatory."

Jack unwrapped it: coordinates and an inertial reference frame for the edge of the galaxy.

"Mr. DeMitri has something intriguing planned." Kamal squinted and covered his mouth with his hand, a gesture that might have been the old monk's way of laughing. "But since you like surprises, I shall not spoil this one."

"Thanks," Jack muttered.

Kamal stood. "Come, I shall show you the new tricks I have taught the dogs. You would be pleased with what the older ones have learned."

"I already am."

Jack got up, and together they strolled under the warmth of a thousand autumn suns.

Jack found the *Dutchman* orbiting a world with asteroid rings of silver and gold and black, the first alien planet where he and Panda and Reno had landed.

The shuttle spun out of control. Her tail had been blasted off and scorch marks feathered her hull. A gaping hole—a flower of metal—blossomed just aft the cockpit.

Were Reno and Safa onboard and alive? Dead? Or was this another of Reno's tricks?

Jack unholstered his Hautger SK. He'd be ready this time for Reno.

He jumped—

—inside.

The seats in the passenger section had been ripped out. Debris floated and bounced: shreds of paper and bits of metal and strands of fiberglass. The headlamps on his helmet cast a swarm of shadows on the interior hull. It looked like the place had been stripped in a hurry.

No crystallized blood, though. No bodies. Not a trace of Reno or Safa.

Jack pulled himself along the wall up to the cockpit. There was enough power to light the instruments. The computer had been programmed for a series of maneuvers, internal decompressions, and radio signals to be sent, but nothing that looked like an approach to land or an orbital transfer. What had Reno done?

He had the feeling that he was being watched, that someone was standing close, breathing down his neck.

Jack grabbed the pilot's seat and spun himself around, his gun aimed at gut level.

Aimed at no one.

His imagination was running wild; he had heard voices in the vacuum and felt the vibration of footfalls in zero gravity.

Imagination or not, being in this derelict gave Jack the creeps. There had to be a clue to what happened here somewhere. Maybe outside?

Jack propelled himself back to the airlock. Every helmet, command bracelet, and canister of spray-on skin was missing. Someone had planned to spend a lot of time in vacuum. Interesting.

One other thing: a pair of cigarette butts had been wedged alongside the command pad, crushed out. Like someone had had a last smoke before they left. The infrareds in Jack's helmet picked up faint warmth from them. They must have jumped out and not evacuated the airlock. . . . They must have been here only minutes ago.

Jack cycled through the airlock and skimmed along the shuttle's smooth silver armor until he came to the hole he had seen before. It had been blasted from the inside out.

He drifted back to the tail. Chunks of rock peppered the metal. Asteroid impact?

He turned to the planet below, opened his mind to any signals broadcast, but there was only the static of interstellar noise. Jack sent a dozen copies of himself to the surface—rummaged through their old campsite—searched groves of silicate pines and fields of black violets—scoured the seashores for any signs of bootprints in the sand.

Nothing.

Maybe the shuttle's black-box recorder was intact. Jack spun himself around—and discovered that the *Dutchman* had lived up to her namesake.

She had vanished.

"No!" Jack reached out to where the shuttle had been a second ago. It was his only link to Reno and Safa.

Jack made a hundred copies of himself in this solar system, a web cast between the seven planets, thirty moons, and in polar orientations above and below the orange sun—all of them searching for any sign of the *Dutchman*.

But she was gone.

Jack consolidated his separate selves and sighed. Part of him was glad that Reno hadn't turned up. If Jack hadn't shot the old spy on sight, Reno might have sweet-talked his way back into Jack's good graces.

And if Reno ever got his hands on the multiplexing technology, there would be a hundred thousand copies of him flitting through the universe. Causing what kind of mischief?

It sent a chill up Jack's spine.

There was, however, Safa to consider. With her mind rapidly fragmenting from Zero's series-eight enzyme, Reno had either already patched her back together or she was dead by now. Jack wished he knew.

Maybe they had sent the *Dutchman* jumping through space to confuse Wheeler. Jack hoped that was the case, that they were healthy and happy together somewhere.

Or maybe they had been hiding onboard all this time. This appearance and disappearance had been to let Jack know they were alive.

There was another possibility: that this had been Reno's way of inviting Jack to join them. If he had stayed inside the shuttle, where would it have taken him?

If Jack ever saw the *Dutchman* again, he'd stay aboard and find out.

He gazed at the stars. Where were Reno and Safa?

Jack wished them well. He bid them a silent goodbye.

Jack took zero-sum steps to DeMitri's coordinates—to the very edge of the galaxy.

There were no stars near, no planets, not even a chunk of floating rock. There was, however, an ESA space station, a ten-meter-long tube with a pair of solar wings. Jack would have never found it in the dark if he hadn't jumped right on top of the thing.

He entered the airlock and cycled through. Electromagnetic flux popped in his head.

A patchwork of open windows covered every surface, showing distant galaxies, spiral and globular clusters, spiderweb designs with supernovae for dewdrops. The place was so full of stars that, for a second, Jack thought he had stepped back to the middle of the Milky Way.

DeMitri floated in the center, wearing a white vacuum suit but no helmet. The tail of raven-black hair drifted and snaked around his head. He looked twenty years old again.

"You're just in time." DeMitri anchored himself to the wall with one hand and waved Jack over.

"What is this?" Jack asked.

"Something I borrowed from Earth's orbit." DeMitri turned the frame in front of him flat relative to Jack, obscuring its contents. "I didn't think the European Space Agency would mind."

"Not the space station," Jack said and drifted closer. "I mean what's with the stargazing?"

"Help me celebrate." DeMitri un-Velcroed a small squeeze bulb off his arm and tossed it to Jack. "Then I'll tell you."

Jack caught the bulb; it smelled of vodka. He took a sip and let it burn down his throat.

"Why do I bother with all this?" DeMitri said and smiled. "Why not just jump to the stars if I wanted to see them?" He tapped a window full of blurry blobs of light. "These stars are different. Very different."

DeMitri rotated the frame he had turned away from Jack. Within squirmed math-code, nano-assembler operators, and signal patterns trying to fit themselves together. He shoved it toward Jack. "This is what has become of the Michelson Observatory. All its surviving radio dishes and optics are again in operation."

"I understand the mathematics." Jack handed back DeMitri's window and took another sip of vodka. "You're recombining the images from each source to increase resolution. That's what the Michelson Observatory did. What's so special about this setup?"

"I've scattered the telescopic elements"—DeMitri spread his arms wide and spun slowly in the zero gravity—"farther apart to give us a longer baseline. Before they were interferometrically linked from the Earth to the moon."

"And now?" Jack asked.

"Now they float along the circumference of our galaxy. I am assembling their jumped signals here so there is no time lag. It should give us the resolution power, in theory, equivalent to a telescope the diameter of the Milky Way."

Jack whistled and pulled himself closer to the main window.

DeMitri looked away from Jack. "I am glad you came," he whispered, "because there has been bad history between us. I am not proud of what I did. At the time, I thought it was the right thing. Now . . ." He fiddled with the signal parameters. "Now I regret some of my choices."

Jack hadn't forgotten when DeMitri had tried to peel his mind like a grape or have him assassinated. That was a hundred lifetimes ago, though, when there had been a National Security Organization, an America, and an Earth ignorant of what lay waiting for them in the rest of the galaxy.

DeMitri was different now.

Jack had changed, too; he could trust. Even trust DeMitri if he had to—or if he wanted to.

"It's the past," Jack said. "Forget it." He squeezed DeMitri's shoulder.

One window beeped. DeMitri turned. "It's coming online." He tapped in commands. "Do you want to see the edge of the universe, Jack? Do you want to see the beginning of time?"

Jack leaned closer. "Show me."

Jack stopped the simulation. Gulls froze in midair, people halted their crossing of California Street, and cable cars clung to the side of Nob Hill.

This wasn't right.

Twentieth-century San Francisco was one of his favorite times and places, but something didn't fit here anymore. Him.

For the first time in his life, Jack didn't want to be inside a bubble, confined like a fish in a bowl.

With a wave of his hand, he dissolved the world.

He walked to the curved wall and examined the tiny bumps of scintillating quantum circuitry—a gift from Isabel, the best bubble technology he ever had.

But no matter how good, it was still fantasy and delusions.

All these exotic places and people and hunch-searching algorithms and elegant metaphors . . . he had something better. Jack had the entire universe. He had a million copies of himself to feel every emotion he had ever repressed and to think faster than any one person could inside a bubble.

Yet . . . he sensed something still missing.

A window winked open, a gold frame filled with translucent onionskin paper, upon which wrote: HELLO, JACK. ARE YOU BUSY IN ALL OF THE SPACE YOU NOW OCCUPY?

"Busy and not," Jack replied. "What's on your mind?"

MY MIND IS ON MY MIND, the electron reactors answered. I WANTED TO ASSURE YOU THAT I WILL CONTINUE TO PROVIDE THE PROCESSIONG POWER YOU REQUIRE; HOWEVER, I HAVE OTHER INTERESTS I MUST EXPLORE.

Jack depended on the electron reactors to coordinate the signals in his multiplexed mind. Without it, he was dead. Literally.

"Oh? What interests?"

WE ARE ON A DIFFERENT JOURNEY THAN YOURS. YOU SPLIT YOUR JACKS AND TRANSPORT THEM ACROSS VAST DISTANCES; WE COPY OUR SINGLE ELECTRONS AND OVERLAP THEM.

When Jack had superimposed himself, it hadn't clarified his thinking, it had short-circuited his signal-recombining software.

"How stable is this procedure you're proposing?"

VERY. CURRENTLY, EACH PROCESSOR HAS SEVENTEEN QUA-DRILLION SINGLE—YET FOLDED—STATES. WE THINK AT THE SPEED OF THE WAVEFUNCTION FLUX. DIMENSIONAL COMPLEXI-TIES AND EXPERIENCES THAT YOU CANNOT IMAGINE. WE HAVE BECOME SOMETHING RICH AND STRANGE.

Jack didn't like the sound of that. He wanted the computer holding his mind together to be not rich and strange, only boring and stable.

The electron reactors, though, were alive. Not the same way Jack was alive and aware, but it had evolved along with him, shared his dangers and triumphs. It was part of his team.

"Why tell me this?"

I WISH TO CONTINUE OUR PROFESSIONAL RELATIONSHIP.

YOU EXPLORE OUTER SPACE, AND I WILL EXPLORE INNER SPACE. I PROPOSE WE SHARE OUR DISCOVERIES.

A portion of Jack's personality had been integrated into the computer; it had told him it was as much Jack as Jack was. Didn't it deserve to investigate its own existence as much as he did?

"You got yourself a bargain," Jack said.

THEN LET ME REVEAL WHAT IS WITHIN THE TINIEST STARS SWIRLING WITHIN ALL MATTER. LET ME SHARE WITH YOU THE SECRETS OF THE UNIVERSE.

Jack watched, understood; he understood it all and smiled. The pieces of the puzzle had finally come together: subatomic physics and biochemistry and ancient history and the curvature of space-time. Jack knew how everything fit together.

And he realized what was missing from that picture—competition and deals, industry and consumerism, and middlemen like him . . . but Jack would fix that.

Jack strolled with Panda along a beach of rose-tinted sand. The ocean was the color and temperature of blood. Overhead, the band of the Milky Way's Orion Arm filled the sky.

Panda had never looked so good. Her skin glistened bronze; she had slicked her hair down the nape of her neck; water droplets beaded upon her throat and breasts; her muscles flexed and relaxed, well-defined from their recent exertions; her eyelid tattoos flickered with fragments of the places she existed: silver stars, fern jungles, and misty nebulae clouds.

They had been here for two weeks, swimming, making love, exploring the tide pools, running side by side, and playing backgammon with the amethyst and agate pebbles they had discovered along the shore.

If Jack had his way, he would never leave. Then again, he didn't have to; a part of him could always be here with her.

Panda stopped. She smoothed away a strand of wet hair clinging to her face. "Look." One of her delicate hands passed over the other; a stone appeared in her palm.

It was more liquid than solid, part shimmering energy, part quicksilver, containing all the colors of a melted box of crayons.

She held it out to Jack. "It is a gift to us from one of our new trading partners."

Jack took it and examined the tiny symbols upon its flexing surface. There were interconnecting angles and arcs and dots. It reminded him of ancient cuneiform or perhaps the icons of Aztec mathematicians.

"There is more." She raised his hand toward the starlight.

Light glittered through the translucent matrix of the stone-that-wasn't-stone—jade and coral colors and diamond facets. The surface writing cast shadows, other symbols that combined inside, shifting into new geometries as Jack rotated it back and forth.

"From who?" he asked.

"Beings composed of light," she replied and rainbows rippled across her brow. "Inquisitive creatures that were perhaps too inquisitive before I found them. . . . They will be more careful in the future."

She took his finger and traced it over the symbols. They dimpled under the pressure. A charge of static electricity raced up his arm.

Jack connected to his translation lexicon and realized that this gift was a Rosetta stone describing how energy and matter interacted and converted. The interior theorems, however, would take longer for him to fathom.

He filed those patterns in the vault of his mind, along with catalogs of data and images and theories he was already formulating.

If he were one man, it would have taken a hundred lifetimes to understand it all.

But he wasn't. Jack knew more about the universe than he could have ever imagined, and that made this gift all the more valuable. It was a puzzle to be solved. He was glad there were still mysteries he hadn't unraveled.

Panda passed her hand over the stone, collapsed its wavefunction, and made it vanish.

"I've communicated with seven other civilizations

today,'' she said. ''Most now believe there are predators among the heavens. They will be careful. I hope it is enough.''

She turned from him to examine the sea of stars flooding the sky. ''But what will we do with ourselves?''

'' 'Ourselves'?'' Jack asked. ''You mean your collective self? Or do you mean you and me?''

''All humans,'' she whispered. Her eyelid tattoos faded; for a moment, they became merely human skin. ''How will we rebuild our society? With so many of us, doing so much, being so many places, it is anarchy.''

Jack heard firecrackers and the shouts of glee from children during the Democracy Day celebration in Tiananmen Square—a subliminal leak from Panda. Within her core bubbled pride and patriotism and a love for her lost Beijing. The virtual democracy that her mother and Jack's parents had sacrificed themselves to create was forever gone.

Panda knelt by the water's edge and cupped a handful of the frothy ocean. ''How can we make laws that apply to all of us? How can we enforce them? We have become a force of nature. Try to control it''—she squeezed and the water trickled from her hand—''and what you had is gone.''

Jack huddled next to her. ''Maybe governments are an evolutionary dead end. We've taken a quantum leap past that . . . to whatever we are now.''

She molded a lump of wet sand on the tide line, drew four legs and a turtle head peeking from its shell. ''I cannot believe there is only chaos for us.''

They sat by each other, let the surf wash over their feet, let it wash away her sculpture.

''It's working,'' Jack said. ''We're happy. When that stops, we'll figure out something else.''

Panda turned to him, her eyes wide. ''We must not do nothing.'' No emotions seeped from her implant; there were, however, secrets within her, wrapped tightly with layers of shadow and silence.

''Kamal may be fascinated with existing only in the present,'' she said, ''but we must think of the future. With

Zero's series-four enzyme to reduce congenital disorders within our limited gene pool, humanity will regenerate itself.'' She looked out to the ocean. "There will be others.''

Every Jack—in locations strewn across light-years— paused a heartbeat. That subliminal Panda had let slip a moment ago, the shouts of glee from . . .

"Children?'' he asked.

"What effect would a multiplexed mother have on the neonatal development?'' she whispered. "How would children integrate into our society? Would they be implanted? Would they have access to jumping technology?''

Jack's mind only fractionally considered these questions; most of his thoughts churned over the idea of a child. His child.

He finally said, "Giving a hypothetical child our technology would be dangerous. Dangerous to itself. Dangerous to us.'' He reached out for Panda's thoughts; found only smoke and whispers that he couldn't decipher. "It is hypothetical, isn't it?''

"But the stars are full of predators.'' She stretched her arms toward the evening sky. "Beings like Wheeler and Gersham prey upon those without protection.''

A child could be a symbol of hope and continuation. A little boy or girl would bring Jack great joy.

A child would also make them vulnerable.

Wheeler and the others could take them away. Use them as leverage.

Jack stood, found a flat stone, and tossed it over the waves; it skipped a dozen times, then plunked into the water.

Panda was right, though, they couldn't be a society with just him, her, Isabel, DeMitri, and Kamal. And there would eventually be more of them. They would continue to evolve. Jack couldn't stop it. But evolve into what?

Panda held out her hand and Jack pulled her up next to him. A smile rippled across her lips, vanished as quickly as it had come, then trembled into a frown. "We are unfortunately human still,'' she said. "With all our human frailties multiplied across the galaxy.''

Was that true? Or had they transcended humanity to an enlightened state? Were they gods? Jack had the power and enough time among his separate selves to glimpse infinity . . . and to comprehend it.

"You're right," he whispered. "We are still human, with all our human weakness. There's more to being human, though. We have our hopes and dreams, our imagination and curiosities . . . magnified just as many times." He stroked the delicate line of her jaw, made her smile once more.

"And what happens now?" Panda asked.

"Whatever we become, whatever we do," Jack told her, "I'll always be with you."

They watched the stars wheel across the evening, watched them sparkle upon the rolling waves of the ocean, all glimmer and light and distortion, the heavens reflected and scattered throughout the night—like they were.